The Road to Lost and Found

A NOVEL

Glenda Cooper

The Road to Lost and Found is a work of fiction inspired by true events.

Names, characters, places, and identifying details have been
changed or are the products of the authors imagination
and should not be construed as real.

Real events in time have been used for the story.
Historical accuracy of persons living or dead are entirely coincidental.

Valley House Press
P.O. Box 65716
University Place, WA. 98464

ISBN: 0985350806
ISBN 13: 9780985350802

Visit the author's website at www.glendacooper.com

FOR MY BROTHER

Memories and Roses

Memories like roses, bloom, and then fade;
sometimes forgotten at the end of the day.

They celebrate happiness; mourn with tears;
bouquets of family marking the years.

Some things are forgotten – the time, or the place;
black and White photos – a forgotten face.

Time passes fast. The petals are spent,
and all that is left is the lingering scent.

~Glenda Cooper~

I'LL HAVE A BEER PLEASE

Lost

*J*immy's Tavern sat on the corner of Sixth Avenue and Division Street. It was precariously situated between the affluent, old part of town and the edgy Hilltop area of Tacoma. For the last twenty years, Jimmy's had seen the neighborhood through family funerals as well as bloody bar fights spurred by racial tensions. The tavern and the clientele had undergone many changes over the years, but had settled into a slightly off-the-main-drag neighborhood bar that sometimes catered to a rough crowd. The working blue collar clientele was usually gone by seven PM, and, like the changing of the guard, the lights would dim, and the Harleys would begin to arrive. The wooden floor had seen better days, but the motorcycle boots that walked across it couldn't have cared less. The dark wooden bar and dim lights helped to hide the dust and the taped-up front window, compli-ments of the last fist-fight when a schooner of beer was thrown through the glass.

John, the bartender, had his series of tattoos on display and one ear-ring that winked through long dark hair. His mustache and beard clearly needed a trim, but he was quick to smile, yet forceful enough to keep the peace among his unruly patrons.

The bar was quiet that night. Three bikes were parked out front, the riders in a serious game of pool in the back room. Two construction workers had stopped in for beer, sitting at the table in front near the broken window.

A couple of regulars, who had clearly seen better and more sober days, were sitting at the bar. John had just grabbed two bottles of Bud and a schooner glass when he heard a banging at the wooden front door. He glanced up as the door banged again and opened slightly. A metal leg appeared to be prying the door open. A few seconds later another bang as the support walker came fully into view, the door propped open by a little old lady's arm, the other firmly holding the walker in place. Every person in the bar watched as she slowly inched her way through the door, taking one step with a tennis shoe foot, then sliding her walker ahead by inches to keep her balance.

John's first thought was to laugh. Boy did that lady get off at the wrong bus stop. His second was for her safety. She looked to be about 70 years old, with short gray hair and wearing a long cardigan sweater that had seen better days. She continued her slow pace until she reached the corner bar stool. Calmly putting her walker aside, she struggled to reach the seat of the bar stool and teetered slightly before she caught her balance. She rested her elbows on the bar, took a deep breath, and slowly looked around the back bar before her tired blue eyes landed on John.

"Evening ma'am. Can I get you anything?"

Her eyes took in his long hair and the flash of his earring. Briefly and unaware that she was doing it, she shook her head in disgust at the tattooed arm, but replied, "Um, yes, I'll have a beer, please."

"Bottle or glass? We have Oly and Bud on tap or long necks."

John noticed the lady looked confused, so he just poured a glass of Bud on tap and set it down on the bar. She reached in her purse and found two quarters, then reached over the bar and handed them to him. John looked at the two quarters and wondered when the last time was she had bought a schooner. He started to say something when he heard a commotion on the street outside.

"Ma'am, did you happen to be driving a white Ford?" John asked as his eyes focused out the window at a car parked squarely in the middle of the street, cars making their way cautiously around, horns honking and fingers flying.

"I dunno." She slowly picked up the glass of beer and took a sip.

Then she reached in her purse again and carefully pulled out a note, which she handed to him. "This is my daughter's phone number. Can you please call her? Her name is Catherine, but she goes by Cat. I think I'm lost. I don't know where I am."

John looked down at the two quarters and the note with a telephone number scrawled on it. He turned around and reached for the phone.

THERE'S NO PLACE LIKE HOME

Two years later
Tacoma, Washington

Cat's silver 350 Z was one of two cars in the parking lot. She had sat there too long staring at the low bay of windows of the nursing home and began to feel the chill. Her restless mind knew that the last two years had changed everything. "No," Cat whispered to herself — a habit she had recently acquired, "it started long before that."

The memories ran through her mind like black and white film clips, rolling backward, stopping only when she saw herself as a young girl in pigtails. Cat smiled briefly. How old had she been then — five, maybe six years old? The smile faded quickly as her Daddy's face flashed behind her closed eyes and she tried to hold onto the memory of the only father she knew. He was her stepfather; she had known him as *Daddy*. The years with him had been cut short. There had been no other father in her life. Time didn't seem to exist before she was five. After that, her life began. Cat wondered how much of that life her mother remembered. Time had changed everything.

Cat took a deep breath and slowly expelled it, leaning her head back against the headrest. Turning off the wipers, she watched as the building in front of her blurred and waivered in the teardrops of rain that formed patterns on the glass. She simply sat there, closing her eyes, willing her mind to be blank, but the pigtailed girl still haunted her.

Cat had been five years old when she and her mom ran away from the life they knew and moved to a small house in the country. Looking back now, the house was only a broken-down cabin. The town wasn't even a *town* at that time; it was a community of misfits, surrounded by untouched acreage and cottonwood trees. Its lone stop sign sat at the intersection where the only two roads in town met. An old brick post office, a small grocery store, a one-pump gas station, and a fish and tackle shop that doubled as a lunch counter sat on the four corners of the intersection. Cedar River ran through the middle of the town, disappeared under a bridge, wound through the woods for about a mile, and eventually ran right past the house where Cat had grown up.

Those were Cat's happiest years. The constant white noise of the river as it rushed over the smooth rocks still coursed through her veins. It had been just a cabin in the woods; she called it home.

Her mother had been a stay-at-home mom who knew all the neighbors and visited with them for hours. None of Cat's friends knew her by anything other than "Mom". She was the mom with the old-fashioned warm kitchen that always smelled of freshly baked bread on a snowy day. She had sewn Cat's new dress for the first day of school and put the finishing touches on her wedding dress fourteen years later. Her mom always had some new vegetable growing in her garden that she couldn't wait to share. In the fall, the house smelled of cedar logs burning in the wood stove, and dill as she put up pickles. The scent of handmade candles, cranberry, and cinnamon, mingled with freshly cut fir branches at Christmas. Cat took those memories with her as she grew up and moved away from home. Every spring, her mom anxiously awaited the arrival of flowers that had been asleep for months. She never failed to call Cat and tell her when they peeked through the ground in the spring – a phone call Cat always looked forward to.

Cat was nineteen and in college when she got the call from her mother that her daddy had died of a heart attack. Her mom had weathered that pain better than Cat, but time did its healing work.

No matter where Cat was, the rushing sound of a river or the smell of fresh grass or the crackle of burning wood outdoors reminded her of home and soothed the little ache in her heart.

As she got older, going home always grounded her. Nothing ever changed. Always comfortable. Nothing "new" was ever expected when she went home to visit; traditions were simply habit. Not only did Cat know exactly what was on the menu for Thanksgiving and Christmas dinners, but she knew exactly which holiday sweater her mom would dig out of her closet and wear when the day arrived. There she was, with that lopsided grin on her face and the makings of hot buttered rum on the kitchen counter. The kitchen smelled of roast turkey or baked ham, depending on the holiday. The sweet fragrance of yeast bread or biscuits permeated the air. The Formica-top table was always set the same, with bold paper napkins and mismatched chairs.

Cat knew that one item during the dinner would be forgotten. It was always that way. The rolls would still be in the warmer, or the cranberry sauce would still be in the refrigerator, or her mom would have forgotten to buy whipped cream for the pumpkin pie. It became a family joke to Cat and her brother Jamie. They'd be eating lamb, and her brother would ask, "Don't we have any mint jelly?"

"Oh shit," Mom would say as she threw her napkin on the table and rushed to the refrigerator to reach for one of her old cut-glass bowls filled carefully with apple/mint jelly, obviously meant for a decorative position at the table, but forgotten until then. Jamie and Cat would shake their heads and chuckle as even that became one of their family traditions.

It happened so slowly Cat didn't see it coming. Her mother started getting tired more often and stopped greeting them at the door. When the grass was over-long and the house needed cleaning, Cat just assumed Mom hadn't quite gotten to it yet. One year her mom forgot to buy the turkey for Thanksgiving. One year she forgot Cat's birthday. Looking back now it was a classic case of denial, and both Cat and Jamie had turned a blind eye to the obvious.

During one visit home, Cat noticed that the garbage hadn't been taken out in weeks and the sink was full of unwashed dishes. It wasn't until then that she began worrying about her mom and checking in on her more often.

Cat was there when her mom was diagnosed with diabetes, but she had assured Cat that she was more than capable of taking care of her medication. Cat believed her. Then she started finding insulin needles and half-used bottles of the drug, unrefrigerated, sitting on the table next to her mom's recliner, along with days of uneaten food. It became common for her mom to sleep all day in her chair, losing track of time. Soon she began losing track of days.

One evening the telephone rang, and Cat's husband Jim answered. Handing the phone to Cat, Jim shrugged his shoulders as if to say he didn't recognize the caller.

"Hello?" Cat asked as she juggled the remote control to turn the volume down on the TV.

"You don't know me. My name is John and I work down at Jimmy's Tavern. Do you have a mother named Madeleine?"

"Yes. Is something wrong? Is she all right?" Cat's voice took on an urgent tone, which alarmed both Jim and the Old English Sheepdog that had taken up residence on the other side of the couch.

"Yeah, she's fine right now. She's just sitting here at the bar havin' a beer. She asked me to call you, and I think her car is stalled out in the middle of the street. You might want to call a tow truck."

As he talked, the story became clear. She had apparently gone out at lunchtime to frequent Ivars, the local drive-through seafood chain. She had stopped for a bowl of clam chowder *to go*. Ivars was mere blocks from her house. When exiting the drive-through, she turned the car the wrong way, got lost, and spent the next seven hours driving around trying to find her way home. She eventually ran out of gas in the middle of the street, parked, got out, and walked to the roadhouse tavern where she asked the bartender to call Cat, but not before she ordered herself a schooner of beer. The bartender gave Cat the directions to Jimmy's Tavern and that was how they found her an hour later, sitting at the bar in a tavern that catered to bikers and thugs, talking to the bartender over a schooner of beer. This was clearly not a part of the city where Cat wanted to linger, so they hurriedly got her mom off the bar stool and headed for the door, thanking the bartender on their way out.

Cat had just been slapped in the face with the realization that her mom was no longer able to take care of herself.

The next day, she called her brother for help. Within sixty days, she and Jamie had moved their mother into an assisted living residence. They packed all of her belongings into boxes that were hurriedly stored in Cat's attic and put the house up for sale.

The decision to move Madeleine did not come lightly. Cat and Jamie both struggled with their options and visited many places before choosing the one that felt right and had nursing staff on-site. The doctors diagnosed dementia, suggesting Madeleine needed supervision over her medical and mental condition. The nurses at the home were all very kind and understanding and far more patient about the onset of dementia than Cat was.

Madeleine didn't take the move very well, and claimed to anyone within earshot that her "daughter put her in a home". The word "home" would always be accentuated with a slight grunt and as much distain as she could gather.

During the next year, Madeleine's dementia worsened, as did numerous ailments, and she was moved into a different wing to receive full-time nursing care. The nurses took very good care of her, peppering the day-to-day routine with friendship and humor. But, through the process of her mom's aging, Cat had lost the mom she had known, and she resented this new person in her place.

That's where Cat sat now, watching the rain through the windshield, just outside "the home". After nearly two years of visiting her mom and watching her memory fade, Cat had come to hate this place. She was tired of Mom saying "I don't know," to every question. The story repeated itself week after week.

"Hi, Mom, how're you doing today? Did you have your breakfast?" Cat would ask as cheerfully as she possibly could.

"I don't know," her mom would reply, looking at Cat's face, as if she were trying to place her.

Cat carried on a one-sided conversation until she ran out of things to say. Then it would become quiet, and she'd just sit by her mom's bed until she fell asleep.

She hated visiting, but she made the trip at least once a week. To amuse herself more than anything else, she began making a game of it. She'd bring flowers, stuffed animals, or pictures to hang on the wall, all within sight of the bed. Each January she'd hang the new fireman calendar in Madeleine's room, which tempted all the nurses and the visiting staff to stay a little longer, maybe visit more often as the months passed when a new sexy fireman's picture appeared on the calendar. It was a ploy to give her mother more company when Cat wasn't around.

Once in a great while, for absolutely no reason, Mom would be a little more alert than usual. During one of Cat's typical one-sided conversations, she was expounding on a new project that her brother had taken under his wing. He was working on a summer music camp for kids. As she neared the end of the story, her mom smiled.

"Daddy would have liked that," Madeleine said, just as plain and normal as ever. Then after an awkward silence, she added, "I'm pretty proud of that kid."

But more times than not there was no response to questions and no reaction to conversation. Sometimes Cat simply watched her sleep. She felt helpless. This was something she couldn't fix. One day, because she didn't know what else to do, she crawled into bed beside her mom and held her until they both fell asleep. An hour later, she woke up to see two staff nurses peeking at them with that "isn't that sweet" look on their faces.

In spite of her failing memory and the deterioration into her own world, she always knew who Cat was. Jamie was not quite as lucky; Madeleine often confused him with her own younger brother, Joe. One afternoon when Cat was visiting, her mom said, "Joe was here this morning."

"Well that's pretty funny, Mom, 'cause Uncle Joe's in Montana. I'd be pretty mad if he came all the way over here and didn't call me. Why do you think he'd do that?" Cat tried to joke with her.

A look of confusion came across her mom's face and she said, "I don't know."

Today, Cat had brought a pencil sketch with her. It was a project that Cat had done many years ago in an art class. It was a pencil drawing of an old farm house; the original photo had been carefully preserved with her Mom's old pictures and photo albums. She had forgotten entirely about the picture until she ran across it recently. Cat and Jamie had been in such a hurry to empty their mom's house and put it up for sale, everything in the house, attic and basement, had been thrown into boxes with little or no organization. The boxes had been up in Cat's attic for over two years. It was continually on Cat's project list of things to do, but she just never got around to it. From time to time, she'd sort through part of a box, but ninety percent of her mom's belongings remained untouched.

A few weeks earlier, as Cat was going through one of the boxes, she found, under a bunch of letters and pictures, a large envelope with Cat's pencil sketches wrapped carefully in tissue paper.

Looking at the drawing now with a more mature eye, it wasn't half bad. The original photo that she had sketched from was also in the envelope. The photo had not weathered as well and had yellowed, almost beyond recognition. Cat believed the old house in the photo was a picture of the house where her mom had grown up, but she wasn't sure. If it was, she decided she'd frame the picture and send it to her Uncle Joe as a Christmas present.

She knew there was only a slim chance that her mom would remember the sketch, but on occasion her long term memory would be a bit clearer in spite of the fact she couldn't remember what she ate five minutes earlier. But even if she couldn't remember, it would give her mom something different to look at while Cat paid her weekly visit.

Cat was tired of replaying things in her mind and had stalled long enough. She flipped up the hood on her rain coat, grabbed the envelope with the photograph and the sketch in it and opened the car door. As she got out and walked across the parking lot, shielding her artwork from the rain, she tried to ward off the feelings of dread that she always felt when walking through the double doors.

"Hi, Nancy." Cat waved at the nurse at the front desk and was almost past her when she heard her say, "I think your mom's in the dining room."

"Okay, thanks", she said, trying not to slow her pace. She was in the "get in, do what you have to do, and get out" phase of her weekly visits. The depression was so overwhelming at times it took every ounce of strength she had to drive over and walk through those doors.

She peeked in the window of the dining room door and saw her mom's walker leaning up against the wall. Madeleine sat by herself at the small table that had been assigned to her. She was staring down at the place mat and picking at something which had captured her attention. Cat opened the door, slapped a smile on her face and said, "Hey, what you doing, sitting in here all by yourself?"

"I don't know." Then she paused for a minute and asked, "What are you doing here?"

"I'm visiting you. What do you think I'm doing?"

"Huh," she said. Her mind might have been slipping away, but she recognized that Cat was giving her a bad time, and she smiled faintly. The quick glimpse reminded Cat of the mom she had lost somewhere.

Cat moved the chair over and sat down beside her mom. She carefully removed the tissue paper from around her sketch and held it up so Madeleine could see it. "Mom?" she questioned, "Is this a picture of the old farm house in Montana?"

Her mom stared at the picture and there was a long silence. Then in a small voice she said, "Ranch." She pointed at the picture and said, "That's the ranch house." As a follow up, which she very rarely did, she continued, her voice shaky from lack of use, "Dad built another bedroom on that side." She pointed to the left of the ranch house. "When Joe and Jennie moved up there in Uncle Ray's old cabin, they used that old bedroom for smoking meat."

Cat's mouth dropped open. She hadn't heard so many words out of her mom in years. Afraid to break the spell, she tentatively asked another question. "You lived up there during the summers, didn't you?"

"Oh, sure I did — in the summer. I'd go up to cook and clean while the boys worked with Dad on the ranch. We'd come down after harvest and move back into the house in town during the school year." Her voice faded off as she closed her eyes.

"Mom?" not wanting her to stop, she quickly asked, "What was it like on the ranch when you were growing up?"

Madeleine opened her eyes and stared at the picture, then said, with half a smile on her face, "It was rocky. The ranch was up in the hills above the canyon. That's where most of us Irish had homesteads. We didn't have much water, no trees, and not even much dirt to farm. 'Dumb Irish farmers!' That's what they used to call us." Then she paused, staring down at her place mat with the frayed edge where she had been picking, and said softly, "it wasn't easy for us growing up."

She stopped talking for a minute as she appeared to be searching her memory. When she started talking again, Cat leaned forward, put her elbows on the table and rested her chin in the palm of her hands. For however long this clarity of hers lasted, she was going to soak up every word and count every minute as a special blessing.

Cat took a deep breath and just listened, smiling at the renewed life in her mom's eyes as she talked.

"You know Dad came from Missouri. He and his brother, Uncle Ray, were the first ones to come to Montana. They filed on their homesteads and built Dad's ranch house in Box Canyon. Then they built the barn and another cabin for Ray.

When Mother died, Gramma didn't want to live up on the ranch and made us stay more in town. Of course I had to take care of Louise at that time. She was just a baby. Your Uncle Joe was probably only five or six. He was a little hellion even at that age. We only saw the older boys when they came down to town for supplies. Once in a while they'd stay for a week or so if the snows were bad. I really missed Dad when he was up on the ranch."

Madeleine's eyes watered a little as she moved them from the placemat to the pencil sketch of the ranch house. Not raising her hand from the table, but pointing at the picture with her index finger, she said, "There was a garden out back. When we were up there in the summer, it was my job to water the garden. Sometimes it took all day with the little trickle of water we had to pump up from the well."

Madeleine paused, searching her mind for something else to remember. Cat could see the thought materialize in her eyes, "then there was the time Ray dug the outhouse hole too close to the house and Gramma pitched a fit." Madeleine smiled. "That was the first time I remember Dad laughing so hard he cried."

She went on, to tell stories about everyday life growing up on the ranch. Some of the stories Cat had heard many times throughout her childhood, but some things she had never heard before.

Madeleine's clarity was vivid. She shared an assortment of disconnected life stories with her daughter that afternoon, and Cat accepted that day as a rare gift.

"Excuse me, Madeleine, would you like a cup of coffee?" The dining room attendant hovered over their shoulders, interrupting the elderly woman in mid-sentence.

For the past two hours, Cat had been fearful of moving, or breathing for that matter, knowing that the spell of her mom's recollection might never return with this clarity. Part of her wanted to lash out at the attendant for interrupting their precious time.

Madeleine blinked a few times and said, "That would be nice." Cat could see in her eyes she was losing concentration. There were so many questions that needed answers. So much more Cat wanted to hear, and yet her mother appeared tired, exhausted really.

"Mom, do you want to walk back to your room and take a nap for a while before dinner?"

"I guess so," she said, getting up slowly from the table and reaching for her walker.

Together, they made the painstakingly slow walk down the hall. Cat straightened up the blankets on the bed and fluffed the pillows, as her mom lay down and closed her eyes. Cat covered her with a quilt and sat for a few minutes watching her. She was exhausted too. Not the "I need sleep" type of exhaustion. She was mentally and emotionally exhausted from reliving the past through her mom's eyes, all the while knowing the moment would disappear in a split second.

Angie, the night nurse, was making her rounds and came into the room nodding and smiling at Cat. "Your mom had a good day today," she said as she checked Madeleine's pulse with one hand and balanced her clipboard in the other. While she was watching the second hand on the clock beat in rhythm with the pulse, she said without taking a breath, "Your mom had the whole rehab floor in stitches this morning. It seems that Madeleine doesn't like the new director very much. Dan, well, he was trying to speed her up a little this morning on the stationary bike. I didn't see it, but I wish I had." She chuckled. "He kept after her saying, 'Come on, Madeleine! You can go faster! You can do it! Come on, get moving; you can do it!' And she just kept getting madder at him until her ears almost steamed. She finally just lit into him and said, 'It's none of your damn business *what* I can do!' She got off that bike and went back to her room and went to bed just as quick as could be. A few hours later, there was an all-out search for her walker. Claims somebody stole it. Come to find out she had been so mad at Dan, she walked right out of the rehab room down the hall to her room and got into bed, leaving her walker right by that bicycle. I got to tell you, I laughed so hard I almost peed my pants. Yep, she was in rare form today."

That sounded so much like her old mom. Cat chuckled to herself as they both walked from her room to the front desk. Standing there, Cat said, "Angie, I don't know what happened today, but she talked to me for about two hours nonstop, talking about when she was a kid, things I never knew before. It was really nice."

"Sometimes that happens. Your mom hasn't crossed that line from dementia to Alzheimer's and she maybe never will. There are a lot of things we don't understand about that. Some days I can't get two words out of her and other days she does okay. I'm glad you were here today," Angie said shaking her head, "though some days, she's a real cracker."

Cat thanked Angie for the story, told her she'd see her later and, waving at the front desk, headed towards her car. More times than not when she left the 'home' she would either be on the verge of tears or spittin' mad. Some days she just wanted to shake her mom and make her be "normal." Not sick. Not old. She just wanted her mom. Other days she hid the frustration under anger, mad that her mom hadn't taken better care of herself, mad that she was the way she was, even mad that she had to deal with it. But today her mom had given Cat a gift, and it was days like today that kept Cat coming back.

THE MISSOURI WIND

Later that evening

"I hope you're okay with having pizza for dinner tonight," Cat said to her husband as she put the plates on the table. "I left Mom's later than I expected. Do you remember that pencil sketch I was going to take to her?"

"Yeah. You said you thought it was a picture of her house in Montana. Did she remember it?" Jim asked as he sat down at the table and reached for a slice of pepperoni pizza.

"Well, it jogged her memory all right. She talked to me for about two hours. She recognized the ranch house immediately and then talked about living up there with Grampa and her brothers during the summers. I just kick myself a hundred times for not asking more about her life when I was younger."

"I think we're all guilty of that. It's just that you don't appreciate it until you get older."

"I suppose. Oh, shoot! I left that sketch in Mom's room. I'll have to swing by tomorrow sometime and pick it up."

"You know, I think it's nice when your mom has good days. You always seem to come home in a much better mood. Most the time it seems that you're so angry with her."

"I'm not angry with her, I'm just angry with the situation. It's so frustrating and it hurts to see her like that. I never know from one day to the next, what I'm gonna find when I walk in that place."

"Do you want me to go with you tomorrow?"

"No, that's okay; I'll just swing by when I'm out running around."

When Cat stopped by the next day, she was hoping for the best. "Hi, Mom, how are you doing this morning?"

"Momma was here to visit," Madeleine said, pointing at a faded wedding picture of her mother and father.

Cat fought with the disappointment for a moment. Then, rather than argue with her, she played along and agreed with her. "Oh that was nice, how's she doing?" she asked distractedly as she picked up some clothes off the floor and hung them in the closet.

"She died," her mom said looking at Cat like she was the crazy one.

And because she was in that kind of a mood, Cat replied, "Makes it kind of hard to visit then, huh?" The moment she said it, she could almost hear her mother's voice from the past saying "Don't you smart mouth me." But instead her mom said, "No, it's not. She visits once in a while. Sometimes Dad comes with her."

Worrying a little about the direction of this conversation and wanting to cut the visit short, Cat picked up the sketch that was leaning against the wall and said, "Well that's good I guess."

"I guess," her mom almost whispered.

"Do you need anything before I go?"

Madeleine looked confused at the question and then said, "I dunno."

"Okay, well, I'm gonna take off and I'll be back to see you on Saturday." Reaching down for a hug she said, "I love you, Mom." But when she looked in her mom's eyes, she saw blank confusion. She took a deep breath, tucked the sketch under her arm, stood up straight, and chanced one more glance at her mom, shaking her head as you would to a child.

Once outside, the fresh air felt good, and with any luck, Cat would get out without tears clouding her vision as she drove home.

She cranked up the radio, slammed her car into reverse, and backed out of the parking space, trying to clear her mind and mentally organize what she was going to do the rest of the weekend.

* * *

The following week, Cat's Uncle Joe came to visit from Montana. Uncle Joe was her mom's last living brother and had always been Cat's favorite. The trip had been planned for a while, but both Cat and Joe had decided not to tell Madeleine he was coming for fear that any last minute cancellation would be too disappointing for her.

About two o'clock in the afternoon, Cat picked up Joe at his hotel.

"Catherine!" Joe reached for her in a hug the moment he opened the hotel door. "You are a sight for sore eyes. Stand back. Let me look at you." Cat took a step back and tilted her head in amusement. The gesture gave her an opportunity to scrutinize her uncle. Thoughts ran rapidly through her mind. *He's starting to show his age. The laugh lines are a little deeper. His hair is a little grayer, and his glasses are a little thicker, but he looks good.*

"So, do I pass inspection, Joe?" Cat smiled and stepped forward looking him in the eye.

"Cat, you and Madeleine have always had the bluest eyes. Dad never could figure out what side of the family those came from." He paused. "Well, come on. Let's go see that sister of mine."

On the way, she and Joe chatted easily. Conversation ranged from his kids and Aunt Jennie to their neighbor, Clara, and her garden. As they got closer to their destination, they both grew a little quieter. Cat was lost in thought, thinking about the phone call she had made to the home earlier that morning. She'd been told that her mom hadn't been very responsive for the past couple days. She wanted to let Joe know, so that he could be better prepared, but she wasn't exactly sure how to do it.

"This looks like a pretty nice place," Joe said as they got out of the car.

15

"Yeah, it's not too bad. Jamie and I didn't want to move her into the nursing area, but we had to. The assisted living wing doesn't have full-time nursing care. They were having some problems managing all her medicine, and her dementia kept getting worse. She even tried to "break out" a few months ago. She got as far as the convenience store across the street. They found her standing in the candy aisle with crumbles of chocolate all over her blouse. They're real good to her here, and keep a closer eye on her now."

"Well, that's good," Joe responded in a short typical Lannen response. Cat couldn't help but smile at the similarity of the word cadence between him and her mom.

"Joe, I need to tell you that Mom doesn't remember things very well." She paused. "Just don't expect too much."

Joe nodded and followed her through the main door and down the hallway. Cat walked in without knocking, breathing a slight sigh of relief to see that she was up and, at least dressed and out of her nightgown.

"Hi Mom, how're you doing? Look who came to visit you? Uncle Joe." She addressed her mom trying to preempt the possibility she wouldn't remember him and cause any uneasy embarrassment.

"Huh," her mom grunted, tilting her head and looking him over.

"Hello there, Madeleine," Joe said. "Jennie sends her regards."

They waited with no response. "Joe, let me get an extra chair from the hallway and we can sit here for a while," Cat said, trying to escape for a minute leaving him alone with his sister.

Today was going to be a frustrating day. Why couldn't she just be normal, visiting with Joe and enjoying her family? Cat could tell this was going to be a big disappointment and it just pissed her off. This was one of those days that made her want to be anywhere but here. She felt sorry for Joe, pretty sure this was not what he had expected. Cat had wanted him to have a nice visit.

She grabbed a chair and slid it into the room, stopping beside Uncle Joe. For the most part Joe and Madeleine were staring at each other. Cat sat down and waited. She was damned if she was going to carry this conversation. She'd just let Joe try to get her to talk.

"Clara put her garden in last week," Joe began, talking in short clips about everyday life in Absarokee. "She gave Jennie the last of the green beans she put up last fall."

Madeleine nodded, either in understanding or about to rest her chin on her chest and fall asleep.

"We had a big 'ole bear come down from the hills and try to get into our back yard, but he decided to mosey down to Jack and Mary's house instead. Scared their dog 'bout half to death."

Madeleine's eyes widened at the mention of the bear. Cat assumed that though her mom wasn't contributing to the conversation, she was listening and possibly understanding. Uncle Joe seemed to be doing okay, so Cat got up and snuck out of the room, leaving them alone.

When Cat returned about a half hour later with a cup of coffee, Joe was sitting on the edge of his chair watching his sister sleep. "Sorry Joe, sometimes she doesn't talk much."

"That's okay. She knew I was here."

"Let's go on back to my house and I can start dinner. Jamie and Mollie will be here in about an hour or so." Cat was glad they were coming down from Seattle. Joe hadn't met her brother's new wife yet, and it had been awhile since she'd seen either of them. Jamie made the trip down to see their mom pretty regularly, but usually he'd come during the middle of the day when Cat was working. The two of them didn't get a chance to visit often.

Joe and Cat had just gotten back to the house when Jamie and Mollie drove in. After all the hugs and hanging of coats, Cat escaped to the kitchen. In her comfort zone, she worked with smooth efficiency. Without skipping a beat, she took a pan out of the oven, punched two minutes on the microwave and closed the cupboard door with her foot.

She'd made a roast with baby potatoes and lots of steamed fresh vegetables. She wanted to bake sourdough rolls, but, with too little time, Jim had offered to make a special trip to the grocery store and pick up some packaged rolls. They were the last thing she had to remember. She mentally walked through the steps, thinking, don't forget to take the rolls out of the microwave and put them in the basket on the table.

As she finished up the final touches of dinner and set the table, everyone had congregated in the living room, including their Old English Sheepdog Morgan who surprisingly, was behaving himself. He had planted himself at Mollie's feet and was sleeping.

"Okay, you guys, dinners ready." Cat held the chair for Uncle Joe and pointed to the far side of the table directing Jamie and Mollie to their places. As Jim was putting Morgan outside, Jamie and Cat argued about whose turn it was to say grace. Jamie lost, and they bowed their heads in blessing.

Their family was never one to miss a meal and the serving platters were passed quickly with everyone's plate overflowing. Nor did they stand on manners too much. Everyone talked at once during most of the meal.

Jamie and Cat were in the middle of a conversation with Joe when she said, "I've really felt bad for Jamie lately. It seems like this past year Mom got you and Jamie confused and she would be forever telling me that you had come to visit."

"Well, that's a pretty good deal I think. I got credit for visiting when I wasn't even here," Joe said in his typical teasing manner. Jamie pretended to pout on the other side of the table as everyone chuckled.

Cat jumped in before another conversation started. "You know a couple weeks ago, Mom had one of her better days and she was talking about Grampa and Uncle Ray. She told me Grampa came to Montana from Missouri. I guess I'd never really heard that story. Was he born there? Or did they migrate there from somewhere else?" she asked Joe.

"Wait a minute," Jamie interrupted. "She talked to you? I can visit for an hour and not get one word out of her and you carry on a conversation about Grampa?"

"Don't feel too put out Jamie. It's not often, but yeah, once in a while she'll throw me a token and she'll have pretty good clarity for a few hours. But when she started talking about Grampa and the Missouri wind blowing, that made me wonder how much of the story I didn't know."

Joe smiled at the reference to the 'Missouri wind'. "That pretty much sounds like Madeleine." Joe paused for a minute and then said, "Dad originally came from Richwoods, Missouri. Madeleine used to say that when two or more Missourians got together they talked so much it was just like the Missouri wind blowing. Most all the Lannens managed to end up in Missouri at one time or another. It was Dad's granddad that came over from Ireland. Dad told us his granddad came over with two brothers. I don't think I ever knew the brothers' names, but James ended up in Richwoods, Missouri, and married a gal by the name of Catherine. That's how you came by your name, Cat. James and Catherine's oldest son was named John Frances. John was Dad's father, your mom's and my grandfather. We were never too sure when they came over from Ireland, but we think they must have immigrated about the time of the potato famine. It wasn't until the early 1900s that Dad and Uncle Ray set out for Montana."

"Mom told us we were part Irish, but she never said too much about the Lannen family history. I guess I just assumed that she didn't know," Cat said as she looked at Joe with curiosity.

"Oh, she knew about it. There are probably a few things she didn't want you kids to know," Joe teased, "but Dad made sure we knew where we came from. I have a pretty good sized file back home with a lot of family documentation. Madeleine and I have a cousin out in California that has been doing some research on the family, too. We compared notes a couple of years ago and got a few more loose ends tied up.

"You know that Jennie and I are of the Mormon religion, and a good part of our faith lies in tracing our family history. We've been documenting the family genealogy research for years. It's been a real interesting project for me, and we've had some interesting characters in our family. If you're interested in taking a look at it one of these days, I'll be sure you get a copy."

"I'd love to have a copy, but in the meantime, I think Jamie and I'd both be interested in hearing what you've uncovered about

Grampa Lannen's Irish side of the family. Let me get this table cleared off and I'll get the dessert," Cat said as she began to pick up the serving dishes, fix coffee, and refill the wine glasses. When she reached into the cupboard and pulled down dessert plates and cups, she remembered the rolls were still in the microwave. Shaking her head, she thought about the funny things that get passed down from generation to generation. "I'll have to remember to tell Jamie about the rolls. He'll get a good laugh out of that," she told herself.

The conversation around the table had continued in a light banter while Cat finished serving the last piece of apple pie, sat down with her glass of wine, and patiently waited.

Uncle Joe, who normally and efficiently didn't put three sentences in a row, took a sip of coffee, cleared his voice and began to tell the story.

"Dad told us that his great grandfather James and his two brothers were the ones that came over on a ship from Ireland. We believe that it was probably around the time of the potato famine." The family all sat spellbound, as Joe slowly began weaving the story together. Outside of a quick swallow of coffee, or the ping of a wine glass, not a breath stirred to interrupt him.

IRELAND TO AMERICA OR BUST!

1845, Ireland

The three boys walked slowly up and down the rows of black curled leaves, knowing that the potatoes lying under the ground were rotting. The stench was nauseous, with insects and flies permeating the air. It had been this way since the winds had blown from southern England carrying a fog of fungus to the countryside around Dublin. The land had become brown and dry, where green hills once rolled until they disappeared over the Cliffs of Moher.

It couldn't have been five years since crops were lush and times were prosperous. As one, the boys looked back on the cottage they called home, remembering how it used to be when Ma and Pa were alive, the sound of the spinning wheel and click of wooden needles still vivid in their memory. They could almost smell the scent of biscuits and chicken stew in the air. Somewhere in the wind they could hear Pa's voice bellowing above the noise of the pigs. In those days, the chickens, dogs, and even the old rangy goat ran through the yard and sometimes even the house. Ma would chase the animals out with the back of a wooden spoon, the same wooden spoon that had found its way to the seat of their pants when their squabbling got out of hand. They remembered all this fondly, but the reality was painful. Long gone was the patch of garden that grew vegetables. Most of the tillable land had disappeared due to drought. Ma had died before the drought took the last of her garden, and Pa died last year when he caught the fever.

Now, in 1845, potatoes were the staple lifeline of Irish households, and all of the crops were failing. Without the crop, the entire countryside was living off wild blackberries, nettles, roots, and weeds. Within six months, one of every five Irish was dying from disease and malnutrition.

"Do we want to stay around here eating tree bark until we can't swallow? This is the second crop to die. I say we pack up. British ships are sailing for North America, and I'd rather take our chances there." Patrick, the oldest of the Lannen brothers, merely verbalized what they all were thinking.

James could understand his older brother's frustration and responded, "Well, if we decide to go to America, we aren't taking any British coffin ship. I've heard too many stories. We'll see about an American ship. The rations are better. But, if we are packing, we gotta all agree. It's all of us go, or none go. Since Pa died last year, we're all we have left here."

"I say let's go," their younger brother Sean chimed in.

The three Lannen brothers made the decision quickly. They sold what livestock remained and pawned everything they owned, including their clothes, to buy passage and to meet the $25 cash requirement for immigration into America. The Lannen brothers would be a part of what America would later term the "first wave" of more than nine million immigrants escaping the plight of Europe over the next five years.

James Lannen was only nineteen when he set off with his brothers for New York. During the fourteen-day trip, there had been much sickness and death on board the ship. James and Sean weathered the trip without incident, but Patrick had been sick nearly the whole trip, losing whatever food he managed to eat. Seeing land and getting his footing on firm American ground cured him immediately, which saved the brothers from having to be quarantined.

At first glance of the new country, the brothers wondered if they had made a mistake. Immigrants were living on the docks and wandering aimlessly, with no money, no means of transportation, and not knowing where to go. Many of them just stayed on the dock, frightened and confused. In the dusk, the three brothers watched as an old man was tripped by two youngsters barely out of short pants before they stole the old man's packet of papers.

The "runners" and thieves were thick, physically attacking the newly arrived families, stealing any money or belongings they might have arrived with. The three brothers managed to avoid the scammers at night by hiding under the lip of the docks. At first light, they ran fast and hard to get as far away from the harbor as they could. When they couldn't run any more, they set about trying to find a meal and someplace to stay.

America had been overwhelmed at receiving wave after wave of famine immigrants brought into both the Boston and New York harbors. The Irish were poor immigrants with few if any belongings and little, if any money. Most had no families left when they boarded the ships. Alone and with no one to help them, they sought each other out for companionship. The Irish settled onto the lowest rung of society, working unskilled jobs on the docks, in stables, or pushing carts. They rapidly became known for their rowdy behavior, fueled by alcohol and boredom. They found cheap housing wherever they could, in musty cellars, abandoned houses near the waterfront, and shoddy tenements.

For the three newly arrived immigrants, transportation was no easy feat. The brothers walked as far as they could until late at night. They stumbled on an alley where several Irish families had congregated in makeshift shanties and looked to be settled for good. The Irish Emigrant Society tried to persuade the immigrants to move to the interior, but they were poverty stricken and tended to settle as close as they could to the port where they disembarked. The Lannen brothers rapidly took stock of this poor Irish community, decided they weren't much better off than in Ireland, and set out for some place they could farm.

Wanting to get away from the coastline and harbor areas, the brothers began their journey west. For several weeks, they simply walked on an overland route, stealing apples and berries alongside the trails. They met with a group of travelers headed for Ohio and followed them to Lake Erie. After doing some odd jobs, they scraped up enough money to buy two horses. They switched off riding double every so often, as they headed into the farm country.

Along the way, they stayed at farm houses or begged to stay in a barn. At times they settled temporarily in various towns to wait out weather and get supplies. They worked for their meals and periodically made a few cents for necessities. At one point they hopped a rail into Ohio. Once there, they stayed and worked for the winter and spring of 1847 before heading out again.

The travel was long and hard. The farther west they traveled, the farther apart the towns were. They'd ride for days on end without seeing anything other than prairie grass. With nothing to distract them except exhaustion, arguments got heated. Patrick wanted to rest, Sean wanted to keep going, and James played the part of the peace maker.

Patrick was suffering another bout of influenza just as they arrived in Madison, Indiana. They boarded their horses at Fisher's Telegraph and Livery Stables and rented a room in the nearby boarding house. James and Sean helped Patrick up the stairs to the room and into the one bed they could afford. James covered his older brother with the threadbare blanket and gave a silent prayer for his recovery. The room was sparse. The small curtainless window over Patrick's bed allowed for little light. There was a chest near the bed, a pitcher of water on a shelf, and a stuffed chair where the two younger brothers took turns sleeping. Patrick slept for most of two weeks before his color came back and his eyes became clear.

James was just coming through the door when he noticed his brother sitting up with his feet dangling over the side of the bed. "Patrick, I see you have finally come back from the dead."

"Yes, I am feeling a little stronger. Where's Sean?"

"He's been helping over at the livery stable. It's kept him busy, but he'll be glad you're feeling better. His feet are itching to head out. He should be back here soon."

"James, I want to talk to you before Sean gets back. I know we agreed that we would stay together, but James, I'm tired. I don't want to ride any farther. We won't find land as beautiful as Ireland once was. This land is rich. The crops will grow. I want to put down roots now. We've been traveling for well over a year. Look around you. This place can be home to us."

"Paddy, this doesn't feel like home to me. Our trip is not over and we cannot leave you. We need to stay together. We're family."

"James, I've made up my mind. Sean won't be happy until he reaches sea water. I don't know what will make *you* happy, but I know you need to go with Sean. Take care of him and try to keep him out of trouble." Patrick stood and put his hand on James' shoulder and pulled him forward in a brotherly hug. "God be with you both."

James looked Patrick in the eyes, sensing the stubbornness in his brother, knowing that he would not change his mind. "All right, Patrick, but when we find our land, we'll send for you." James reached for the door, pausing once to nod at his brother, and left the room.

Reaching the livery stable, James found his brother in a stall, putting hoof ointment on an old draft horse. "Sean, you and I are going to be leaving. Let's get our supplies packed."

"Isn't Patrick coming with us? Is he all right?" Sean asked.

"Yes, he is feeling better, but he's going to stay here for a while so he can rest and get well. We'll go on and come back for him later."

Sean accepted that answer and eagerly got the horses ready and supplies loaded. Within the hour, James and Sean were heading south toward Louisville, Kentucky. From Louisville, they'd ride due west to St. Louis, the largest town on the frontier and gateway for westward travel. Their plan had been to join up with some wagons in St. Louis and continue heading west, but their supplies and money ran out. James knew that St. Louis' proximity to the

Mississippi River made it a principal trading center, and, as he had hoped, they had been able to work and find shelter for the winter.

Sean could hardly wait for spring to arrive before his feet were itching to ride. Without waiting for a train of wagons and with few supplies, the boys headed out, riding along the river for as long as they could before turning west, toward Washington County, Missouri.

James and Sean had been riding for a while, and were looking for a place to rest when they rode into a little town called Richwoods, Missouri.

Richwoods consisted of the town proper, with farms and ranches on the outskirts. It seemed like a friendly place. The settled farmers might even offer jobs from time to time, particularly at harvest time. Unlike Ireland, there were no rolling hills, but the soil was black and fertile. The crops they passed were stout and healthy.

On the main street, a bartering stable stood next to a farming goods shack where they stopped to get directions to some place to eat and rest. As luck would have it, the bartering stable was owned by an Irish fellow named Flanagan who directed the boys to the Irish side of town, instructing them how to get to the Flanagan household.

As they rode down the street, nearing the Irish side, they heard the laughter of children and Irish tunes. The streets were filled with the Gaelic lilt that James didn't realize he had missed. The houses were quaint, but clean. In the dusk, some houses had candles and lanterns lighting the windows, giving off a warm yellow glow across the porches. Since it was nearing the dinner hour, walking by each house offered a host of smells: bread baking, mutton stew, colcannon, and frying onion and potato pancakes, smells that James had not sensed since leaving Ireland. As his stomach growled with hunger, he rapidly became fond of this place.

They had been invited to sup with the Flanagans. Mrs. Flanagan was a tiny little thing who ruled the roost at supper time. Whenever new Irish arrived in town it was cause for celebration, and relatives came from out of nowhere to join in. While not at all fancy, it was the best meal the boys had eaten since long before they left Ireland. James began feeling the longing of a permanent home. Hearing the conversation around the table and watching Mrs. Flanagan move gracefully and easily as she served the stew, James was reminded of all he had lost. He finished his supper in deep thought.

After supper, as was tradition, the Irish men of Richwoods congregated out on their porches to partake in alcohol and conversation. With their tongues loosened by the drink, James and Sean began arguing. At twenty-one, James had decided, much the same as his older brother had, that he wanted to settle. He was tired of traveling and, unlike his younger brother, saw Richwoods as a place to plant roots. Sean, on the other hand, wanted to continue going west. He had heard that gold had been found in some place called California.

The argument escalated to fists. The following morning, with his fat lip and black eye, the youngest Lannen lit out of town. As it happened, a family was making the same route to California, so Sean joined them and left Richwoods. At the very same time he was riding out, James was at the land office, filing homestead papers.

James built his homestead, farmed his land, and invested in livestock. He had become good friends with his neighbors, John Flanagan, on the east side, and Philip Munday and Philip's son Peter, whose farm bordered to the south. Between the three of them, they'd share crops, barter, and hire out for harvesting and planting. The three families became very close.

James liked spending time at the Mundays and ate there often with the family. Philip's oldest daughter, Catherine, was quite pretty and had an easy way about her that appealed to James. It was hard for him not to want to spend time there. He had never seen anyone with eyes quite that blue before, or skin quite that fair. He only had to look at her mother to see how time would take her. Catherine was the spittin' image of Mary Ann Munday, only without the lingering Irish accent of her homeland.

"Catherine, why don't you fetch James some more biscuits?"

"Oh, please the saints, Mary, I never thought I would say this, but I cannot eat another bite," said James. "Thank you ever so much for the delicious supper, but I think I'll take a walk for a bit." With that, he pushed himself away from the table and headed out onto the porch, thinking once again about Catherine and how he could spend a lifetime looking at her. Perhaps it was time to broach a conversation with her.

"Catherine, may I talk to you for a bit, on the porch, if you don't mind?" James asked as they were just finishing up another exceptional supper of mutton stew and sour milk bread.

"Of course, James, let me grab a cover and I'll be right out." Catherine wrapped a shawl around her shoulders and followed James onto the porch. James turned toward her as she came through the doorway. "Catherine, I'd like you to come and sit beside me for a moment. I have something to talk to you about." Catherine sat beside him on the step and wrapped the shawl more tightly around her to ward off the chill.

"I've talked to Phillip and he gave me his approval to marry you."

"Oh, really?" Catherine asked, her blue eyes challenging James.

"Yes, and I thought we would wed before the harvest."

"Oh, really, that's what you thought, aye?" Catherine raised her eyebrow.

"Well, yes."

Catherine left the porch, slamming the door behind her, leaving James in a quandary as to what he had done wrong. Confused, James started walking down the road toward his farm when he heard Catherine's voice from the window. "Perhaps, James, you should think about asking me if I *want* to marry you, instead of asking my father — that is, unless you want to marry my father." And with that parting remark, Catherine was gone from the window.

It was nearly two months later, after the harvest, before James got up enough nerve to ask for Catherine's hand. Having been coached by Mary, James asked Catherine if she would have him for a husband, and Catherine readily accepted.

They set the date for the following June, and on June 13, 1850, James and Catherine married in St. Stephan's Catholic Church. The entire town turned out and the whiskey flowed, with an Irish party, the likes that had not been seen in those parts before.

Within a year, Catherine gave birth to their first daughter, Mary, named after Catherine's mother. A second daughter was named Bridget after James' mother. Bridget was followed by John Frances in 1861, and with four more children following within the next eighteen years: Catherine, Nellie, Margaret, and finally Edward in 1879.

But John Frances, the oldest son, was his father's pride and joy.

JAMES' SON, JOHN FRANCES

1884, Richwoods, Missouri

Twenty-three-year-old John Frances rode across the field, taking a short cut to the ranch from the main road. As he rode, his mind wandered. He wasn't expected home until tomorrow, but he had something important to talk about to his dad. His dad was probably still working in the barn, finishing up for the evening. His mom was probably fixing dinner and his sisters would be doing their dinner chores.

John Frances had been surrounded his whole life by girls, with two older sisters, two younger sisters, and his only brother being too young to do him any good. John fondly remembered his older sister, Bridget, walking him to school. As a young boy, John had studied hard but never quite took a liking to the books. He did fair in school, until he left his studies at sixteen and began working more on the farm. He worked shoulder to shoulder with his father, planting, harvesting, and working the stock. By the time he was nineteen, he hired out from time to time doing jobs for other farmers, making money to help the family.

During the past year, he had taken on jobs that had kept him away for weeks at a time, spending nights in the next city and sleeping in ranch houses. He was not expected home that evening and Catherine was just sitting down to feed little Edward.

"Bridget, can you take the girls out of here? "Catherine asked, "I'm trying to get Edward to eat, and they are offering too much distraction." Bridget took seven-year-old Margaret's hand and herded her sisters, Nellie and little Catherine, out of the kitchen.

Mother, I thought you said John wasn't coming home tonight, but it looks like he's coming in from the field with Papa." Bridget was standing on her tiptoes trying to get a better look out the window at the field in the distance. Distracted, she let go of Margaret's hand and the three young children ran out the door to meet their father.

"Well, I thought that's what your father said this morning."

"Guess I'd better throw another potato in the pot," Bridget offered. "I'll go down to the cellar and see what we have."

Father and son were dark, tall, and lanky. They carried themselves similarly and bore a deep resemblance to each other. While James still spoke with a slight Irish brogue, John Frances was pure, soft, deep Missouri drawl.

Hearing their boots on the porch, Catherine went to meet them both at the door. It was still hard for her to believe that her son was all grown up. She was happy to see him and to be able to spend this unexpected time with him this evening. She didn't see him often enough when he was away working.

"It's a good thing you showed up when you did. Another hour and you would have gotten biscuits and water for supper," she said, smiling with a bit of a tease in her voice.

"Catherine, John Frances has something he wants to tell you," James said, joining in the light conversation. Placing his hand on John's shoulder, he slightly nudged him forward. John just looked at the floor, slightly embarrassed, and was quiet for about ten seconds, took a deep breath, and then said, "I asked Clara to marry me and she turned me down."

"What?" Catherine's voice clearly jumped an octave. Clara had been the interest of John's life for the last two years, and Catherine had so been hoping she would be a member of their family.

"Nah, I'm just kidding you, Mom." John's eyes sparkled when he could catch his mother off guard. "She said yes."

Catherine reached up to give her son a hug, "Oh John, I like her so much. I'm so happy for you, for you both!" And as Catherine pried all the details out of John, James just smiled and shook his head knowing no stone would be left unturned when his wife got done with him.

And, in 1885, John Frances, at the age of twenty-four married Clara Davis, who was five years younger. They built a small house near James and Catherine, sharing the barn and some outbuildings. John ran his own cattle and helped his father with his farm. Three years later, on February 29, 1888, Clara and John gave birth to their first son, John Michael Lannen.

JOHN FRANCES' SON,"MIKE"

1909, Richwoods, Missouri

John Michael Lannen, who had always been called Mike, was the oldest of four brothers and two sisters. His closest brother, a mere two years behind him, was James Raymond, who they called Ray.

Mike and Ray were terrors growing up. Whether it was shooting crows, riding horses, or just being someplace where they "shouldn't otta been" they did it vigorously. Where one found trouble, the other wasn't too far behind.

In their early teens, Mike and Ray were at a community picnic in Richwoods where it seemed the whole town had turned out. There was a large amount of beer consumed and all the empty bottles were left on the picnic grounds. The following day the boys went over to pick up all the bottles at their mother's request. It didn't take them long to discover that there was a little beer left in each bottle, so they carefully collected it all, snuck off down by the river and drank it. They were as sick then as the time they ate the sweet chew tobacco that they stole from Ole Man Coogan.

John Frances was tickled to death with his two sons, but Clara had more in store for him, and gave birth to four more children: George, Marie, Edmund, and Catherine Alice.

George and Edmund were too young to join in the older brothers' shenanigans and the girls — well — were just girls. That left Mike and Ray best friends as well as brothers.

Mike and Ray did everything together. The two grew up very like each other, sometimes even finishing each other's sentences. They were as close as two brothers could be.

John was adamant that his two sons get educated, so both boys were schooled until they were fourteen. After that, they spent all their time learning to ranch and farm, at the elbow of their father. In addition to working their own land, they both did odd jobs for friends and neighbors during their teens. The money they made helped in some small way to provide food and to run the ranch and farm.

Twenty-year-old Mike had been working up in St. Louis for the winter doing odd jobs, and eighteen-year-old Ray had been putting in some time at a neighbor's ranch. Now that they were older, they didn't see each other as much, but they still had much in common, and they usually thought along the same lines. Because of that, Mike didn't like the direction that this particular conversation was moving.

"I'm telling you, that's what I heard. The mountains and fields are as green and lush as Ireland itself," Ray said, dramatically spreading his arms toward the land.

"Ray, you've never been to Ireland," Mike responded in a deadpan voice.

"I know, but I've listened. Neal Flanagan's brother just got back from Montana and he got himself a homestead of 160 acres and he's going back next month. I just want to see it for myself, Mike."

"Yeah I've heard the same thing, but the timing's not right. If you left now, I'll be the only one to help Dad with the planting and he's not gonna be too happy about that. So if you're dead-set on leaving now, you're gonna be the one to tell him."

"You're going to be the one to tell who?" their dad questioned as he walked through the door, removing his hat and hanging it on a peg. His eyes calmly scanned the doorway to the kitchen wondering what Clara might be planning for supper.

"Dad, I want to go to Montana," Ray said, grabbing his father's attention. "Mike and I have been talking, and some people we know are running cattle and farming crops on some homestead land there. And Dad, their farms are doing really good and they're making money. You can farm ten acres to one plat."

John was quiet for a minute, looking at each of his sons and knowing they were about the age they'd be leaving soon, one way or another.

"I guess there ain't nothing I can do to stop you." John looked from one son to the other. "Your mother ain't gonna like that much, but you're of age, boy. Besides, I've heard the same stories, and if I was still a youngun' and in your boots — can't say as if I wouldn't be thinking the same."

"Mike? Are you okay with it?" Ray softly asked his brother. Mike's opinion was important to Ray and always would be. "If I leave now, I could just take a quick look around and be back to help harvest in the fall."

The response came fast. "Yeah, go on; get out of here." Mike had to suppress a smile. If the truth were known he'd been thinking along those same lines. And Ray was primed for an adventure. He'd just sit back, take care of things around the ranch, and wait for Ray to report back.

Ray left in the spring of 1909. Several Richwoods families, including some of the Flanagans and their neighbors, the Letchers, had migrated and were homesteading in the Stillwater County region of Montana. That was the direction Ray was headed.

Ray was as good as his word. He returned to Missouri that September to help Mike with the harvest. The following spring he went back to Montana for good, and Mike went with him.

Neither one of the boys had any idea what they were getting themselves into. Mike was the thorough one of the two, and thought the best thing to do was to solicit as much advice as he could from their neighbors and friends. For every successful homesteading story, there were three more of failures. One neighbor had staked property by a nice river that turned out to be a dry bed for nine months of the year. Another suggested that they have their own source of wood on the property to lessen hauling time and fatiguing horses. Mike took in all the advice and suggestions, but in the end, twenty-two-year-old Mike and his brother Ray left Missouri for Montana with nothing to go on but common sense.

When Mike and Ray finally arrived, Montana wasn't exactly as Mike had expected. Montana had a drought winter in 1910, and the hills that time of the year were not green and lush. They were more dry and brown, smelling of dry dirt and thistle. But the vast land had a lot of possibilities. Still, snow-covered mountains rose off in the distance, and both the Stillwater and the Yellowstone Rivers were high in their banks. From the looks of things, there were plenty of animals for hunting. Figuring they wouldn't starve anytime soon, they decided to give it a try.

They rode toward the Beartooth Mountains and stopped near the mouth of the Stillwater River in Box Canyon. The canyon sat just on the outskirts of an old Indian settlement named Fishtail. Land sites contained good spring water and plenty of wood close by, fulfilling two critical requirements on Mike's list.

They rode back into town and filed on two sites in Box Canyon. Each site was 160 acres, the maximum number of acres allowable under the Homestead Act.

President Lincoln had enacted the Homestead Act in 1862. Part of the stipulation was a requirement to build a house on the property. It had to have four walls, one window and one door, with a minimum square footage. The owner had to live on the homestead at least six months out of the year, and had to fence the entire 160 acres.

The two sites that Mike and Ray filed on were adjacent to each other. Working together the boys began fencing the property. The two houses that they erected were only seventy-five yards apart, just barely meeting the variance requirement. Together they built and shared the same barn and outbuildings, which seemed an economical solution for them.

Since it takes some time for a ranch to be self-supporting, both boys worked for other ranchers part of the year until they got money enough to build their stock and plant the ground with hay and cattle feed.

They kept in touch with their family in Richwoods, reporting their progress when they had time to write. Their dad looked forward to the sparse letters and shared the boys' stories numerous times with anyone in Missouri who would listen.

A few years later, their dad's youngest brother, Edward, followed his two nephews to Montana, and their uncle filed a homestead claim that joined Ray's on the south end of his property. A little later, Mike and Ray's brother, George, came to Montana and filed claim on property that bordered their Uncle Edwards.

A large part of the Lannen compound was nothing more than a rock valley with steep sides, which was not suitable for farming. Several other Irish claimed property high in the hills on either side of the Lannens and tried to make a go of it. The Irish just seemed to band together and gravitate toward the hills.

Generations later would laugh about all the crazy Irish buying up the rocky hills that they couldn't farm, while the Germans and the Skandies took their homesteads out on the lush valley floors. For the Lannen brothers, it was very difficult at times, but they were managing with hard work and a lot of luck.

Finally, in 1914, John and Clara decided to follow their sons to Montana. They sold everything in Missouri, packed up little Edmund, Marie, and six-year-old Catherine and headed to Montana. They stayed with Edward for a season, helping him meet the percentage of cultivation necessary to "prove up" and gain title to the property. Once that was done, John and Clara sought out their own home and school for the three youngest children. Still raising a family, and not used to this hard life, Clara preferred a few necessities and balked at living up on the hills.

John and Clara decided to rent a little house in the town of Fishtail. The house had been one that Mike and Ray had rented from time to time when they weren't up on the ranch. The house needed some repairs and a new roof, which John worked on when he wasn't up on the ranch helping his sons. Clara enrolled the children in school, planted a small garden, and added a woman's touch to a house that had previously not been much more than a ranch-hand bunk house. Clara was much happier in town, but she was hungry for companionship with other women. She missed her embroidery circle of friends in Missouri, so she set about meeting her new neighbors. The Hagamans had just gotten back into town and Clara just happened to have put up additional blackberry jam. She grabbed two jars, put them in a basket and headed out the door.

Jacob and Maria Hagaman were seasonal homesteaders. They only lived in Fishtail during the planting and harvest season. When winter set in, Jacob moved his family to Belgrade, away from the harsh mountain weather. Each year, when the Hagamans came from Belgrade to the ranch, they brought their children and extended family with them. A regular train of wagons and horses would show up early in April. The Lannens, and particularly Mike, looked forward to their return each year. Jacob was a good source of news from west of the mountains, and news didn't always get to Box Canyon very timely. In addition, the Hagamans' daughter, Elsie, had just turned twenty-two and Mike had taken a liking to her. Mike and Ray often helped Jacob with his crops, particularly when the planting was ready. In exchange for that help, Jacob readily invited Mike and Ray to supper. After supper on one of those evenings, Mike and Elsie were outside the ranch house talking near the split rail fence. "I was real glad to see Jacob brought the family down early this year," Mike said to Elsie, leaning his arm over the top rail of the fence.

"Well, school was out for the babies, and Dad wanted to get the planting in early."

"Makes sense." Always short on words, Mike fought hard to think of something else to say. "I heard your brother filed on the site just north of me."

"Yes, but Wallace has never finished anything he's started. He says he's gonna build a cabin in the north corner, though we'll see."

Mike paused, scuffing his shoes in the dirt and looking everywhere except directly at Elsie. His eyes focused on a point off in the distance.

"Els, I was thinking that you might consider staying down here and getting married."

And without a beat of hesitation, Elsie said, smiling, "I might consider."

Without a bit of fuss and little else to say about the matter, Mike and Elsie set the wedding date for spring of 1916. At her parents' insistence, they were married in front of friends and family at St. James Catholic Church up in Belgrade. Immediately after the wedding, Mike took his new bride back down to Fishtail and they moved into the small and very rustic homestead ranch house.

Throughout the next year Mike and Ray built a larger house not too far from the existing cabin for the newlyweds. They used the old original homestead building as a work shed and relegated a corner of the old cabin as a "smoke house" where they butchered pigs and cured ham.

Mike built a spring box near the new house that served to refrigerate their food. Then he dug a root cellar into the side of a bank next to the kitchen door. Elsie kept busy putting up canned goods and managing the house garden so she could keep potatoes, carrots, and apples in the cellar all winter.

The ranch by that time was totally self-sustaining. It had survived drought years and flourished in others. Mike eventually bought the Fishtail rental that John and Clara lived in, as well as several other neighboring homesteads near the ranch, including his father's. Mike and Elsie were doing well.

After some consideration, Mike decided to go full bore into the cattle business. He never farmed very many acres anyway, only a few for his own use.

For the next several years Mike and Ray worked, farmed and ranched together. Then one day, quick as could be, Ray up and met a gal named Ella from a neighboring farm and married her.

Elsie's brother Wallace, as Elsie had predicted, never finished his homestead terms and had sold his ranch to Mike. Ray and Mike painstakingly moved Wallace's partially completed log cabin, one log at a time, onto Ray's property giving Ella a decent home. The cabin sat right next door to Mike and Elsie. The compound was growing and Elsie was glad for the female companionship.

Two years after Mike and Elsie were married, she gave birth to their first son. Mike took Elsie to Belgrade in her eighth month to stay with Jacob and Maria. With the heavy snows and the isolation of the canyon, Mike wanted Elsie in town and safe. Maria brought her own grandson into the world, on January 22, 1918. Elsie named him Earl Michael Lannen. They sent word to the ranch to tell Mike that Elsie and his son were doing fine, but Elsie stayed up in Belgrade until the hardest part of winter was over. Once the snow started melting, Mike brought his wife and his first-born son back down to the house in Fishtail.

Four years later, in 1922, Elsie gave birth to their second son, Frances, at their home in Fishtail. Elsie's mother came to assist with this birth too. She stayed on to take care of Elsie and their four-year old son Earl for a few months.

At that time, Montana was experiencing a failing economy that was coming right after another round of drought years. Banks were going broke and depression was hitting the state, long before the rest of the country would be faced with what would be termed the Great Depression. Mike and Elsie's lives were about to change.

* * *

Present

Holding up his coffee cup as a recognized signal requesting a refill, Joe continued, "Dad lost a little money in the bank, but he'd been pretty frugal. He provided the best he could for his family and anyone else who might have needed food or a roof over their heads. If Dad had it, he shared. Though he didn't practice formalized religion very much, he lived his life in a very religious manner. He had a strong sense of what was right.

"Four years after Frances was born, Momma was pregnant again. On April 1, 1926, your mom, Madeleine May, was born in Fishtail.

"Seems like that was about that same time Ray contracted TB and him and Ella moved to New Mexico for his health. That was real hard on Dad, 'cause he and Dad had been real close for a number of years. Ray and Ella bought up a dry goods store down there in order to make a living. Dad tried to manage the whole ranch by himself and rented out Ray's cabin. He always thought Ray would return, so he pretty much kept everything just the way it was. But Ray never recovered. He ended up dying in New Mexico, and a little later on, Ella came back by herself and moved into the cabin on Ray's part of the homestead.

But with Ray gone, Dad's work increased. With your momma just being born, times got pretty tough."

Joe paused again as much to rest his mind as to have a swallow of his freshly refilled coffee. The break lent itself to Cat and Mollie loading up the dishwasher and putting the rest of the pie away. While they were working, a side conversation continued in the dining room.

For Cat, just listening to the way Uncle Joe talked with the slow Montana drawl reminded her of her mom. They both had a way of lazily peppering their speech with peculiar phrases that made Cat smile. She was enthralled with the way the words flowed, as much as the story itself.

With the kitchen back in order, they returned to the dining room and took their seats at the table. Without skipping a beat, Joe continued. "Madeleine never had any friends to speak of, outside of us. If Dad hadn't felt so strongly about getting an education, she probably never would have even gone to school. She didn't have much use for anybody there. Although I seem to recall one girl that she used to talk about, I think her name was Dorothy, but I don't recall her last name.

I think Madeleine was probably about twelve or so when I really started understanding what she was going through.

DO YOU REMEMBER MOMMA?

1938, Absarokee, Montana

"Maddy, don't let them tease you like that. I think you're nice."

"Doesn't matter."

"Are you sure you have to go straight home?"

"Yes."

"Well, your gramma sure is a mean one . . ."

Twelve-year-old Madeleine kept walking with her head down as Dorothy's voice faded to the background with a hypnotic-like patter as they each went their separate ways.

Every day it was the same old thing. Her school mates taunted her about her short boy-cut hair, her sturdy shoes, and her clothes. That day they wanted to know if her jumper was a hand-me-down from her grandmother's flour sack underwear.

No matter how much she wished otherwise, she had to go home and do chores. Her grandmother was very strict about getting all her chores done, helping to get dinner for her four brothers and taking care of her little sister. It would be easier in a few months, when her two older brothers, Earl and Frances, who was just turning sixteen, went up to the ranch with her dad.

No one else understood the relief of three fewer mouths to feed, fewer clothes to wash and a little reprieve from her older

brothers' incessant teasing. Although, she would have given anything and put up with all of the teasing if she could just go with
them this year. She missed her dad painfully when he went up to
the ranch.

Some days more than others, she missed her mother. It didn't
seem like four years had passed since her mother died. Since then,
her grandmother Maria had moved to a little house in Absarokee
to help take care of the baby, as well as Madeleine and her little
brother, Joe. Mike had bought the rental house at Maria's urging,
claiming the ranch was no place to raise children. Maria was getting up in years at that time and, as Madeleine got older, more
responsibility was heaped on her. There were just no easy days.

Madeleine was old enough to remember her momma. If she
shut her eyes really tight, she could feel what it was like when her
mother wrapped one arm around her and one around Joe and
held them close. Madeleine would never understand why her
mother died and why no one ever talked about her. A little piece of
armor surrounded her heart that day, and the weight of the world
landed on her eight-year-old shoulders.

Whether it was explained to her, or whether she just knew, it
would be up to her to see to things now. Her six-year-old little
brother had looked to her for guidance, and a sickly new-born
baby needed care. Without too much time for grieving or reflecting, Maria just showed up and moved in to take care of the house
and kids, and Mike headed up to the ranch to take care of the
cattle.

It's not as if Maria had too much say in the matter. Her husband Jacob had died in 1931, and though she had tried to keep the
ranch house, it wasn't easy for her to manage by herself, in spite
of leasing out all the acreage and barn. Mike had come to her not
two weeks after Elsie died and offered Maria a roof over her head
and support if she would move in and help with the kids and the
house. She belligerently saw the sense in letting Mike sell what was
left of her house and asking her to take over the raising of his family, even though she was sixty-seven at the time.

They all eventually settled into a routine that was centered on hard work and long hours. During the winter months, Madeleine's dad and older brothers came down from the ranch for longer periods of time to escape the winter snows. The small house in Absarokee that her dad had bought to accommodate Maria was closer to town, right across the street from the school that Madeleine and Joe attended.

Wedging school into the normal household schedule was inconvenient for her grandmother's routine, but schooling was not taken lightly by Mike. He insisted that all his children get at least the basic requirements. Mike's formal education ended after eighth grade when he lived in Richwoods, Missouri. He could read, write, and do basic arithmetic, but he absorbed a lot on his own. He had a good head on his shoulders, listened, and used good common sense. For being a farmer and rancher that had seen little of the world, his knowledge and opinions were wise and never faltered from what he felt was the right thing.

Madeleine thought he was the smartest man ever. Not only did he know everything about ranching and farming, but he also knew about things outside of Montana, and places she'd never heard of. Over coffee and red-eye gravy at breakfast, Mike and his oldest son, discussed the state of the whole world as news came out in the weekly Absarokee paper or the nightly radio report. Events in Europe had come to the forefront of their conversations lately.

At twelve, Madeleine didn't have any idea where Europe was. Nor did she understand much of what her dad and brothers talked about. Taking care of her little sister, Louise, and trying to live up to her grandmother's expectations took up most of her day.

"Madeleine, you're going to have to learn to clean these corners better or we'll be finding mildew in here."

"Yes, Gramma."

"And don't you 'yes, Gramma' me with that tone. Put some elbow grease into those corners and quit being so lazy. Between you and Joe, I'm surprised that anything gets done right around here. Where is that boy anyway?"

Madeleine knew where Joe was but wasn't about to tell her gramma about the fence- post and dirt lean-to in the barn that Joe had built to play in.

Lately, Joe had taken to waging a war on magpies. When he was younger, he spent hours in the barn hiding in wait for the magpies to appear so he could throw rocks at them. More recently Frances had given him an old rifle and a few bullets. Now, especially on rainy days, he went up in the barn with a book and his twenty-two rifle and lay in the hay loft. Every so often he would look through the cracks of the barn to see if any magpies were around. Madeleine was glad that he was a poor shot; for the time being the magpies were generally safe.

Madeleine never let on to her gramma where Joe was. There were times on her way to the garden when Madeleine, too, went into the barn and just sat for a while. She knew nothing about the outside world of women. Oh, she heard girls at school talk about fashion, music, and movies, but the world began and ended each day in that farmhouse.

It wasn't even a reprieve to leave the house to go to school. She and Joe would walk up to the schoolhouse, where they'd split up and go to their respective rooms. The seven other girls in her class had long curly hair, as was the fashion then. Most of them looked to wear store-bought dresses and warm heavy coats. The bleached flour sacks that Gramma had used to make her slip and underwear left an itchy desire of jealousy.

Madeleine wasn't very good in school. She never had the answers when asked. And if she did have the answer, she never spoke up. She was very conservative with her words; it was the Lannen way. "Don't take twenty words to say something when five will do," her dad would say. So to her teachers and other students, it always seemed like Madeleine didn't know the answers in class. On top of that, it was difficult for her to complete all her homework without time to herself when she got home. Other than Dorothy, none of the other girls ever talked to her. More likely, they whispered or said hurtful things that Madeleine didn't understand. Life had gotten in the way of her childhood and the sooner she got done with school and those girls, the better off she'd be.

LOST INNOCENCE

1941, Absarokee, Montana

"No, you cannot go with your friends, and if I were their mothers, I would have them scrubbing floors for a month of Sundays." Gramma sternly gave this type of lecture to Madeleine every time she asked to go somewhere and participate in normal fifteen-year-old girl activities. "Just how do you expect dinner to get cooked, or do you think it's just going to cook itself?"

Joe, a normal thirteen-year-old brother, smirked in the next room listening. He could picture Madeleine's set jaw and resignation that she wasn't going anywhere that night.

Joe was excited because Dad was bringing his brothers, Frances and Earl, down from the ranch, and they'd be home for a few days. Since Frances graduated school the previous year and Earl got married, Joe hadn't seen too much of them. Frances had always been home with him during the winter school season. This last year, it had only been Madeleine walking with him and Louise to school. And they had to walk slowly because Louise was only in second grade and still a baby. Joe was old enough to walk by himself, but his gramma insisted that they all go together, which only led to more ridicule for Madeleine.

At fifteen, Madeleine's life was changing in ways she didn't understand. Two years earlier, her gramma had come to her with what looked like a stretchy bandage of some sort and told her to fasten it around her chest and wear it from then on. It was uncomfortable and she didn't understand what she was being punished for — but she didn't ask.

Last year, at school, she had a real scare. She had a stomach ache when she woke up first thing in the morning that had gotten worse throughout the day. She thought maybe the milk had gone bad or something, but by afternoon the pain was nearly unbearable. When she got home after school she went directly to the outhouse. She was bleeding. At first, she thought she'd had an accident. That evening, she snuck down and hand-washed her underclothes so that her gramma didn't find out.

By the second day the bleeding got heavier, but she was afraid to say anything to anyone. Secretly, she thought she was going to die, like her mother. Again, she hid her underclothing from her gramma. She tried to stay in bed, claiming nausea, but when it didn't stop the third day and, in fact, looked like she was bleeding worse, she gave up trying to hide it and told her grandmother.

"Well, I was wondering when that was going to happen," her gramma said, and left the room, leaving Madeleine in a state of confusion and fear. When she returned, she had a stack of small rags. She proceeded to further humiliate Madeleine by sticking rags in her underwear. "Wash them yourself when you're done with them and use 'em next month."

That was Madeleine's entrance into adulthood. She never knew why this went on month after month. But she would likely never tell Gramma again if anything happened to her. She would die first.

At fifteen, when the other girls from her class were going to the movies, she was stuck home on a Friday night. Her only reprieve was that she would get to see her dad the next day. She missed spending time with him. Maybe he would take her with him when he went to get more ranch supplies. She liked riding in the truck as he did errands. She couldn't wait until school was out and they all made the move up to the ranch house for the summer where she'd see her dad every night.

* * *

The next morning Madeleine and Joe were busy doing chores when Joe heard the truck pull in. Glad for the distraction, he dropped the feed bucket and ran outside to greet his dad and brothers.

Hey, Joe, why don't you help me with these?" Frances hollered at his little brother from the bed of the truck as he was unloading milk cans and empty supply containers from the back.

Joe came running. He adored his brothers and couldn't wait until he was old enough to stay up on the ranch all the time.

"How long are you going stay down this time? Can you stay long enough to go to the dance tonight? Aunt Catherine is playing up at Stillwater. I heard Madeleine talking about it. She and Gramma got into a fight last night. She couldn't go see her friends. I want school to be over. Do you think we can go to a movie? Are you going to be here for Christmas?"

Joe was full of questions and all his stammering gave Frances ammunition to tease Madeleine and get under her skin a little, one of his favorite pastimes when he was in town.

Carrying in the empty grain sacks, Frances sought out Madeleine and said, "I'm thinking of driving up to see Margaret and ask her to go to the dance tonight in Stillwater. Do you want to ride up?"

Madeleine's eyes narrowed and she shot daggers at him. He knew well that Margaret was her arch nemesis and Madeleine couldn't stand her. But she weighed her options carefully before responding. She really wanted to go to this dance and Frances was her only way of getting there. So she answered him with one word.

"Yes."

"All right then. We'll be leaving here at six, so if you aren't ready, I'll be leaving without you." Frances turned and walked back to the truck grinning all the way. Frances didn't even like Margaret. He was only going to ask her to the dance to irritate Madeleine, and he knew he had.

Madeleine's irritation at Frances turned to glee when her dad walked through the door, removing his hat and stepping through the threshold in one graceful movement. He hung his hat on the peg by the door, grabbed the newspaper, and headed to his favorite chair.

"Madeleine, how're you getting along?"

"I'm fine. Do you want me to fix you something to eat?"

"No, I expect Gramma has supper planned soon. Maybe some coffee, if you get a minute."

"Where's Earl? " Madeleine asked.

"He and Betty will be along a little later. We dropped him off at Betty's folks. I think they're planning on going up to Stillwater a little later tonight."

Madeleine poured her dad a cup of coffee and delivered it to the table beside his chair. Whenever Mike came down from the ranch, he liked to catch up on world affairs by reading the backlog of newspapers and listening to the news on the radio.

Left alone, they didn't pay much attention to the news, but when Dad and the boys came down, there was always a lively discussion as news events were discussed and argued around the table. They talked about President Roosevelt and the Nazis and, more recently, about friends of Frances and Earl who had been activated as part of the Montana National Guard.

Mike set the December sixth newspaper down to take a gulp of the hot coffee while Madeleine sat on the arm of his chair telling her dad about frivolous things from school and that Frances was asking Margaret to go to the dance. Unable to control himself, he said "Well she seems like a real nice girl," knowing well that the rivalry existed and he could also get Madeleine's dander up.

Gramma was watching their conversation and the relaxed way that Madeleine and her dad bantered back and forth in the familiar way of a daughter and father. The more she watched, the grimmer she got. "Madeleine, why don't you come in here and help with supper now. Let Mike read his papers."

When Madeleine went to the kitchen, Maria took her by the shoulders and sternly looked at her. "You do not sit on your father's lap in that flaunting way. You're almost grown, and that's not good behavior for a girl your age. You keep your distance and act like a proper lady, though I don't know why I even try. You're never going to amount to anything more than a farmer's wife, if you're lucky."

Madeleine turned away, her feelings hurt, but the tears remained unshed. Silently, she picked up a potato and began peeling as Gramma set the potato water on the wood stove.

Joe, who was once again lurking and listening from the other room, felt bad for Madeleine. He knew how she felt about their dad. It was almost the only time he saw her smile.

According to plan, Frances picked up Margaret and, at ten minutes to six was outside honking the horn. He knew Madeleine would not be ready and planned his arrival early just to irritate her a little more.

She came rushing out of the house with Joe in tow, her comb and a small mirror in one hand, buttons on her sleeve still undone, and a scowl on her face. She and Joe got in the back seat where she finished combing her hair. She proceeded to cross her arms and not say one word to Frances or Margaret all the way to Stillwater.

The Stillwater community hall held dances often, crowded with kids and adults alike. The music was always lively and loud. With few places to go on a Saturday night, it attracted people from as far away as Billings and Columbus.

Aunt Catherine, her dad's sister, was one of Madeleine's favorite relatives. Catherine, her husband Cody and her two cousins, Rex and Buddy, all played instruments ranging from fiddles and washboards to saxophones and banjos. While Madeleine had no talent for music, she loved to listen, especially when her Aunt Catherine and Cody were playing.

She sat against the wall, sipping punch and tapping her foot, wishing she knew how to dance like some of the other girls. She felt like she never quite measured up to others her age. In one respect, her life didn't afford her the time to learn social skills. Responsibility and the role she played in her family aged her beyond her years. Yet in another respect, without a mother to talk to or without girlfriends to confide in, she was very naïve about life. She never had any fascination for the boys she knew. After growing up with her brothers, she looked at them as more of a nuisance.

She did notice lately, though, that some of the boys she had known all her life were beginning to look older, and some even tried to talk to her. She didn't know why that should make her nervous, but she covered it up by acting angry or just ignoring them. And of course, being a Lannen, she wasn't much of a conversationalist anyway.

"Hi Madeleine, did you just get here?" The boy shuffled his feet as he stood in front of her.

"Yes."

"Do you want to get some punch?"

"No."

"When the band starts playing again, would you like to dance with me?"

"No."

"Okay, then . . . well, I'll see you around." Dejected and uncomfortable, the boy left to join a couple of his friends on the other side of the room.

About that time Earl and Betty showed up and came over to sit with her. She liked Betty. She was like a big sister and she was looking forward to the summer up on the ranch with Betty and Earl living next door in Uncle Ray's old cabin.

"Hi there, Madeleine," Betty said, scooting in next to her sister-in-law. "I thought I might come down to town just before Christmas and help get the house set up. Maybe you and I could make some candied fruitcake for the holiday. Since this is my first Christmas with Earl's family, I'd like to be able to bring some cake to Aunt Catherine and Marie before the holiday if I can get Earl to take me."

"Oh, Betty, I'd like that. But I probably need to ask Gramma if it's okay."

"That would be real nice, Madeleine; it would give me a chance to get to know you a little better. We could talk just like sisters."

When the evening finally came to an end, everyone piled into their cars and headed back home. Madeleine had enjoyed seeing all the people and listening to the music. She was still thinking about what Betty had said about sisters. It would be very nice to have someone to talk with sometimes. It had been a good night, in spite of the fact that Frances flaunted Margaret all over the dance floor.

She was exhausted when she went to bed that night. All the chores she had done and her dad coming home and the dance at Stillwater, finally took their toll on her. She fell fast asleep.

Sunday morning came too soon. Madeleine got up, dressed, and went to get Louise up and dressed for church. They faithfully attended St. Michael's every Sunday that the weather allowed. Gramma had made a batch of hot grain cereal, which Joe had already managed to spill on his shirt, so there was a ruckus going on in the kitchen. Whenever Dad was home, the house smelled like pipe tobacco and strong coffee. Madeleine breathed in the smell, enjoying the scent.

Frances drove them to Mass. They usually lingered after church visiting with neighbors, but since the boys had to get supplies for the ranch, they hurried home and changed into their work clothes.

It was just a normal Sunday after church. Chores were getting started and milk was being brought in. Chickens were being fed and Gramma was taking stock of supplies for supper when Earl came slamming through the wooden screen door.

"Dad! Turn on the radio! The War Department is makin' an announcement. Them Japs just attacked Hawaii. I heard it when I was down at the store." Frances followed Earl and grabbed for the radio dial to tune in the broadcast. Everyone stood in silence and listened:

"From the NBC newsroom in New York: President Roosevelt said in a statement today that the Japanese have attacked Pearl Harbor, Hawaii, from the air. I'll repeat that. President Roosevelt says that The Japanese have attacked Pearl Harbor in Hawaii from the air . . ."

MOMMA'S OLD WEDDING GOWN

Present

"The way I remember it," Joe said, "we all started talking at the same time, half-way listening to the rest of the radio broadcast. I remember seeing Madeleine standing there in the doorway just watching us. I don't think she understood what was going on, but the next day Aunt Catherine came over and told us that both our cousins, Buddy and Rex, were enlisting to go to war. She was crying and all worked up. I think she just about scared Madeleine half to death.

"Come to find out, Rex couldn't get in the Army, 'cause of his bad eye. Buddy went in and was killed before the first year was out. That just about broke Madeleine's heart. She didn't usually cry 'bout nothing, but she cried and cried then.

Most all of the folks in Absarokee had sons or brothers that joined up. The farms couldn't get worked with all the men gone. More and more of our neighbors around Absarokee left, selling all their cattle and leaving their farms empty. The crops all went to seed. Things got bad for a while. We had a hard time making money the next couple years. That war came and tough times just came with it."

* * *

1944, Absarokee, Montana

Once the war had begun, a lot of things changed in Madeleine's life. It was more difficult to get supplies into the stores, so the size of their garden doubled. Everyone had to work harder just to survive. Gramma Hagaman was getting older and Madeleine had taken up even more of the slack in the family. Louise was ten and Joe was of the age to spend more time at the ranch and less in town.

Madeleine had turned eighteen a week earlier and, while her birthday came and went without undue celebration, Joe presented her with a piece of chocolate candy that he had bought with his own money at the Fishtail General Store. Maria hadn't felt too well the evening of her birthday, so Madeleine fixed the dinner of fried chicken and mashed *spuds,* as Mike called them, with chicken gravy. It was enough of a birthday present having her dad and brothers down from the ranch.

With her birthday over, Madeleine looked toward her high school graduation. While she wasn't sure what she was going to do, she was looking forward to getting out of school with a diploma. It was important to her dad, and that made it important to her.

With only ten graduates in the class of 1944, Absarokee High school combined the graduation ceremony with a prom dance on the same evening.

"I don't care about the prom. It's a big waste of time, if you ask me," she told Joe when he asked her if she was going to the dance. And that's exactly how she felt about it; that is, until a friend of her cousin Buddy asked her to be his date.

Madeleine tried to push the thought of Buddy from her mind. His death was still too raw to think about, so she focused on her immediate problem. Tradition had it that the girls all wore formal, floor-length gowns for graduation and prom. If she only needed a dress for the prom, she probably wouldn't go. But since she needed a dress for graduation, she didn't know what she was going to do. Two of the girls in her class had shopped in Billings and bought brand new dresses which they continually talked about. She was sick of listening to them.

Like all girls on the cusp of womanhood, she had dreams. It's not like she had no imagination, but then her dad's voice of reason would bring her back to reality.

"Don't look at the left-hand side of the menu for what you want to eat, look at the right-hand side for what you can afford."

And she knew they couldn't afford to buy a fancy dress in Billings, and she knew she was going to have to talk to her gramma about it. Betty had offered to come down and help do her hair for the prom, but that didn't solve the problem of the dress.

She wiped her hands on the towel, hung it on the peg, and left the kitchen, slipping into her gramma's bedroom.

"Gramma? Are you awake? Can I talk to you for a minute?"

"Yes, what do you need child?"

"I'm going to be graduating soon."

"Uh huh."

"Well," Madeleine paused, took a deep breath and then just blurted it out. "I need a dress for graduation and for the prom dance."

"Dance? You need a dress for a dance? Joe needs new pants and Louise needs shoes."

"No, not just the dance — I need a formal dress for the graduation ceremony and I would be able to wear it for the dance, too." Gramma was so quiet Madeleine thought she might have gone back to sleep.

"I'll talk to your dad tomorrow."

Feeling like she had just been dismissed, Madeleine left the room.

A week later, Gramma sent Joe up to the attic storage area to pull a box down. Once Joe handed the box to Gramma, she set it carefully on the kitchen table and opened it. Inside was their mother's old wedding gown. The white ivory color had yellowed with age and parts of the lace had deteriorated. Maria slowly pulled her daughter's wedding dress from the box and held it up to her face, trying to breathe in Elsie's scent. Then sadly, she held the dress away from her and examined it carefully.

"What's that?" Madeleine asked, as she entered the room.

"When I get done with it, it's going to be your graduation dress."

"What? I can't wear that!"

"It will work just fine. I'll tear out the seams and we'll fit it for you, and I'll change this neckline a little, let the hem out . . ."

"I can't. It's yellow. It's old. Everybody will laugh at me. Gramma, its Momma's wedding dress." She choked out, "I don't like it, and I won't wear it."

Joe watched Madeleine's face fall. Her eyes were holding back tears. And he felt bad for her. Madeleine was like the mother he didn't have, and he knew more than anyone the disappointments she carried and how hard life had been on her.

"I can give you some money, Madeleine; I have some dollars from working on the Flanagan ranch," Joe blurted out.

"Oh don't be silly, Joseph," Gramma said. "She'll be just fine with this dress. It was a beautiful dress. Once I get it fixed, she'll see."

Joe wasn't so sure.

Maria was a good seamstress though and, using Elsie's old pedal sewing machine, she ripped seams and sewed and cut and refashioned the old dress. Still she couldn't do anything about the uneven yellowing on the material.

When it was done, the dress did look better, but Madeleine still hated it, as much for the meaning behind it as the dress itself. She had no other options. She had to wear the dress, but she didn't have to like it. While other girls had new pink and blue dresses, she was to wear a yellowing remade wedding dress that looked just like a remade wedding dress and a stubborn frown on her face.

She refused to have a good time at the dance and she refused to stay any longer than absolutely necessary. While she didn't know exactly what she was going to do, now that she was graduated, she knew she was going to get out of Absarokee.

That evening with diploma in hand, she packed the dress back up in the box and had Joe return it to the attic. She hoped she never saw that dress again and hoped she never had to see any of those people from school again. She'd been embarrassed beyond belief.

Within two weeks, she was packed and moving to Billings to look for a job. Her cousin Jack, who lived in Billings, had found a walk-up apartment for her. With her dad and Joe's help, they moved her in with the minimum number of necessities. Mike paid her first month's rent and prayed that she would be able to make it on her own.

She wasn't qualified for any job. Even though many jobs opened up to women because of men vacating to the military, she had no skill or any money for training. She had no experience other than keeping the house, cleaning, cooking, and taking care of her brother and sister. She had no luck at restaurants, or soda fountains, or the ticket office at the local theater.

But, happily, after two weeks she was offered a job on the belt line at a food cannery. She eagerly accepted it and began working.

She even met a nice girl in her apartment building. Mary Ellen was from Columbus and had just moved to Billings the year before. If she happened to be at home when Madeleine came home from work, she would come over to visit, and more times than not they'd share dinner.

NOT JUST ANOTHER BIRTHDAY PARTY

Present

"Things seemed to be going okay for Madeleine. I think it was a big weight off Dad's mind. Up until then he wasn't sure if she was going to end up back home or not. I don't know too much about what went on up there in Billings. But after she left, Gramma took to her bed most of the time, and Louise had to take up most the slack for both Gramma and Madeleine."

Joe paused in his story telling to stretch his legs. His eyes looked tired. "I'm afraid I'm getting worn out," Joe said to no one in particular.

"I'm so sorry, Joe. I know we've kept you up," Cat said. "But I really love hearing Montana stories. Mom never talked much about it." Joe finished the last drop of his coffee and stifled a yawn. "We probably need to get you back to the hotel, so you can get some sleep."

The group began to break up, lingering a little longer, saying their goodbyes.

"Thanks for dinner, it was really good," Jamie said, giving Cat a big bear hug. "Mollie and I'll drive Joe over to his hotel. You've had a long day too, and besides, you get to see him tomorrow when you take him to the airport."

"That would be great, if you want to, Jamie. Thanks."

Jamie, Mollie, and Uncle Joe left the house and Cat picked up the last of the coffee cups. While Cat was finishing up in the kitchen, she was thinking about what Uncle Joe had told them about her mom's childhood. She missed her mom; she missed how her mom used to be. Even though her mom still lived in the "home", she wasn't the same person. She wasn't the same Mom Cat remembered and not the same Mom she heard about that night. Having Uncle Joe talk about the ranch and their growing up years made her feel the connection to her family. She finished up in the kitchen, started the dishwasher, turned off the lights, and followed the sounds of Morgan wrestling on the bed with Jim. Standing in the doorway, she smiled at them. She had a strong connection to this family too.

* * *

The next day, Cat drove over to the hotel to pick up Joe and drive him to the airport. She was sorry to see him go. He was like an extension of her mom, before her mom became such a stranger.

"If you remember when you get home, Joe, send me a copy of the family history you've been working on. I'd love to take a look at it," Cat reminded Joe as she gave him a hug at the gate.

"I will. You take care now." Joe released her and started to head for the end of the security line when Cat remembered that she was still holding the brown-paper-wrapped package that contained the pencil sketch of the ranch that she'd had framed. Waving him down, she handed it to him and said, "Don't open this until Christmas. It's just something I want you to have." He nodded.

Cat watched him walk through the gate toward his terminal, the picture under his arm. She waited until he was out of sight before she turned to leave.

For the next several weeks, Cat's visits with her mom were punctuated with a series of "I dunno's" and they settled back into the same frustrating routine.

* * *

With the spring, came her mom's birthday. Cat tried to get everyone together at the "home" and have a little celebration. Jamie and Mollie came down, and Cat and Jim brought a small birthday cake and some presents, but her mom was preoccupied with a stuffed teddy bear that Jamie had brought. Madeleine must have felt it was her duty to wander through the halls and introduce "Teddy" to all the nurses. She didn't seem to care whether her kids were there or not. To Cat, it was like sadly watching a child. It hurt her, and the only way she knew how to handle hurt was to be angry.

"Well this was a pleasant visit, wasn't it?" she said sarcastically, as they sat in the family room with discarded wrapping paper and presents strewn around. Her mother had taken no interest in them.

"Don't be so hard on your mom," Jim said. "If she wants to wander around the halls with the stuffed bear and it makes her happy, that's fine with me."

"I think it's kind of cute," Mollie said in her naïve manner. Cat shot her a look, rolling her eyes. Cat had wanted "the Hallmark moment", the "Currier and Ives Christmas," the Norman Rockwell magazine cover with the nice little old gramma celebrating a birthday with her children. Life has a way of throwing you zingers, doesn't it?

Jamie and Mollie started packing up the presents and throwing away the discarded paper in the obvious move recognized as "the party is over".

Jim and Cat tracked down her mom, who was holding court in the dining room with her teddy, and walked back to her bedroom with her. She seemed strangely preoccupied, holding the teddy tight as she sat on the edge of her bed. Jamie and Mollie came into the room to say goodbye. "I love you Mom, happy birthday," Jamie said. "We'll see you soon." He turned to his sister, their eye's meeting in sibling connection, hugged her, and whispered, "It is — what it is. I love you."

When they had left, Cat helped her mom into a flannel nightgown and put her and the teddy to bed. Cat exuded frustration when she yanked the covers up to her mom's chin. "We have to get going, Mom. Happy birthday! " She had just turned to leave, giving Jim that look that says "we're out of here", when she heard her mother's small voice behind her. "You know, you're a lot like your father sometimes."

Cat swung around and caught her unusually steady eye. "What do you mean I'm like Daddy?"

"No . . . not Daddy." Madeleine paused to clear her throat. "I meant your real father." Cat couldn't look away and knew somehow that her mother was trying to organize her thoughts. She'd seen that look of determination on her face before. Madeleine continued in a very weak but steady voice. "You can be very cold when you want to be." She paused, looking Cat in the eye. "It's hurtful." Madeleine shut her eyes but continued speaking. "Your father's family was very English. They always acted, I dunno . . . I guess the word would be . . . reserved. I always thought they were a cold bunch, though." Madeleine paused again, taking a slow breath, and then opened her eyes. For a moment, she looked at Cat as if she hadn't seen her for a long time. "You've always had a tendency to be that way; I guess you came by it legitimately." She had a half-smirk on her face. "As much as I tried to look the other way, you still took after him some."

This was an odd conversation, first because Madeleine was actually carrying on the conversation and secondly, because speaking of her real father had always been a taboo subject. No good or calm word had ever been said about him. Even invoking his name would cause her mom to scrunch up her face in disgust. Without waiting for Cat to say a thing, Madeleine continued talking, her voice growing stronger as her memories became more clear.

"Glenn's great-great grandfather came from England — came from a long line of farmers, but you would have thought Glenn's mother was a descendent of the queen herself. I told you I never knew anything about them, but I did. Your father told me I should lessen the burden."

Cat sat down slowly on the chair beside her mom's bed and watched her face. What burden was she talking about? Of course she knew that her blood father was English. Her mother had told her that much years ago. She'd always known she was English-Irish. But it was always said accusingly, as if it were a bad mix of blood.

Madeleine closed her eyes and the silence stretched uncomfortably. Cat wasn't sure if she had fallen asleep or not when she began to talk again. "Jonathan . . ." she paused, "your great-grandfather's name was Jonathan. His parents emigrated directly from England, and when they got here, they settled in Michigan." She paused again. "Your great-grandmother's name was Evangeline."

Cat felt Jim move closer into the room and stop short as he heard Madeleine talking. He very quietly leaned against the wall, crossed his arms over his chest and listened silently.

As the old woman held her teddy bear tightly, she began slowly. "I think it must have been right after the Civil War ended; Jonathan and Evangeline were married."

ROSES AND RUNAWAYS

Late 1800s, Ionia County, Michigan

Not long after the end of the Civil War, Jonathan Barker and Evangeline Conner were planning a wedding in Ionia County, Michigan. Ionia County was a small area in the central part of the state surrounded by rolling hills of farmland and wheat fields, generously spider-webbed with creeks and tributaries of the Grand River. It was beautiful country, not unlike the Yorkshire Dales area of England itself.

Years earlier, a wave of French-Canadians had tried to settle in Iona County. But by 1876, the British chased them out and the county became primarily of English descent. This was exactly how the English preferred it. English lineage and heritage was very important to the core of the community and was reflected in every aspect of life. Many of the homes were replicas of their homes in England. The town shops ordered cloth and yarn from Great Britain, along with glassware and even art. Well-to-do children were taught the Queen's English with its carefully rounded vowels, to preserve the dialect which gave them prestige and class over the commoners.

Both Jonathan and Evangeline were one generation removed from the mother country. Most of the upper-English families in Iona County married within their social class. Marrying mixed blood was frowned upon. Jonathan and Evangeline were very confident of their lineage, since both families had come to America at about the same time. Both families arrived through New York Harbor. Both families had staked their original homesteads in Michigan and were solidly part of the upper-crust in the county. The two families knew and respected each other and, in fact, had been in business together for years. Both the Connor and the Barker families were very pleased with this union.

In the spring of 1876, Jon and Evangeline said their wedding vows before the rector at St. Patrick's Episcopal Church. The church held nearly one hundred of their neighbors and family in witness. Evangeline was a beautiful bride, wearing a dress with a crinoline hoop skirt ordered from England. Her lace veil with the floral motif had belonged to her mother. She carried a bouquet of the palest pink-nearly-white tea roses, her favorite flower.

A modest celebration followed the ceremony that included a light supper, a double layer fruit cake with white frosting, and music and dancing until early into the following morning. The wedding was talked about for weeks.

The newly married couple moved immediately into Jon's home. Jon, a furniture maker by trade, owned part of the lumber mill as well as a substantial piece of property on the outskirts of the county. The beautiful white Victorian two-story home sat on the edge of town. Like most of the homes in that area, his was heavily influenced by European design, sporting the popular Victorian décor with a wide wrap-around porch, formal parlor, and large dining room. The main floor was appointed with gas lighting and classic chandeliers. The house was filled with beautiful polished furniture, buffets, and upholstered chairs. Many of the pieces had been built with Jon's own imagination and skill. Evangeline had very little to do to the house itself, other than add a woman's touch.

She spent the first few years filling the house with heirlooms, collected from both of their families. She added her own special touches with needlework, crochet throws, and trunk covers.

The house itself faced hundreds of acres of "great field", which extended as far as the eye could see. Numerous outbuildings spotted the parameter of the field. A large barn closer to the house was used mostly for tools and storage of their wagons. Fortunate to have moderate wealth, they chose to board their horses at a livery stable closer to town.

They did a small amount of farming, mostly for their own use, and kept a few cows. However, that wasn't their primary source of income. Jon's income came from lumber, as did most of the residents of Ionia County. His lucrative hobby as a craftsman with fine wood both gave him a creative outlet and added substantially to their financial coffers.

The Barkers were doing very well. When Evangeline gave birth to a son two years after their marriage, their life turned even better. They named their new son, Royal Conner Barker.

"Oh, Jon, look at him. I swear he gets bigger every day. And look at him smile." Evangeline held Royal, making cooing noises and watching her son giggle as she nuzzled him.

"Yes, I do rather think he looks a lot like me. Wouldn't you agree?"

"Of course he does, dear. I don't believe I've ever loved anything so much. We shall have a dozen children. I cannot bear not having the sound of a baby in our home. It is the happiest voice I've ever heard." Jon smiled at his happy family. However, a second child did not come easily or soon.

Two and a half years later, in 1881, after two miscarriages, Evangeline was pregnant again. She was very weak, and had been ordered to bed by the town doctor to protect the unborn child. While she was bed-ridden, fever went through Ionia County and their young son Royal took sick and died. She had been unable to help him, and his death devastated Jon.

Two months later, barely escaping the fever herself, Evangeline gave birth to a second son named Glenn Lee Barker. Though they still mourned the loss of their first-born, the new baby helped to move them past their grief.

Evangeline's mother came to help her while Evangeline gained back her strength.

"Honey, I brought you some roses from my garden. Do you have a vase I can put them in?" Evangeline's mother was thoughtful in remembering how much her daughter loved tea roses.

"Yes, Mother, my cut glass is in the far cupboard."

Evangeline's mother chose a vase that she had given Evangeline and began arranging the roses. "I cut some extra, and took them up to the cemetery."

"Oh, Mother, I can't believe we've lost him. Baby Royal was so sick, and I could do naught for him. Jon is beside himself with a broken heart, and will not soothe the baby. I fear that he doesn't love him."

"This has been a difficult time for everyone. Give him time to mourn. He will heap love upon Glenn the same way he did with Royal, and the same way he will to the rest of your children."

"I do hope you're right, Mother. I know I need to get out of bed and get on with life, but I have nothing to look forward to except the baby."

"Evangeline, you used to spend hours helping me with the flowers. You seemed to enjoy it so much. Perhaps you need your own roses to care for. I'm sure that Jonathan could find a place in the garden to plant a bush or two. Roses bring you life. You could nurture them in memory of Royal."

"Yes, I will talk to Jon. That is a wonderful idea."

And at Evangeline's request, Jon planted a rose garden next to the house. The roses helped to heal her, and she spent all her spare time pruning, weeding, and cutting her beautiful tea roses, filling vases and displaying them throughout their home enveloping the rooms with their fragrance.

Evangeline would have liked more children, but it wasn't meant to be, so all her attention was heaped onto Glenn's small shoulders. Jon was afraid to open his heart to Glenn and instead used rules and discipline as his means of communication with the boy. Jon was a strict father with high expectations. He had buried his ability to love a child with the loss of Royal. Young Glenn could earn his father's approval, but he never gained his love. Glenn bore the brunt of his father's pain.

Glenn was taught early to respect and fear his father. Jon worked hard, and expected his young son to work just as hard. He expected, no demanded, a lot from Glenn. The boy was taught early to help with chores and punished soundly for forgetting.

Impeccable manners were taught and enforced from the time he could walk. He was educated in the proverbial "little red school house", drilled on spelling, geography, and reading. He was expected to use proper etiquette at all times whether at home or away. Evangeline wished with all her heart that Glenn had siblings to share his burden. Had that miracle occurred, she was sure Jon would not have such heavy expectations for Glenn. She was very concerned that Glenn was missing out on his childhood. Because she was a little fearful of Jon herself, she simply tried her best to keep peace between them.

"Glenn, you are required to sit up tall at the table when you're studying," Evangeline gently reminded him, as she arranged a bouquet in one of her crystal vases.

"Yes, Mother." Glenn straightened his shoulders.

"You have been doing quite well in schooling lately, have you not?"

"Yes, Mother."

"Then why don't you put your books away and see if your friend Robert is out and about. Your father isn't going to be home until late tonight, so it'll be our secret. Run along now."

"Thank you, Mother." Glenn rapidly closed his books and ran to put them away. He was making his way towards the door at a run when he ran back to give Evangeline a strong hug around her waist. He breathed in her scent, smelling of flowers, and then ran for the door. Evangeline grinned, watching out the window as he disappeared down the road.

At an early age, Glenn began following his father through the fields, absorbing all he could about farming, a childish attempt to gain his father's approval. Jon allowed him to tag along and, for the most part, put up with his company and an endless stream of questions while he tended the crops and animals. Jon took Glenn to the wood mill on occasion, and Glenn became a sponge of information in hopes that his father would be proud of him. The minute school was dismissed, Glenn sought out his father and followed him around until dinner time. After dinner, Evangeline worked with him on his studies before they lost the evening light.

Sometimes his mother talked to him about his day and laughed at his childish humor. He could almost always talk her out of a peppermint stick or a piece of hard candy, with the promise not to tell his father.

Glenn was only 10 years old — still a child really, when Evangeline became very sick and quite unexpectedly died in the middle of the night. There was no hint of a problem. His mother had fixed dinner the night before. They had eaten beef and the puffy yellow biscuits that Glenn liked, with gravy. His mom had retired early without pushing Glenn on his studies, and he had disappeared quickly to the barn, just in case she changed her mind.

The next morning, there were strangers in his house and his father was more remote than usual, only talking to the doctor from town. No one talked to Glenn or even recognized that he was there. He hid in the hallway trying to listen to their conversations, but they were speaking too low, so he hid in the barn for the rest of the morning.

The neighbors that bordered the east side of the farm took Glenn home with them. It was there that he was told his mother had died.

Glenn didn't see his father for weeks. His grandparents came and took him to their house in town, where he ate, slept, and studied — always waiting for his father to come and take him home.

Jon never did take Glenn home. Distraught at Evangeline's death, he turned to his parents for help in raising his son. For the next few years, Glenn lived with his grandparents in a home that smelled of age. His father mourned for far too long and eventually settled into a routine that did not accommodate a twelve-year-old boy. As time went on, Glenn saw less and less of his father.

When Jon did visit, he brought small gifts for his son but spend most of the time talking to his parents. When Jon left, Glenn stayed behind. His mother's death had been painful for young Glenn; he missed her dearly. At night, he sometimes thought he smelled her roses, and would lie awake for hours breathing deeply. Glenn could have once been a part of his father's life, but in time, a son didn't fit into Jon's lifestyle. Glenn's pleas to his father fell on deaf ears.

As he grew older, he became angry and bitter about his father's lack of attention. He and his best friend Robert hung out together whenever they could, and got into their share of trouble, much of it instigated by Glenn as he rebelled against both his father and grandparents.

Robert and Glenn were as close as brothers and swore to be best friends for life. But at sixteen, Robert and his family moved away to Billings, Montana. Robert's father had lost his job and needed to go where there was work. The move was swift, and Glenn felt the loss as if it were his mother's death all over.

Many families from Michigan and Minnesota were migrating to what they called the "true" west following the direction of the railroad. Billings just happened to be a stop in that direction.

Robert and Glenn stayed in contact by writing letters to each other. Robert told him all about his adventures in Montana and how horses and wagons filled the streets. Cowboys carried guns and walked around with large hats and boots. Robert made it all sound like a grand adventure, exciting and sparking Glenn's imagination with visions of a faraway place and the only friendship Glenn had known.

Not surprisingly, in 1898, at seventeen, Glenn ran away. He didn't stay in Michigan to see his father remarry later that year to the widow Clara. He didn't stay to finish school. Instead, he followed the railroad west.

He stopped in Billings long enough to meet up with Robert, who by that time, was sweet on a girl and had new friends. Glenn continued on to the next stop on the railroad line, Livingston, which lay just beyond Billings, with far more population and industry and hope for a better opportunity for a job.

Glenn was very adept at numbers. With a few simple lies about his age and background, he began learning a trade at the Livingston Land Company, recording homesteads and managing the records for platted land sales.

Glenn easily made friends. He was well-mannered, polished, and had a grand sense of humor. The men took him under their wings teaching him much about business and even more about the private doings of men. At the land company and on his rounds, he took to wearing a ten-gallon Stetson. He enjoyed the attention and the stature it granted him. Like a chameleon, he moved easily between being a cowboy and being the man-about-town spending his evenings in poker and drinking clubs.

Always miserly with his money and careful with investments, he never lacked for anything, but always held the fear of being without. His nose to the grindstone, he centered his life on his job with little time for anything else.

Years passed swiftly, with his job occupying his days and his socializing, and drinking in the evenings. He didn't lack companionship, but had no concept of family or the desire to start one.

QUITE THE CATCH FOR AN ENGLISHMAN

1911, Livingston, Montana

As Glenn neared thirty, he still lived in the same house he had purchased when he was nineteen. He had never married, but that didn't mean he was lonely. While he enjoyed a reputation as a well-heeled socialite sometimes accompanied by wealthy ladies of status, he could party with the bawdiest. Although he was frugal with his business investments, he would throw his money and position around whenever it suited him. Many times that would gain him the attention of women who wanted nothing more than a ring on their finger and a stake in his money.

Whenever a woman got too close to him, he'd take a trip and not make it known. He'd simply stop calling on her. It wasn't beneath him to even be hurtful. While his graces could have used improvement, he had a good reputation for business, and his career was successful. In the social circles he was known as "quite a catch" with his good looks and outgoing personality. Although content without female company, he was never at a loss if he needed a dinner companion for some occasion.

It was at one of these occasions that he met twenty-one-year-old Mary Eleanor Ewald, the youngest daughter of one of Glenn's customers. She was very pleasing to the eye and possessed an impeccable English background. It was the first time that Glenn posed the thought of sharing his life with someone. She reminded him of his mother. She even smelled a bit like roses — a scent he never forgot.

On December 7, 1912, one year after they met, he wed Mary in Livingston, Montana. Nine years younger than Glenn, Mary was only twenty-two years old when she became Mrs. Glenn Barker. She had spent her whole life in Livingston and was aching to leave. Mary always had her sights set on a higher social ladder, so when Glenn was offered a position several years later with a branch of the Montana Land Co. in Billings, she eagerly set about convincing him to accept.

Billings was developing fast into a social Mecca, with theaters and clubs. The additional money Glenn could be making and the thought of living in the "new city" excited Mary.

Billings was also becoming a very diverse city. German settlers were cultivating the rich farmland in the valley. The English were developing the core business districts. Within the bounds of the city, mansions were being constructed by Swiss immigrants. It was Mary's hope to own one of those mansions and bring her English culture to the inner circle of Billings. She could become the socialite there that she could never be in Livingston.

"Mother, you know I will miss you and Papa, but Glenn has promised that we will come back to Livingston to visit just as soon as we get settled. And you can come stay with us on the holiday, so you don't have to drive the buggy back and forth."

"Well, I think Glenn has some rather grand ideas," her mother stated dourly. She was not necessarily as taken in by Glenn as her daughter was.

"We're going to look at the mansions when we go to Billings next week. Glenn says the new city is growing fast, and he can make lots of money there; it's going to be so exciting."

"Don't expect too much until you see what you get. Papa's not too sure about that land company. He read in the news that they're running out of property in Billings. Fact is the county is sending the Irish up on hills to homestead, telling them to farm the rocks.

And those crazy Irish don't know any better. You can't trust them, you know that, don't you?"

"Oh Momma, you're just going to have to have some faith in Glenn. He says this is a good opportunity and I believe him. You know I heard that Billings even has a yarn store that carries threads all the way from Europe."

But Mary didn't get her mansion. Glenn was more provident than she had imagined. While he had thrown his money around in the past to impress her, he now tightened the purse strings. He was also rightfully concerned about talk of a downturn in the economy and was savvy enough to understand the implications.

While Mary had her heart set on a grand house, Glenn settled on purchasing a modest house just off Main Avenue in a practical neighborhood, close to the land company.

After her initial disappointment, she resigned herself to making the home and her life as pleasant as she could. Mary was outward and energetic, joining women's clubs, as well as the sewing and quilting circles. She filled their home with beautiful handmade crocheted pillows, quilts, throws, and intricate lace doilies. Her skill with fancy yarns was enviable, and she taught the skills to her lady friends, making her quite popular in her circle.

Even though Glenn had stopped short of buying Mary her mansion, she did not want for expensive furnishings. If Mary needed or desired something, Glenn managed to get it for her. He had a piano brought over from Minnesota. Bone china was shipped from New York. Finer things that were not available in Billings were sent away for. While Mary was not exactly the grand dame she had intended on becoming, the couple was socially set.

* * *

For the next six years, Glenn did very well at the land company. But in 1918 when banks began to tighten up and money was harder to come by, he changed careers and decided to start his own business. As a hedge against the economy, he took a lease on a feed and general store that was less than a mile from home and proceeded to learn the grocery business. No matter how bad the economy got, he knew people needed food and supplies.

He named the store Barker's Grocery and stocked it with everything: fresh produce, baked goods, canned items, housewares, tools, feed and grain. He would make this into a neighborhood general store that even bartered for goods when necessary.

With everything from consigned farm equipment to candy, business was doing well. Within the first year, he hired some help to manage the store and was making a neat profit on his own.

Two years after opening the store, Mary proudly announced she was pregnant. She had begun to think she would never have a child. On October 31, 1921, she gave birth to a son and heir, Glenn Lee Barker, Jr. He would be Glenn Sr. and Mary's only child. Mary wanted more children, but after a miscarriage, Glenn stopped pursuing it, afraid he would lose Mary too early, like his mother.

* * *

Present

"So that was that," Madeleine said in a matter-of-fact way, as if the whole issue had just been put to bed. Then she said, almost as an afterthought, "Your father was the only child they ever had and not too long after that, Glenn Sr. began drinking heavily, spending most of his time either at work or at the clubs, leaving your father's rearing up to Mary."

About that time, the floor nurse brought in a tray of food for Madeleine's dinner. Cat appreciated the stealthy service and thanked her. Her mom had stopped talking and began picking at a roll on the food tray when she looked up at her daughter and asked, "Do you need to get home and start dinner?"

Cat glanced quickly at Jim, who had long since pulled up a chair, transfixed with the story. "No, we're fine; if I get hungry, I'll just pick at your fruit cup," Cat said, plucking a grape and popping it into her mouth. "That is, unless you want to kick us out," she said jokingly, trying to keep the moment light, hoping with her whole being that her mom would continue talking.

As Madeleine picked up her fork and scooped up a bite of mashed potatoes, they waited for her to swallow. In a very small voice, she continued. "Your father grew up a lot different than we did." She paused, taking another bite. "His folks had a pretty nice house in Billings. Mary had to have the best of everything. You know all my good cut glass dishes were passed down from her." She paused for a moment. Cat let the comment slide, since she and Jamie had long since packed up all her mom's dishes and stored them in the attic.

"From what I heard, your father was a little contrary when he was young." She chuckled a bit. "Oh yes, Junior was a handful. 'Junior'! I hadn't thought about that in years. Your grandparents nicknamed your father *Junior*. He hated that name. When he was young, probably eight or nine, Mary made him take piano lessons. He hated those lessons too. They must have done some good though, 'cause when he was older, he was a really good piano player. He could play just about anything when he put his mind to it, but he didn't play very often. I don't know why. He was kind of like you are with your piano." Her voice trailed off and she paused again. Though she was still looking at Cat, it seemed as if she was looking through her, reaching for memories of the past.

* * *

1930, Billings, Montana

"I don't know why I have to practice this. I hate that old lady," Glenn whined.

"Junior, you just practice that piano and be grateful that your father still sees fit to pay for lessons."

"But I want to go outside," he whined. "Johnny and Red are waiting for me."

"Well you aren't going anywhere. You finish your practicing and don't shame God for wasting your talent. Those boys can just wait on you. Last time you were with them, you got into trouble sneaking into that movie theater and your father blistered your backside. Is that what you want again?"

"No, ma'am."

Glenn's mother settled back in her chair, picking up her crochet hook and concentrating on which stitch she had missed before her nine-year-old son began his daily outburst over the keyboard. Mary did her best to ignore the incorrect notes and settled her thoughts on how her life had changed lately.

While the rest of the country was just starting to feel the pain of the 1929 stock market crash, Montana had been in a deep depression for years. Between the years of 1920 and 1928, more than half of Montana's banks failed. Once the failures started, it spread like the drought. Depositors withdrew funds and the money fled east. Folks unable to get jobs followed soon after. The Montana economy basically collapsed.

Prior to that, Billings had been growing at an industrious rate and Glenn Sr. had worked hard at being a part of that growth. It had been a much happier time for Mary. It was difficult to watch homesteads board up and the trains fill with families they had known for years. Farming and ranching had collapsed and there was little employment to be found. Luckily, Glenn Sr. had always been the frugal sort; even though the Barker Store didn't do as much business as it used to, it was still a lifeline to the neighborhood. He couldn't afford to hire help, so he spent most of his days at the store himself. Although the money wasn't what it once was, he had invested lightly and some of his private endeavors continued to pay. With some belt tightening and budgeting, they had adjusted.

It appeared to Mary that part of that adjustment was spending more and more evenings at the local clubs with his friends, bemoaning the economy and what President Hoover was likely, or not likely, to do to improve things. Since Prohibition in 1920, alcohol was illegal, but that didn't stop more and more clubs and nightspots from sprouting up in the seedier parts of town. The speakeasies and backrooms sold plenty of bootlegged whiskey and, as soon as one was closed down, two more opened. The law chose to turn a blind eye to most of them. Since money started getting tight, Glenn's hours away from home seemed to get longer. He was often out until well after Junior was in bed, and most nights when he did come home, he fell asleep in the living room chair.

Mary spent a few precious moments longing for the past, remembering when she wasn't quite as thick around the middle and her looks didn't belie her 39 years. Well, enough feeling sorry for herself. She picked up her needle and continued to crochet.

Junior cared little about the economy or his father's late hours. What he cared about then, was hanging out with his friends and perhaps sneaking into the downtown pool hall. At nine years old, there were more important things to do than to pluck keys on the piano or take the lessons that were forced on him.

Seeing his mother slump slightly in the chair with her eyes closed, he snuck off the piano bench and made for the front door, allowing the screen door to slam behind him. He took one big leap off the porch, avoiding the stairs, and began running down the sidewalk, turning right at the main road heading over the four blocks to Red's house.

Red's house was not as big or as nice as Glenn's, but, for all the cracked paint on the outside, the inside was warm and friendly. He didn't have to worry about polished wood or crystal glass figurines or forgetting to wipe off his shoes. In spite of not having much money, Red's parents were fine people. Red's dad always talked to him like a grownup, and his mom was very friendly. The house always smelled of sweet rolls or something baking, mixed with spicy sauce and garden flowers. Unlike Glenn's parents, Red's were full of laughter and quick to give out hugs and cookies, or both.

Red's older brother even had his own car. And once in a while when he wasn't busy, he'd drive the boys down to the movie theater or to the pool hall. After the last bout of trouble, the movie theater was off limits, but not as long as they didn't get caught.

As Glenn rounded the corner, he saw Red and Johnny sprawled out on the sidewalk in front of the house with two sacks of marbles between them. After a playful greeting of slapping and punching each other, Glenn leaned back on his elbows to relax on the cool lawn.

Staring up at the clouds, he wished he could move into Red's house. Then he wouldn't have to be home when his dad came home. It just like he couldn't do anything right these days, and his dad was real quick with a backhand, especially when he came home late from the club. The boy had learned rapidly to mind his manners around his father and disappear as quickly as possible.

He also learned that not getting caught in a lie was well worth the lie itself. That alone saved him from punishment nine times out of ten. Whenever he did get caught, he just figured that it made up for all the times he didn't. It was all about playing the odds.

"Hey, Red, whatcha say we go downtown?"

"Naa, can't tonight. I have chores and homework to do. I'm just not like you."

"What do you mean?"

"You never bring home a book," Red scowled, "and you still get A's all the way down the teacher's column."

"Yeah, I don't know why that happens. It just comes easy for me I guess. What about you, Johnny?"

Johnny had been concentrating on a shot with his marble. "I don't know, Glenn; I probably ought to go home." As Johnny sat up and looked over, Glenn noticed the black eye."

"Geez, Johnny where'd you get that shiner?"

"Ahh, I fell and just got bumped."

Glenn knew better than that and had been witness to more than one fight between Johnny and his dad. Johnny's dad always got mean when work started getting slow. Johnny and Glenn shared a bond in that quiet understanding.

BUT, YOU HAVE TO BE
EIGHTEEN TO ENLIST

1937, Billings, Montana

Six years later, with his sophomore year just ending, Glenn was cornered by a lively little brunette between classes. "Glenn, are you going to the dance tonight?" Clair asked.

"Yep. I'll be there. I'm picking up Red and his girl in Pop's truck."

"This is just gonna be the best dance ever," she continued. "We're all meeting afterwards down at Kate's, so if you aren't doing anything after, you could stop by." Clair was hoping he would come. She'd had a crush on him for their whole sophomore year and hadn't been able to talk to him much more than between classes.

"We'll see." Glenn wandered off down the hall. He didn't have any interest in the high school dance in spite of the fact that Clair was growing up to be quite a looker.

Glenn had grown tall and lanky, with an air of confidence about him that made him appear much older than his sixteen years. Girls liked him. But most important to him, he had finally outgrown the nick name of "Junior".

The school was sponsoring the dance and the potluck as a fundraiser, hoping to raise enough money to help with the building of a new high school. They were outgrowing the existing school and everyone in the town was eager to have a new one built within the next couple of years. This was the first big dance the school had planned in a long time, and the entire student body seemed to be talking about it.

While Glenn was supposed to be on his way to class, he decided at the last minute that he'd ditch the rest of the day and go downtown. Maybe he'd see if there was a movie playing.

Movie arrivals were undependable getting to Billings since the Hollywood black list had been made public. Those aggravating church people were shutting down more movies than ever got shown.

As he walked along Main Avenue, his eye caught a sign in the window with big black letters claiming "Montana National Guard Needs You!" He'd heard of the Guard and saw some of them on weekends wearing uniforms and marching on their way to gun practice. Slowing down to a stop in front of the window, he stared at the black letters of the advertisement. He thought he might look into that later. He tucked the information away in the back of his mind. *Wouldn't Pop just come out of his chair if I enlisted?* The idea became more attractive the more he thought about angering his father.

Two hours later, he picked up Red with his most recent girlfriend, and the three of them walked into the school gym, following the sound of music and the smell of food. The gym had been transformed into a dance floor and eating area. He and Red had snuck some cigarettes earlier, and Glenn tapped down the left-over pack in his pocket to keep them out of sight. He filled up a plate of food and sat down with some friends.

Between the music, the jokes, and the laughter, his mind kept wandering back to that National Guard sign. Maybe tomorrow he'd stop in and talk to the guy in charge and see exactly what you needed to do if you were thinking about joining up.

The room was suddenly becoming stale. "Come on, Red, it's still early, let's go down to the hall and play a little pool. I'm getting a little tired of listening to these crooners. At least the music swings down there."

"Geez, Glenn, if I get kicked out of there one more time, my dad is going to hang me from a tree."

"Oh, Red, your dad wouldn't lay a hand on you. If he did, your mom would probably beat the tar out of him."

"Yeah, I know, but, he was real mad last time."

"No buts. Come on," Glenn said as he led Red through the crowd to the door. They made for the truck, picking up Red's girl on the way out, and dropping her off at her home. Then Glenn headed downtown parking several blocks away from the hall. The moment he opened the truck door, he could hear the music and laughter coming out of the place.

Glenn grabbed Red, still protesting, and headed for the crowd that was entering the pool hall. Both he and Red looked older than their age and had been sneaking into the hall for years. As long as they didn't cause any trouble, the bartenders looked the other way. And up until now, the boys usually just played some pool, had a soda, and were on their way. Lately, though, the bartenders noticed that they had been mingling more and more with the regular customers, particularly the women.

They had even seen Glenn dancing with a particular girl on occasion. That was the last night they got kicked out. It didn't help their case much that they had bootleg whisky and cigarettes on their breath when they got home.

As they entered the hall, strains of dance records from the jukebox filled the place. The beat was alive with a Tommy Dorsey tune, and the dance floor was packed. "Augh, geez . . . here we go again," Red muttered with resignation. While Glenn headed across the dance floor, Red headed the other way to get a soda.

For the most part, they had been fairly inconspicuous that evening. But when the jukebox finally wound down, hungry for more coins, Glenn wasn't quite ready for the evening to end, and he did something he almost never did. Oh, Red had seen him do it before, but the times were few and far between. Glenn grabbed a chair and slid it up to the piano. Taking his thumb and running it from the treble to the bass, he began playing a bass beat that slowly took on a boogie rhythm. A few feet started tapping; a couple of girls, with the aid of excessive drinking, began dancing with each other on the dance floor. The base rhythm turned into a recognizable Benny Goodman song. Glenn was drawing the attention of the crowd.

Glenn knew he was about two minutes from getting thrown out on his ear, but he couldn't resist the popular jazz music. And true to form, a group crowded around the piano. Following a rousing finish, he hit the door fast, meeting Red outside.

"I don't know how you do that Glenn. Anyone who can play that stuff by ear like you, should do something with that talent. You should be in a band or something. Why don't you play more?"

"I don't know. Just don't want to."

"Well it's a damn waste, if you ask me." Red had been down this conversation road before and knew it was useless.

"Hey Red, can I ask you something? I'm thinking about joining up with the National Guard. What do you think?"

"Geez Glenn, you can't. You have to be eighteen to join up." Red listened to himself saying those words and knew just as sure as he was standing there, Glenn was going to join up and he'd lie about his age.

DEAD PEOPLE DON'T
CARRY ON CONVERSATIONS

Present

Cat noticed a motion out of the corner of her eye and saw the night nurse and the young nursing aide standing behind the curtain in the doorway. They had been listening to Madeleine tell her story. They were amazed, since they had barely heard their patient talk at all, outside of "Yes, No" and "I dunno."

Madeleine started to get restless and shut her eyes for a few minutes. The nurse took that opportunity to come in and give her the nightly insulin shot. She nodded her head in Cat's direction with a half-smile while she was attending to the task. As soon as she was done and had left the room, Cat asked, "Mom, why didn't you ever share this with me before?"

"Oh, I dunno. I guess the last time we talked, I finally forgave him." She paused and, in a whisper that her daughter could barely hear, "He told me that I should tell you what I could remember — that it would lessen the burden. He said that I needed to do that soon."

"Mom," Cat asked tentatively, "what are you talking about? Who talked to you?"

"Your father — He came here to see me — and we talked," she said with dead-pan seriousness.

"Mom," she questioned, almost afraid of the answer, "When do you think my father was here? Just exactly when do you think he visited you?"

"I dunno." She looked confused. "I think it was last night."

Cat glanced over at Jim, with a "can you even believe this?" look, and by the time she turned around, her mom was asleep, with the teddy crushed to her neck. Cat stood up, removed her mom's shoes, covered her up and kissed her forehead, whispering "Good night, Mom."

They left the room and Cat leaned against the hallway wall, shutting her own eyes for a minute. She heard Jim whisper. "Wow . . . I've never heard her talk so much. I take it you didn't know any of that about your father? You know, not the part about his nocturnal visit from beyond, but the part about him growing up?"

"Nope. She never told me a thing about my father when I was young. I never knew any of the history. I don't remember anything about him, and whenever she did allude to him, it was bad. He left us when I was about five years old and the only Dad I ever really knew was my stepdad."

Jim was quiet as they turned and walked down the hallway towards the door. Cat silently wondered about her birth father's life, and what had possessed her mom to talk about it now.

The cool outdoor air chilled her as she turned to ask, "Don't you think it's weird that Mom thinks my father visited her? She must have been dreaming or something." She looked at Jim for confirmation, but he just kept walking, deep in thought.

On the drive home, Cat was lost in her own world, remembering all the things her mom had said. It had been like listening to a stranger's life story. She wasn't sure how she felt about it and needed time to digest it all.

"Are you okay?" Jim broke the silence as they drove into their driveway.

"Yeah, I guess I am. It kind of pisses me off that she never told me any of that before. But yeah, I'm okay." And then with a little smile in her voice, she said, "I have to tell you one thing though.

Next time she comes out of her stupor, I've got some questions for her!"

* * *

The following Saturday, when Cat visited, her mom had very little clarity of memory. Cat could tell that before she even entered the room, just by looking at her from the doorway. Sometimes, like today, her mom looked at her with an almost vacant look in her eyes. She dreaded the day that her mom might not even remember who she was. She smiled her fake smile and walked into the room.

"Hi, Mom, how're you doing?" She set her purse on the chair and picked up a few pieces of clothes that were scattered around. As she hung them in the closet, she asked, "Did you already eat lunch?"

"I guess so," her mom said, watching Cat move around the room.

"So, what did you have to eat? Anything good today?"

"I dunno."

Cat turned to look at her. This was clearly not going to be a very long visit. Taking a big breath, she began the usual one-sided conversation. "So, I heard from Jamie yesterday, and I guess he and Mollie are going camping around the Point. Do you remember that summer when Daddy took us camping around the Peninsula? That was the best vacation." She paused, waiting for any type of response. Her mom continued to watch her as she talked. It struck Cat how frail she looked; her eyes looked tired and old. There was no other way to describe them. Her mom started fidgeting with the silk binding of her blanket.

It didn't seem to Cat as if visiting made a difference one way or the other. Maybe it was just supposed to be good for her soul. Maybe it was just some kind of payback. She turned instantly sad — heartbroken really. Leaning down close to her mom's face, she softly said, "Mom, I'm gonna go. You look really tired. I'll let you get some rest." Her mom moved her head just a little so that their eyes met and held. Cat's hand found its way to the thin hair on the old woman's temple and she softly stroked her face. Fighting back the tears, Cat forced a smile and gave her a little wink. In response, her mom blinked both her eyes and scrunched her face a little, as if it were an effort. Cat sat there quietly touching her mom for a few minutes before leaving.

* * *

Madeleine died four nights later. Cat's mom died in her sleep. The following week was hectic. Cat called her brother; she called her uncles and told them about her mom passing. She told her brother she'd take care of things at the "home" while he handled some of the funeral arrangements.

Cat drove into the parking lot of the nursing home and rapidly walked up to the front door, holding it open for an elderly man making his way outside. Passing the front desk, she stopped to talk to the attendant for a minute. "Hi, Gloria. I just drove over to pick up Mom's things."

"I'm so sorry for your loss. I really liked your mom. I'll walk down with you," Gloria said as she fell in step with Cat. "I'm so glad that you were here the night she passed. It's nice that you got to spend that time with her."

Cat paused in the hallway, confused, and said, "I wasn't here that night; I haven't been here since Saturday." She figured that Gloria had gotten the days wrong.

"Well, that's strange. I was on duty that night and when I checked on her at midnight, she was awake and told me you had just left. Well actually, now that I'm thinking about it, that isn't exactly true. She said Louise was visiting and just left, so I just assumed she was confused and meant you."

"That *is* really weird." Cat paused for a minute, and then continued, "Louise was Mom's sister – but she died a couple years ago. Mom always mixed up our names when I was young. I think I always reminded her of Louise because she pretty much raised her like a daughter. But Gloria . . . I wasn't here that night."

They both continued their walk to Madeleine's room in silence. Gloria helped Cat pack the few pictures and mementos that she wanted to keep. Before leaving the building for the last time, Cat stopped back by the front desk.

"Hi, Nancy, how are you doing? Gloria and I were just packing up a few of Mom's pictures and things. Is there some way I can arrange to have her clothes and other belongings donated somewhere?"

"Absolutely," Nancy said, grabbing a pen and a piece of paper. "Just let me write that down and we'll take care of it for you. And I just want to tell you how sorry we all are. I really liked your mom. Can you please let us know when you're going to have the funeral? I think some of us might like to attend."

"I sure will. Thanks, Nancy," Cat replied, making a mental note to send the "home" some flowers for the front desk. They had been so nice to her mom; it was the least she could do.

A VERY UNORTHODOX SURPRISE

A few days later

The funeral would be sparsely attended. Uncle Joe, her mom's last living sibling, was coming in from Montana. Uncle Andy, Aunt Louise's husband, was flying in from Florida.

Jamie, Mollie, Jim and Cat were the only other immediate family. Madeleine had outlived all of her friends. Doris, an elderly aunt, wasn't spry enough to spend time at the funeral and burial, or what she referred to as the "ordeal", but called Cat to express her condolences. Before she hung up, she added, "I always liked your mother. We were good friends."

Because there would be so few, Cat decided to plan an early dinner where they could reminisce a bit after they finished at the cemetery. Even Father Duncan had accepted the invitation for dinner.

Father Duncan Mychajlo was a pleasant surprise. Short of calling "rent a priest" if there were such a thing, Cat wasn't sure how they managed to obtain the services of a Catholic priest since neither Jamie nor Cat were practicing Catholics. In spite of the fact that Madeleine had plenty to say against the Catholics as a whole, she would have wanted her final blessing to be of the Catholic faith.

Cat sort of stumbled upon Father Duncan. The funeral director had a friend, a priest who occasionally made himself available for just this sort of thing. They agreed to meet with him. He was a little unconventional in many respects, not like the staunch Roman Catholic priest who had put the fear of God into Cat as a child. Father Duncan, originally from the Ukraine had an unusual way of looking at things. *Unorthodox* might be a little too strong a word, but whatever it was, he struck a chord with her.

The relationship with Father Duncan began with a very short conversation by phone to agree on a time to meet. Father had offered to come to Cat's home, and Cat, of course politely agreed. After all, he was a priest.

As the appointment time grew closer, Cat's Catholic upbringing bubbled to the surface, even though she wasn't sure she could even remember the words to the Act of Contrition. She cleaned and re-cleaned, dusted and re-dusted, arranged cookies on a plate, made coffee, and paced, keeping one eye on the driveway.

Jim was quick to point out how ridiculous it was that Cat was so nervous, stating the obvious, "What's the big deal? He puts his pants on one leg at a time." She wasn't so sure, and visualized God frowning at her husband for even saying such a thing. She continued pacing.

She watched as Father Duncan drove into the driveway. He was younger and looked friendlier than she expected. Her vision of the eighty-year-old priest in robes, with incense burning, making the sign of the cross as lightning struck her, quickly vanished.

Even Jim was taken back. Instead of a scepter and dangling rosary beads around his waist, here was a pleasant looking fellow in street clothes, with nothing but a notebook and pen in his hand. Within ten minutes, he had entirely diffused Cat's anxiety.

"Father, I'm not really a practicing Catholic anymore, and Jim is not a practicing anything, so I'm glad we found you and that you're willing to do this. I know Mom would have wanted a priest," she told him rather apologetically. "I was very nervous to talk to you."

"There's no need to be nervous around me. I'll do whatever a priest is called upon to do, and that includes weddings and funerals, house-blessings, and block parties. Whether you are Catholic or not is quite beside the point. I don't care if you're Catholic, Orthodox, Lutheran, Presbyterian, Jewish, Buddhist, Shinto, Emersonian, Harley Davidson, or Gypsy Rose Lee." He paused smiling, then continued in a more serious tone, "I believe that all of us carry a gift of the beauty of the Spirit, and so I can even serve those who don't believe in the Spirit. I meet people where they're at, learn something of their experience and the way they talk to each other about life, how they take care of each other in good times and hard, and then help them to do that a little better when they need it. And along the way I try to give them a little stretch ahead.

"I would like you to know that I am always available to serve you and Jim, as you are now and however the future unfolds. That said, don't fret about me stepping overboard into the holy moly depths of spiritual theology and 'The Second Coming'."

The priest was easy to listen to. Some of his questions were difficult to answer, but all were designed at getting to know the family dynamics. He added a lot of insight into the hurt and frustration Cat had felt watching her mother's deterioration. Cat felt comfortable sharing with him the anger she had toward her mom's weaknesses — how she never took responsibility for her health. She resented that they ended up taking care of her in the end. She was angry that God saw fit to take pieces of her mother's mind before her body. Cat was even angry that she was angry. In her openness with the priest, she confessed, "All my life I have fought being just like my mother. I've worked so hard to *not* be like her." Cat began tearing up.

Father Duncan changed the subject and in short time had them laughing and remembering better times, alleviating some of the tension of Cat's frustration. He was what they needed. He moved them from focusing on the negative to remembering the positive. He moved Cat's anger to laughter.

"I know that you don't want to be like your mother, but whether you know it or not," he counseled, "you'll find bits and pieces of her life embedded in yours. All children pick up traits of their parents without realizing it. It might be a phrase, a word, or some sort of mannerism, like how you smile or laugh. You will see. In the coming months and even years you will say or hear something that will remind you of her. Embrace those moments. Don't reject them. It's what she has left behind for you."

Father Duncan's advice gave Cat a moment to pause. Up until right then she had tried as hard as she could to be as unlike her mother as possible. But Father Duncan made here think about the larger picture. She was a part of her mom and that's what made her the person she was.

After about three hours, which was about two hours more than Cat had anticipated, Father Duncan felt like an old friend. At some point during that time they had moved from coffee to a new wine Cat had discovered. Even Father Duncan decided that he was rather partial to Pinot Grigio after polishing off his second glass.

Since her brother hadn't been able to attend this initial meeting, Father agreed to drop over on Sunday afternoon after Mass so that he could at least meet and talk to Jamie and Mollie.

On Sunday, Cat knew that Father Duncan would be coming directly from Mass, so she decided to serve a light lunch. She was busying herself in the kitchen when Jamie, Mollie, and Father Duncan all arrived simultaneously. While Jim corralled them in the living room, Father Duncan set about asking Jamie questions. Before too long, Jamie was regaling Father with stories of what it was like growing up with Cat as a sister.

Cat was bringing out the last of the sandwiches when she heard the end of one particularly embarrassing story. As the roar of laughter burst, she teasingly pointed at her brother and said, "Okay, Buster Brown, that's enough of those stories!" Then it hit her. Her mom used to say "Buster Brown". Cat had used the terminology all her life and never thought about where it came from.

"That's too funny," Jamie said, noticing how quiet Cat had become. "Mom used to call me that."

"Yeah, I know," she said, looking directly into Father Duncan's eyes, "and she used to call me 'Sis'." Quickly recovering, she announced, "Come on, you guys, sandwiches are on."

Out of laziness, Jamie and Cat seldom said grace. But on necessary occasions, like Christmas or Thanksgiving, they reverted to reciting the stoic Catholic blessing. This time was no different. As kids, they used to see how fast they could say it, running all the words together until it sounded like a foreign language. Cat didn't feel that was probably appropriate, so while they bowed their heads, she recited, "Bless us, oh Lord, and these, thy gifts which we are about to receive from thy bounty, through Christ, our Lord. Amen."

Sandwiches were plated, fruit was picked at, and glasses were filled with iced tea. Father Duncan asked about their dad. Jamie deferred to his sister, and she responded. "Well, he was Jamie's real father and my stepfather." But, she added quickly, "He was really the only dad I knew. He died when I was nineteen, the year after I graduated from high school. Jamie must have just turned . . . thirteen."

"And your mother never remarried? " Father asked.

"No, she had a few boyfriends from time to time, but mostly she had neighbors and friends in the Valley. They all sort of looked out for each other."

"Do you remember Fred?" Jamie asked Cat, shaking his head and scrunching his nose up as if he had just smelled something spoiled.

"Oh, yeah, he was like a bad penny, couldn't get rid of him." Cat stopped short as she and Jamie stared at each other for a moment. They both burst out laughing, to the confusion of everyone else. Cat looked over at Jim and said, "*Bad penny* was another one of Mom's sayings." Jim smiled, and Cat caught Father Duncan's amused expression out of the corner of her eye.

She was still thinking about the bad penny statement as she began clearing the table. She rinsed off the dishes and brought in the pitcher of iced tea, catching the tail end of Jamie's story.

"So I'm talking to Mom on the phone, standing in the middle of the dorm hallway in my underwear, and she's telling me how she was at the neighbors and had a few too many drinks and on her way home, she ran into the bushes," Jamie said gesturing, dragging out the story dramatically. "I said, 'Oh, my God, Mom, are you okay? Is the car okay? And she said, 'Oh, I wasn't driving; I was just trying to walk home. I got scratched up some in the blackberry bushes, but I'm fine'." Everyone broke out in laughter imagining both the phone conversation and Madeleine trying to walk home under the influence of their neighbor's very toxic Black Russians.

Mollie stopped laughing long enough to wipe the tears from her eyes and say, "When I hear Jamie telling stories like that, I can't believe that she's the same person I knew. She sounds like she used to be a real firecracker!"

Cat was still chuckling as she refilled the last glass with tea. "Well she could be pretty funny at times," she said. "I'm sorry you didn't know her then. She would have liked you."

They finished the details of the service that afternoon, with Father Duncan making schedule notes and seeking last minute information.

SO THIS IS WHAT FAMILY FEELS LIKE

One week later

The day of the funeral went according to plan and was perfectly executed. Father Duncan did an exceptional job at piecing together the family. Jamie had put together a video and music tribute that probably no one except him and Cat understood. The long drive out to the cemetery in Maple Valley was the first time Cat had been back since moving her mom out of her house. It also would probably be the last time she would go there. Cat allowed Father Duncan one "holy moly" minute as he said a prayer in Latin. It was somehow appropriate.

Sitting on a metal chair as a makeshift pew, Cat's eyes kept wandering from the wooden casket to her dad's headstone. She felt a sense of peace. She knew her mom was safe and that her dad would take care of her from here. It was during one of those moments that Father Duncan startled her out of her remembrances by asking if anyone wished to say anything. Cat felt Uncle Joe move, slowly standing and walking over to Father Duncan. "Father, if you don't mind, I don't have anything more to say, but I brought some homemade Montana potpourri from Clara, one of our neighbors in Absarokee. Clara and Madeleine grew up together and she thought Madeleine would like to take a little bit of Montana with her. So, if I can have just a minute, I'd like to sprinkle some of this on Madeleine's casket." As Joe finished his explanation, he reached into his pocket and sprinkled the small bag of dried Montana flowers on the top of the casket. Father Duncan bowed his head and silently said a prayer.

Joe carefully stepped down off the single riser that surrounded the casket and slowly made his way back to the chair beside Cat. When he sat down, he reached over and covered her hand with his.

Cat would be the first to admit that she wasn't a touchy person. She wasn't a hugger and never let her hand linger on anyone's arm. She was very protective of her personal space and cognizant of people who tried to invade it. But Uncle Joe's hand covering hers felt like the most natural thing. For the briefest moment, the connection felt as if there was static electricity in his touch. She thought *this is what family feels like.* Again, Father Duncan interrupted her thoughts by asking if there was anyone else who wanted to speak. With no response, the small group broke up and visited for a few moments. But now it was over.

The family headed back to Cat's house where she'd planned an early dinner with time to relax and visit with her uncles. Jim had suggested that she keep the meal simple, but her entertaining, no matter what the situation, tended to take on a life of its own.

The simple ham dinner had mysteriously grown to include numerous salads, Irish soda bread made from scratch, deviled eggs, fresh vegetables from the local farmers market, parsley-dipped baby potatoes, pickles and olives and cheese and several bottles of Pinot Grigio, which had become Cat's and Father Duncan's new favorite wine.

Once they got to the house there was a bit of settling down. A pipe and a few cigarettes were enjoyed outside on the porch before everyone finally congregated in the dining room.

For a moment, Cat stood in the doorway and watched the unusual mix of people. Father Duncan was listening to Uncle Andy regaling him with fishing stories as Mollie made sure Andy's scotch glass was never empty for fear he would remember that he was telling bawdy stories to a priest.

Jamie and Joe were in deep discussion about something. Looking at the uncanny resemblance of the two standing together, Cat could understand how her mom's mind might have tricked her from time to time and confused the two.

She sliced the last of the Soda bread and delivered the final salad bowl to the table as Jim was opening another bottle of wine.

As if directing traffic, she pointed to people and chairs as everyone obediently sat. They bowed their heads and Cat took the lead. "Father Duncan, I want to thank you so much for your blessings today, but I'd like to impose upon you one more time to bless us, this meal, and to offer safe travel home for my uncles."

Father Duncan smiled and said "I think that was pretty sneaky of you in passing the gavel." Bowing his head, he prayed. "Heavenly *Father, we ask you to bless this food, those who grew it and those who prepared it. We also ask your blessing on Madeleine, Andy, Joe and all those who have come to you this day as a family uniting themselves in your love. Amen.*"

And with that, the serving plates were lifted, along with the old familiar argument on which way they are supposed to be passed. The dinner conversation swirled around Cat, as she became reflective. Her mom would have liked having Joe and Andy here. Cat hadn't realized how much she'd missed the connection to family until Joe had reached over to touch her hand during the service.

With conversations going on in several directions and no one pointedly talking directly to her, she allowed herself the luxury of thinking about the potpourri made from Montana flowers that Uncle Joe had lovingly placed on top of the casket. She pictured the roses that Father Duncan had asked them to carry and then place on the casket to represent a part of their hearts. Her mind recalled snips and flashes of the day, and she just let it wander. Cat added very little to the conversation, outside of a few agreements and smiles as she passed serving plates. Looking around the table, she took a deep breath and felt at peace.

As dinner began winding down, Father Duncan, with true curiosity asked, "So, Joe, tell me about Madeleine. Cat told me that you had done a great deal of discovery on your family history. I was led to understand you come from Irish stock. As a matter of fact, the blessing I said before this meal was an Old Irish Catholic blessing."

"Yes, Father, I have spent a little time digging into the family history. I brought Cat a package of genealogy papers I had promised her earlier. Through my research and a cousin of ours, we've traced the Lannen family to Ireland in the early 1800s."

"I have quite an interest in genealogy myself. If you don't mind my asking, I think it would be a rather fitting end to this day if you could share a little of Madeleine's past with us here."

And though he hadn't meant to share with anyone other than Cat, Uncle Joe went through a good deal of the documentation that he'd brought, pointing out interesting pieces of history and always tying the stories back to Madeleine.

Father Duncan was enthralled with the story of Madeleine's life and impressed with the documented history that Uncle Joe had managed to come up with. He was full of questions, which Joe happily answered. As the afternoon went on, Jamie and Cat were both emotionally raw with everything that had happened earlier that day and both were uncharacteristically quiet.

Cat was startled out of her memories by Father Duncan. "Your mom was quite a person, growing up in that time with the problems that had befallen her. It would have been a hard time for any human being, let alone a girl of her age. It must have been a hard life for all of you." He looked at Joe.

"Well, it certainly had its moments," Joe responded. But we didn't know any better. I think as Madeleine got older, it got tougher for her." Joe paused, collecting his thoughts. "And after she went to Billings, I stayed up on the ranch with Dad most of the time, and Louise had to take over most of the chores in town. I think it was harder on Louise than it was on me."

Andy, who had been pretty quiet for most of the evening, agreed with Joe. "Yeah, I know Louise didn't like it very much with Madeleine gone." He paused. "She said that it was a lot of work and she missed having Madeleine there. I don't think their Gramma was getting along too well at the time either."

"Uncle Andy," Cat turned to bring him full into the conversation, "did Aunt Louise talk much about the time Mom lived in Billings? I know she lived there for a couple of years and that she and my real father met there, but I'm not sure how that all happened. Mom didn't talk much about that time at all."

Andy thought for a minute and replied, "No, Louise never said too much about it either. I don't think she saw Madeleine very much during those years, least not what she ever mentioned to me. I know a little about your father at that time, and I know Madeleine was working there in Billings when she met Glenn. Your dad and she were both working for Northwest Airlines back then — that's where they met. I didn't meet Glenn until we both got stationed at the National Guard in Yakima, after the war. It was pretty quiet on base and we used to spend some time together when we were off duty." And then, looking guiltily at Father Duncan, Andy added, "And there might have been a little beer involved on occasion."

Father Duncan just smiled at him, clearly not offended.

Out of the corner of her eye, Cat saw her brother lose interest in the conversation once it turned to Cat's real father. Jamie was getting restless, and yet, this was part of her mom's life too. She shot him a look, with one eyebrow raised, that clearly said *shut up and sit down.* Like any good little brother, no matter how old he was — he sat down. However, also realizing that the hour was getting late and Father Duncan might need to make a graceful exit, Cat said, "Andy, we know so very little about Mom's life at that time, if you could share even a few stories, I would really love to hear them. I'm beginning to know more about my mom now that she's gone, than I ever did when she was here. If you could think about that for a minute while I pick up a few things; we can get Morgan fed and I'll make some more coffee." Then directing her attention to Father Duncan, who stood up when she addressed him, Cat said, "I know it's getting late and I don't know what your schedule is, but I think we might be reminiscing for a little longer. You're certainly welcome and I'd love to have you stay if you want to."

"Okay!" Father Duncan eagerly said, and quickly sat down. She smiled at him, recognizing then that he wanted to stay. He appeared to be as entranced with the stories as they all were.

It seemed like everyone disbursed for a few minutes. Jim went to make Morgan's dinner. Andy took his pipe and went out to the back yard, and Joe went with him to stretch his legs. Everyone managed to congregate back in the living room at about the same time.

In an effort to keep the conversation light, Cat said, "Okay Andy, spill the beans and tell me what you know about my real father. I haven't told Jamie this . . ." she caught Jamie's direct look out of the corner of her eye . . . "but a few months ago when I was visiting Mom, she had one day of very clear memory and she started telling me about when the Barkers came over from England and about my great-great grandparents. I have no idea how she remembered all those names and dates, but she did. Her eyes were so clear that day. She was lucid and very matter-of-fact about it. She said it was time she told me the story. I have to assume that what she told me was true; of course, she also said that my real father had visited her at the home one night, not long before she died." Cat intentionally left out the part of the story where her aunt Louise had supposedly visited her mom on the very night that she died.

"Well, let me see; where do I start?" Andy began, "Keep in mind that Glenn didn't talk much about himself unless his tongue was loosened by a beer or two, and, at that point, I might have had a couple beers and probably couldn't hear all that well." Andy couldn't help but sneak one more glance at Father Duncan as he chose his words carefully. "The way Glenn told the story was that when he was in high school, the City of Billings was in a depressed state. There weren't any jobs available, and, from what he told me about his family, they weren't real close. So he just decided to enlist in the National Guard before he even turned eighteen."

TELL MOM I'LL WRITE

1939, Billings, Montana

The Great Depression had thrown millions of people into hard financial times. The people of Billings suffered not only a lack of jobs, but were at the mercy of yet another drought. Families struggled to make ends meet any way they could. Part of the answer for many men was to join the Montana National Guard unit. The stipend for being a part of the Guard provided a meager addition to whatever financial income they might be earning.

In Glenn's case, he enlisted in the Guard in July 1939 by lying about his age. He was seventeen and just graduated from high school with little hope of getting a job. After the initial six-week training, it had seemed like a part-time job. Once a month he reported on a weekend, for gun or hand-to-hand training, usually finishing off on Sunday by standing guard or helping with new enlistees. The Guard only tied up one weekend a month, so it didn't intrude on his social life. And it afforded him some gas money.

The following year, in view of pending Nazi aggression in Europe, President Roosevelt called all National Guard units to active duty throughout the country. Glenn received written orders for activation with terms and options for full enlistment.

With few resources available and no interest in working for his father at the store, Glenn decided to enlist for a five-year term in the hopes of getting out of Billings.

Later that afternoon, when he returned home, his dad was standing in the front yard with a beer, watering his precious roses. Junior swore that his dad cared more about those damned roses than he did about him. When Junior announced his decision to his dad, it was met with an argument.

"Dad, it's a good job. It's not like I can find one around here anyway."

"You can't find a job, 'cause you don't want to work, you lazy son-of-a-bitch. You could have worked at the store. You think this is an easy way out, don't you, Junior? You think the Army is going to put up with your attitude?"

"Well, Dad, that's just about what I figured you say. You never have been supportive of anything I did. Don't know why I thought this would be different."

"You got a mouth on you, boy. You don't know the first thing about what's going on over there in Europe. You think this is just one big game. Well, I am not gonna be there to bail you out."

"I didn't ask you to. I didn't ask you for shit! Just thought I'd let you know, I'm leaving in the morning. Tell Mom I'll write." As the door slammed behind Junior, Glenn Senior took a long pull from his beer, and turned the hose back around on his roses. As far as he was concerned, he no longer had a son.

The next morning, young Glenn stopped by Red's house on his way to the train station. Red's mom had baked a batch of peanut butter cookies and had wrapped up half a dozen for Glenn to take with him.

"Glenn you take care of yourself now and stay safe. Okay?"

"Yes ma'am, I will. Thanks for the cookies. That was real swell of you." Glenn looked at her and then reached over and gave her a big hug before turning to slap Red on the back.

"Come on, Red, let's get that jalopy started and get me to the station."

"So where're they sending you for training?" Red asked, as the screen door slammed behind them.

"Orders say Camp Murray. The Guard sergeant said it's in Tacoma, Washington and that it rains 365 days a year there. Guess we'll see." Glenn waited for the motor in Red's car to finally turn over and spit black smoke out of the tailpipe. Smiling and shaking his head, he gave his friend a fake punch in the arm as they peeled out of the gravel driveway. Glenn was looking at this as an adventure.

WHEN IT RAINS IT POURS

1940, Tacoma, Washington
Camp Murray

In September of 1940, with the activation of the Guard and the increased enlistment, twelve thousand men descended upon the Camp Murray field training camp. Camp Murray was just South of Fort Lewis near the town of Tacoma, Washington.

The Fort lacked facilities and equipment to handle the large influx of men. Even food was in short supply. The army scratched for any kind of equipment and supplies to accommodate the influx of men.

Glenn and his unit were issued leftover World War I field uniforms, complete with flat-brimmed campaign hats, World War I helmets, bootees, wrap leggings and riding pants, plus fatigue uniforms of blue cotton. Glenn became one of the many faceless, ragamuffin enlistees to begin a year of training at Camp Murray.

Glenn and some of his fellow recruits were assigned to live in tents because there weren't enough barracks to accommodate them. The camp seemed to attract the rain; winds whipped through the hand-me-down tents, and fog settled in nightly. Camp Murray was referred to as the wettest camp in the United States, and Glenn was beginning to understand why. As he lay on his cot the first night, he found it impossible to go to sleep. He was cold and wet and wondered if he hadn't made a huge mistake.

As weeks wore on, slight improvements were made with the living conditions, and Glenn began to fall into a routine. With the climate and conditions, Glenn was lucky to have escaped a reoccurring flu epidemic that hit his unit during the winter. It wasn't until April 1941 that they were able to slowly move the five miles through mud to newly built barracks. Hard walls were a heavenly sight for Glenn's eyes.

In spite of the setbacks, the rigorous training program continued, including the hated ten mile full-pack march each Monday morning, followed by a full review every Wednesday. Glenn worked hard. He was pushed both physically and mentally.

By early summer, Glenn's unit was ready to try out their infantry skills. They were loaded onto trains and sent to Hunter Liggett, California for maneuvers. For a month, they did mock exercises that mimicked an invading fleet, and they were charged with defending the coastline.

Glenn was happy to be in a part of the country where it wasn't raining. When he first arrived in California, he stepped off the train and turned his face into the sun, letting it warm his face. For him, the maneuvers and training were beside the point – this was like a vacation.

By the time they completed that training mission in California and returned to Camp Murray, Glenn's active duty orders were waiting for him.

In November, a month after Glenn turned 20, regiments were being cut out of the group to be sent to the Philippines as replacements for American troops who were ready to rotate home. Glenn was in one of those groups and on December 5th found himself on board a train, headed toward San Francisco.

He was going to be stationed at an Air Force facility in support of the airfield in Luzon. Since he was trained as an airfield technician, he was pretty well guaranteed to have a roof over his head and not be sleeping in any jungle fighting Nazis. What little he knew about the Philippines led him to believe this was the adventure he had been waiting for.

In spite of the fact he was shoulder to shoulder with other soldiers, he was able to let the train lull him to sleep. In that half-sleep state, he thought about his last trip home to Billings.

Knowing he was finally going overseas, he managed a quick furlough and flew home to see his mom and dad. Thinking about it later, he wished he had saved his leave. His dad never changed, and they had more words before he left.

Both Red and Johnny had enlisted in active forces by that time, but they all had been separated, and the mail wasn't too reliable. As usual, Glenn had spent more time on leave at Red's house than his own. He had spent most evenings at the pool hall, but food and alcohol rationing put a damper on any fun he had hoped to have.

He'd never been to San Francisco or the Monterey Bay area, but his schedule left him there for most of the weekend, before he was to fly to Hawaii on the following Tuesday. From Hawaii, they would be flown to Luzon. His orders said he was to embark from Fort Ord which was just about two hours South of San Francisco. He guessed he better catch some shuteye while he could.

By early Saturday afternoon, the train stopped. Glenn joined the drill of pulling their duffels, getting checked off the train and onto the platform. Hurry up and wait; it was always the same story. Seems like he spent half his life standing in line. There was a lot of nervous chatter and joking, with a few hats being used to slap each other playfully as the men waited to load onto buses for transport to the Fort.

Once there, Glenn checked in and was assigned a bunk in the barracks. He and the other arrivals waited for roll call and last minute instructions and then were dismissed to find the mess hall and the base clubs. Skipping dinner and heading for the club, Glenn and two other guys found the bar easily and settled down on bar stools.

Glenn ordered for his friends. "Can we get three beers over here?"

"Yes sir, where are you headed off to?" the bartender asked.

"Philippines," Glenn replied proudly.

"I got a brother over there; part of the USAFFE; makes no sense to me "Forces in the Far East"; he's at Clark Field; says General Marshall is loadin' them up with B-17s. Here you go — three beers."

"Thanks," the three said in unison.

"Well, here's to no more rain and not missing our plane." Glenn picked up the beer bottle and drained over half of it in two gulps.

Somewhere around midnight, the trio left the noisy, smoke-filled club with nothing but beer and peanuts in their stomachs. They found the barracks and fell into their bunks. It was now Sunday morning, December 7, 1941.

Glenn's head pounded as the screaming siren woke him from his beer-induced sleep. Someone had a small radio in the barracks and the words could barely be heard above the static. Orders were given to fall out – NOW! All leaves were cancelled. The Japanese had just attacked the U.S. Navy at Pearl Harbor. Until further notice, Glenn's unit was officially stationed at Fort Ord.

Outside of the Fort, word spread throughout the Bay area. Thousands of people gathered at the ocean beach to gaze into the Pacific in disbelief. Less than one hour after the attack, defensive mines were being laid in San Francisco Bay.

All members of the Armed Forces in San Francisco were recalled to duty to take up battle stations. All normal maritime operations in the Bay were brought to a halt. Police were ordered to stop all soldiers and sailors on downtown streets and send them to their duty stations.

Military guards took up posts on the Golden Gate Bridge to search the vehicles of anyone who looked Japanese, for explosives. The Western Defense Command received a report of Japanese ships thirty miles off the coast of California. A cargo vessel reported that it had been torpedoed. Both were incorrect reports. Just the same, panic ensued at each report, true or otherwise.

The following day, President Roosevelt's war message to the Joint Session of Congress was heard at 9:30 am. Every radio in San Francisco was tuned in to listen to 500 words that would ring in remembrance throughout history. The entire barracks listened without breathing:

"Yesterday, December 7, 1941 – a day which will live in infamy – the United States of America . . . was suddenly and deliberately attacked by naval and air forces of the Empire of Japan. . ."

Following the president's declaration of war, Mayor Angelo Rossi issued the following proclamation:

"To the people of San Francisco. . . I have declared an emergency in San Francisco. Under the powers conferred on me in this circumstance, I have coordinated all the proper departments of the City and County of San Francisco with the program of the Civilian Defense Council. . ."

San Francisco experienced its first air raid and blackout at 6:15 that evening. Permanent orders were issued, and Glenn remained at Fort Ord for the next year.

* * *

Present

"And there he sat," Andy concluded, "on the California coast. Not exactly what he had in mind. But after all was said and done, it was a good thing he didn't go to the Philippines."

As if a light bulb had gone off, Father Duncan looked at Andy and whispered, "His orders were for Luzon in the Philippine Islands? The death march of Bataan took place just a few months after the bombing of Pearl Harbor, didn't it?"

"Yes sir, it did, and that's exactly where Glenn was heading before he was derailed with the Pearl attack." Andy stifled a yawn. "When he finally did go overseas, I don't know exactly where he was stationed. I know he spent some time near the Salomon Islands and that he went through Honolulu a couple of times. It always sounded like he had a fondness for Hawaii." Andy's voice trailed off and he looked lost in his memories.

Cat was beginning to feel guilty keeping Andy for so long. It had been a long day. She looked around the room and decided that they needed to call it a night. "You know, I really appreciate you guys coming for Mom's funeral. I didn't expect you to, but I'm glad you did. I guess I needed to have family around after all."

By earlier agreement, Jamie and Mollie had offered to take Joe back to his hotel after dinner. "Joe, are you just about ready to head out? Mollie and I will give you ride whenever you're ready."

"I'm ready whenever you are," Joe responded as he walked over to give Cat a hug goodbye. And to Father Duncan, he reached out to shake his hand. "Thank you very much, Father. You did a good job on the service. Madeleine would have liked that." And they headed towards the door.

Andy had rented a car and was going to visit a friend in Seattle the next day. While he wasn't at the mercy of a ride, he was ready to leave too.

"Andy," Cat said, "I appreciate you sticking around to talk. Thanks so much for coming over and being here with us today. Like I told Joe, you didn't have to come, but I'm very glad you did."

Andy stood as she leaned over to give him a hug. "I liked your mom a lot," he said close to her ear, "I'll miss her."

Father Duncan walked out with him, but not before telling Cat that he would be calling to check on her.

It had been a long and stressful day. As Cat curled up on the bed a bit later, she was treated with the sound of what she knew to be 130 pounds of sheepdog galloping down the hallway. With one massive leap, Morgan hit the bed beside her, happy to have everyone finally gone so he could re-take control of the house. Cat closed her eyes as the dog curled up against her. The last thing she remembered was hearing Jim trying to coax Morgan off the bed. She smiled.

THINGS THAT GO THUMP IN THE NIGHT

The next morning

The morning light was barely starting to crack though the blinds of the bedroom to shine on Jim and Morgan who were lightly snoring simultaneously. Jim rolled over, his eyes still closed, willing himself to go back to sleep.

Thump! He opened one eye to see that he was alone in bed. He heard another thump and rolled over to look at Morgan, still lying stretched out on his blanket beside the bed, both eyes open and staring at the ceiling. Thump.

"What the hell is that noise?" Jim asked of no one in particular. He threw back the covers, grabbed his pants and struggled to put them on in his half-sleep state.

Morgan was equally curious, but based on his demeanor was certainly not threatened by the noise. They both moved down the hall trying to determine where the sound was coming from.

After listening for a minute, Jim walked out the front door and into the garage. The ladder was propped up against the attic opening and the noise was coming from that direction. He climbed up until his head cleared the opening, and there he found Cat.

She had thrown on a pair of jeans that had seen better days and an old, faded, Notre Dame sweatshirt. Her hair was tied in a hasty pony tail that had worked its way half out of the band. He watched her sitting amid boxes and papers that had been pulled into the center of the attic where the light was better. Her head was bowed in deep concentration as she studied what appeared to be a photo album.

"Good morning," he said, causing Cat to jump and drop the book.

"Oh my God! You scared me!"

"Well, I'd like to ask what you're doing up here. I figured you'd be here at some point going through your mom's things, just not quite so early in the morning."

"I'm sorry, honey. I just couldn't stand it. After hearing the stories last night, I know there are pictures and letters here in mom's boxes that'll fill in a lot more detail of her life and my real father's life, too. Some of these pictures I've seen a hundred times before, but I never really *looked* at them."

"How about if I go down and make us some coffee, and I'll bring you a cup."

"Well actually, as long as you're awake, can I hand you down a couple of boxes and I'll go through them in the house?" She handed down four boxes filled with papers and the photo album she'd been looking at. They carried them into the house.

With the contents of the boxes spread out on the office floor and a coffee mug in her hand, Cat systematically started going through letters, postcards, and memorabilia. Some of the boxes she'd uncovered earlier that morning were those that she and Jamie had hurriedly packed the day that they moved their mom out of her house. But there were other boxes that had been packed carefully, almost lovingly, by Madeleine herself, years earlier.

"You know what gets me?" Cat asked, almost talking to herself, but knowing Jim was within earshot. "Mom never said two good words about my real father the whole time I was growing up. I don't know if it was a self-defense thing, or what happened between them. But that night at the home when she started talking about the Barker family and what happened when my dad was younger, he sounded like a pretty normal guy. So, I'm thinking . . . Okay, maybe he wasn't as bad as she'd led me to believe. And then

I remembered these picture albums of the two of them, pictures that were taken in Anchorage when they were first married. When I found them in the attic, I looked at the pictures more carefully — I mean really looked at them. And for the first time, it dawned on me that Mom was smiling. She looked happy. He had his arm around her and they looked like they were in love. Not at all the way she led me to believe her marriage was with him. Look at these pictures." Cat opened the photo album to the page in the middle of the book and turned it toward Jim.

The book was made up of heavy-weight old fashioned black craft paper, with each picture held in place by white corner holders that had turned yellow with time. Pointing at the white writing on the black pages beneath each picture, Jim asked, "Is this your mom's writing?"

"No, I think it must be my father's. There are hundreds of pictures in here and each one has comments written under them. Do you know how long it would take to put this together? This doesn't look like the work of someone who didn't love his wife a great deal."

Most of the pictures in the album Cat had been studying were taken right after her mom and dad were married and moved to Alaska. There were the prerequisite pictures of the surrounding landscape and mountains, along with pictures of friends and parties and picnics. The ones she liked best were of the two of them just living life — her mom cooking in the kitchen, the two of them sitting on the porch in the evening, her dad throwing snowballs, and the two of them just relaxing.

"I feel like there is a whole part of me that I didn't know existed. I know it sounds hokey, but it's like I'm discovering my past. And look," Cat said, pointing at the album, "he was meticulous. He cataloged all the dates and places. I found a whole box of letters he wrote to mom, that I haven't even begun to look at yet. She must have saved every letter. "

"Sounds to me like you aren't going to fix breakfast yet, huh?" Jim asked.

"No, I'm gonna fix breakfast." She laughed at him. "It's just that I'm on information overload right now. I'm not sure what I'm gonna do with all this, but I don't think I can stop until I know the whole story."

"Can I, maybe, make a suggestion?" Jim asked tentatively as he looked directly into her eyes. He paused, almost as much for effect as to make sure Cat was listening to him. "Why don't you do with it, what you do best? Why don't you write it? Write the story of your mom's life. You've been looking for a new project to write about anyway, and I think this is good for you — to know your mom in a different light as a real person, not as the mom you grew up with and not as the mom you visited in the nursing home."

Cat thought for a minute and then said, "Huh. Maybe I will." She looked around at all the attic boxes and papers in disarray. "We'll see," she said shrugging her shoulders. "So, what do you want me to make for breakfast?"

For the next week, Cat read and re-read letters and notes, capturing dates whenever they were available. By the fourth box, she had every flat surface in the office covered with chronological bits and pieces of her mom's life. That life that she found so boring when she was growing up had taken on a new dimension. For the first time, Madeleine wasn't just her mom; she was a daughter, a sister, and young woman with all the dreams and longings for love and family. She was more than a mother; she was a person that had become a stranger. The more Cat discovered, the more she wished she could have known that stranger better.

Jim was right, there was a good story there, but as Cat looked at the boxes and stacks of notes and bundles of letters with Post-its abounding, she knew her first step was to put some organization and structure to all this information. So, that's exactly what she did.

She needed to consolidate what she knew so far. Sitting at her computer, Cat opened a new Excel spreadsheet. She took a deep breath and imagined her mind a blank slate. She tried to change her thinking to take the emotion out of it and look at this as a project. She ran dates on the left hand side of the spreadsheet, from 1850 to the present and, with the help of Uncle Joe's research, began filling in dates connected to her mother's life. In the second column Cat added dates from her birth father's life. She was looking for the commonalities, the intersection. How did they meet? What was happening in the world at that time? She added information about historic events, music, movies, and fashions that were popular at different points throughout the years. She wanted to get a sense and feel of the time and put what she knew of the history into some sort of perspective.

After getting the initial information down and organized, Cat had on the computer screen before her, a skeleton of two families running parallel, with many empty cells and more unanswered questions.

For the next several weeks, all this information percolated in her mind. Her work on the timeline ran in bits and spurts. All her thoughts, questions, and research ended up as notes on the spreadsheet.

She mulled over her uncles' conversations and found herself on the Internet googling for different things, reading history of the potato famine, of immigrants, Montana homesteading, and early days of WWII.

When she ran out of things to research, she went back to the attic and picked through boxes. Some of the things she found were as familiar to her as her mom's homemade bread. There were pieces of memorabilia that had been a part of her childhood: a butter dish of her mother's, doilies crocheted by her grandmother, framed pictures, figurines, vases and things that took on new meaning. Some, she knew the story of; some she could only guess. A round hat box revealed a folded airplane ticket from Billings to Seattle, a pillbox hat with a veil attached, and reminisces of a corsage that might have held small tea roses and baby's breath.

With each new box she learned more of her mom's story. Not the story that her mom conveniently told, or didn't tell, but the real story of her life.

There among the attic boxes, Cat found her birth father's military records, his discharge papers, letters that had been written but had never been mailed. There were dozens of letters on military stationery addressed to his mother and father, still sealed and unmailed, tied together with a piece of twine. There were notes and letters between Madeleine and him when he had first gone to Anchorage. Cat painstakingly read and reread everything, looking for minutia details that would lead her through their lives, both separately and together.

Little by little, their lives began to take shape. It was like a jigsaw puzzle. Every piece of the puzzle that fit into place added detail to the picture. How old was her mom and what was she doing the year Glenn enlisted in the army? What brought them together? Why did they get married in Seattle? How long did they live in Alaska? What were they like when Cat was born? What really happened to them?

Large pieces of their lives began to fill chapters. She was immersed in the project. When she slept, she dreamt the story. When she got stumped, she'd take a week off and come back to it with renewed perspective.

Then one afternoon, Cat's writing came to a screeching halt. She didn't know what to write next. Was this what writer's block felt like? Something was nagging at the back of her mind. She was missing something. She made the conscience decision to give it a rest for a while.

About a month later, in late autumn, it was one of those cloudy, rainy days that Cat was so familiar with in the Northwest. She called them the "gray" days. The morning light doesn't come up until late and the darkness descends early in the afternoon. The midday is punctuated with clouds, drizzle, and fog. That Saturday was one of those gray, rainy days.

Jim and Morgan had taken up residence down in the garage, doing whatever guys and dogs do in their garages. If she strained her ears, she could almost hear the football game on the radio. Cat decided it was a good day to head back up to the attic and put some order to the boxes and the mess she'd created earlier in the year. If she didn't get a path cleared, they'd never find their Christmas decorations and she knew it was well past time to throw some things away.

The attic had been very organized before she and her brother had reduced most of their mom's house to boxes and hastily stowed them up there. She and Jamie had not exactly been meticulous when they moved their mom's belongings. Madeleine had been sick; they had taken advantage of their mother's illness and her dementia. They took Madeleine to the hospital, and by the time she was well enough to leave, they'd moved her into an assisted living home. Within thirty days, she and Jamie had packed the house, given away the furniture, cleaned and listed the house for sale.

They had moved fast, trying to avoid the emotional baggage that would reduce them both to tears. Their mantra was, "this is the best thing for mom." Without much fanfare, they threw everything in cardboard boxes and brought them to Cat's house. And there they sat, still crowding the small attic. Yes, it was past time to do some cleaning.

After several hours, Cat had cleared a path to the back wall and was well within reach of their Christmas decorations. Several boxes had been thrown down to be destroyed or given away. She'd been labeling and organizing the remainder of the boxes, but it entailed opening and digging through the contents of each box, silently cussing out her brother and herself for not being more organized when they did this the first time. She was half way through the boxes against the back wall when she opened a box that revealed an antique accordion on top. She smiled as she remembered kicking that thing around the house as a kid. This wasn't a box that she and Jamie had thrown together. This box had been taped and labeled by her mother years earlier, a conclusion based on how steady her writing was on the label.

Under the accordion, Cat found files and documents belonging to her stepfather, his distinct perfect handwriting still on the labels, faded, but very legible. Memories washed over her as she saw his handwriting on contents and notes. She remembered rainy days sitting for hours at the kitchen table with him as he worked with her on her penmanship. She practiced and practiced until she could mimic his perfectly formed cursive writing. She could almost feel his hand hovering over hers, guiding her pencil to make perfectly sculptured letters. She was as familiar with his writing as she was with her own.

She opened an envelope and pulled out a copy of his birth certificate, staring at the name on the document; *Everett James Peterson*. She smiled at the thought that her brother carried their dad's middle name. Still holding the birth certificate, Cat kept digging in the box, running her fingers over pictures, ticket stubs, and programs. Near the bottom of the box, she lifted out his old watch and a familiar tie clasp.

Her heart hurt, holding the little pieces of memory that her mom had so painstakingly wrapped in sheets of newspaper. She could almost feel her daddy standing behind her.

As she continued looking through the box, she found dates on the packing newspapers. Her mom had closed this box three years after her stepfather had died. The pain of losing him was as strong then as it was when she was nineteen. She had been as close to him as she'd been removed from her birth father. And yet, it seemed that there was more to know filed away in this box; missing pieces of his life. Missing pieces of her mom's life; missing pieces of her own life.

WHAT DO YOU DO WITH
A BOX OF MEMORIES?

Three weeks later

Tacoma, Washington

"I'm so glad you called me; I have lots to tell you," Cat said to Father Duncan as they left the pickup line at Starbucks and found a table.

"Well I had a counseling session that took me close by and thought if you were home, it would be nice to grab a cup of coffee. And I'm curious to know how you're doing."

"I'm doing well, Father. I decided to do a little family research on my own. It actually has turned into a huge project. I found some of Mom's photographs, letters, and documents in some boxes in the attic. So in addition to giving me more history on her, I'm also documenting history on my real father. But before I go any further, I need to ask you something, Father. It's kind of a strange question, but do you believe that when people die, they sometimes lurk around to help or guide you?"

"I'm not sure *lurking* is the correct terminology, but sure, why not?"

"That sounds like a guess, not a fact, Father. Are you placating me?"

"No. It isn't a guess or a fact; it is belief — and faith. I see no reason not to believe that in death the energy of the soul can inspire from some plane of existence. Or I guess in layman's terms, why not?"

"Well, I believe it. There were just things that happened after my stepfather died. I believe that he somehow stayed close to me – to help me, to protect me, maybe even to guide me in the right direction. At first, he came to me in my dreams. Then one day, someone that I thought loved me, slapped me and knocked me to the ground. Before I even hit the floor, I felt my stepdad at my side, willing me strength. After that, I just knew if I needed him, he'd be there. He's guided me through every major crisis in my life. If I stumbled, he gave me balance. Then as I grew older, I felt him less and less – until recently. When I found some boxes in the attic that belonged to him, I could nearly feel his breath and smell his aftershave." Cat decided to lighten up the conversation. "So, in a nutshell, he and I have been hanging around in the attic lately going through boxes." Cat paused for dramatic purposes, as Father Duncan's right eye-brow lifted. This was no mocking, only a subtle gesture to continue.

"I really truly believe in my heart that he is helping me, guiding me, if you will, on my research." As she paused, they both took a drink of coffee and set the coffee cups back down.

"And again, I ask, why not?" he said shrugging. "Has he helped you discover anything that has surprised you?"

"As a matter of fact, I think he has. About a month ago, I stopped researching because I felt like I was missing something in my mom's life. Sometimes it helps if I take a break and gain some perspective before I continue. Anyway, to make a long story short, a couple weeks ago, I felt this need to go back up in the attic and, I swear, he led me to a box that contained memories of him. I'm talking about his discharge papers, legal documents, notes, sketches, and some little things that I thought Mom had gotten rid of years ago. I didn't even know that box was up there. But even more interesting, when I was going through that box, it dawned on me what I was missing. I can't figure out my mom's life without including both my father and my stepfather. They were both a part of who she was." As Cat continued explaining to Father Duncan, her sentences ran together at a fast pace.

"My stepfather's life hadn't been a part of my original project, but he led me to that box. That box contained the remnants of a life I knew and loved well. My stepfather's birth certificate was in one of the bottom files. I sat on the floor of the attic and stared at it for the longest time. Everett James Peterson, born in 1921, the same year as Glenn Lee Barker Jr., my real father. My writer's instinct that had been stagnant for a month went into overdrive. I tried to put together how my stepfather's life differed within the timeline of my father and my mother? Clearly, this isn't the path I had originally headed down, but bits and pieces of my stepfather's life began seeping out of his files and into my notes. I found the missing piece of my mom's life — my stepfather." Finally Cat took a breath and waited for Father Duncan to say something.

"Seldom is the path that you originally choose the same path at the end of the journey. I think you have chosen well. I hope you will find what you're looking for."

"I'm not exactly sure what that is, Father."

"You'll know it when you find it. It's a journey."

They finished their coffee and left Starbucks with a promise to get together again soon. Before the coffee shop disappeared from her rearview mirror, Cat's mind was sifting through the life of her stepfather.

When Cat returned home, she immediately powered up the computer. With her latest treasured box sitting beside her, she added another column to her spreadsheet and began documenting pieces of information on her stepfather's life. There were huge holes, with very little on his early years. In fact, now that she thought about it, he had never talked too much about his life. And as she had so often done this past year, she wished she'd asked more questions and taken more interest in the people she loved when they were still alive.

There was only one person still living who knew her stepfather when he was a child –Aunt Doris. Cat also knew that this was a long overdue visit.

LONG OVERDUE . . . LONG OVERDUE . . .

The following week

Aunt Doris was well into her eighties and had been the wife of Howard, Everett's older brother. Doris lived about forty miles from Cat and Jim, in a studio apartment built at her daughter and son-in-law's home. Cat hadn't been there before. For the past ten years, she had only talked to Doris on the phone, mainly giving her health updates on her mom. She felt guilty at not staying closer and hoped that her spontaneous visit would be received well.

She'd called Margaret, Doris' daughter, and made arrangements to visit.

Doris was still a slight bird of a person. She'd always been a tiny woman, but age seemed to have shrunk her even more. Regardless, there was still strength in her hug when she answered the door.

"I was wondering if I was ever going to see you again. Did Jamie come with you?" She asked, looking around.

"No, I'm sorry he didn't, Aunt Doris. I made the trip by myself this time. I'm sorry I didn't come visiting earlier."

"Oh, that's fine, that's fine. You come in and sit down; let me turn this TV off," she said leading the way into her living room area and turning the TV down, but not entirely off. "I was sorry to hear that your mom died. When I lived next door to her, we spent a lot of time together. She was a nice lady. You've grown up to look like her some. I heard she had some trouble at the end. "

Cat smiled at her aunt's comparison to her and her mom, and replied, "Yeah, she struggled a little bit with remembering things."

"Well, don't we all; don't we all," Doris mumbled.

Cat had forgotten about Doris' habit of repeating the last few words of her sentences. The familiarity of it made her smile.

"Doris, I was going through some of Mom's old boxes and found a bunch of Daddy's papers and things. I was just wondering how much you knew about Daddy and Howard's childhood when they were growing up. I remember his mother, Ruth, but he never spoke about his father or grandparents, or anything like that. The only one he ever talked about was Aunt Jen. She always seemed more like a mother to him than an aunt."

"That's true, she was, but actually Jen was Everett's great-aunt." She paused for a minute as if remembering something. "She came across the country in a covered wagon with Ruth's mother a long time ago, long time ago. Can I get you some tea?"

"No, I'm fine thanks. Can I ask you a funny question?" Cat paused. "Was Daddy Swedish? I never quite knew if he was Swedish or Irish? You know he could speak with a pretty good Irish brogue when he wanted to."

"Oh" she chuckled, "he learned that Irish stuff from the Brothers at Briscoe, but he had Swedish in him. Everett's great-great-grandfather came directly from Sweden. You know what they say, Swedish is as Swedish does, or something like that." Doris rambled from one thought to the next. "Yes, they immigrated here in the late part of the 1800s, as I heard. Ended up in Minnesota, they did. The traveling, as I heard it, was quite an ordeal. It took them a couple years to get here, with all the problems. We didn't talk about it too much. Family didn't talk too much about anything. Your Uncle Howard was your dad's half-brother, did you know that? Nobody ever admitted that openly. But I think Madeleine knew that — yep, I think she knew that."

Cat leaned over to pick out an orange piece of sugared candy from the candy dish. She popped it in her mouth and made herself comfortable on the flowered couch in Aunt Doris' living room, watching her aunt, as she appeared to be filtering lives through her mind. Then Doris sat down in her rocking chair, carefully fluffing a crocheted pillow behind the small of her back.

"Hmmm . . . Where do I begin?" And then, mumbling to herself Aunt Doris whispered, "Where do I begin?"

FROM SWEDEN TO AMERICA

1860, Sweden

At the end of the 1860s, Sweden had been struck with a series of crop failures. The year 1867 became known as "the wet year" of rotting grain, while 1868 became the "dry year" of burned fields, and 1869 became "the severe year" of epidemics and hungry children. Collectively, they were called the "starvation years". With increased hunger and disease, there was a major exodus from the country.

Many European countries were experiencing draught, disease, and depression during this time, so Swedish immigrants were not alone in their exodus from Europe. A large majority of them were lured to America with promises of free land, independence, and a better life.

Mass immigration to the U.S. began around 1865 and continued through 1915, until more than a million Swedes had immigrated through New York and Boston harbors.

The ships were poor and crowded, with little food or fresh water, and many didn't survive the trip. With the rough water and poor conditions, seasickness was prevalent, and sleep was difficult.

The trip was long and tiring, to say the least, but even when they landed on American soil, the Swedes were usually only at the halfway point of their migration. Few stayed in the East.

Seeking farmland to the west, they'd make the rest of their journey by horse, carts, rail, or by walking on trails. Some were lucky enough to take paddle steamers or tugs across rivers or through the Great Lakes to ports like Chicago.

In 1879, Dan and Clara Peterson made the difficult decision to emigrate from Sweden. They had been married for less than two years, had seen nothing but difficult times, and were looking forward to another drought year of poor crops. They clearly could not see a future for themselves in Sweden. Clara's older sister and her husband had immigrated to the United States several years earlier and had settled in a place called Minnesota. They had successfully obtained property through a homestead, built a small house and barn and, according to their letters, the crops were flourishing. That powerful magnet had lured Dan and Clara to follow after her sister.

They packed a few bags of personal belongings, vacated their home and starving crops, and, at the age of thirty, Dan carried their bags aboard a ship headed for America.

Since they traveled with very little, they had little to barter with, other than a small nest egg, the last of their inheritance from Clara's father, who had recently died. Upon landing, they secured passage by rail from New York Harbor to Syracuse, New York, on their way to Buffalo. While it was only 150 miles from Syracuse to Buffalo, the trip took nearly a month of hitching rides and walking. Once Dan and Clara got to Buffalo, they were able to take waterways nearly all the way to Minnesota. Dan, who was a strong barrel-chested man, hired onto one of the steamers for free passage through Lake Erie and up the St. Clair River to St. Clair Lake.

They were able to ride a paddle tug up to Mackinac Island, a port town on Lake Huron. From his work on the water, Dan had enough money to buy their passage from the port of Duluth to St. Paul by rail. All in all, it was a long and taxing trip.

Clara's sister lived just outside St. Paul and, according to her letters, there were more and more Swedish people moving into the area and homesteading in the county. So much so, that they called the place "Little Sweden".

On the eastern border of Minnesota, many counties became almost totally owned by Swedes. The houses were very dense, with little property. The original homestead acreage had been subdivided by families numerous times, leaving some of the immigrants with nothing more than land to build a house on and a community or family farm from which to work.

When the Petersons arrived, they marked their claim in Minnesota on the easternmost borders of Minnesota and Wisconsin. Dan filed for a full Homestead in 1881. Within the next year they built a rough cabin and dug a well. They also had an outhouse, a partial barn and the beginnings of a garden. The fields they planted the year before were doing well, and their cellar was full. America was, indeed, the land of promise.

In 1883, Clara became sick and, after a painful miscarriage, lost their first son. She didn't get pregnant again until 1888, bearing a healthy son, who they named August Daniel Peterson, Jr. and called Little Danny. When he was just two years old, he got a little brother, Vernon Anton Peterson, born in 1890. Dan and Clara were both very happy with this addition to their family.

Propped up in bed with Dan by her side, Clara was admiring her newest son, counting fingers and toes and touching chubby cheeks.

"Clara, have I told you how much I love you? I know how much you have given up, and this is not exactly the life I promised you when we married."

"Daniel, you have given me this and more," Clara said, holding the newborn baby close. Teasingly, she added, "And what about those promises you think you gave me? I'd like to hear them now please, as I never recall hearing them before."

Dan smiled at her and then at the wee bundle. "I'm thinking Danny may get a run for his money with this one. He'll not have you all to himself anymore."

"And I'm thinking, 'nor will you'. Now run along and let me feed him before he gets cranky."

Dan left the room, thinking about his good fortune. He now had a home, crops enough to keep away hunger, good friends, and family. It was enough for now, but not for long.

Two years later, the county was wild with rumors about gold being discovered in the Klondike. There was a mad rush to the territory of Washington, which was becoming very prosperous as a last stop for miners heading north to Alaska.

As families migrated through Minnesota from the Corn Belt states, the gossip spread fast. Some were on their way to the Klondike and some were just looking to get jobs that supported the gold rush. Dan heard that jobs were plentiful, and fortunes were being made with the lumber mills that produced and transported most of the lumber along the west coast and Alaska.

Friends who had moved to Washington told of the mountains and ocean and the mild weather. They spoke of crops that did not burn in the summer and freeze in the winter. They spoke of new cities being built and great opportunities. They told of fortunes being made. The more Dan heard, the itchier his feet became.

Though it was not an easy decision, in 1898, Dan uprooted his wife Clara and his two sons, ages ten and eight, and moved to a lumber town in Washington called Seattle.

LITTLE RED HEADED GIRL

1899, Kalispell, Montana

While Dan and Clara were settling into their new life in Seattle, a baby girl was born in Kalispell, Montana to Charles and Elizabeth Moore. Four years before, Charles and Elizabeth had left Missouri in a covered wagon on their way west. Elizabeth's older sister, Jenifer Margaret came with them. At age twenty-three, Jenifer was three years older than her sister and had always assumed the mother role in their relationship. Charles was glad she had come with them; Elizabeth, being a young bride, needed the company of a female.

They had made it as far as Kalispell when a hard winter hit and their supplies ran out. They had only enough money to rent one room in a boarding house, where they stayed that winter. The following spring, Charles hired on at a farm, and he and Elizabeth took a cabin on the property. Jen did some cooking and cleaning for the owner of the boarding house and he allowed her to stay in the apartment free of rent.

When Elsbeth, as Jen called her sister, got pregnant, their plans of traveling further were put on hold. Unfortunately, Elsbeth lost that first child, but was pregnant again within the next year. With the help of a local mid-wife and with Jen by her side, Elsbeth gave birth to a screaming red-headed baby girl that they named Ruth.

Charles, like many across the country, had also listened to the ongoing news of the gold rush and was anxious to continue west. Without a homestead of their own and no consistent job prospects, they made plans to leave as soon as Elsbeth was able to travel.

Four months later, they were packed and on the trail headed through Idaho and eastern Washington, finally settling in some tenant housing north of the city of Seattle, in western Washington.

Charles found employment on the docks and made good money compared to farming. The work was hard but paid well. Elsbeth, Charles and their daughter Ruth settled into a family routine. Within the next several years, Jen met a gentleman, fell in love, and got married. They took a house not far from Elsbeth and Charles, and nine months later, they were the proud parents of a baby boy.

Early one day in 1913, Charles had gone off to the docks, Ruth had gone to school, and Elsbeth was doing some sewing at home, when there was a knock on the door. When Elsbeth opened it, a foreman stood there to inform her of an accident on the docks. Charles had been off-loading freight when a binding broke. He was very sorry, but Charles had been killed. Elsbeth fainted.

With no means of employment and a thirteen-year-old daughter, the future looked bleak for Elizabeth, but she was resourceful. A year later, she met and married as a matter of convenience, a widower named Joseph St. Michael. Joseph brought with him two daughters, Thelma and Evelyn. Little Ruth despised the two younger girls and was even more upset when Joseph and Ruth uprooted the family and moved south of Seattle to a city called Georgetown.

At nearly the same time Jen's only son caught influenza and died. The stress was too much for her. She left her husband and moved to south Seattle to be near her sister.

In short order, Jen became part owner of a boarding house where she lived, renting the additional living space for a fee, giving her income. She was very self-sufficient and, at thirty-nine, reasonably happy, never lacking for male companionship, but not looking to be married again.

She was still close to her sister and enjoyed her company. However, with the two St. Michael girls and Ruth always in some sort of snit, Jen distanced herself from the family. Joseph was a little too "French" and snooty for her taste, insisting on only the best for his girls. His insistence on piano lessons and parlor games and fancy restaurants and cars was unnerving for Jen's Missouri blood.

"Jen, are you sure you aren't going to be able to come for Thanksgiving dinner?" Elsbeth asked.

"Oh please, Elsbeth, if I have to listen to that pompous ass again over dinner, I'll lose it on the floor."

"Don't be so mean. He takes good care of us, and I don't know what I would have done without him after Charles died."

"Well, don't hold up dinner on my account. I have a date and I fully intend to enjoy myself this year. Who knows? Maybe I'll marry him the next time he asks. It would be a good excuse to have all my holidays at home."

WWI WAS SUCH AN INCONVENIENCE

1914, Seattle, Washington

Daniel Jr. and Vernon, the Peterson brothers, both worked at Yesler's sawmill. Dan Sr., their father, had died nearly two years earlier and the responsibility of the family fell to the boys. They both quit school early and went to work at the mill with their dad. When Dan took sick and died, it was an easy transition for the boys to continue working to provide income for their mother and sister.

At twenty-six and twenty-four respectively, neither Danny nor Vernon had much of a social life and took their family responsibilities seriously. As was often their habit, they walked the two miles from work together and talked. Their conversation rounded to a new family that had moved in next door.

"Did you see the red-headed girl? She looked old enough, did she not? Seems friendly enough," Vernon remarked to Danny.

"I don't think she can be but sixteen, but she'll be a looker, sure enough."

As they rounded the corner the subject of their conversation was sitting on her front steps reading a book. She looked up and waved a neighborly wave. Danny noticed Vernon put his head down and turn beet red.

"Auuugh," Danny teased, "You like her, don't you."

Vernon ignored his brother and went into the house. Yes, he liked her. She was just about the prettiest thing he had ever seen. Her name was Ruth Moore and she was from Montana. They called her Ruthy and her family had just moved here with three daughters.

During the next year, Vernon had worked up enough nerve to talk to her and, with a little prying, found out that Ruthy was only fifteen, even though she looked several years older. At twenty-four, Vernon thought it was wise to put any romantic interest aside for now. Still there was no doubt about it, she was going to turn some heads in another couple of years and Vernon wanted to be there. He was just going to have to wait.

Two years later, in 1916, WWI was smoldering and many young men were leaving to join the services. Ruthy thought that was highly inconvenient since she just celebrated her seventeenth birthday and was now allowed to go out without a chaperone.

She decided she would call herself Ruth St. Michael, as it sounded more regal than plain ole' Ruth Moore. She never endeared herself to her step-sisters, Thelma and Evelyn, and they in turn resented Ruth's use of the St. Michael name. But at seventeen, she wouldn't have to put up with them for much longer.

Ruthy had a couple of suitors who had shown interest in her. Of course, there was always Vernon, next door. Stable, solid, responsible, mature, Vernon. But the boys she wanted, that were her age, were fixated on the war. That's all they talked about. Several of her school mates had already enlisted and gone to Europe. Surely she was going to be an old maid and that just wasn't acceptable.

About that time, Vernon came through the gate and interrupted her thoughts.

"Ruthy, can I talk to you?"

"Sure. You're home from the yards early."

"I quit the mill today. Ruthy, I'm gonna be going away. I've decided to enlist and I'm wondering if you'd write to me when I'm gone."

"Oh, Vernon, not you too! Everyone I know is leaving, and I'm stuck here. I don't want you to go too." Ruth's mind was working overtime. She knew that Vernon had a crush on her. He was a nice enough sort, but she had always thought of him as a fall-back guy. Now she felt panic at losing that too.

"I've done my share of thinking about it and I think it's the right thing to do. I'm leaving tomorrow. "

"Well, doodle, I'm not very happy about that at all, but if your mind is set on it, of course I'll write to you."

And sure enough, Vernon enlisted and he and Ruth struck up a more serious relationship through letters and postcards, when Vernon was able to send them. With the war in full swing, Vernon had asked Ruth to wait for him and told her that when the war was over, he wanted to "call" on her. So while she agreed in her letters to wait for him, it didn't stop her from falling in love with a very visible Seattle businessman who, unfortunately, was married.

They were both very secretive about the relationship, with promises being dangled about divorce and a future together. When the lies stopped, Ruth's heart was broken. The affair had lasted for a full year before Vernon came home to officially propose marriage to her.

When the proposal came, the response was not at all what Vernon had expected. "Vernon, I'm pregnant."

"I see." Vernon paused. "And is he going to marry you?"

"Oh, Vernon, he can't. He's married and I'm so stupid. I'm so sorry, I know I said I'd wait for you, but it was all a big mistake."

"Ruthy, I love you and I would still like to marry you. I'll raise the baby like it was my own, if you'll have me."

And with limited options, Ruth and Vernon were married. Seven months later, she gave birth to a son, who they named Howard Vernon. Two years later, in 1921, at age twenty-two, she gave birth to another son who they named Everett James. And a year after that, they had a daughter, Virginia Ann.

"Ruthy, I have to go now, are you going to be okay? I'll be spending the night up in Colby, so I'll be home tomorrow."

"I hate that job of yours. You know what they call those boats, don't you? The Mosquito Fleet. Why can't you get a normal job in the city, something closer to home? I can't stand being here alone with these kids all the time."

"I can't help it, you know. We have to take a cargo run on the high tide for delivery to Grants after the scheduled runs. We can't make it back until the tide turns."

"Well, it's embarrassing to even tell people what you do, that's all. They say those boats are only fit for the Chinese."

"Well, those people must not need a paycheck." Vernon leaned down and gave Howard a pat on the head, gave Ruth a kiss on the cheek, and left the house with his duffle in tow.

Vernon accepted Howard as his own and never showed favoritism toward his own blood son, but Ruth was another story. She always favored Howard. She never really got over her affair and never really loved Vernon as she should have. That was a favoritism that did not go unnoticed by the rest of the family.

Nearly three years after Virginia was born, Ruth begrudgingly became pregnant again, giving birth to another son, Gerry Anton. During that time, Vernon had become very ill.

For weeks on end, he was unable to get out of bed. He ran high fevers and favored easy infections. Doctors labeled it the "soldier's sickness". While there was very little known about the disease at that time, over ten percent of the WWI soldiers brought this illness home. For years, there would be no obvious symptoms; it was called a latent disease.

When the illness finally manifested itself, it infected bone marrow, lymph glands, vital organs and the nervous system. More than half of the people that were infected with this disease lived full lives in remission; the remainder eventually succumbed to the disease or caught secondary illness that would take their lives.

Because Ruth had little patience for sick people and was unable to take care of four children and a sick husband, she committed Vernon to a VA hospital in Palo Alto, California, for treatment. He never came out of the hospital — and Ruth never looked back.

It didn't take long for Ruth to get on with her life. At twenty-eight, her looks had held up and nightlife had grown around her that she was anxious to enjoy. Barely able to live on military benefits covered under the VA, she found that she could supplement her income by playing piano at the Mission Theater as background music for silent movies.

Many times, without a babysitter, she was forced to take Howard and Everett to the theater with her. As they huddled under the piano, Ruth played her evening set. It wasn't uncommon to have to wake the two boys when she finished, so she could take them home.

She began dating men of means who could show her a good time. She didn't think twice about dropping off her children with Vernon's family for days at a time. And when that didn't work, her Aunt Jen, who had a soft spot in her heart for Everett, was an easy target for babysitting.

Jen had married Harry Porter, a businessman from Seattle who traveled a lot, leaving Jen with a good deal of time to babysit the boys. Since Ruth needed help, she even made peace with both Evelyn and Thelma to help with raising her children.

Ruth dropped her Peterson name and began using the name St. Michael again, and her social life went on, as if it had never been interrupted by marriage and children.

* * *

Present

"Yes, Ruth was something else, something else," Doris said. "Oh we got on okay, but it wasn't easy. She got harder to get along with as she got older. I just never paid her too much never-mind. No one ever talked about, or knew for sure about Howard's father, and she just wrote Vernon off, quick as could be, once he got sick."

Cat added to that thought, "I remember her a little bit. I don't know why, but we didn't visit her very often. I'm not sure Mom got along with her very well. She said that Ruth thought the world owed her a living."

"Well that's your mom for you," Doris said chuckling. "She never minced her words too much. That's one of the things I liked about her. She spoke her mind. Oh, not often, mind you. But when she had enough, she'd let loose and give you the what-for but good."

Not wanting to change the subject from her stepdad, Cat pushed on. "So, Ruth just went on her merry way until the boys got old enough to send to boarding school? I remember Daddy telling us stories about Briscoe." She was mentally willing Doris to continue.

"Yes, and then there was Briscoe. " Doris paused for a thoughtful moment. "That caused a big riff between Ruth and Jen. In the end, Ruth got her way and enlisted the two oldest boys into boarding school. Ev must have been seven or eight years old. Scared to death, he was. Ruth had let Howard do his first year in Georgetown Elementary, but she just rounded up both those boys and sent them off like a bad package. She'd have sent Virginia off too if she could; that child was a hellion from day one. But Briscoe was a boys' Catholic boarding school run by the Franciscan Brothers. Outside of the nuns that minded the paperwork at the school, girls weren't allowed in Briscoe."

THE SMELL OF CHILI SPICES

Briscoe Boys School, Kent, Washington

In 1929, an ivy-covered three-story brick building sat on the floor of Kent Valley, just south of Seattle. The two steeples, like bookends, arose high over the chapel building on one end and the monastery on the other.

The Briscoe Memorial School was home to thousands of boys — a haven, for the unwanted. Anywhere from 100-160 boys, ages 8-15 would attend Briscoe at any given time. The boys were cared for and taught by the Franciscan Brothers. The brothers lived under the Roman Catholic umbrella taking vows of poverty, chastity and obedience, but they were not ordained as priests.

Between the Chapel and the Monastery, where the Brothers lived and slept, there were classrooms and dormitories for the boys. Through the walkway, away from the classrooms, sat the mess hall; adjacent to an industrial size kitchen. Three times a day, the hall would be full of young boys, with the appropriate noise level, as they devoured their meals. The hall would remain silent the rest of the day, with the exception of the footsteps of Brothers and certain boys that would be assigned kitchen duty for those days. Voices could be heard from the kitchen.

"Everett, come smell this," said Brother Frederic, as he rolled his thumb and forefinger together, pulverizing the dry herb.

"This is the scent of cumin. My sister sends it to me for my chili, to use in my old family recipe. You cannot buy this here in Seattle"

Everett held his nose too close to the scent origin, backing away quickly as his nose adjusted to the pungent smell. "I taste this smell in your chili when it is served in the hall."

"Ah, Everett my son, that is the fine distinction of spices, when you can taste the smell of the spice."

For all the things that Everett hated about being at Briscoe Boys School, the one thing he looked forward to was kitchen duty with Brother Frederic. Brother Frederico Marin made the best chili in the world and somehow believed that it was his mission as a Franciscan Brother to pass his Mexican culinary heritage onto young Everett, a willing, yet somewhat misguided subject.

Brother Frederic had taken young Everett under his wing, somehow sensing from their first meeting that he needed a friend. He remembered meeting young Everett's mother.

He had met Ruth St. Michael, on the day of application. She had easily handed money across the desk, signing papers that would reserve room, board, and religious training for both her sons. The well-dressed gentleman with her appeared uncomfortable and anxious to get the meeting over with. His eyes purposely avoided Brother Frederic's, as well as the crucifix over the head of Sister Clara of St. Dominic, the administrator of acceptance at the time.

St. Michael was Ruth's stepfather's last name. Brother Frederic had read the background material on the application and knew that Ruth's husband had been very ill and sent to a VA hospital for treatment and that she had wasted no time in divorcing him and taking back her presumed maiden name. At barely thirty years old, she had a full life ahead of her that did not include the raising of three sons and a daughter.

She didn't hesitate in affixing her name to Everett and Howard's application for admittance. She signed her name firmly, rose, accepted her coat from the gentleman and quickly left the room. Brother Frederic hadn't seen her since.

Yes, he had met Ruth and he remembered the first day the two boys were brought to school with their functional brown suitcases and frightened eyes. An aunt had led them through the door to the office. She had kind eyes and, while she gave the oldest boy a proficient hug, she pulled the younger one to her, wrapped her arms around his chubby body and hugged him tightly. Tugging on the front of his cap, she allowed her eyes to fill with tears. As she turned to leave she cast a glance towards Brother Frederic that reflected love and concern.

Taking stock of the two boys, Frederic led them to their rooms. Oh yes, Everett would be a handful. He was a sizable eight years old, with a cherub face, a mop of curly hair, and eyes full of the devil.

Everett had a creative streak. Channeling the boy's creativity was a challenge for all the brothers, but Frederick enjoyed the time he was able to spend with Everett in the kitchen teaching him to cook.

"The secret to good Chili is in the spices and in simmering the sauce for a long time to make the beans very tender. And always stir to keep the heat even so that all of the spices open up in the sauce." Frederick closed his hand around the wooden spoon and Everett's chubby hand to demonstrate the figure eight stirring motion in the commissary-size pot.

Everett loved cooking and listening to the Brother with the slight accent. Brother Frederic had interesting and colorful stories with moral solutions that were always challenging to figure out. He sometimes talked with his hands in larger-than-life gestures, a flare of drama that appealed to Everett and amused him for hours, breaking up the monotony of school routine.

Everett heard the sound of church bells over the kitchen noises and, in spite of wishing to stay there a little longer, he knew he had to get to Mass.

"Come back after penance and I'll let you put the bread in the oven and you can be my tester of the chili." Everett heard Frederic direct his voice down the hall, as he was running on short chubby legs towards the chapel. He knew he had earned himself an extra bowl of chili that night.

Everett quickly found his pew and knelt, pretending to pray. It was easy to let his mind wander during Mass listening to the music of the choir. He was fascinated with the harmonies and overtones that echoed throughout the chapel. The music helped to take his mind off his hunger. As his stomach growled, he took solace in remembering that tonight they would be supping on Brother Frederic's chili and crusty bread. He could almost taste the chili as it was still simmering in the kitchen over the wood stove, just down the hall from the Chapel.

LAD, WOULD YOU LIKE
A NIP OF THE IRISH?

1935, Georgetown, Washington

Summer break would be coming soon, and at fourteen, Everett was looking forward to being united with his brothers and his sister. He missed seeing them for months on end. Howard was now going to regular school and Ev was anxious to hear what that was like.

Life outside of the school was always uncertain for Everett. He never knew whether he would be going home or to Aunt Jen's, or if his mother would have a new boyfriend. Even when Ruth was home, she never stayed ther for very long.

Everett remembered very little of his dad, and what he remembered most was the dark bedroom and smell of sickness. Even as a young child, Everett knew his mother resented having to take care of his dad. Then one day she told him his dad went to a hospital to get better, but he never came back home.

After that, the boys saw even less of their mother. She came and went with men and suitcases. She would be gone for days and buy funny hats to wear. They'd sometimes stay with their aunts. Everett liked staying with his Great-Aunt Jen the best.

Aunt Jen cooked big dinners, a good thing since Everett always brought a large appetite. Even though it was just the two of them, she always set the big table, and they'd linger while eating and talk about everything. She'd often fix chocolate for dessert, one of his favorites. He loved her house. It smelled of flowers and warm baked biscuits. She had a garden just outside the back door where she liked to spend hours cutting and weeding, her big sun bonnet tied under her chin.

Everett would sit in the garden with her, talking and helping her weed and water. Jen offered Everett a glimpse into her life, as an independent woman. She was also a talented artist, dabbling in water paint and oil, with always an encouraging word of support for Everett's artistic talent. But most important to Everett, she lavished attention on him and laughed with total abandon at anything and everything.

Sometimes the two younger children, Virginia and Gerry, stayed with Ruth's step-sisters, leaving Howard and Everett at home to fend for themselves. Being the oldest, Howard took charge of minding Everett. In reality, they both came and went as they pleased. Everett's interests were varied and much different from Howard's. With music and art running through his veins, and a mother who eagerly paid to get rid of him, Everett's summer hours were full with piano and violin lessons from the old lady who lived a half-hour bike ride away.

"Hey fatso, what are you carrying?" The two boys approached him as he was riding to his lessons. They looked much older than Everett. "Let's see what you got kid?"

Balancing his violin case on his bike was difficult at best, but knowing that he carried the quarter in his pocket for his lesson and having been threatened by his mother to protect his violin which was on loan, he tried to peddle faster. The boys grabbed at his bike, as he, the bike, and the violin went down, sprawling clumsily onto the pavement.

"Not again," he thought out loud. They wouldn't take his money or violin again. He stood his ground despite the blood running down his knee, and, with all of his might, took a swing at the taller boy. His fist connected with a nose, spurting blood over the both of them. Surprising himself, he turned to the second boy, with all the strength he could muster and a hatred that only a threatened boy can feel. He watched as the boy grabbed his friend. "Come on, let's get out of here and leave the fat boy alone."

With the chain on his bike loose, his violin case cracked, blood on his shirt, and a stream running down his leg, Everett grinned. His quarter was still intact. He picked up his bike, balanced his case, and walked the rest of the way to his lesson. He was a little surprised at himself for taking the swing, but he learned he didn't need to be afraid. He could defend himself if he needed to. He was still uncomfortable with the thought of violence and vowed that he would always try the peaceful approach first, but he would never again feel like he was defenseless.

Piano and violin lessons didn't last long. Nor did the drum or accordion or trumpet lessons, but Everett did have musical talent. The instrument that he finally landed on was his voice. He found that he had nearly perfect pitch and enjoyed singing more than playing any instrument.

With summer over, he returned to Briscoe School and became engaged in the church choir. He had a knack for harmony and his tenor was a good addition to the mature voices of the Brothers. In the choir he found a refuge and certain enjoyment in learning to sing harmony lines and blend chords with the men. Even chapel held more interest for him, knowing that while others had to sit quietly in prayer, he could raise his voice in harmony, during hymns, presumably to the heavens and allow his mind to be elsewhere for a time.

"Everett, what are you doing back here, lad, spying on us?" Brother O'Malley hid the small bottle behind his back, tossing a pleading look to the two other Irish Brothers in his company.

Under the pretense of additional choir rehearsal, the Brothers had slipped behind the monastery to have a nip of the Irish and blend their voices in old Irish country songs that were not welcome in the Franciscan order or the church halls. It seemed the more Irish they drank, the more Irish their brogue, and the farther away from heaven their Irish lyrics became.

Everett picked up the brogue and the tunes quickly enough, but the camaraderie and the laughing, with the aid of liquid Irish, gave him connections that he had somehow missed in his life.

The Irish brothers of the Franciscan order never gave him away. They allowed him to escape into their world of the Irish homeland and family with those stolen moments of Irish tunes. Within the confines of the school, Everett's interest revolved around music and the hours spent helping Brother Frederic with the cooking. Those were the only two things that he remembered fondly from his childhood.

"I would think, Everett, after all these years, you would not find such enjoyment in the kitchen." Everett smiled up at Brother Frederic but did not miss a beat in the slicing of the onion he was working on. "I hear from Brother John that your music is very advanced. God must have smiled on you and gave you the good talent. I can't carry a tune in a bushel, but I can cook. I can still teach you a thing or two about cooking."

This was Everett's last year at Briscoe. He would miss helping Brother Frederic in the kitchen and listening to his stories. It wasn't lost on him that Brother Frederic was one of the first and only friends that he had when he was brought to the school. There were few people Everett would miss when he advanced, but Frederico was one.

Stealing a biscuit on his way out the door, Everett headed to practice.

KEEP YOUR FRIENDS CLOSE . . .
AND GIRLS CLOSER

1936, Georgetown summer

As a teenager, his last summer before entering high school took on a different perspective. With a paper route giving him a small amount of money and his mother on yet another trip, Everett biked to the beach at Seward Park, about four miles away, and spent the day on the lake. He was not very good at most sports, with this short legs and stocky body, but he had a natural talent for swimming.

Lake Washington was a public lake used heavily for boating and swimming during the summer. The city lifeguards offered swimming and diving classes, as well as regular competitions as a part of their summer curriculum. Everett was a mainstay competitor in the swimming club events and he nearly always won, or at least made an impressive showing. The swimming club was a good source of camaraderie. He made friends easily among both girls and boys, but girls were still somewhat of a curiosity to him. They were sure nice to look at, but he didn't understand them yet with all their giggling and shrieking.

Everett didn't care what anyone looked like on the outside and always went straight to the heart. Because of that, he had befriended an unusual group of misfits. There was the tall, gangly guy who couldn't put two words together intelligently, but whose heart was big as gold. The chubby girl that Everett had saved from being teased one day was so funny once you got to know her that she would have you in tears, gasping for breath. And then, there was a boy who was missing a couple fingers and whose face had been scarred from a fire when he was a baby. Ev had found the boy sitting by himself, holding a lost mutt, when Everett coaxed him into friendship. Whether male or female, Everett was very protective of his eclectic group of friends.

This would be his last break before he started Cleveland High School. He hadn't actually been up to the high school yet, but thought he might snoop around before the summer was over. He could nearly see the high school from his apartment in Georgetown. It sat high atop Beacon Hill and overlooked the Duwamish River and Georgetown valley.

He had read the general information about the school. He knew it was named for Grover Cleveland and that the school proposed to represent the "high-water mark of personal virtue and patriotic service", or so the brochure quoted. The school mascot was the Aquila, an eagle. The sport teams were active; the music and drama departments were what they called progressive and, best of all, it was co-ed. Yes, he was looking forward to High School.

* * *

1939, Cleveland High School

By 1939, Everett's last year at Cleveland High School, he was almost running down the hall. There were few classes that Everett enjoyed more than a cappella choir in his senior year. That day he had lost track of time.

Everett's stride was not very long and he looked somewhat comical as he rounded the corner to the music room, half walking and half running. And then he heard something behind him and stopped short of the door. In one of the private practice rooms, a clear and very precise soprano was singing and playing a most hauntingly beautiful melody. He tip-toed to the door for fear of disturbing her, and when close enough, he looked through the small window in the door. He listened for a few minutes and then quietly turned the door knob and snuck into the room.

Masayo stopped playing and singing immediately, jumping up so fast she nearly knocked the metronome off the piano. Her eyes immediately fell to the floor, bowing her head in Everett's direction.

"I'm sorry, I'm so sorry," she said as she tried to walk past him to reach the door. Everett recognized her as Masayo Nishimura, another senior who had several classes with Everett. She was of Japanese decent and was known for both her shyness and her intelligence. She'd been on the honor roll all through high school with straight A's. She was tiny girl with slightly tilted eyes, tan skin, and dark black hair. It surprised him to hear that voice come from the obviously uncomfortable person now trying to escape the practice room.

"Wait! You have a beautiful voice. Why didn't you join the choir?"

"No, I cannot be in choir."

"Why?"

"Scholarship more important to parents," Masayo said, in her clipped English.

"Masayo, that was a beautiful song. What's the name of it?"

"It is American from 1927," she said proudly. "It is called, 'Someone to Watch Over Me'. I was singing in Japanese language."

"I've never heard anything like that before. Where'd you learn to play the piano? You're very good."

"Thank you."

"It's okay if you're in here. No one will bother you. Please, play another song; I'd like to listen; I promise I'll be very quiet."

And so began a friendship. Everett and Masayo often met in the practice room, skipping their study hall class. She was a very accomplished pianist with, as Everett often told her, a voice like an angel. Masayo didn't have very many friends and Everett had a kind heart.

Masayo lived in Japantown, just off of Jackson Street towards Maynard Avenue in the south end of Seattle. Japantown was another world. Paper lanterns hung outside Japanese owned shops. Across from the Fuji hotel was Kobe Park, a place for families to spend quiet Saturdays. The park was lined with cherry trees and the most unusual flowers. Japantown was on the other side of Main Street, on the hill away from the piers and traffic, a calming retreat in an otherwise busy area of town. Not many people were familiar with Seattle's Japantown even though it was four times larger than Chinatown.

Chinatown claimed the city blocks just east of the downtown nightclub area, where rows of signs and sandwich boards marked the location of the major nightclubs up and down Jackson Street. There were twice as many unmarked clubs tucked away in basements and back room parlors. Beginning early in the evening when the music started, Asian faces disappeared and white folks dressed in their finery filled the streets on their way to an evening of jazz and dancing.

Everett had walked Masaya home on several occasions, as much to keep her company as to skirt the edges of the jazz area of downtown. The music coming from speakeasies in the underground and on street corners fascinated him. He sometimes lingered in the area long after dark to see couples disappearing down alleys and into smoke filled rooms where music flowed.

When the sun began to set, Masaya always picked up her pace, not wanting to be caught out after dark. It could be a rough part of town, and she needed to be safe at home with her family.

Near the end of the school year, Masayo received her scholarship and was set on going to the University of Washington. Everett took her out for a soda to celebrate before he joined the rest of his class in the courtyard for the senior annual signing party.

"Everett, thank you so much for being my friend and for letting me play the piano for you. You have a very kind heart."

"Masayo, those were the best study hall hours I had. Are you sure you don't want to join the party in the courtyard?"

"No, I must go home. My grandmother is ill and I need to go."

"Well okay then, I hope she's all right. I'll see you at graduation tomorrow."

And Everett walked over to the courtyard at the high school, where everyone had arranged to meet. He greeted and talked to classmates as he passed them on the sidewalk.

"Hi Dot, are you going to the dance tonight?"

"You bet I am. Will I see you there?"

"Now that I know you're gonna be there, I wouldn't miss it."

"Oh, Ev, quit flirting with me," Dot said in a sing-song voice while theatrically batting her eyelashes. "I'm gonna miss talking to you every day. Promise me that we'll get together this summer, you know, just to catch up."

"You bet. Save me a dance tonight." Everett continued on his brisk pace, briefly considering that he may have missed an opportunity by only becoming friends with Dot. Yet, he'd see her tonight at the dance.

This was the last dance and celebration before graduation. What a year this had been. There was absolutely no doubt about it, he had a great time in high school and this last year was the best. He was, however, getting a little maudlin about all the friends he'd be leaving behind and probably never see again.

With his outgoing personality and good humor, he had made some very good friends. He had joined the boys club, the vaudeville group, band, choir, and the photography club. He'd had a major role and a lot of fun in the senior play, and had won some competitions with the swimming club. Even though he had a lot of creative interests, he was a very good student and did well in the core studies, well enough to apply to Linfield College in Oregon.

Linwood was one of the best drama and arts schools around. It was also one of the oldest colleges in the Northwest, a popular liberal arts college down in McMinnville, Oregon. One of his music teachers had spoken highly of it. Lacking any other direction and respecting a music professor's opinion, Ev decided to apply there with high hopes of acceptance.

Right now, though, he needed to hurry. The annual signing party had already started in the Cleveland High main courtyard and he wanted to get as many signatures as he could. Turning the corner, he stepped into the middle of a throng of classmates.

"Hey Ev, I'm so glad you made it before I left. I really enjoyed working with you during the opera; I hope you keep up the good singing!"

"Thanks Wanda, I had fun with you, too."

Two more girls walked up, both talking at once. "Everett, you should not get so sentimental when you write in people's annuals. I really have enjoyed spending high school with you. I wish you the best of luck at Linfield. Okay?"

"I know what you mean, Jeannie, about him getting all sentimental," Jackie chimed in. "You just shouldn't say such things, Everett. Now I'm mad at you for making me get all watery." Then, putting a fake pout on her face, she teased, "Oh and the next time you try sneaking into my bedroom window at night, I'm going to have to let the dogs out on you."

Jackie and Jeannie, both giggling and shaking their heads, left him there and were off to get more signatures in their annuals.

"Hi Everett," a tall blonde said as she reached for his annual. "I just wanted to say that even though I only met you this year, you're a pretty swell kid and I think you have a pretty swell sister, too. I wish you both all the luck in the world."

"Thanks Donna, I had a good time in art class. I'll tell Virginia what you said about her."

A dark-haired girl came around the side of the building, excitedly waving her annual. "Everett! I'm so glad I found you. Would you sign my book?" She quickly opened her book to the page featuring the operetta "Mikado", where she and Ev both had lead parts in the production.

"I'd love to, but only if you give me a hug." They exchanged a quick hug. "I'm so glad you came to the annual exchange. "Here you go." Everett handed his book over to her. "Sign mine; here's a pen."

"Ev, I want you to know that you are an amusing and talented boy. And didn't we have such a good time at the cast party? Thank you so much for being my friend. And good luck next year." She reached over to give Ev another hug, and then walked away smiling.

The dance and senior celebration that followed were bittersweet. Ev couldn't help but feel the confusion of numerous emotions. He masked that very well by dancing with every girl in the place at least once, settling on a pretty senior to drive home that evening.

Now he stood with his graduating class thinking about the finality of it all and how truly uncertain the future was. He liked the ceremony of the graduation, the caps and gowns, the reflective music and speeches. He had never let on to his classmates that he didn't get accepted into Linfield College.

It was just as well, since the private college fees were more than he would be able to afford. His second choice school was the University of Washington, which solved the housing issue since he could live at home.

But he needed to get a steady job for the summer to afford the tuition fees, and that would be a challenge. There weren't many jobs available for students; many families were still struggling with the fallout from the depression.

He had heard about a program called the Civilian Conservation Corps that might be a possibility of employment for the summer. They had recently opened up that program for shorter terms, other than the normal six months. He had an appointment the following day at the CCC office in downtown Seattle.

The next morning, Ev sat in the hard metal chair and listened as the recruiter drawled on. "So, as part of President Roosevelt's New Deal, he passed the Emergency Conservation Work Act. We know it as the Civilian Conservation Corps. Here in the Northwest, the CCCs have done a lot of good work and employed a lot of men that otherwise could not get jobs." The recruiter went on to explain to Everett and the two other boys, "Primarily, our assignments up here are to fight forest fires, replant the forests, manage flood control, help with community safety and, right now, we have a big project going on up north, putting in natural rock barrier walls along roads bordering government property."

Ev carefully read all the material. There were few require-ments: you needed to be a U.S. citizen, unemployed, and unmar-ried between the ages of eighteen and twenty-six. The typical enlistment was for six months, but they offered a three-month summer enlistment which was right up Ev's alley. This would give him tuition for school and a temporary job for the summer.

He enlisted and was promptly assigned to the forestry unit, where he worked fighting forest fires and helping to replant Doug-las fir trees in the foothills near North Bend and Snoqualmie.

He liked working in the forest and didn't mind the physical labor. The only thing he didn't like was the significant damper on his dating life. He missed going to Seward Park and seeing his friends, but he made the best of the weekends. In short order, he nearly had the tuition saved for the first school quarter.

A DAPPER SORT OF A FELLOW

1939, University of Washington

Everett paid his tuition and claimed his classes, heavily laden with music and drama courses, and began his attachment to the University of Washington. Though he knew a drama or music career was unlikely, he followed his heart.

By 1939, the University had gained a strong reputation in music, arts, literature, philosophy and science, and it was easy enough for Everett to lose himself in the expressive arts.

As he knew would happen, Everett ran into several people that he had gone to school with from Cleveland High, not the least of which was Masayo. Masayo's classes were weighted with science and math, but that did not stop their paths from crossing.

"Masayo, I still can't talk you into music, huh?"

"No, I can't. I have to study to be doctor, but I hear you sing with your friends on the quad last week. Sound good. Nice."

"Oh, that was our old quartet. We sang together when we were in vaudeville class last year. I'm trying to talk them into joining the talent competition for Campus Day. You're going to come, aren't you?"

"Oh, I don't know, but I will see."

"Come on, I'll walk you over to the hall."

Ev had run into his vaudeville quartet friends strictly by accident. He hadn't known they were at the University, and when he saw them, they just couldn't help themselves, resurrecting a barbershop medley they had learned in high school. Their impromptu performance in the middle of the Liberal Arts Quad drew quite a bit of attention from the students and faculty, prompting one upper-classman to stop Everett on his way to the hall.

"So, do you belong to a group? And then in response to Ev's questioning expression, "your singing back there."

"Oh, no, those were just some of my old classmates. We were in a vaudeville class together."

"Well you have a really good tenor; if you're not doing anything tonight, some of us get together and sing barbershop over at Meany Hall. If you get a chance, drop by. We usually get there about seven."

"Oh, yeah?" His interest piqued. "What room do you meet in?"

"Well, the rooms change all the time; just head towards Meany and follow the sounds. You can't miss it. Oh, by the way, my name's Harry," he said, extending his hand for a handshake.

"I'm Everett," meeting his hand. "Maybe I'll see you later." With that, the two boys separated, going in opposite directions to class.

Everett was able to meet his tuition for the remainder of the freshman year by doing odd jobs. He worked in a soda shop a few hours a day and got a part-time job with Howard doing some handyman work in a Georgetown apartment building.

By juggling his school schedule, he was able to free up an evening or two a week to pursue his new hobby, singing barbershop over at Meany Hall. He had recruited his old vaudeville classmates to join him, and they formed their own quartet that sang from time to time at one of the Georgetown movie houses. In spite of his busy schedule, he still managed to woo a girlfriend or two.

Everett had grown into a dapper sort of a fellow. His short, stocky frame was offset by his confident carriage. He held himself high, but without conceit. He had an unassuming nature and an open heart that would get broken several times. He liked women, and they liked him. He was easy to talk to, funny, smart, and always a gentleman. His dating was sometimes stunted because he lacked permanent transportation, but he was able to borrow Howard's car if he needed.

Howard was the sensible, analytical brother. As the oldest, he took his sense of responsibility serious. He had saved his money and bought a bankrupt furniture store. Out of the rumble and dust, Howard revived the store and was making it successful. He worked sales during the day and did the books and furniture repair at night. Many nights, Everett came to the store and helped his brother with the repair and paint. It provided Everett a couple of bucks spending money and the use of Howard's car when he needed. It was a beneficial arrangement for both of them.

The two brothers had been dependent on each other growing up and were still close, talking to each other almost every day. But while Everett lived his life with a wink and a smile, Howard was more thoughtful and sedate. Ev liked him not only as his brother, but as a man.

When Everett got home that evening, his telephone was ringing.

"Hello?" Ev answered, still distracted by his thoughts.

"Ev, I tried calling you earlier. Did you just get home?" Howard's voice sounded stressed on the other end of the phone line.

"Yeah, I just walked in the door. I was at barbershop practice. What'd you need?"

"Gerry called. He got picked up and didn't want to call Mother. Geez Ev, I don't have the money to bail him out again."

"What was it this time?"

"I guess he was in downtown Seattle last night and got in a fight. Cops came," Howard said in short spurts.

"Even if I had the money, I wouldn't bail him out. Let him sit there."

"Yeah, that's what Doris said. But he's our brother." Howard repeated the same mantra that he had tried on his wife with the same type of response from Everett.

"Don't try to make me feel guilty. I'm not going to feel sorry for him; he brings this all on himself."

"I figured you'd say that. It's okay, I'll figure out something."

Howard hung up and Ev, still holding the phone, slid to the chair. Gerry had been in fights since he was ten. Now that he was a teenager, the fighting and repercussions were increasing. He felt sorry for him to a certain extent and it hurt because he was the little brother. But he and Howard had gone through a lot in their young lives and they had worked hard to put it all behind them. Sometimes you just have to grow up.

Gerry wasn't Howard's responsibility. Everett knew Howard was only trying to do what he thought a big brother should do. Feeling guilty, Everett had probably been a little short with his brother on the telephone. He'd call Howard back tomorrow and see what he could do to help.

I'LL BE WAITING FOR
YOU WITH BELLS ON

1940, Seattle, Washington

The following summer, Ev was working a few part-time hours at the soda shop, and had applied for a job at the Boeing Airplane Company. Earlier that year, Boeing had been allocated a significant amount of money by the Army Air Corps for design and testing of the Model 345 Airplane. That plane was the basis for the B-29 bomber. Boeing was growing in leaps and bounds due to the warplane effort and hiring workers for the summer in order to complete those orders. Ev's employment application landed on a desk in one of the warplane shops and he was hired for the summer.

By the time fall quarter started, he had enough money scraped together to enroll. The Boeing schedule allowed him to work hours in the evenings and, with the aid of a few loans from Aunt Jen, he was able to limp through his sophomore year.

Out of economic necessity, he had given up on the drama classes and substituted math and short-term business courses. With that additional background, Boeing hired him for a full-time position the following summer, 1941. At that same time, Everett found himself in a defining relationship with a young woman he had been seeing for a couple of months.

"Okay, so how'd it go? Did you get the job?" Barbara Jo Parker asked as she sat at the counter waiting for her soda.

"Yeah, they said I could start on Monday. Forty hours at least through August. I'm working full time and Howard is loaning me his car. I figure if I'm careful, I can get two more quarters in, and maybe they'll keep me on part-time during school."

"That's great. I think we should celebrate. I get off at six and my roommate is out tonight. Why don't you come over and I'll fix you dinner. Probably won't be much and you're a better cook than me, but I'd like to cook for you, for a change."

"Six it is then. I'll walk you back. I have some things to do this afternoon, but I'll see you tonight."

"I'll be waiting for you, with bells on."

As Barbara wrapped her arm in his, Everett walked her back to work, lingering a block from the shop to kiss her goodbye. Everything seemed to be looking up for him. Barbara was fun to be with, smart, and had legs that didn't stop. His money problems were on the back burner and he had a beautiful woman cooking dinner for him. What more could a guy ask for?

Several months later, Ev finished up his classes and was on his way to meet Barbara. It was cold for early November and the used car he bought didn't have a heater, so it was a miserable ride to her apartment.

Barbara's roommate had moved out in August and Ev spent as much time at Barbara's as he did anywhere.

"Honey, are you home?" Ev said, coming through the door.

"I'm in here," Barbara called from the bedroom.

As Ev walked through the door he could feel something wasn't right. Barbara was sitting on the edge of the bed, staring at the closet with tears in her eyes.

She turned to look at him and said in a quiet monotone voice, "Honey, I don't know how else to say this. I'm pregnant." And the tears began to fall. To his credit, Ev went to the bed, sat beside her, and wrapped his arms around her as she sobbed.

"Oh, God, I'm sorry, I'm so sorry," she whispered through her tears.

"Baby, it's not your fault. Don't be sorry. It'll be okay; we'll get through this." Ev was calm and reassuring on the outside, but he felt like a truck had hit him on the inside. His chest ached with what he knew to be the right thing to do.

He slowly unwrapped his arms, lifted her chin and kissed the tip of her nose. He stood up, then dropped to one knee reaching for her hand. "Barbara, will you marry me and have my baby?"

She was shocked and confused. "Oh my God! What are you doing?" She dropped her head into her hands. "That's a real nice offer, but . . . " and the tears flowed again.

"Barbara, stop crying for a minute. This isn't just a *nice* offer. I am serious. Honey . . . will . . . you . . . marry . . . me?" he said very slowly and deliberately, pressing her to respond to the question. Barbara looked directly into his steady eyes for a moment and, after a brief hesitation, responded. "Yes!" she said, dropping to her knees and allowing herself to be held tightly.

Ev pushed the hair off her face and kissed her. And even with her swollen eyes, he looked at her and said, "You're beautiful, and I love you."

Within the next week they were married by a Justice of the Peace. Ev moved in permanently to her apartment until they could think of a better arrangement. And they prepared to celebrate their first Thanksgiving as husband and wife.

Two weeks later, they lay in bed one morning listening to the radio. In awe of the rapid changes in her body as the baby grew, Ev liked to hold his hand on her stomach trying as he might to feel the life. In a state of half sleep with his hand on her stomach, he heard in the background:

"We interrupt this program to bring you a special news bulletin. The Japanese have attacked Pearl Harbor, Hawaii, by air."

Ev bolted straight up out of bed, grabbing for the volume control of the radio.

TRUST IN FAITH AND DNA

Present

Aunt Doris put down her tea cup. At some point during the story, Cat had heated water and made two cups of tea, all the while listening intently to the story.

"I remember when the baby was born. Oh he loved that baby more than life itself. Of course, that was during the time we had blackouts because of the war. Yes that was a hard time for all of us . . . hard time." Pointing to a box that was sitting on her bookshelf, Doris said, "I think there are some pictures in that box. You can have them if you'd like. Most of that stuff came from Aunt Jen. There's some letters and postcards and things – I don't know what all's in there, but it doesn't make any never mind to me."

Sensing that the story telling had come to a close for the day, Cat thanked Doris for the tea and the conversation and rose from the couch. "I'll try to come back and visit you again soon. I'll bring Jamie with me next time."

"Oh, that would be nice."

"You take care of yourself, okay?" Cat gave her a goodbye hug and then she tucked the box under her arm and turned to leave.

Just as she was getting into the car, she heard Doris's voice from the porch. "Drive careful, Cat." Cat smiled and waved as she pulled out of the driveway.

When Cat got home, she could hardly wait to go through the box. It offered more pieces to the jigsaw puzzle, and she began sketching out another chapter in her book.

She was in such deep concentration as her mind raced and her fingers flew across the keyboard, she didn't notice when Jim set a tuna sandwich and Diet Pepsi on her desk. She didn't remember eating it. She was so distracted putting this history onto paper that she didn't notice it get dark and didn't pay much attention when Morgan lay down by her feet and started to snore.

Later that evening Cat was totally absorbed in making notes from Aunt Doris' memories, when she caught a movement out of the corner of her eye. She turned to see Jim standing in the door-way.

"Don't you think it's time you came to bed now? It's after midnight. You've been at this all day."

"Yeah, I'm just about done; I've come to a good place to stop anyway. I think I've found a striking point in history that centers my three characters. I have enough background with all three families to bring the timeline to 1941 with the bombing of Pearl Harbor."

"Huh . . . interesting. I take it that's why you've found a new interest in World War II," Jim said, as he locked the front door and headed for the bedroom. Cat followed him.

"I guess so. I never paid much attention to the war before and, now that I'm mentally on the brink of it, I don't know how I'm going to consolidate the whole of WWII within a few chapters of this book." Cat paused, thinking about how she wanted to attack that part. "I don't think I want to elaborate too much on the war itself, just the effect it had on my characters," she said, crawling into bed. "Isn't that funny? I know them now as characters." Suddenly feeling guilty for the time she'd been spending away from him, she added, "Honey, I'm sorry I've been working so much on this book lately." She rolled over and cuddled in the crook of his arm. She'd finally resigned herself to stop calling the project "research", or "my writing". She was finally convinced that what she had was the beginning of a book. No longer just the story of her mom's life, her mom was still at the center, but the story itself had taken on a life of its own.

"Are you sure you don't need a break?" he asked softly. "You've been at this thing for six months now." Cat could feel his breath against her hair as he talked with nothing but concern in his voice.

"I know. I'm sorry, but you know something? I have never done anything in my life that's been so difficult and all consuming, but, so incredibly rewarding. I mean, it was one thing trying to pick through and document my mom's broken stories, but the research on my father and my stepfather . . . the history and trying to tie everyone's lives together . . . I don't know . . . it feels like something is driving me forward. When I started, I thought this was going to be a story about Mom and maybe my real father, if I found enough information on him. But then I realized that so much of Mom's life was shaped by both my father and my stepdad. I couldn't ignore everything I was uncovering.

"It's funny, I was just talking about this to Father Duncan the other day. I've always felt that my stepdad watched over me. After his death, I always felt like I had the proverbial angel over my shoulder; that presence helped me make decisions in my life. I used to talk to him all the time." A smile automatically came into her voice, "I would totally talk out loud to him and carry on one-sided conversations. As I got older, and time went on, I felt him less and less. And you'll be interested to know, that after you and I got married, I didn't feel him around very much. It didn't feel like he deserted me, I just figured that he must have known I was in good hands and you'd take care of me. But with all this writing and digging up the past, I've felt him more strongly lately."

Cat lay still for a moment. "Can I tell you something really weird that happened?" Without waiting for an answer, she continued, "I knew my stepdad had been married before, but I didn't know any-thing about his first wife. He never talked about her. He told us once that he had a daughter named Sharon, but that his wife took Sharon and left. Sharon was only three at the time, and he never saw her again. I don't know why, but his wife didn't allow him any contact with his daughter. He never talked about that part of his life. I never knew what his first wife's name was.

"When I got to the part in my book where I was trying to fill in that period of his life, I needed to give her a name. I can't tell you how many times I've done this during the last six months; I just closed my eyes for a minute and put myself mentally in his shoes at the time. I remember this so clearly because I actually said out loud, "If I were my stepdad, I would probably marry someone named . . . Barbara." And the name felt right, so I used it. Then when I talked to Aunt Doris, she actually confirmed that my stepdad's first wife was named Barbara. Now, is that weird or what? I know he put that name in my head. Just like I know now that my real father appeared at the home and talked to Mom before she died and that Louise visited her. I just believe it."

Jim, who had never had any extra-sensory experience and balked at believing that dead people might somehow talk to you, was characteristically quiet. Then he whispered, "Yeah, that's pretty weird."

They both lay there quietly in each other's arms until Cat heard the evenness of his breath in sleep. As she rolled over, she whispered into her pillow, "Daddy, thank you for trusting him with me. I'm safe, and I love you both."

"I love you too, honey." While it was Jim's voice that Cat heard in his quiet sleep, she knew her stepdad was echoing the words. With a half-smile, she fell sound asleep.

* * *

During the next couple of weeks, Cat tried to give herself a break from writing. She'd left both her stepdad and Glenn on the cusp of Pearl Harbor, and her mom had moved into Billings during the war years. But the story kept percolating in her mind, always there, waiting to be written.

Finally she decided to revisit the box that held Glenn's war records and letters, reading everything again. He had been to some very active bases, and she felt the war years were critical to his personality. His letters explained how time was changing him. In order to do this part of his life justice, she knew she was going to have to understand more about the war itself.

If she was going to tackle that mountain and move the story of Glenn's life through WWII, she needed to do some significant research. When she wasn't on some search engine reading about the war, she was pulling articles and scanning books for background about air bases, troop movement, specific skirmishes, and the politics surrounding the war itself. It was a daunting challenge that left her with more questions than answers. Blogs and personal recollections put faces and feelings into the otherwise historical accounting of the battles.

She had somehow gleaned enough information in generalities to timeline Glenn's military records, dates, and whereabouts in relation to active fighting and troop movements.

She decided the only way she was going to get through the war years was to take what she knew for certain, along with the research, and see if her birth-father's hand would guide her. Once again, she put her trust in her DNA and her faith in guidance from beyond. She knew Glenn had been on leave in Hawaii in 1942. She sat down one morning and began to write.

THE JOURNEY INTO HELL

December, 1942 – Honolulu, Hawaii

Glenn liked Hawaii and could imagine it as the island paradise it was before Pearl. Constant reminders of the devastation remained. There was an eerie silence near the harbor and a lingering burnt-oil smell in the air when the trade winds blew just right. Even though it happened over a year earlier, the people of Hawaii and the military remained on edge.

After Pearl, Glenn and his regiment were permanently stationed at Fort Ord as part of the military action to enforce blackout conditions and to present unified military strength on the West Coast to protect against invasion.

When Glenn left the Camp Murray boot camp in Tacoma, he was in the second regiment to have orders for the Philippines. Had he been in the first group to ship out, he would have missed the Pearl Harbor bombing by three weeks and been at Luzon in the Philippines in that deadly April of 1942.

Even though he heard fragmented news reports, the story became clear as to what happened in the Philippines, and he was bewildered at how and why he came so close, but avoided two horrific disasters, Pearl Harbor and Baatan. When he heard the first news of Bataan, he felt violently ill, knowing he was within weeks of experiencing it himself.

On April 9, 1942, American and Filipino troops on the Bataan Peninsula of West Luzon Island in the Philippines were fighting to survive against the Japanese. With little ammunition and low on food, more men were dying from hunger than from enemy fire. On the afternoon of the ninth, they surrendered to the Japanese by raising white flags, T-shirts, and whatever other white articles they had.

The Japanese soldiers took the men prisoners, but there were more men than they had anticipated and were unable to transport all of them by truck to the prison camp in San Fernando. The only way to move the men was to have them march the seventy miles. The United States press quickly dubbed that distance the "Baatan Death March".

The men were not in good health, dehydrated and malnourished. The march was slow and the Japanese were flush with victory; the stage was set. Japanese soldiers killed men without provocation. They withheld water and food, taunted and tortured, with more than a thousand lives lost.

Glenn never understood why his luck of timing landed him in Fort Ord at that crucial time. But there he sat in Hawaii with a new set of orders. After maneuver training in Kailua for sixty days, the air troops were being sent to the Solomon Islands.

Serious fighting took place within that group of islands in the strongholds of Gilbert and Marshall islands. By February, Guadalcanal was finally secured by the US, and Japanese resistance on the islands ceased.

The Marines renamed the captured Japanese airfield on Guadalcanal. Glenn flew into Henderson Field to assume his new duties. His regiment had been instructed to unload all their supplies in the daylight hours because the Japanese were still mounting night raids.

The U.S. troops that remained were suffering from malaria and dysentery. Glenn's orders were to assist with airfield maintenance and offer support for the coordination of outbound and inbound troops, and to manage the off-loading and inventory of supplies. On constant surveillance for snipers and stragglers, Glenn's first few months at Henderson opened his eyes to the real war.

"Goddamn, I hate this place; I've had diarrhea for a month," the sergeant spat at Glenn. "I'm tired of the bugs. I'm tired of the heat. I'm tired of you. Get this stuff off-loaded so I can get out of here."

"Yeah, we're all tired, so shut the hell up," Glenn mumbled just out of earshot.

In May, a typhoon hit the base, driving them out of the tents and makeshift barracks. It wasn't until the following July that supplies were replenished and the field was back in decent repair. All branches of the military were used again using Henderson field for fueling, maintenance and medical.

Part of the airfield's outer buildings were turned into makeshift housing which afforded some privacy and a more comfortable bed than the GI cots in the barracks. Glenn was able to secure one of these buildings for his living quarters because of his need for close proximity to the airfield supply houses. Even with the upgraded quarters, he never got used to the heat and humidity, or the smell of rot. The night raids and gunfire kept him jittery. Goddamn, he hated it here.

In only six months, he had seen more death and destruction than any man should have to deal with. He counted the days until his tour was over.

* * *

1943, Henderson Field, Guadalcanal

The nights were the worst. Glenn half slept, half dreamed. He grew accustomed to the sound of another bomber limping in. Three others shared the makeshift hanger. The first two had come in with little damage. The third had been shot up pretty well, with one casualty taken off the plane. Even though the rest of the crew walked away, there remained obvious signs of gunfire, and one engine sat at a precarious angle, smoke pouring from it.

The smoke burned his eyes as he watched the latest B-17 make a rocky landing, unsteady, but safe on the ground. He watched as medics drove jeeps to off-load boys who were his age or younger. Two were carried off and covered immediately. From his vantage point, three others slowly emerged, with torn, blood-soaked rags holding arms and heads together.

He waited as the plane was brought within forty feet of the maintenance shack before he grabbed the hanger hook and release tool to open the trap door. His breathing became labored and he could feel the blood pounding in his head as he walked toward the belly of the plane to pull open the hatch.

As it opened, dark brown liquid dripped across the casing from the cargo hold and onto the runway, followed by an arm, severed by a stream of bullets. Bone, skin, torn muscle and blood fell to the pavement. Horrified, he couldn't stop staring at the fingers still wrapped around the St. Christopher medal. He couldn't breathe for the stench.

Glenn bolted upright in bed, covered in sweat, his stomach churning. He could hear someone breathing, loud and unsteady, before he realized it was his own breath. The nights were the worst. One bloody hatch after another haunted his dreams and kept him from getting a full night's sleep.

He got up, unable to shake the visions in his head. He pulled on his fatigue bottoms and walked outside barefoot, hoping the cooler air would clear his head.

His job was officially listed as a field mechanic, but he had been assigned to the maintenance squad, cleaning up the planes and getting them ready for mechanical repairs. On the nights when he was alone, he was haunted by what he found – dog tags, body parts, pictures and mementos – that he threw carelessly into a metal box.

He needed a beer and a cigarette. Going back inside, he opened the small icebox and took out the last quart bottle of beer, letting it burn down his throat before reaching for his cigarette pack.

The quarters were small, but with enough room to bunk down any number of his brothers that came to call at night with their own nightmares. When the generator was working, the beer was cold. But many nights, warm beer was the order of the evening, compliments of the supply clerk who managed to confiscate his share as it moved through the airfield supply.

Glenn cheered himself up with the thought he had only two more months.

He finished the last of his beer and stubbed out the cigarette. Sleep had eluded him. With his mind racing, he threw on his unlaced boots and left the barracks area to walk. They hadn't had any raids for quite some time, and in another hour, the sun would come up.

Then he heard the low unmistakable sputtering of planes heading toward the base. It wasn't uncommon having planes drop in at night, usually unannounced and undetected. Even though he wasn't on duty, he knew he wouldn't go back to sleep. Might as well go down to the airfield.

He lit up another cigarette and was heading back to retrieve his shirt when he heard an explosion. Looking up at the lit sky, he saw one of the planes in full fire, falling directly onto the field. He took a deep drag of his tobacco and blew it out slowly and just stared into the sky where the plane had just been. Now he could add charred bodies to what he had seen. He prayed there would be nothing left for him to find.

He felt the second explosion behind him at the same time that he heard it. As he was knocked to the ground, gunfire began above him. He crawled closer to the barracks wall, still stunned, when he felt his arm in pain and saw his shirtsleeve was in tatters. He'd been hit. Everything went black – he awoke in the hospital barracks with his arm fully bandaged. "How are you feeling?" the medic asked as he gave him a shot.

"I guess I'm okay. What happened?"

"We had some planes coming down on the field and got hit by a raid. Your arm picked up some shrapnel. I cleaned it and tried to pick out as much as I could see while you were still knocked out. I know there's still more in there, but I don't have the equipment here to do anything more than patch you up. I think it'll heal just fine for now. You're going to be on medical leave for a while, so we're sending you back to Hawaii to have them take a look at it."

Glenn could have kissed the man. To get out of this hellhole and go back to Hawaii was worth getting shot.

Several weeks later, Glenn finally got access to the hospital phone to make a call home.

"Dad? Yeah, I'm in a hospital in Hawaii. (pause)

"Yeah, no, I'm okay, I just got some shrapnel in my arm." (pause)

"How's Mom? Last time I talked to her, she wasn't feeling too good." (pause)

"Oh, yeah? Well tell her I called and I'm okay. I'll write when I can." (pause)

"Yeah, I'll do that."

"Are you okay, Bud?" the corpsman in the next cot asked as Glenn hung up the phone.

"Yeah, my dad can be a real son-of-a-bitch, that's all."

"Barker!" someone yelled from the doorway. "We got your orders and it looks like you're getting out of here."

Staff doctors had removed most of the metal pieces from Glenn's arm, but some small ones remained imbedded because they were too close to the nerves. With any luck, he'd never notice them. He supposed that was good news, since it hurt worse with them poking around in his arm than it did if they just left him alone.

His orders returned him to Henderson for sixty days before he was transferred to an allied base in India.

* * *

1944, Allied Base, India

Glenn thought India was as unusual place to be stationed, but he wasn't complaining. The country was an unwilling participant in the war and was only an Ally by default, since they were still under Great Britain's rule. He hadn't seen much of the base yet, but he dumped his gear in the "shack", and found a bar right outside the main gate.

Being in a new place, his nerves were a little on edge as he stepped through the door, letting his eyes adjust to the dim light.

Inside felt cooler. American music came from a radio sitting on the edge of the bar. Several soldiers still in uniform sat at the tables. Glenn took a place at the bar alongside another sergeant who looked like he could use a refill.

"Welcome to the local cantina, Sergeant," the soldier said as Glenn sat down.

"Well, this doesn't look too bad." Glenn took in the back bar and eating area. "I just might be able to sit out the rest of the war right here." He ordered two beers. "I'm Sergeant Barker, Admin Operations. I just got in."

"Yeah, you're a lucky son-of-a-gun, Barker. Admin duty is for the weak of heart. If you'd been here a couple months ago, you might have seen some action."

"Yeah, coming in here I heard you chased the Japs off a supply road."

"Burma Road. Long as the Japs had that road we couldn't get supply planes out of here without going over The Hump — and that was an ugly run."

"The Hump?"

"See them mountains over there? Them're called the Himalayas. Only way to get supplies out of here was to go right over the top. That's The Hump."

The Burma Road was seven hundred miles of dirt highway that represented China's last overland link with the outside world. Reopening that overland route was a huge mission and critical to the balance of the campaign. With the Road reopened and the airfield cleared, the supply traffic through the base increased rapidly. Glenn was given the title of Air Technician, in charge of all incoming shipments of parts and equipment, to include weapons. He and his staff inspected and moved the supply to a delivery area, tagging appropriate items for transport.

All in all, it was an eight-to-five office job with a few daily trips back and forth to the supply warehouse. After hours found him at the local cantina, the officers' lounge, or the restaurants that catered to the Americans and British. He avoided the mess hall at all costs.

His mail finally caught up with him. He hadn't received any mail since he was stationed on the islands. He had called his dad from the hospital in Hawaii back in January, more because he wanted to check on his mom than talk to his dad. Other than that, he hadn't had any contact with home. He picked up his mail, threw it on his bunk, and left for dinner without looking at it.

Later, he thumbed through the packet and found a letter from Red's mom, which he would open later. There was a card announcing a change of address from one of his buddies at Henderson and a letter from his father.

Opening it, he read: "Glenn, your mother died on February 8. Respectfully, Glenn L. Barker, Sr." That was all it said. Glenn glanced at the date of the letter – March 14. Clearly, the note was an afterthought written a month after his mother had died.

The letter from Red's mom was more informative and the sympathy was sincere. Glenn never wrote back nor called to acknowledge his dad's letter.

He didn't sleep that night. He had been periodically plagued with sleepless nights since Henderson. He'd discovered that staying awake was preferable to the nightmares. Tonight would be one of those nights.

Six months later, Glenn received his last set of orders. He was being sent to the United States Army Garrison Yongsan in Seoul, Korea.

* * *

September, 1944 – Seoul, Korea

As early as 1940, Korea had been militarily active, with Kim Gu declaring war on Japan in 1941. In 1944, the U.S. military was faced with the possibility of fighting the Japanese on Korean soil.

Garrison Youngsan was the headquarters for the U.S. presence in Korea, known as the United States Forces Korea, or USFK.

Glenn was once again airfield and warehouse bound in a hot and humid part of the world, only this time there was an even more unbearable stench than the last. The air, water, and food reeked of a sour, deathly stink.

The better barracks were taken over by Special Services, leaving hard cots in tents for the regular Army and Air Corps. The bugs were insistent, and it wasn't unusual for bites to get infected. Diarrhea and stomach flu symptoms attacked everyone, and there was little variation to the meals. With almost no fresh food, the meals were limited to C rations for the most part. These consisted of mostly meat and hash combinations. Troops ate rice every day to supplement the rations.

A supply plane left cases of "D" rations, which was the army excuse for a chocolate bar. Made with dry milk, cacao fat, and oat flour, the bar was of sawdust consistency. Glenn survived on rice and rations and, periodically, a bootleg supply of alcohol that might come through the base.

The leader of the Korean army, Kim Gu, was trying to unite the different sectors of the Korean armies, and the United States had agreed to send a U.S. Office of Special Services team (US/OSS) to work with the Korean Independence army. However, both countries had ulterior motives. The U.S. wanted the land to fight the Soviet Union and Korea wanted the military aid to liberate Korea from Japan.

Neither country got what they wanted. The dropping of atomic bombs on Hiroshima and Nagasaki on August 6 and August 9, led the Japanese government to search for ways to end the war. On August 15, 1945, Japan surrendered unconditionally.

South Korea was thrown into turmoil because the U.S. did not have a clear policy on how to handle the situation in Korea after the surrender.

Glenn had been aware of the trafficking of the OSS and the Korean armies across the China border. An OSS detachment assigned to the Korean Army was caught within the borders of China when the surrender occurred. The transport planes with the returning OSS came through Yongsan, leaving the Koreans in China.

The Soviets had invaded North Korea and the U.S. military orders were to move out of Garrison Youngsan. Within thirty days the camp was vacant. Glenn was being sent home for discharge. A quick stop in Hawaii for a couple days R&R and then onto a troop carrier bound for Oakland, California.

The minute he landed in Hawaii, he took a shower, bought the biggest steak he could find, with all the fixin's, and nearly drowned himself in ice cold beer.

He was on his way home.

* * *

Present

Cat moved the curser to the top left of the screen and selected "file-save-file/close." For a moment she just sat there. Taking a deep breath, she stood up and sought out her husband.

With Morgan on her heels, she found him sleeping softly in front of the TV, with a death grip on the remote control. While she wanted to jump up and down and celebrate, she chose to let him nap, and curled up beside him on the couch. Morgan was not inclined to do the same and planted his butt firmly on Jim's feet. Using his "indoor voice", Morgan asked politely in his own way for Jim to wake up and pet him — which he did.

"Are you done writing for tonight?" Jim asked in a sleepy voice, as he scratched behind Morgan's ears.

"Yeah, I'm done. I just got my dad through WWII. I might have to ask you to read that part, just to see if I have any glaring errors in the timeline, but it feels right. Do you want me to fix you a sandwich? I think I deserve a glass of wine and something to eat to celebrate. "

"Have you thought about what you're going to do with this book when you get done with it?" Cat was busy looking in the refrigerator for something to fix quickly.

"Yeah, I've thought about it. In fact I was telling Father Duncan last week that when I finish it, I was thinking of binding it and giving it to my brother for Christmas. You know how I always do one special family present for him? I think this book would be really special. In a way, I'd not only be giving him the story of Mom's life, but his history and my history, too."

"I think that's a great idea. You really need to share it with someone. You've put so much work into it," Jim said, as he got up to let Morgan outside.

And with that normalcy, Cat opted to open a bottle of champagne and fix a couple of ham sandwiches for dinner as they carried on small talk, anything other than talking about family history. Cat had been so preoccupied with her own project, she was suddenly curious about what was going on with her husband.

"So, how is your car coming along?"

Since Jim retired, he had a renewed interest in, and now the time to build a Street Rod, something he had always wanted to do. Cat knew he was just putting the finishing touches on a 1956 Chevy Belair. He'd worked hard getting it completed and in show condition so that he could participate in a series of competitive car shows. Cat hadn't been down to their garage for months and hadn't seen the final product of all his effort.

"I'm just about done with it. I need to finish the wheels, and then I should be ready to go. I'm thinking about maybe taking it over to Spokane next month."

Feeling guilty at being so self-absorbed lately, she asked a series of questions and patiently listened as he rambled on about car things she didn't understand and had no interest in. What she *was* interested in was how animated and excited his voice became as he explained in detail about his Ram Jet 350 engine, exhaust system, and VDO gauges. Cat feigned interest in the detail, loving to hear him talk about a hobby that he loved. She smiled at him and thought how lucky she was. In the end, Cat agreed to go to the first car show with him.

When Morgan heard them talking about the "car", he thought they were going for a "ride". He jumped up, overly excited, on his way to find his leash, skating across the entire kitchen floor and running head on into the cupboard doors. Standing up and clearly forgetting where he had been headed, he spied the last of his Kibbles on the floor and began chasing them around. Jim and Cat both burst out laughing. Morgan was such a duffus sometimes.

Later that evening, they watched a little TV, and Cat cleaned up the kitchen during the commercials. The three of them retired to the bedroom for the nightly fight about who got to sleep on the bed and who was going to sleep on the dog blanket on the floor. Morgan always lost, but he consistently tried, regardless of the obvious outcome.

For the next few weeks, Cat thought about how she was going to proceed. She'd left her stepfather with the bombing of Pearl Harbor and her real father at the end of the war. Her mom was somewhere in between the two. She knew she was at a point in her mom's life where Cat had actually heard some things, firsthand. She recalled bits and pieces of conversations and small details that her mom had told her during those few times that Cat actually listened. By comparing those stories to the black and white pictures from the attic boxes, the memories were becoming more vivid.

The next time she sat down at the computer, the words flowed easily.

MILES AND MILES OF GREEN BEANS

Summer, 1944, Billings, Montana

"Look Madeleine, I'm not just saying this because I'm the sheriff; I'm your cousin, for God's sake. When you got the job here, I promised Mike I'd keep an eye on you, and Mary Ellen is not the kind of girl that you should take in as a boarder."

"She isn't going to be a boarder. She's going to be a roommate. We just thought that if we got an apartment together, we could split the cost."

"Madeleine . . ." Jack wondered how he should put this. "She takes money for favors . . ." He paused . . . "from men. We know her and her friends downtown. "

Madeleine thought for a moment, both seeing his point and thinking about how Mary Ellen looked perfectly normal to her.

"She is not the kind of woman I want my little cousin making friends with. And that's the end of the discussion. Now, if you want me to give you a lift downtown, we'd better git goin'.'"

Jack dropped her off at the cannery, where she'd been working since July. It was a job she didn't particularly care for, but at least it was a job. It afforded her the small apartment and tight living expenses in the city.

Madeleine had left Absarokee right after graduation. She needed to get out on her own and, since there wasn't any employment in Absarokee or Fishtail, her next best choice was Billings. She took the first job she could get and refused to think about failing because that would mean returning to live with a grandmother who had already accused her of being nothing but material for a farmer's wife.

At the cannery, she took her place along the line of other women as the conveyor belt started sending green beans down the line. They picked out the spoiled ones and sorted the good ones for canning. Today it was green beans — miles of green beans. She hated the days the fruit came down the belt for sorting. For days afterward, the whole warehouse smelled like rotten fruit. Most of the fruit they picked out ended up as fruit cocktail. She vowed never to eat fruit cocktail from a store-bought can again.

The women talked among themselves as they picked and sorted. Madeleine had not made friends with any of them. Most were war brides with husbands overseas, and the conversation often turned to the current events of the war.

She found the talk depressing and tried not to think about Buddy, but she couldn't help it. When her aunt Catherine broke the news to her – she didn't very often cry, but she had cried then. It wasn't fair. She didn't understand much about the war or why it took him. Thinking about it made her sad.

The women had moved on from discussing a recent letter received from a husband, to how they'd give their eyeteeth for a pair of nylons, unavailable since the war started.

Madeleine just sorted beans and let her mind wander. She thought about what Jack had said and thought about Mary Ellen and how it was none of his business what she did. She missed Joe and Louise and thought about how they were doing up on the ranch this summer. She missed her dad so much, it hurt sometimes.

Joe was sixteen that year, finally old enough to be of some help to Dad up on the ranch. But that left Louise alone to help Gramma with the cooking, cleaning, and the garden. She was glad that Earl and Betty were living up on the ranch in Uncle Ray's old house next door to her dad's. At least that would give Louise some company and help. None of them would be back down to Absarokee until school started in August. Maybe she would try to go home for a visit when they came back.

When the buzzer sounded and the conveyor belt stopped, they finished up the line, boxed the rest of the beans, and set the boxes on the platform for pickup.

Discarding her cover up, a sad substitute for an apron, she followed the rest of the women to the storeroom to retrieve her coat and purse.

On her way, she walked past the company bulletin board, ignoring information about Victory Gardens, advertisements for War Bonds, and the latest handwritten For Sale signs, her eye caught an advertisement from Northwest Airlines for teletype training.

According to the flyer, skill training was being offered at the St. Paul main office for the airlines. The notice offered a three-month training course, with boarding available, and a guaranteed job if you pass the course. She pulled the flyer from the board, folded it, and stuffed it into her purse. She'd think about it later when she got home.

Her apartment was about a mile away from the cannery. Some days she hit the schedule just right and she got a lift, but most days, she just walked home.

Her apartment was on the second floor and consisted of a main room, a small kitchen, bedroom, and a bath. It was a step up from a studio apartment, with only a few items of furniture. Gramma had sent her off with some bleached flour-sack towels and a few kitchen essentials. Madeleine insisted on a kitchen to save the expense of eating in a cafeteria, although tonight, she was going to splurge on an egg salad sandwich on the way home. While waiting for her sandwich, she pulled the flyer from her purse and re-read the words.

* * *

A few weeks later, Madeleine found herself in Absarokee, talking to her father. "Dad, I really want to do this. I called and got all the information. The school is for three months and they will arrange for me to live with a family and work for what they call 'room and board', so it won't cost me anything to live there and I've saved a little money for the entry fee. If I work really hard and pass the school, they promise me a job at an airline office, maybe in Billings."

Mike looked over the well-used, folded up flyer and thought that he didn't trust any offer that promised a job. But Madeleine needed to do something to get herself started. She had worked in that miserable cannery place for four months and she'd never been given a lick of help, not that he had any help to give her.

It hadn't been easy on her. She was eight when Elsie died, and the full weight of the loss and stepping into a mother's role had been hard on her. If she had been a son, he would have known better how to guide her. He was at a loss and felt guilty that he hadn't known what to do and left her rearing to Maria. He'd had to deal with his own sense of loss, and buried himself and the two older boys in the ranch business.

"So, you say this schooling starts in November? I suppose if we are going to go, we ought to figure out when we should leave."

"Dad, you mean you would take me all the way there? I figured on taking the train. I already talked to Jack and he said he could put my stuff in his shed for a few months."

"Well, I think if you have your head set on this, I'll drive you myself and make sure you get where you're supposed to go. We ought to probably go before it starts snowing. Since I'm already in town, might as well get going as soon as we can."

"Thanks, Dad, that would be swell. I only have to take some clothes, so I won't have too much to pack. Rex is going to drive me back to Billings, and I can be ready in a couple days. They have a boarding house where I can stay until they get me placed with a family. I'll call them as soon as I get back."

And so, Madeleine left Absarokee with a plan. Rex took her home to Billings. She packed up her clothes and apartment. Jack took the few things she had and stored them in his shed as he promised, and she stayed with him until her Dad picked her up and headed east to St. Paul for a new chapter in her life.

THE QUICK BROWN FOX JUMPED
OVER THE LAZY DOG'S BACK.

1944, Minneapolis-St. Paul

Northwest Airlines was incorporated in Minnesota in 1926 with its principal place of business in St. Paul. It was originally a commercial airline carrying people, property, and mail predominantly in the territories of Minnesota, North Dakota, Montana, and Washington.

Since the war began, more and more of the maintenance operations were being managed by women, who took over jobs previously held by men. This left a void in trained office staff. In order to fill that void, Northwest hired a full-time training staff to give unemployed women the skills to work in the offices. They offered skill courses in typing, steno, shorthand, teletype, accounting, and ticketing. They typically advertised for these secretary and office classes on flyers sent out to various cities that had Northwest offices and airfields. It was one of those flyers that landed in Madeleine's hands and prompted her trip to Minneapolis-St. Paul.

She and Mike drove for fourteen hours from Billings to Minnesota. Madeleine had been given the information for a boarding house, but they decided to stay overnight in a hotel and face the house and admissions processing in the light of day.

During the admissions process, Madeleine was told she would not be staying in the boarding house after all. The school had already made arrangements with the Bullock family for a live-in situation that entailed babysitting two children in the evenings and doing domestic service for the family on the weekends. This was very agreeable to her, so her dad drove her to her new temporary home, met the missus and saw to it that Madeleine got settled. After a quick hug and a promise to call, Mike was on his way back home within the hour.

Mr. and Mrs. Bullock were very well off. They had a nice house made for entertaining, which they did often. Madeleine had never seen such fine furniture before. As she took in the polished wood, glass cabinets with crystal dishes, delicate framed pictures, and fragile mirrors, she felt large and clumsy. Afraid of breaking something, she crossed her arms tightly in front of her as Mrs. Bullock showed her around the rest of the house. Madeleine was given use of the guest bedroom, which contained a bed, two dressers, a closet case, two small tables and a comfortable chair. The children seemed well-behaved, and the school was close enough for walking.

As Madeleine took in her surroundings, she felt something in her pocket and realized that her dad had slipped her some extra money. She knew, without him saying, that those dollars were for her in case of an emergency. It was just like him not to make a big deal of it, but to make sure she would be okay. As she fingered the paper dollars, she smiled and silently thanked him.

The school didn't start for two more weeks. She had time to get acquainted with Mrs. Bullock and figure out their routine so she wouldn't disrupt their family. It was important to her that she did a good job and not mess this up. It was a generous offer and without it, she would not be able to afford this training.

Madeleine learned a lot from Mrs. Bullock, who was very picky, it seemed, but also very patient. Towels needed to be folded in a certain way. No loose ends were to be seen, only the fold faced out in the hall closet shelf. The table needed to be set a certain way; knives, forks, and spoons needed to be parallel and even. Napkins were folded evenly and flat. She learned how to make hospital corners with sheets. Everything needed to be perfect — everything clean — everything polished, dusted, and shining.

Some evenings Madeleine fixed light dinners for the children and listened while they read, or she read to them. Once her school started, she had her own studies in the evening. All and all, it was a nice arrangement for both her and the Bullocks.

She worked hard in school, learning to type, learning shorthand and learning how to use the teletype machines. She quickly became competent in typing. Even in her dreams she would type over and over, *"The quick brown fox jumped over the lazy dogs back,"* until she easily mastered fifty words a minute, the minimum for a passing grade.

The other girls in her class were from a variety of states and they were all quite friendly. She made a few casual friendships, but her schedule didn't allow much time for socializing. She went home in the evenings and did her chores, but late at night she would get homesick.

She missed Billings and she missed her family.

Christmas season was busy for the Bullocks. They decorated the house with a nine-foot tree, evergreen swags, holly, and candles placed everywhere in crystal candle holders and decorated with fresh holly.

There was planning to be done for a formal holiday dinner party, which became part of Madeleine's duties. And since the Bullocks were out socializing nearly every night, she would put the children down and have the nights to herself. She'd spent some money on dish towel material, which she embroider as a Christmas present for Mrs. Bullock, and she'd picked up small gifts for both of the children.

Madeleine was surprised on Christmas morning to be presented with a holiday gift from Mrs. Bullock. She tore open the box in her excitement and discovered it contained a new skirt and a sweater set for her to wear on her first day of work when she passed her schooling, which she did near the end of January 1945.

After getting her completion certificate, she took the train home to Billings, where her dad picked her up with Joe in tow, and drove her back to Absarokee. It was good to be home. Madeleine had received confirmation before she left school that there was a job interview scheduled for her at Northwest Airlines in Billings. When Madeleine went to the interview, she was hired immediately, and set to start work after a short break at home in Absarokee.

CARRIED ALONG WITH THE CROWD

1945, Billings Montana

Northwest was a good company to work for. It had changed from being a mail carrier to passenger service and was rapidly expanding. In 1945 the passenger planes flew through the Dakotas, Montana, Spokane and Seattle.

In addition to passenger service, Northwest had joined the war effort by flying military equipment and personnel from the continental United States to Alaska and the Aleutian Islands.

The Billings, Northwest Airlines field was a beneficiary to all that activity. It had become a convenient migration route for soldiers to and from military bases, as well as a major route from Fort Lewis to the Corn Belt.

Madeleine had worked in the Northwest Air office for six months and liked her work. The offices weren't much to look at. They had been pretty well stripped bare, turning over all excess supplies and furniture to the military. The walls, ceiling, floors, and most of the file cabinets and desks were basic office chipped-paint gray and mismatched. The arms on the chairs had been taped together in many layers, and the whole place could have used a good cleaning. Madeleine couldn't help thinking on her first day that Mrs. Bullock would have had them all scrubbing that floor with a toothbrush until it gleamed.

She made a few friends with other women, and the boss was pretty nice, so she didn't feel she had much to complain about. But more than the women she worked with, she liked the pilots and officers who came and went through their office during the course of the day.They were always friendly, with a smile, a joke, or at least a wave. Sometimes they'd stop in the offices and regale the women with stories — where they had been or where they were headed.

The women had moved a picnic table closer to the building so they could sit outside and eat lunch or visit during coffee breaks. Madeleine liked to eat her lunch there late in the afternoon when the planes started landing. She could spend hours watching the people coming and going across the airfield and through the building.

Soldiers disembarked at the Billings airfield on their way to other states, and the women were always excited when a new batch of soldiers wandered the airport while waiting for connecting flights.

Two full planeloads of soldiers already had landed, and it was barely noon. Even though it was only the first part of September, an early storm had backed up connecting flights to Chicago, so more people than usual were milling around.

One group of soldiers from Fort Lewis, in various states of Khaki dress, congregated around the office picnic table in a blue haze of cigarette smoke. They all looked content drinking their sodas and listening to a radio someone had set on one of the benches.

The women inside did their best to pretend that they weren't watching them, carrying on their typical office conversations among themselves.

"Did you see that last batch of boys? Holy cow! Makes you wonder what we are going to look at when this war is over," Paula said. "Of course, if the war was over, all the boys would be home. But then of course, they'd just be boys from Billings, and who needs that kind of disappointment?"

"I don't care where the boys are from; I just want more of a selection than that four-eyed Avery down the hall," one of the secretaries chimed in.

"Oh, Avery ain't so bad," another voice popped up.

"That just goes to show you how desperate we are," Paula continued, as she stared out the window. She stood up rapidly and raised her voice, "What the hell is going on out there? Turn up the radio! Quick, somebody turn up the radio!"

"This is the day we have been waiting for since Pearl Harbor," President Truman announced, *"I have accepted Japan's surrender. This is the day when fascism finally dies, as we always knew it would. The war is over."*

Madeleine stood with the other secretaries at the window and watched the soldiers on the field as they yelled and jumped and pounded their fists in the air. Someone came bursting in the door and grabbed Madeleine in a big hug, jumping up and down.

She was caught off-guard, but as she was being bounced around, she saw that some of the women had tears in their eyes, and others were getting hugs from soldiers pouring through the office doors.

And with that short announcement wild celebrations erupted. Most of the women vacated the office to join in the excitement. Someone grabbed Madeleine's arm, and the next thing she knew, she was being carried along in the throng of people.

Celebrations began. The Northwest Airlines office remained closed for the rest of the day.

* * *

Present

"Wow!" Jim said softly, his eyes still closed. He had slumped down on the couch, resting his head against the back of the cushion as he listened to Cat read from the computer screen. He had been subconsciously petting Morgan's head as he listened. "Wow," he repeated. "That's really a different perspective of your mom – one I didn't know."

"I know what you mean. It's like three different moms. The mom I knew at the nursing home wasn't the mom I grew up with;

199

and the mom I grew up with wasn't the mom I'm writing about. I don't think I knew her very well. God, I wish I'd asked more questions when I was a kid. I wish I'd taken more of an interest. You know? It just makes me feel sad and guilty now. I was so frustrated and angry with her at the end."

"Well you can't beat yourself up about it. Think of it this way. You're taking a rare opportunity to get to know her now. But, I understand what you're saying. I wish I'd known all of this about your mom a long time ago. It would have helped me understand her a lot better."

"That's about the nicest compliment you could have given me. Father Duncan said pretty much the same thing. I've been sending him a chapter or two as I get them polished. He calls it a life journey. It's made me learn a lot about Mom, but I think I've learned a lot about myself too. At this point, I'm just tapping into good old fashion DNA to carry me through the rest. "

"So, how are you going to end this book?" he asked. "Where is it going to stop?"

Cat expelled a deep breath and rolled her eyes. "I don't know. It's almost like these characters have their own direction and I'm not in control. I guess we'll just have to wait and see. Anyway, I wanted to read you the part on the war years; I thought you'd find that interesting."

As her computer powered down, she moved over to the couch and Jim continued the conversation. "Even though you took a lot of liberty with four years of war, I got the point that this isn't about the war. It was just something that touched all their lives, part of their history."

They sat there in silence for a few minutes. Morgan moved around on the couch to squeeze his head between the two, requiring both to scratch behind his ears. All three of them shut their eyes and let their thoughts drift.

* * *

The following week, Cat met Father Duncan at the Olympia Shari's restaurant, not too far from his church. It had been some time since she sent him new chapters, and she'd printed out her most recent chapters for him. For some reason, Father Duncan's approval was important to her. He kept her centered. She don't know how else to explain it.

"Hey Father, I brought you a present," she said as he held the door open for her. They had once again timed their arrival perfectly, driving into the parking lot together.

"And how are you this morning?" he asked as they were led to a booth in the back.

"I'm doing great. I brought you some more chapters and I'm in a really good place. The writing is going fast with very little to edit."

"Oh good; I'm looking forward to the read." He hefted the printed pages and raised his eyebrow at the weight of the chapters.

"Yes, I know. I've done a lot of writing, and it's a lot of pages."

"So have you found what you're looking for yet?"

"Nothing earth shattering, and I can't imagine there's much else left to discover since I know firsthand how this all ends. I'm just not sure how I'm going to write it yet."

They ordered coffee with cinnamon rolls and carried on small talk for a short while before Father had to leave. He lifted the ream of paper that held her recent chapters, exaggerating the weight by slumping over in pain, which made her laugh.

She liked the easy-going relationship with Father Duncan. He sometimes asked hard questions. And he sometimes offered unsolicited advice. But he genuinely seemed to have an interest in her research and seemed to enjoy her sharing. He encouraged her to keep going. She wondered if he was right, that she still might find something unexpected at the end of this journey. Her mind took a sideways turn and she pictured the pot of gold at the end of the rainbow. She thought, "How very Irish of me to think that way," and almost laughed out loud. She sat in her car and watched him drive out of the parking lot. He made her smile.

As she pulled out onto the highway, her mind began taking stock of where she'd left off with her stepfather. It was so easy for her to write his life. With her mom, the discoveries were painful. With her real father, they were just discoveries, but with her step-dad, it felt good. She felt as if he was guiding her through every page, making the words flow smoothly. She still had to fill in a lot of years with very little to go on, but she had absolutely no doubt that she'd nailed his story true.

I DON'T CARE WHAT PEOPLE THINK

1942, Seattle, Washington

Five months after the bombing of Pearl Harbor, Barbara was six months pregnant. She had not had the easiest of pregnancies. After the morning sickness subsided, she was unhappy and hormonal. The changes in both of their lives had been enormous.

Ev had quit school without thinking twice, taking full responsibility for the role of breadwinner and husband.

Pearl Harbor was an obvious source of stress for the entire nation. Immediately following that tragedy, everyone in Seattle took steps to follow blackout procedures which amounted to putting heavy black paper over windows and eliminating all house lights. No headlights were allowed on cars and the streetlights were dark from eleven every night until dawn the following morning.

Barbara felt claustrophobic and depressed living in the dark, as it seemed, for large periods of time. In spite of the fact that some of the blackout process had been significantly lessened, telephone and radio was limited. With Ev at work the better part of each day, boredom had set in.

Ev tried to understand what she was going through and offer support, but the constant whining and nagging sometimes got to him. He no longer went to sing barbershop in the evenings, trying to avoid accusations and jealousies.

One day, Barbara didn't feel well and didn't need the surprise visit from Virginia, who had just driven off, leaving a somewhat cryptic message. Thirty minutes later, Barbara met Ev at the front door.

"Your sister was here," she snapped.

"That's unusual, what'd she want?"

"What did she want? She had a message about your girlfriend."

"What are you talking about? What girlfriend?"

"Oh, some Jap girl you dated. She made me write her name down. She said her name was Maisy or something like that. She went to music camp or some kind of camp and for some unknown reason, she thought you would be interested."

Concern set in rapidly. "Barbara," Ev said very slowly, "what exactly did Virginia say? Where's the note?"

"It's right here. She said they came to the University to take that girl to a Camp Harmony. See? She wrote that part. For some reason she thought you'd care. You don't, do you? And then she told me to give you the message or she would come back here and she was kind of threatening. Ev, I don't want her ever in this house again. She is so rude to me."

Everett didn't listen to the rest of her rampage. He grabbed his jacket and headed out the door, letting it slam behind him. He needed to go somewhere, but he didn't exactly know where.

He had heard about Executive Order 9066. Japanese Americans were being forcibly relocated from their homes to what they called internment camps. Camp Harmony was an unofficial name given an assembly center in Puyallup. At first, the camp had been set up as a place "to identify, detain and process" Japanese-Americans for their safety, and move them to a relocation center in Twin Falls, Idaho.

He'd heard these things, but he really hadn't expected it to happen to anyone he knew. Ev raced over to Virginia's apartment. He wanted to hear directly from her what had happened on campus.

When Everett left Virginia's, he felt sick as he drove back home. Virginia had offered additional information. The authorities had pulled the school records, obtaining addresses of all the families of the Japanese students. The families were also to be "detained for processing" that day. He learned that Masayo's mother, father, grandmother, and two little brothers also were taken.

It was nearly dark and they were still under partial blackout orders, so he didn't turn on any house lights when he entered. He saw that Barbara had gone to bed, and he went in search of a beer and a cigarette.

He thought about the beautiful voice he had spent so much time with. They had both started the University at the same time, she with a scholastic scholarship and he by sheer luck and hard work. By his sophomore year, his hours had become sporadic, and their paths didn't cross. When he was married and quit school, it was all rather sudden. The last time he saw her was in January when he drove up to the University to get his grades and a copy of his transcript. He had spotted her on one of the school benches.

He knew that the public was being hard on the Japanese since the attack on Pearl Harbor. Even the Chinese on campus had taken to wearing badges that said "I AM CHINESE", to differentiate between the hated Japanese and the Chinese students.

All of that meant nothing to Everett, and he wanted her to know that if she ever needed anything, or needed to talk, that he was there.

"Everett, you have always been a good person. Other students will not like you talking to me."

"You know what, Masayo? I don't care what other people think. I know you've had a rough time, and I don't think it's right."

"I don't think so either. Some people have been very mean. Faces stare at me and I feel like creeping into a hole," she said. "Then when I walk up The Ave, there was a white lady who came toward me and said 'You dirty Jap' and she spat on me." Masayo's eyes filled with tears just thinking that someone she didn't even know could feel such anger toward her. Ev leaned over and put his arm around her, trying to make her feel better.

When he left her that day, he was the one who was angry, angry that she'd been made to feel lesser somehow. She wasn't responsible for the war. She was more American than many Americans.

Now, nearly four months later, he wished he could do something to help her and her family, but he knew that he couldn't. His heart hurt thinking about it. What kind of a world was he bringing a baby into? But bring a baby into this world, he did.

* * *

1945, Seattle, Washington

He had done everything he could to secure his job at Boeing. He'd been working there a little over three years. He had even gone to night school to learn Turret Lathe Operation and took additional war production training.

Ev worked at Plant 2 on the west side of Boeing Field across the Duwamish River and just outside the city limits. B-17 bombers were now being produced there. Plant 2 operated three shifts, seven days a week, and employed thousands of workers. Ev had steady hours with benefits and a good reputation among his co-workers and his supervisors.

To help make ends meet, he had taken a second job for the last six months working part-time as a sign painter. He liked painting; at least he could use his art skills. But having a second job took him away from his daughter more than he would have liked.

Reflecting now on the last four years was difficult. Leaving the University in the fall of his sophomore year was a necessity. Taking responsibility for the pregnancy was easy. Trying to make a marriage work when you are only twenty years old was impossible.

He and Barbara had really nothing in common, except Sharon. Sharon Lou, his daughter, was born on July 21, 1942. She was almost three years old, and the place in his heart that she held, ached, it hurt so bad. The love that he wished he had for the mother fell entirely on the child.

From the day she was born, Everett loved holding her. He would sing to her for hours watching her expressions as she wrapped her tiny hand around his finger and held on tightly.

He was in awe when she took her first step, and he laughed at her childhood seriousness when she carried on full, one-sided conversations with him.

Now, on his way home from work, he looked forward to whatever antics she may have been up to. He could just picture walking through the door with her running toward him, lifting her up into his arms and listening to her babble on about something as serious as a lost shoe.

He hoped that Barbara had her at home tonight. She had taken to dropping her off at Uncle George and Aunt Evelyn's house during the day while he was at work. He didn't mind them babysitting once in a while, but it was beginning to be more often than not. Her only reasoning was that she needed time to herself. He could understand that once in a while. Except for those afternoons, Barbara was a very attentive and loving mother.

In another year or so, Sharon could start kindergarten, at least half the day, and Barbara had told him she wanted to get a part-time job. He knew that a lot of women worked, but he was the byproduct of a mother who was never around, and he knew what that does to a child. He had a good deal of respect for women and their careers, but more respect for a mother. He thought women gave up too much and that a child needed a mom to be home. At least that was what he had always envisioned a "family" to be. He wasn't fond of the idea of Barbara going to work. This topic had caused more than one heated discussion and was still friction in their relationship.

He knew he was coming home a little earlier than normal. He usually didn't get home until after five, sometimes closer to six. But, with the Memorial Day holiday coming up, they were juggling some hours around to meet all the military inspections before Tuesday. To compensate for the afternoon off, he would be going into work earlier than normal in the morning.

Since it was only a little after two, he still had the whole afternoon ahead. With the unusually warm weather, he thought, maybe Barbara and Sharon would like to take a drive to the lake this afternoon. He and Barbara could use the change of scenery, and Sharon would enjoy playing by the water.

Everett turned onto their block, drove around a parked car that looked vaguely familiar, and pulled into his driveway. Turning off the ignition, his attention was drawn to the sound of the engine. He made a mental note to check the spark plugs this weekend; it was probably about time to change them again.

Grabbing his jacket and lunch sack from the back seat, he walked up to open the door, hoping to hear Sharon's squealing voice on the other side yelling, "Daddy, Daddy! Daddy's home!" But he was met with silence. A shadow of disappointment crossed his face. The house felt empty.

He thought he probably should have called Barbara before he left work so he could swing by and pick up Sharon at Evelyn's. Walking into the kitchen he felt a little irritated that his wife wasn't home and scanned the countertops looking for a note. He grabbed his jacket and headed down the hallway. First he heard the radio playing and then he heard voices. Oh, good, he thought, they are home.

Opening the door to the bedroom only provided a kaleidoscope of scenes. Later, he would remember only shattered pieces of the next thirty minutes. In slow motion, Barbara turned to look at him as she stood beside the bed, a cigarette dangling in her fingers. She was wearing a loose pink satin robe that he didn't recall seeing before. A man was sitting on the rumpled bed, his shirt casually half-unbuttoned. As Ev took in the scene, his subconscious registered the radio playing a Bing Crosby song; he would never remember which one.

His eyes locked on hers and held in confusion. "Is Sharon at Evelyn's?" he asked in a painstakingly low whisper.

Barbara slowly looked down at the floor and in a nearly inaudible voice said, "Yes."

He must have turned around and walked out. He didn't remember closing the door. He didn't even remember getting into the car. But there he sat in his car, outside Aunt Evelyn's house. He needed to calm down. He didn't need his anger showing and he didn't trust himself.

When he finally knocked on the door, he put his hand up to stop Evelyn from opening the screen. "Can Sharon stay here tonight? I'll pick her up tomorrow?"

"Sure honey, what's the matter?"

"Oh, I just need to take care of some things and I have to be at work early, so if it's okay, I'll pick her up tomorrow afternoon?"

"That's fine. Is Barbara okay?"

The painful look on Everett's face spoke volumes, "Yeah, I'll see you tomorrow. Give Sharon a kiss for me." He turned and left the steps and headed for his car.

I MISS MY DAUGHTER

1945, Oakland, California
Oakland Army Base

Everett gave Barbara the opportunity to file for the divorce. He knew it was likely she would leave the area and he'd lose access to his daughter. He needed to bury the ache in his heart, so he made the quick decision to join the Army and get out of Seattle for a while. On June 19, 1945 Ev enlisted in the Army and was immediately stationed at Fort Lewis/Camp Murray, for boot camp. While he was no lover of guns or violence, he was methodical and accurate, earning the M1 Sharpshooter status in rifle training.

He was offered Non-Commission Officer training, passing with flying colors. Shortly thereafter, he received orders to be stationed at the Oakland Army Base, in Oakland California. It was during his NCO training that the bombs had been dropped on Hiroshima and Nagasaki. He breathed a sigh of relief when he had heard, hopeful that he wouldn't see any fighting.

His status at that time was that of a Noncommissioned Officer, Tech 5. As part of his responsibilities, he supervised eight to ten soldiers. Currently his role was doing administrative activities in connection with special orders for soldiers returning from overseas duty.

Since the Japanese surrender, an increased number of troop ships were coming through Oakland, unloading soldiers being discharged and making their way home. These soldiers needed processing and transportation to various bases, and were causing a coordination nightmare.

That day, he and his men were supervising the unloading of troops at the docks, for troop inventory totals. They logged in the disembarking soldiers, the troop movement, and destinations for record in the permanent files.

Ev didn't like working on the docks; it meant a lot of standing. Plus he hated it when the injured were brought off. He always got a little nauseous when he saw the amputees. Most of these kids were younger than he was. They had been half way around the world, only to come home with arms and legs missing; that is, if they were lucky enough to come home. He wondered if the war had been worth it.

A new ship had docked earlier that morning from Hawaii. As the soldiers slung their duffel bags over their shoulders, they walked down the long pier to where Ev and one of his men stood at the gate with their clipboards, instructions, and orders.

"State your name, air number, and hometown, Private," Ev said, as the boy handed him his orders.

"Private First Class Brown, 455-34-3246, Seattle, Washington, Sir."

"That's my hometown too, Private. You'll want to meet in Building A. You'll be on your way home by tonight. Good luck, son."

Making a notation on his list, Ev turned to the next soldier.

"State your name, air number, and hometown, Sergeant," and he reached for the sergeant's packet of orders.

"Sergeant Glenn Lee Barker, 426-31-7879, Billings, Montana, sir."

"Welcome back to the States, Sergeant Barker. Your briefing will be in Building C at the end of the dock; go right and follow the signs."

"Thank you, sir," Glenn said as he hiked his duffel back over his shoulder and proceeded down the dock.

Six hours later Ev rotated off the dock and back into the administration building to file his paperwork. Back in the barracks, he had his own paperwork to take care of. His final divorce papers had arrived. He had signed them, and needed to get them back into the mail. He missed his daughter.

BIG BROWN EYES

October, 1945, Billings, Montana

"**H**oly Cow, here he comes again. Have you ever seen such big brown peepers on a guy?" Paula asked, staring out the window at the new maintenance officer coming toward them. The Northwest Airlines office had resumed business at breakneck speed since the end of the war, and the office secretaries made a full-time job out of watching the soldiers come and go.

"Oh, Paula, sit down. You spend more time looking out the window at the crew than you do working. Avery is going to have your hide one of these days," Stella cautioned cryptically.

"Well, what do you care? You're married. Some of us have to keep an eye open for what might be, and boy, I think he could just be what the doctor ordered."

Madeleine was at the front counter when the soldier who had captured the discussion came swaggering through the door.

"Hey Doll! I have some paperwork needs delivered. Where do you want it?"

Paula mumbled under her breath, "I'll tell you where I want it."

"You can just leave it here on the counter. I'll take care of it," Madeleine said, seemingly immune to his charms.

"So, when are you going to let me buy you a cup of coffee?" he asked.

"What makes you think I drink coffee?"

"Well then, how 'bout a soda?"

"Maybe." She responded just as one of the pilots walked up and handed her a mileage log. "Here you go, Madeleine, have a nice weekend." The pilot gave her half a wave on the way out the door.

"Madeleine, huh? I'm Glenn." He leaned on the counter, grinning, his eyes full of mischief.

Madeleine's phone rang and she reached to answer it before she had to think of a response. He gave her a quick wink and, with the smile still plastered on his face, he left. He'd be back tomorrow.

* * *

It was going to be Glenn's twenty-fourth birthday next week and he had just started his job at Northwest Airlines in Billings. Three months earlier he had been in Korea counting the days until he would be discharged.

So much had happened in a short period of time. On August 8, the United States dropped an atomic bomb on Hiroshima, Japan. The uncertainty of Japanese repercussions put everyone on high alert at the Korean base. Two days later, another bomb was dropped on Nagasaki, Japan. When the rubble finally settled on August 15, Japan accepted terms for a cease fire and the ultimate end of the war.

On September 2, when the agreement of surrender was officially signed aboard the USS Missouri in Tokyo Harbor, Glenn was en route to Hawaii to begin processing out of the service. After a brief stay in Hawaii, with some much-needed sleep and decent food and drink, he boarded a troop ship headed for Oakland, California.

He couldn't wait to be back on American soil. When the ship docked, the soldiers threw their duffels over their shoulders and walked the long pier to the stationed NCO waiting at the gate.

"State your name, air number, and hometown Sergeant." The NCO turned the page on his clip board and reached for Glenn's packet of orders.

"Sergeant Glenn Lee Barker, 426-31-7879, Billings, Montana, sir."

"Welcome back to the States, Sergeant Barker. Your briefing will be in Building C at the end of the dock. Go right and follow the signs."

"Thank you, sir." Glenn said, as he hiked his duffel back over his shoulder and proceeded down the dock. He could hear Officer Peterson behind him saying to the next soldier, "State your name, air number, and . . . " Out of earshot , he headed to Building C, where he was briefed and transported to an airfield for his final official military destination at Fort Douglas, Utah, before going home.

On September 27, he was officially discharged and flew to Billings where Red, recently discharged too, met him at the airport, and they proceeded to the first local bar.

"Oh boy! I can't even tell you how glad I am to be out. Never thought I'd miss this place."

"To us!" Red lifted his beer in a mock toast. "I know what you mean. I've been stateside for the last year, but only got home a month ago."

"How's your folks?" Glenn asked.

"They're doing okay. I was sorry to hear about your mom last year. I thought maybe they'd let you come home on leave. I see your dad around once in a while."

"Yeah, with the mail being so slow and Dad not writing very often, I didn't even know she was sick until it was too late." He paused to take a long pull on the beer bottle. "I couldn't have done anything, but . . ." Glenn shrugged.

"You gonna stay over there? You know you're more than welcome at my house; Mom would love to see you. Besides, the way she's been cooking for me since I got back, I think I've gained twenty pounds. You might as well enjoy a few good meals. It'll take the pressure off me."

"I might take you up on that, until I find a job and get on my feet."

"You ought to come down to the airport and see if you can't get a job at Northwest. They've been hiring maintenance lately and are partial to us soldiers."

"Maybe I'll do that in a day or so. Right now, we're having another round, and then we are going to go find someplace to order the biggest Montana steak I can find."

Red had been right. When Glenn talked to Northwest, they sure could use his experience and gave him a job in the warehouse managing inventory and logging air supply shipments.

For the past two weeks, the highlight of his day was dropping off the paperwork at the office. Some of the girls liked to talk and flirt and waylay him, which he didn't mind at all, as the office was always cooler than the warehouse, and the view was a lot better. But that one brunette never paid him much mind. Hard as he tried, he couldn't get her to smile. It had become a real challenge. But at least now he knew her name — Madeleine.

WHAT KIND OF
GIRL DO YOU THINK I AM?

October, 1945, Billings, Montana

Glenn had just flat worn her down. After nearly two full weeks of him leaning over the counter making jokes, batting his eyes, and asking her out for coffee, sodas, movies, and dinner, Madeleine finally ran out of excuses.

"Come on Madeline, it's a party. It just happens to be on Halloween night. I promise if you don't have a good time, I'll take you right home."

"I don't know."

"We'll have some dinner, listen to some music, maybe do a little dancing. It'll be fun."

"Oh, all right. But I'm not wearing any costume. If I have to wear some sort of get up, I'm not going."

"No, it's not that kind of party. It's not a costume party. It's just a dinner party. I'll pick you up at seven. Okay?"

"Oh, okay," she said, shaking her head in resignation, "I just have this feeling I'm going to be sorry."

She'd finally accepted a date with him on Halloween night, figuring going to a party would be better than staying home in her stuffy apartment. She was very glad to know it would *not* be a costume party. As he had planned, he picked her up and drove straight into downtown Billings to a steak house and bar that was known to be the best place in town. She'd heard of this place from her friends in the office and knew it was fancy. She couldn't imagine having a party here — it would cost a fortune. Getting out of the car and heading to the door, she began getting a little leery about this whole evening, but for the time being she would give Glenn the benefit of the doubt.

They were seated and given menus. But before going any further, Madeleine said, "I don't think this is any party; I think you'd better take me home."

"This is a party, Madeleine, my party. This is my birthday and this is how I want to spend it, with you."

"Oh, you're so full of hogwash," she said, reaching for her purse.

"Honest, Madeleine, look, my military ID has my birth date on it." He pulled his ID from his wallet. "Today's my birthday. And I don't have anyone I'd rather celebrate it with, than you."

She paused, looked at the ID and then at him. "Huh. That was a pretty sneaky way of you getting me here."

"Yeah, but it worked, didn't it?"

It had worked. They talked and ate and had drinks. He was witty and made her laugh. Her naiveté was a source of amusement to him, and he teased her mercilessly — something she was used to after growing up with three brothers. She unexpectedly had a great time. No one had ever quite made her feel like she was the center of attention before. Even though he had been a perfect gentleman, he made her feel rather uneasy — a little nervous and short of breath. She liked him.

A few days later, Madeleine agreed to go to a movie with Glenn at the local movie house. They shared popcorn and soda. He started making it a habit of stopping by the administration office and talking to her while she was eating lunch, much to the chagrin of the other women in the office. All this attention made her feel kind of giddy inside; she'd never had anyone jealous of her before.

Thanksgiving came and went, and Christmas was around the corner. Glenn had insisted on getting Madeleine a small Christmas tree, which sat naked in the corner of her apartment. Earl and

Betty came up to Billings bringing her some fruitcake, and Betty insisted on helping her buy some ornaments and small decorations for the tree and for her apartment.

Madeleine enjoyed spending time with Betty. She was family and she was someone that she could talk to and confide in. Betty was an easy listener. "So, Madeleine, where did you get the tree?" Betty asked, as she was helping Madeleine hang ornaments on the branches.

"Oh, well a guy I met got it for me."

"A guy you met? This sounds a little serious, if he is going to buy a tree for you and spend Christmas with you."

"Oh, he's not spending Christmas with me. He just thought I ought to have a tree. I don't know why; I'm not going to be here on Christmas; I'll be down in Absarokee."

"Well, I think it was a nice gesture. Are we gonna meet him?"

"No, I don't think so."

"Madeleine. Do you like him?" Betty asked very seriously.

"Yeah, I guess I do." Madeleine hadn't really thought much about it until she said it out loud to Betty. But yes, she was beginning to like him very much.

Madeleine and Glenn spent an early Christmas together, with Madeleine fixing fried chicken and homemade pumpkin pie for dessert. She figured chicken was close enough to turkey and would just have to do. The following day, she headed back down to Absarokee to spend a couple of days with her dad and family. She didn't tell them about Glenn.

That following April of 1946, Madeleine celebrated her twentieth birthday, with Glenn taking her out on the town. They doubled dated with Red and his latest girl. After dinner, they decided to go to the Club to enjoy some music and dancing. After too many beers, Glenn regaled the small after-dinner crowd with a rare treat at some ad hoc piano playing.

"I don't know why he doesn't play more. We used to sneak in here once in a while and he'd get going on that thing until a crowd showed up, then he wouldn't play anymore," Red told Madeleine as they were sitting at the table.

"I didn't even know he could play. He's never said anything. He really doesn't talk much about himself," Madeleine said, absolutely in awe of the music coming from the piano as Glenn's fingers moved across the keyboard.

"Yeah, I know. He doesn't say too much about anything. We've known each other since we were kids though. We've been through a lot together." Then he was interrupted as Glenn broke into a simple rendition of "Happy Birthday", which prompted everyone in the Club singing directly to her. Madeleine's face turned red and she was embarrassed to no end at the attention. No one had ever made the world circle around her before. She didn't know if she was mad or happy. He just had a way of getting to her.

Madeleine was falling for him. There was no doubt about it. And Glenn felt the same about her.

Madeleine was glad that they both worked for Northwest. It was most convenient. She could see Glenn nearly every day and their lives had grown into a very comfortable routine.

She would have liked to keep everything the way it was, but over the past few months, there had been a lot of changes at Northwest. Several from the office had transferred to other cities, making the airport and the paperwork busier and busier every day. All this was happening when the airline was in the midst of changing its focus, with new passenger routes and an eye toward the Orient.

Since the end of the war, the Northwest Airline military cargo route to Canada, Alaska, and the Aleutian Islands became nearly nonexistent. But the passenger routes had increased to accommodate the influx of military personnel and their families that remained in Anchorage and the outlying areas. Both the Territory of Alaska and passenger aviation were exploding with new business. Glenn had watched these changes with interest.

In June of 1946, Northwest Airlines was awarded the primary domestic route to Alaska and the "Great Circle" route to the Far East. The advertising department tagged the airline "Northwest Orient Airline". They started staffing up with maintenance and warehouse crews in the Anchorage, Alaska, area.

In August, three new air routes converged in Anchorage. Northwest Airlines was awarded the direct flights between Seattle and Anchorage, Anchorage and Minneapolis-St. Paul, as well as the Anchorage/Chicago route via Canada.

Both Merrill and Elmendorf military airfields in Anchorage were transformed into passenger and cargo airports, almost overnight. Glenn was offered an opportunity for promotion and transfer to Anchorage to help the Airlines through that transition.

"So that's the deal. I'd like to take the transfer. It's a lot more money than I'm getting here, and Mad, I want you to come with me," Glenn cajoled.

"Alaska, huh? And just how am I gonna come with you? And just what am I going to do up there?

"Honey, marry me, and come with me."

"What?"

"I love you. And I want you to marry me and come with me to Anchorage. It'll be great. I'll make you happy, Mad, I really will."

Many things went through Madeleine's mind, especially her grandmother telling her she'd never be anything but a farmer's wife and how she'd begun to believe that herself. She also worried that Anchorage took her that much farther away from her family.

In the end, Madeleine decided to marry Glenn, but that she needed some time to clean up loose ends. Glenn transferred to Anchorage and Madeleine stayed in Billings with the promise that they'd get married after the first of the year. She couldn't help remembering how much she had missed her dad when she was in St. Paul and how happy she was to be near him again. Even though she told Glenn she would marry him, she wasn't sure if that is what she really wanted to do. But at least she'd bought some time.

Glenn transferred to Anchorage. For the next several months they wrote and called each other, and Madeleine warmed up to the idea of both being married and moving to Anchorage. That year, at Thanksgiving dinner, she told her dad of their plans and he was deeply pleased about the news. He had always felt that Madeleine had gotten the raw end of the deal in life, so he was happy for her. She deserved someone to take care of her for a change.

As an employee of Northwest, Glenn could take free hops down to Billings periodically to see her. And at Christmas he gave her a gold locket made from Alaskan petrified stone with a real gold chain. She put Glenn's picture in the locket and wore it every day.

Because of his erratic work schedule, they were unable to make wedding plans until well after the first of the year. He finally got some time off and they made plans to meet in Seattle in March to get married. They could both take a free hop to Seattle, get married, and she would return to Anchorage with him. She wanted this marriage to be done right and insisted on being married by a Catholic priest, but had no idea how she was going to arrange everything from Billings.

As luck would have it, Glenn had a distant cousin in Seattle. Laurie and Floyd Harland had been close to Glenn when he was growing up. Madeleine had met the Harland family before and was now about to enlist the help of Laurie Harland.

"MA-7-2784 in Seattle, Washington, please."

"Connecting. . ."

"Hello?"

"Laurie? This is Madeleine Lannen in Montana."

"Madeleine. Oh gosh, it's good to hear from you. How are you doing? Is everybody okay?"

"Yes, Laurie, everything is fine. I'm gonna be out your way next month and I thought maybe I'd call and ask you a couple of questions."

"Absolutely, what do you need? How long are you going to stay? Where are you staying?"

"I'm only staying in Seattle a week. Laurie, I'm getting married."

"To Glenn? Oh my God! When did he ask you? And you're coming to Seattle? You have to tell me everything."

"I will, when I get there." Madeleine smiled at Laurie's excitement. "Glenn's going to fly down and meet me in Seattle, and we want to get married there, on Saturday the 22nd. Laurie, I want to get married by a Catholic priest and thought you might be able to help me."

And so the conversation went.

Laurie was a godsend. She arranged for the priest, insisted on getting Madeleine flowers, and took care of a multitude of details that Madeleine found difficult to manage from so far away.

Madeleine flew into Seattle on the 17th. Glenn picked her up at the airport and they went directly to get a marriage license. Within the next five days, she and Laurie went shopping for dresses and hats, and even arranged for dinner after the ceremony. On Saturday, the 22nd, at three in the afternoon, Glenn picked up Madeleine at Laurie's apartment and presented her with a beautiful white corsage of tea roses with the palest of pink centers. It didn't matter that she and Laurie already had gotten a wedding bouquet; she loved flowers, loved the corsage, and would use them both. They were married in the County-City building on Warren Avenue in Seattle, by a Catholic priest. Glenn placed a plain, fine gold band on her finger and promised to love and cherish her. The heady smell of roses from her corsage filled the small room as he kissed the bride.

It had been a busy few days. When she turned twenty-one in another week-and-a-half, she would be living in Anchorage as Mrs. Glenn Barker.

PRETTY GRAY HOUSES, ALL IN A ROW

1947, Anchorage, Alaska

The woman at the front door was balancing a coffee cake in one arm while holding onto a little blond boy with her other hand.

"Mrs. Barker? Welcome to the neighborhood and welcome to Alaska. Glenn told us he was flying down to Seattle to bring himself home a bride. I'm Shirley Colby and this is our son, Eric. We live right next door in that gray house. You would think they would find another color to paint these houses. I feel like painting mine bright pink!" Shirley exclaimed as she pushed the coffee cake in Madeleine's direction.

Caught off guard and not completely over the last few busy days, Madeleine stammered, "Oh, I wasn't really, um, expecting, oh, I'm sorry, come on in. I'm Madeleine. "

"Nice to meet you, Madeleine. Actually I don't have a lot of time right now. I just wanted to drop off this coffee cake and introduce myself. Maybe we can make some time to visit in a couple of days when you get settled. But if you need anything, you just drop on over. Tom, that's my husband, is off on Saturday. I'll come over and see if you need any help getting settled."

"I don't think that's necessary; there really isn't much to get settled. But I'm hoping one of these days, I'll find the coffee pot, so I could at least fix you a cup of coffee and we could cut into this cake. It looks delicious!"

"Well that would be real nice. If you aren't doing anything to speak of on Friday morning, maybe I'll drop over then, if that works for you. It's been awhile since I've had any time to relax with some coffee, especially since there aren't that many women up here in the boonies. Maybe I'll see you then, okay?"

Shirley and her son left, waving at Madeleine from the main sidewalk as they went next door to their house.

Madeleine turned around in the doorway and looked closely at the inside of her house, as an outsider would. Great, she thought, we have one table, two chairs, and a couch. I haven't even found more than one cup in any of the cupboards. I don't know how I'm going to be expected to fix dinner. I need groceries, some linen, towels, plates, and some silverware. Madeleine looked at the clock. She knew Glenn was not going to be home until late. And without second guessing herself, she grabbed her coat and began walking the mile to the nearest store.

She was freezing when she got to the "Main Store". It was a two-story building. Staples, such as sugar, flour, canned food, bread, and the very few fresh items were on the first floor. Near the back were some paper products, bolts of material, ammunition, knives of the hunting variety, and alcohol. The pickings were slim, but Madeleine filled up two bags with groceries, paper plates, plastic forks, spoons, soap, and some other necessities.

Madeleine didn't realize that even though it was nearly April, it began getting dark at two-thirty in the afternoon. With the dark, it became colder. The mile home with the two sacks of supplies seemed to take hours. Her feet, ears, nose, and fingers were freezing. Then, to make matters worse, all the houses looked alike and she lost her direction. By the time she found her way home, she was more than mad and frustrated.

"It wouldn't have killed him to stay home one day just to make sure I was okay," she muttered to no one in particular. "Damn near froze to death out there. Some honeymoon this is."

When she warmed up, she heated some canned soup in the only pan she could find. Bread, butter, soup, and coffee cake were going to have to do for the night's dinner.

By the time it was eight o'clock and Glenn still wasn't home, she ate some soup, curled up on the couch with two blankets and fell fast asleep. She woke up, still cold, an hour later as he was coming through the door.

"Where were you?"

"Oh, I'm sorry, honey; some of the guys took me out for a drink to congratulate me on getting married."

"Would've been nice if you'd come home and celebrated with me. I damn near froze to death out there trying to buy some food for dinner."

"You shouldn't be going out in this weather, honey. I'm sorry. I go in late tomorrow, so I'll take you shopping for some things in the morning. And I guess we better buy you some gloves and a heavier coat. Do you forgive me?" And then with that disarming smile of his, "I sure would like some of whatever smells so good."

Madeleine relented. It was hard not to. "Oh, sit down; I'll get you some soup. Not much of a first dinner though."

Glenn grabbed a quart bottle of beer out of the refrigerator and a glass on the way to the table and thought, "A guy could get used to having someone to come home to, someone to fix dinner and take care of things. Yes, everything is going to work out just fine."

But, for Madeleine, there were many strange challenges. After the snow and the dark came the gray. The neighborhood was gray. The houses, cars, and buildings were all the same drab gray. Part of this was due to left-over camouflage from the war. Part of it was simply because, as the sunlight hours increased, Madeleine saw more and more of the same. The snow and ice were dirty, coating everything in its path with gray slush.

Trees were sparse and grass was nonexistent. Madeleine lived for the days that Glenn was off work. They took in movies and visited shops in downtown Anchorage. She loved taking a drive to the mountains or going up to Lake Spenard to enjoy dinner and a fire in the lodge. They'd driven all around the area and had even spent some time whale watching up on Cook Inlet.

Tom and Shirley Colby, their neighbors, had become good friends. Shirley and Madeleine would visit, have coffee, and go shopping often for supplies. When their hours fell right, Tom and Glenn would commute together to the airfield, leaving Shirley with a car during the day. Once in a while they'd pack up three-year-old Eric and go to the theater or park in downtown Anchorage. Eric finally got over his shyness and felt comfortable around Madeleine. He sat for hours near her, or on her lap. Madeleine began to feel the first stirrings of wanting a family of her own.

Near the end of June, the weather unexpectedly spiked into the eighties. The five of them spent several days out at Lake Spenard keeping cool and picnicking on the shores.

"Madeleine, you need to get yourself a swimming suit so you can get in here too," Glenn suggested in a matter-of-fact tone. He was shoulder deep in the lake, treading water as he watched her slowly wade into knee deep water.

"I don't know how to swim."

"What? How can anyone not know how to swim?"

"Just where in the world do you think I would have learned how to swim? If I would have ever been any place where there was swimming, Gramma would never have allowed it. I've just never been anywhere to learn how."

"Well then, I guess I'm just going to have to teach you." And playfully, Glenn swam under water until he saw her legs, reached for her ankles and gave one big yank, coming up laughing.

Madeleine, whose feet had been pulled out from under her, landed unceremoniously on her butt — legs in the air and spurting water. She was fuming. She didn't talk to Glenn for the entire drive home. She'd been more frightened than embarrassed, and didn't know to handle it other than to get angry. She swore she was never getting near that lake or any other water like that again.

After the dunking incident, the rest of the summer passed far too rapidly. They had finally fallen into an easy routine. Glenn's work had lightened up and he had regular hours. With the summer came long days of sunlight, with dusk coming very late in the evening. Several times a week, they joined neighbors and friends for barbeque or hosted get-togethers at their house, playing board games or poker.

Tom and Shirley went on vacation to the lower forty-eight and, as neighbors do, Glenn and Madeleine offered to watch their house and feed the dog for them. One evening as Madeleine was cleaning up after dinner, Glenn went over to check on their house and feed their "mutt" as he referred to the neighbor's spaniel.

Madeleine finished up and sat down to have a cigarette, an activity she'd recently taken up, but hadn't really decided if she liked or not. Of all of the acquaintances they had, she was one of the few who didn't smoke and, quite frankly, she just got tired of turning down cigarettes when they were offered. Smoking made her feel more a part of the group and Glenn thought it was kind of sexy. So in spite of the initial burning and occasional coughing, she persisted until it felt semi comfortable to her.

When Glenn didn't return, she decided to go next door and make sure everything was all right. She heard the piano the minute she got outside the Colby's gate. The door was still unlocked so she quietly let herself in.

Glenn was sitting at the piano reading some sheet music and playing, concentrating so hard, he didn't hear her come in. The spaniel was sleeping by his feet, snoring softly. She sat on the couch — just watched him and listened to the music that filled the small front room. This wasn't the horsing around piano she'd heard him play before; this was something complex and grand sounding. She didn't know what the music was, but she was enjoying the sounds and was awestruck to know that it was coming from him.

She broke the silence, "We should get a piano so that you can play."

Glenn stopped momentarily and then continued the last stanzas of the song, listening as the last few notes faded away.

"Nah, I just wanted to know if I could still do it. Sorry, I didn't mean to be over here for so long. Did you get everything done?"

"Yeah, but then I got kind of worried that you weren't back yet." Glenn got up and went to sit on the couch beside her, moving one of Eric's toys to make room.

The spaniel had followed Glenn and was eagerly looking to get a head scratch. "Maybe we ought to get a mutt one of these days." No more was said about a piano, or about his solitary piano playing in the faint light of the neighbor's house.

With winter came the dark again. Madeleine didn't mind the snow so much, but the dark was depressing. Glenn was working more and more hours and she was left to fend for herself for long periods of time.

She knew that Glenn often stopped for a drink with the crew after hours, and was tired of him getting home late. So she took to fighting fire with fire. She decided if he wouldn't come home, she would go to him. She began showing up at the commissary bar and having a beer, just to keep company with someone while she waited for Glenn.

The establishment was very lenient about allowing women inside the bar, recognizing that the wives were bored and there wasn't much to do in the dead of night. So, Madeleine figured out a way to pass some time.

"Hi, Bill, how're you doing?" Madeleine asked the bartender.

"Hi, Madeleine, what can I get you? You waitin' for Glenn?"

"Yeah. I don't know what I want. A beer just doesn't sound good tonight."

"Well then you have come at a very good time. I've been mixing up a little something back here called a daiquiri. And I need a taster." He poured an icy glass full of something that smelled of pineapple, topping it with two maraschino cherries on a toothpick.

Madeleine sipped it carefully, deciding it wasn't too bad, even though the first taste made her pucker a little.

She and Bill carried on a friendly conversation, and Bill explained to her that he had tended bar in Hawaii and was afraid he was losing his knack at mixing something other than beer and Jack Daniels. "No one up here orders anything that's a challenge to make. Once in a while I just feel like mixing up something different. My problem is that I need a guinea pig to be my taster from time to time."

Agreeable to anything that helped to pass the time, this became a new routine for her. She stopped into the bar a little early every day to try some new concoction that Bill had cooked up from his old recipe book. He had to improvise a little more than usual, as bananas, fruit, and some liquors were difficult to get in Anchorage. Some of the drinks she liked; some she rejected. She learned that slow gin fizzes were lethal and she'd gotten sick on those, but it didn't take her long to find out that fruity rum drinks went down pretty easy.

It wasn't an ideal situation, but Madeleine looked forward to those afternoons, to pass the hours while she waited for Glenn.

GET ME OUT OF HERE!

1948, Anchorage, Alaska

Glenn came through the front door, throwing his pack, coat, and lunchbox on the closest chair, and headed into the kitchen where Madeleine was fixing dinner.

She remained with her back to him, taking a pot off the burner before she turned. "Well, my period started again, so I guess I'm not pregnant. I thought maybe I might be, but . . ." her voice trailed off in a sigh.

"Oh, honey, I'm sorry. I know how disappointed you are. I was hoping too. You know something though? You're gonna make a good mom one of these days. When the time is right, it'll happen." He opened the refrigerator and pulled out a beer, popping the top and heading into the front room.

"That's that, I guess." Madeleine was more than disappointed. She had mentally prepared herself to be pregnant, imaging what it would be like to have a life inside her. But it wasn't to be, at least not yet. She was beginning to wonder if something was wrong with her. Her sister-in-law, Betty, told her to stop worrying and that it would happen when it was meant to happen. That was easy for Betty to say; she already had three children.

The stress of getting through the long dark winter, faced with the muddy black snow and the unending gray days, were a little more tolerable when she thought she might be having a baby.

She'd even been thinking about baby names and how to fix up the spare room as a nursery. She thought that a baby would give her the "family" she was missing.

Madeleine turned off the stove, dropped the dishtowel on the counter, and followed Glenn into the other room. Sitting beside him and laying her head on his shoulder, she tried to pull herself out of the funk.

"Mad, how would you like to move?" Glenn asked, then paused. "I know it's been hard on you up here and I've been thinking about something. The Air Corps has been advertising for reserves to take over some permanent jobs in the States and I've talked to one of the recruiters."

"What does that mean?"

"It means we've got an opportunity to transfer out of here. They have positions open in Hawaii and in Yakima, Washington. I guess my question is, if you're up for it, where would you like to raise your kids?"

"Are you kidding me? You're not kidding me are you? We could leave Anchorage and move to Washington? That's not too far from Montana. I could get over to see Dad and Louise and Joe — and everyone. Please say you're not kidding me." And then she added, "I really hate it up here, honey."

"No, I'm not kidding." He was thoughtful for a moment, then added, "And here's another thought. If I'm going to be leaving Northwest, we might as well take advantage of a hop into Billings. If I can get the time off, maybe we can go visit your dad for a bit."

All of Madeleine's disappointment over the pregnancy gave way to the need to have her family near.

Glenn was able to take the days off and they flew into Billings the following month. Her dad and Frances picked them up at the airport and drove them to the house in Absarokee. Some things had changed, but some things stayed the same. Gramma wasn't well, so Madeleine stepped in and helped Louise with the cooking and household chores as if she'd never been gone. She didn't mind that at all; it gave her some time to talk with Louise now that she was nearly grown.

"Louise, hand me that knife and I'll help you with the potatoes."

"I'm so glad you're here. How long can you stay?" Louise handed Madeleine the knife and a pail of unpeeled potatoes, then picked up and began snapping the green beans.

"We're going to stay for about a week or so before we go back up to Anchorage. If things work out right, we might be moving to Washington."

"How far away is that? Can I come visit you? I wonder if Gramma will let me. Oh who cares; I'll just ask Dad."

Madeleine chuckled. "Yes, you can come visit, and I'll get home a little more often. So, Sis, what's been going on around here?"

"Well Catherine and Cody played up in Billings last week, and Rex has a girlfriend. She's real nice, Madeleine, you'll like her. And I guess you know all about Frances getting married. In fact, last I heard, Frances and Jane were going to have a big 'ole dinner for you and Glenn on Saturday, and I heard they were invitin' just about everybody. I think you went to school with Jane. They got a big 'ole ranch on Nye road just outside Fishtail. It's gonna be a real big party."

Yes, Madeleine had heard that Frances married a local gal she went to school with. Madeleine remembered her well. She'd been a year behind Madeleine at Absarokee High School. Jane had been one of those girls that had everything that Madeleine didn't — the looks, the popularity, the money, and the best prom dresses from Billings.

Jane's parents owned a large ranch just outside Columbus. Their cattle and horses were impressive. They owned thousands of acres of farmland along with a few hills and valleys. Their acreage ran off and on for thirty miles and was planted in hay, alfalfa, and other grass for feed. To see her at the rodeos or riding her horse — wide open — across the fields was a thing of beauty and grace. She always had the best horse. She always had the best of everything. You could almost dislike her.

As Jane grew up, though, she wasn't just a good-looking cow girl; she worked her folk's ranch as hard as any man and she had a good head for business. Frances was a bit rough around the edges for Jane, and Jane was a bit spoiled for Frances, but as unlikely a pair as they were, they fell in love.

When Frances and Jane married, Jane's father bought them a new two-story ranch house right outside Fishtail. He also gave them four-hundred acres of land that they seeded in hay and grain for their horses. Jane came with a healthy dowry. With her money and drive, and Frances' strong back, they put up several barns, a show ring, numerous outbuildings, and hundreds of fenced acres for their cattle. Their ranch was pristine. Chicken coops were clean and painted with white trim. The gardens were impressive, both with flowers and food. The pond held a few ducks that lazily swam around, adding to the ambiance. Even the pigs were well-mannered, or so it seemed. Everything looked perfect right down to the enamel-white double swinging chair on the front porch.

Jane jumped at the opportunity to show off their home and ranch and spread the word throughout the family that they were hosting a family reunion barbeque.

Madeleine was thrilled to be able to see everyone at once and catch up. She had nephews and nieces she hadn't met, and Louise was right – Madeleine liked Rex's girlfriend a lot. Madeleine introduced Glenn to her family. Glenn hadn't met any of them, except her dad during one of his hops down to Billings when he had first moved to Anchorage. For being a city boy, he held his own in the conversations, even though he knew little-to-nothing about horses, ranching, or farming.

When they had exhausted Madeleine's family, Glenn put his own family differences aside and, at Madeleine's insistence, they stopped to visit Glenn Sr. The visit was uncomfortable, with very little said between the two men. Still, she felt better for having tried.

When they left Montana, she felt renewed and able to manage another four months before Glenn could arrange his transfer. They had made up their minds to transfer to Yakima, with a tentative date at the end of August. When the transfer date arrived, they left without looking back.

When they arrived in Yakima, they found a house to rent on the outskirts of town in a quiet neighborhood. The house wasn't too much to look at, but it was furnished with most of the necessities. Glenn reported to the Air National Guard Station in September and began his new job as warehouse foreman. Madeleine set about fixing up their new home.

One night, Glenn brought home a little black cocker spaniel puppy which they named "Blackie". Madeleine immediately fell in love with the black fur ball, and after a short stint at housebreaking, she settled in just fine as the third member of their family.

SISTERS

1950, Yakima, Washington

The drive from Yakima to Billings takes about ten hours. Madeleine and Glenn had made the trip three months earlier to celebrate Christmas in Absarokee. Gramma had taken ill and was in a nursing home, so Louise and Madeleine fixed Christmas dinner. Earl and Betty brought down the turkey from their farm up in Livingston. Louise raided the cellar for potatoes and vegetables that Gramma canned last fall. Madeleine baked biscuits and a sweet potato pie for dessert. All Madeleine wanted for Christmas was for her dad to promise that as soon as the roads were clear in the spring, he would come to Yakima and visit them. Madeleine held him to the promise, and when he drove up to the house that spring evening, Madeleine was visibly relieved that he had arrived safely.

Glenn carried Mike's bag into the house and put it in the guest room. They carried on small talk while Madeleine went to get some coffee.

"Here's your coffee, Dad. I'll be right back. I have to run down to the grocery to get something for supper," Madeleine said as she set the hot mug on the porch railing.

"All right. I'll be right here on the porch with this worthless black mutt of yours." Mike's eyes always twinkled when he was teasing.

Madeleine gave him an obviously forced smile, then grabbed her purse and headed out the door.

Glenn watched as Mike tapped his pipe on the bottom of his shoe, pulled out the foil sack from his pocket, loaded, and lit the pipe, filling the air with the pungent aroma that was so much a part of him.

Glenn decided to join Mike on the back porch and lit his own cigarette. They both sat in companionable silence enjoying their ember of choice and looking at the dark sky.

After a couple of slow deep puffs on his pipe, Mike began, "You know that Madeleine's gramma died here a couple weeks ago."

"Yeah, she told me. She's kind of worried about Louise."

"Yep, that's pretty much what I thought."

"Is there anything we can do?"

"Well," he drawled, "I can't take her up on the ranch right now. She needs to finish school, and most times there won't be anybody down in Absarokee. I can't have her staying alone down there."

"Why don't you have her come here? Madeleine would like to have her here anyway."

"Well, that's what I been thinking, but I know you and Madeleine are just starting off and all. Madeleine's spent most of her life taking care of kids."

"Yeah, but Mike, we already talked about having her live with us the minute we heard Maria had passed away. She was gonna go and get her a week ago, but we knew you were coming out and we wanted to talk to you first."

Mike took his time considering that, then looked Glenn directly in the eye as if he was sizing up the kind of man he was. After taking another long drag from his pipe, he simply said with the most economical of words, "Okay then."

When Madeleine got home Glenn told her that Louise was going to come to Yakima and move in with them. In typical Madeleine fashion, she took it all in stride, as if it really wasn't important. She simply said, "Good." But inside there was never a doubt in her mind that Louise was coming to Yakima with or without anyone's agreement or approval.

Louise still had one month left before finishing the school year in Absarokee. She was going to stay on for the first part of the summer to help her dad and brothers up on the ranch. By August, she'd be on her way to Yakima, reacquainting herself with her big sister.

Mike thought that with Maria gone, there were a few items of Elsie's that rightfully should go to Madeleine and Louise. One of those items was the old treadle sewing machine. Elsie had sewed everything on it before she died; it was the same sewing machine that Gramma had used to sew a yellowed wedding dress into a prom gown. There were happy and bitter memories tied to that machine.

Joe and Frances painstakingly built a box that would hold the machine so they could ship it by train. They packed the box with some of Louise's clothes, handmade quilts, dresser scarves, doilies and other handmade items, pictures, linens, and Elsie's old postcard album, adding protection for the machine and giving the treasured belongings a new home with Madeleine. Louise and the box arrived in Yakima safely, the first week in August.

Glenn and Madeleine had both worked hard at getting things ready around the house so Louise would feel comfortable. They had painted the spare guest room, cleaned and fixed some furniture, and bought more. They wanted to make the accommodations as nice as they could for her. They shouldn't have worried, since Louise was just as happy to be with her sister as Madeleine was to have her there.

Ignoring the additional expense, they enrolled Louise in the Holy Rosary Private Catholic School for girls. The Holy Rosary School dated back to the 1890s. The school, the Church, and the parish hall were the center of the Catholic community in Yakima. It was Madeleine's thought at the time that Louise would be safe with the Catholic nuns, and she felt comfortable that Louise would get a good education. She never regretted her decision.

Louise was outfitted for the required school uniforms, making the issue of clothes easier. They bought study supplies, toured the school, met some of the nuns, and tried to make the transition as easy as they could. Louise adapted quickly to the new surroundings, even though she'd never been outside the fifty-mile circle around Absarokee. She liked her new school; she loved living with her sister and Glenn; but like Madeleine, she missed her dad and Joe.

Shortly after Louise moved in, they celebrated her 15th birthday. Glenn took both his girls out on the town for dinner.

By the time Louise was in her junior year at Holy Rosary, she'd grown into quite the young lady. She was a head shorter than everyone else, with a petite build, an easy-going sense of humor, and a great smile. Madeleine loved her like a daughter.

Even though Louise attended a girl's Catholic school, she didn't miss out on male attention. One day she sat on the front porch with two neighborhood boys who went to the public school. Harold, who they all called Harry, and Jimmy were entertaining Louise by betting each other they couldn't swallow a live goldfish.

Madeleine heard Louise scream. By the time she got to the porch, sure enough, Jimmy had accidentally dropped the live goldfish right down his throat and swallowed it. Louise was making gagging sounds and Harry was doubled over laughing.

Madeleine just shook her head and went back inside to start dinner. The last years hadn't been the easiest, but having Louise around had been a blessing. Madeleine missed her brothers, and it had been over a year since she'd seen her dad. She was hoping that he and Joe could come to Yakima for Thanksgiving.

She heard Glenn's car pull into the drive and was hoping he was in a good mood. He'd had difficulties at work lately, having been passed over for a promotion he'd counted on. She was getting tired of him coming home every night with another complaint about his job. Madeleine did her best to hide her frustration over the complaints, but it wore on her.

She hated the nights he woke up with nightmares. He'd always seemed to have trouble sleeping, but lately he would wake up with cold sweats, get up, and not come back to bed. She hated that he would sit up until all hours of the morning drinking beer. And she really hated the nights that the anger got directed towards her. She did her best to hide all of this from Louise.

But that night, she had some news to tell him, and she hoped he would be as happy about it as she was.

"Hey, honey, that kid out there ate one of your goldfish." Glenn chuckled as he came in the door.

"Yeah, that's what I hear."

"What's for dinner?" he asked as he automatically made his way to the refrigerator, grabbed a beer and sat down at the table.

"I was thinking about macaroni and cheese and some of those green beans we picked." Madeleine took a beer glass out of the cupboard and set it on the table for Glenn. "Doctor says I'm pregnant." She looked at him for a reaction.

"What? Are you kidding me?"

"No. He says that's why I haven't been feeling good in the mornings."

"How are you feeling now? Sit down. Are you sure, this isn't just another drill or something?"

"No, I don't think it's a drill. I think this is the real thing this time."

Glenn didn't know quite what to do. After years of talking about it and trying to get pregnant, maybe it was finally going to happen. He just sat there rubbing her arm and staring at her, looking for some change to occur. "Have you told Louise yet?"

"No, not yet. I will." She stood up and began setting the table for dinner.

THERE'S YOUR DAMN SODA CRACKERS!

January, 1952, Yakima, Washington

Those were the worst two months. Every morning began with acute morning sickness, culminating with hours on end spent either in bed or on the sofa with sheer fatigue. In the evenings she felt better. Louise was always helpful, but school and activities came first.

Madeleine would have liked Glenn to be more supportive and understanding, to baby her, to give her some needed help around the house. Instead, he had taken to stopping more and more often at the local bar after work.

Part of her didn't blame him. She'd been hormonally crazy lately. But there was a part deep inside her that wanted him to be with her. Madeleine didn't understand everything that was happening to her body, or what to expect, and she wasn't comfortable talking to anyone about it, including her doctor. And there was always the nagging fear that something would happen to her as it did when her mother died giving birth to Louise.

When all of Madeleine's issues were added to Glenn's dissatisfaction with his job, they had reached a new low.

"Are you sick again?" Glenn asked almost accusingly.

"Yes, I'm sick again."

"Geez, Mad, I wish there was something I could do."

"There is something you can do. You can ask me if I need anything once in a while."

"Do you need anything now?"

"I need some soda crackers, but we don't have any. It's about the only thing I can keep down."

"Fine," Glenn mumbled as he walked out the door, letting it slam behind him.

Madeleine very seldom cried; she just got mad. She was still mad when she heard him return thirty minutes later carrying a commissary-size case of saltine soda crackers, plunking them down beside the sofa.

"There's your damn soda crackers." And he left.

Now Madeleine was mad – and sick.

***

It was April before Madeleine started feeling better. By then she felt as big as a house. Louise was just finishing up school, with plans to spend the summer on the ranch with her dad and brothers.

Since Madeleine finally got over her morning sickness and started to feel better, she wasn't mad at Glenn all the time. She was still pissed off about the soda cracker incident, but he had become a lot more attentive to her, helping with dinners and helping her fix up a space for the baby crib. He acted genuinely happy, and looked forward to being a father.

In May, they put Louise on a train for Montana and had settled down to wait out the last three weeks.

The first sharp pain came at one in the afternoon on Saturday, June 14. After feeling pretty well that morning, she began cramping a little after noon. Glenn drove her to the hospital. After seventeen hours of labor, at six on Sunday evening, Madeleine gave birth to a daughter. Glenn wasn't there when his daughter was born.

A month before, Madeleine had pressed Glenn for help in considering baby names. The only thing he was adamant about was that they absolutely would not name a son, Glenn Lee the third. He had hated his name from the time he was a kid and refused to pass that name on to any child. As a matter of fact, he didn't want any names from the Barker side of the family passed onto any of his children. Other than that, he had no other opinion on names, and just told Madeleine to "pick one."

She'd settled on Terrance Michael, if the baby was a boy, and she'd been thinking of Catherine for a girl's name, but had not settled on a middle name. She still was undecided when she went into labor. Since Glenn wasn't there when she was born, and Madeleine was pressed to give a name for the birth certificate, she made up her mind immediately, giving her daughter four names. "We're naming her Catherine Lee Conner Barker." Madeleine took the name "Conner" from Glenn's grandmother, Evangeline, and then she added "Lee" just to spite Glenn. Glenn was furious.

FRIENDS – UPSTAIRS, DOWNSTAIRS

August, 1952, Yakima Washington

Two months later, Madeleine was home with the baby when Louise called. "Hi Sis, I'm at the train station. Was Glenn gonna pick me up? I just got in a little while ago and I've been looking for him, but I can't find him."

"Oh shit. Yes he was supposed to. Was your trip okay? Let me call him. He'll be right there; just stay put."

Madeleine hung up and dialed a number.

"Sergeant Anderson."

"Yes, is Glenn Barker there?"

"No ma'am, I'm not sure where he is."

"Well damn it. Is this Andy? He was supposed to pick up my sister at the train station and she's there and I can't find him. I don't have the car and I've got the baby here."

"Well, I can pick her up."

"You can? Oh, I'd appreciate that so much. She's just come in from Billings and I told her to stay put."

"No problem. I'll get her home in a little bit."

When Andy arrived at the station he thought Louise was just about the prettiest thing that he had ever seen. He slid her suitcase into the trunk of his car and then, remembering his manners, held the car door open for her, latching it securely after she settled into the front seat. He drove her to Glenn and Madeleine's and then lurked around for quite a while before heading back to work. If he got up the nerve, he was going to call her to go to the movies on Saturday, and he sure hoped she would.

Andy and Louise dated during her senior year and they became quite the item. Andy was a permanent fixture at the house. In the spring of 1953, they were preparing for Louise's prom and graduation. She was leaving right after graduation to spend the summer back in Montana and hadn't quite decided what she was going to do after that, or how Andy was going to fit into her life.

Andy was worried about Louise going to Montana and hoped she'd move back to Yakima after the summer. He was going to miss her. Madeleine and Louise were sitting at the kitchen table talking about that, when Glenn walked through the door and abruptly told her, "I quit my goddam job and I'm going out for a beer!"

Once Glenn made up his mind to quit, he just as quickly decided they were moving to Seattle. He had heard from his childhood friend, Johnny, that they were hiring supervisors at the Todd Pacific Shipyards. Johnny had relocated from Billings to Seattle about a year earlier and was doing well at the shipyards. Even if he didn't get on there, Glenn thought the odds were better of getting a job in Seattle than in Yakima.

Glenn had been having a difficult time getting along with his foreman for six months. The last time he was passed up for a pay raise, he'd had words with him and things had gone downhill rapidly from there.

Madeleine was angry at Glenn for making all these decisions that would uproot her life when they had a new baby, but she didn't have a choice.

Within a month, they packed, moved, and found an apartment in an area just south of Seattle, called Georgetown. The building was an old brick three-story, on the corner of Ellis and Warsaw Street, just off the Boeing Airfield property. Their apartment was small and dark. They were lucky to have rented on the ground floor, avoiding the use of the narrow and steep stairs that ran between floors.

The apartment made Madeleine feel a bit claustrophobic and, to make matters worse, it poured rain for two weeks. The baby was coming down with something and had been fussy for days. When all that was added to the loud planes that went directly over their apartment every hour on the hour, Madeleine was none too happy.

If there was a bright spot in all this, it was that Glenn was hired at the shipyards almost immediately. Madeleine met Lavern and her daughter who lived in the apartment above them. They had a nice conversation standing on the front stoop as their daughters played on the stairs. Madeleine missed having someone to talk with since Louise had gone, so it was pleasant to have some female conversation. She and Lavern began a routine of having coffee together after Glenn left for work.

"I'm glad you guys moved in downstairs and that the girls get along so well," Lavern said as she refilled Madeleine's coffee cup.

The two were sitting at Lavern's kitchen table, watching as her three-year-old daughter Maria held onto little Catherine's hands, trying to get her to walk with her.

"I'm not quite all the way settled yet. I'd like to get some material and make some lighter curtains for the kitchen. It's so dark and dreary. I like the yellow in here. It sure brightens it up." Madeleine admired the kitchen area.

"Morrie left me the car today, so if you want to take a run to the fabric store, we could take the girls and get out of here for a while."

"Oh, I don't know how to tell you how much I'd like to do that. I need to get some material to make Catherine some more dresses; she's growing out of things faster than I can keep up."

Lavern didn't say anything; she just left the room and came back a few minutes later, placing three sacks full of clothes in front of Madeleine. "Here, see if Catherine can use any of these. Maria has already grown out of them and I was just going to give them away."

Madeleine was speechless. She pulled a little coat out of the sack, and a wool skirt, and little tops made from quality material that was like new. "Oh my God, look at these. Lavern, I can't accept these clothes. They're so expensive."

"Like I said, if you can use them, great. I was going to give them away anyway."

So, as little Maria grew out of her clothes, Lavern gave them to Madeleine, and a friendship was cemented.

For the next year or so things settled down for Madeleine and Glenn. Glenn seemed to be doing well at his job. They were back into a comfortable routine for the most part. The baby was healthy and growing. Louise married Andy in 1954 and he had transferred to Seattle with the Army Air Corps Reserves, so that Louise could be near her sister. They rented a house not too far from Georgetown.

Madeleine and Lavern became best friends. Their two girls spent every waking hour together. Lavern had another baby, a boy this time. While she was pregnant, she had helped Madeleine sew curtains for her apartment and watched the kids while Madeleine painted her kitchen a light yellow.

With the additional baby, Lavern and Morrie decided to put a down payment on a house in Burien. Even though she talked to Lavern by phone every day, Madeleine got a little restless. She missed having Lavern upstairs. She missed a yard and wanted a garden. She would have liked some place where Catherine could play outside.

Eventually she convinced Glenn that they needed to move. Since he had a little money saved up, they started looking to rent a house. They didn't want to move too far away from Boeing field and the Todd warehouse, but they did want to move far enough to get away from the hourly noise of the airplanes.

After several weeks, they found a house in their price range, located in a neighborhood north of Beacon Hill, on Renton Avenue just off Lucille Street. It was very small, with only one bedroom and a storage room that could be converted to hold a child's bed and maybe a small dresser. The back yard contained a wall of nine-foot-high blackberry bushes; the front yard was a postage-stamp-sized mud puddle.

Glenn was tired of looking for houses, so he told Madeleine, "We're either taking this one or we aren't moving anywhere." Madeleine took it.

YOU ARE SUCH A LITTLE DEVIL . . .

1953, Georgetown, Washington

When Ev got out of the Army, he returned to Georgetown and stayed with his Aunt Jen for a couple of months. He was working at both Howard's furniture store and the Todd Shipyards, weighing his options at the time. He finally rented a small apartment and applied for a new job up near Concrete. He also reconnected with an old fast-and-loose buddy named Jimmy whose wild lifestyle and gumption soon had Ev in partnership with him, renting a cabin in the country. Jimmy was one of Ev's best friends, but they were as different as night and day. Jimmy wanted the cabin for parties and beer, while Ev saw the country as an escape, for solace and relaxation. They compromised with Ev staying there during the week and commuting to work and Jimmy filling the weekends with entertainment.

On one of those weekends, Jimmy was just leaving Normandy Park where he had picked up Hazel and her friend Gloria. They were going out to the cabin to party in the woods by the river. Hazel was always up for anything. If there was a party or an adventure in the making, Hazel never hesitated, convention be damned.

Jimmy and Ev had known Hazel for years. They had both dated her, but in the end she made a better friend than a girlfriend. She could be a little fickle, a little spoiled, and a lot wild. Coming from a well-to-do family that lived in the upper end of Normandy Park, she always had discretionary income, which was why Jimmy had left the shopping for supplies up to her.

He was not disappointed. The trunk of his old car was packed with beer, wine, food, ice, and a bottle of "Jack". Her friend Gloria was the brunette to Hazel's blonde. Hazel invited her along because "us gals got to stick together."

It was a bit of a drive to the river. As Jimmy drove, the trees seemed to intensify and the more it felt like driving deep into another world. Hazel was fascinated with the cotton that was falling like snow from the trees. She hadn't been to the *campsite*, as Jimmy called it, so she didn't know what she was getting herself into. But she had heard plenty about the parties on the river from both Jimmy and Ev.

As they were driving, she let her mind wander, thinking that theirs was an unusual friendship. She thought of Ev as the nice one. Jimmy could be a little unpredictable and crude at times, but Ev was always the perfect gentleman. He seemed a lot more stable. Hazel could appreciate that in a guy. But she also liked Jimmy's spontaneity. She loved them both, but boy, Hazel thought to herself, if you were ever in a "pickle", you would call Ev, cause Jimmy would be nowhere in sight.

They turned off onto a dirt road, drove over a little bridge, and immediately hit huge mud holes, bouncing the girls around. The road kept getting narrower until they finally stopped at a clearing where the trees seemed to touch the sky.

Hazel heard the roar of the river before she saw it. "Oh, Look at that! Have you ever seen anything so beautiful?" Her strappy high-heeled sandals gave way to bare feet before the car door was shut. Within ten seconds, Hazel was knee deep in the river with the water rushing around her legs. Gloria was not far behind. As the two girls squealed and laughed, Ev watched them, with a grin on his face. There was nothing he liked to see more than a couple good looking girls splashing each other in the river.

The guys had just settled in with a beer when they heard two more cars drive in. The two cars were filled with guys and gals sitting on their laps. Loud laughter was coming from the open car windows. Both cars were honking horns at each other. Ev thought, "it's going to be a long day, and a longer night."

Hours later the sky was turning a deep red, and sparks from their bonfire played against that canvas. Most of the food had been eaten, but the beer was still flowing; several conversations were going on at once.

Throughout the afternoon, people had dropped by with fishing poles, swimsuits, and more beer; a full blown party had been in progress for the better part of the day.

The girls had long since given up on shoes, had tied their shirt-tails up, and put their hair in pony tails. Jimmy brought his ukulele and was playing a humorous number as Hazel was trying to juggle her Jack Daniels and dance around him at the same time. It led to some boisterous moments of laughter among the group.

For a moment, Ev mentally stepped outside of himself, as if watching the shenanigans from afar. So many things had not gone as he had hoped they would. He had hoped that time would give him the ability to see his daughter, but Barbara refused to respond.

Even though he finally got the job at the shipyards, he still wasn't sure how long that would last. Renting this property with Jimmy was probably a luxury he could not afford, but whenever he escaped the city and drove out here, the sound of the river washed over him and he felt like he could breathe.

He had been thinking lately that, with a little work, he could live out here in the valley permanently. He'd save money on the rent of his apartment in town. If he worked on it in his spare time, he could probably get the cabin sealed up enough to hold the heat for winter. He was good with wood, but it needed a lot of work.

The rough cabin certainly wasn't much; most of it was still two-by-four studs, intended only as a fishing shelter. He and Jimmy had used cardboard boxes from the furniture store to nail over the studs to keep out the wind. On those nights when it got too late to go back to town, they roughed it.

There was a hotplate in the cooking area and an old table with two chairs. They pulled in electricity and had a wood stove for heat. The plumbing and septic had been jerry-rigged to afford a toilet, but there were possibilities.

"Ev, honey, do you want another beer? I gotta pee first, but I'll bring you back one," Hazel hollered at Ev, rousing him out of his musings.

"Maybe I better come with you. Make sure you don't get lost." Ev grinned and tugged on the tie of Hazel's shirt.

"You are such a little devil," she teased, as she sashayed away.

WHEN YOU COMIN' HOME?

1956, Georgetown, Washington
Joe's Bar

Joe's Bar was a friendly neighborhood bar that sat squarely in the heart of Georgetown, just off the main exit to Boeing Field. On the border of the military supply field, it faced tree-lined streets of converted brick military housing.

The bar catered to regulars, who filled the room with cigarette smoke and laughter. Joe the Bartender and his niece, Nancy, ran the place, with Nancy in the kitchen, throwing out daily specials and bar grub. Unescorted women were not allowed to loiter, promoting a family atmosphere. It was a place where men could wind down with friends after work or the lonely could find friendly conversation, a schooner of beer, and a good meal.

The wooden bar had seen better days. Remnants of an old spittoon trough ran under the feet of the customers that crowded the bar. Nothing was free, but Joe was known to float a schooner or two for the regulars or a down-trodden soul.

In the back, a few worn-out chairs and linoleum top tables sat near a juke box that was never played. The wooden floor was a little unsteady in places, causing more than one joke when someone stumbled on their way to the door.

Joe's was more than a bar. It was a place where lives played out. On this particular day, the bar was full of regulars, Ev among them, having a beer with Bill, an old friend at one of the back tables.

"It's called Dorre Don Campsites," Ev was saying." I own the property with my friend, Jimmy. We've got a cabin out there. I have to tell you, you can't even see the sky for all the trees, and it's right on the river. Come on out with me this weekend and take a look. I have a few friends that are dropping by, but you're more than welcome to stay there until you get your feet back on the ground."

"Thanks Ev, I think I might. Want another beer?" asked Bill.

"Sure, but put it on my tab."

* * *

After renting the river property for two years, Ev and Jimmy had gone in together and purchased the property on contract from ole man Stanford. Jimmy was such a wander-about though; he was seldom around. He had just returned from Hawaii and called Ev to put him on notice that he was back in town. Wherever Jimmy went, a party was sure to follow.

As far as Everett knew, Jimmy didn't even have a permanent home. He just bounced from place to place and enjoyed life to its fullest. With a quick sense of humor and flashing blue eyes, he was never without female companions. He was a good friend with a good heart, and Everett trusted him.

When Jimmy originally found the cabin on the river property with its thick stand of forest and the rush of water from the Cedar River, his eyes saw stars. They had begged and borrowed money so they could rent the property and cabin. Mainly it was used as a party destination when Jimmy was in town and as a fishing cabin when Ev stayed out there alone. Then, the owner decided to sell it.

"Come on, we can do it," Jimmy urged Ev.

"Jimmy, you always have wild ideas, but I have to say there is something about this place. I could picture fixing this up and living here for the rest of my life."

"I can picture doing a lot of other things here. Just think, Ev. We could own this place. By the way, did you see what's growing down there on the bank? That's crazy tobacco. We were smokin' some of that on the islands. It's good stuff."

Ev tried to return Jimmy to the conversation at hand. "If we do this, we need to do it legal. We need to have an attorney and record it. I need to have it buttoned up, 'cause I never know where you're going to be from one time to the next. We might need to do some sort of partnership or something. But, if I decide to build onto the cabin, I need to know that you're okay with that."

And so the conversation went until Jimmy and Everett signed the deed for partial lots 30, 31 and 32 of the Dorre Don Campsites in Maple Valley. Because the property sat right on the Cedar River which ate away land, only partial lots were left. And though the cabin was still basically a fishing cabin with a roof, Everett had plans to close it in, which he did with scrap wood and used sheet rock. He added an oil stove, some used carpet, and finally boarded up the hallway so that there was a solid roof on the way to the bathroom.

* * *

This particular weekend, Jimmy was bringing a new girlfriend out for some fun, along with a barbershop buddy of theirs named Jack Johnson, and his girl. They were going to be out sometime on the weekend. But right now, Ev was just relaxing at Joe's with a beer, trying to help his friend Bill by offering him a roof over his head until he got on his feet again.

Joe's Bar was the half-way point between the city of Concrete, where Ev now worked and the Valley. He liked to make the convenient stop to break up the long drive home. Joe's was also located near Howard's house and a mere four blocks from his favorite Aunt Jen, who always let him stay with her, in the event he didn't feel up to driving home after a few too many beers.

Everett had been listening for an hour, to Bill complain about losing his job and all his girlfriend problems. Always willing to help an injured bird, Everett offered him sanctuary in the Valley. With Everett, there were never any strings on his generosity. If he had it, he would freely share it.

Bill was grateful for the offer and gladly accepted. They decided that they'd meet the next night right after work back at Joe's, so they could drive to the cabin together.

With only a couple of swallows of beer left, Bill and Everett were momentarily distracted by the laughter coming from three men sitting at the bar. Aided by several hours of drinking, their voices competed with the radio as well as other conversations surrounding them.

The group at the bar seemed harmless enough. Regardless, Everett made the quick decision that it was time to leave Joe's and maybe drop in on his Aunt Jen to see what she might have cooking for dinner.

As they were settling up with the bartender, bright sunlight lit up the dingy bar as the door opened and a woman walked in. She headed straight for the bar where the three men sat. Angling herself between the barstools, she tapped on the shoulder of one of them.

"Glenn, when do you think you might be home? You know, you said you were coming straight home tonight. I couldn't wait dinner any longer; I had to feed Catherine. It would sure be nice if you got home in time to see her before she went to bed one of these nights."

Her voice faded off into the background as Everett and Bill headed for the door.

"Look, meet me here tomorrow at four," Ev said. "Bring some beer and some sleeping bags or ponchos if you have 'em. We'll build a bonfire and just unwind a little before Jimmy gets out on Saturday."

"It's a deal. See ya then, Ev, and thanks."

As Everett drove out of the lot he didn't notice the little girl playing in the back seat of a parked car. He did notice however, the woman coming out of the bar and heading to the car. A part of his mind registered that she wasn't too hard to look at, but based on the look on her face, she was not a happy woman.

Not giving it much more thought, he sped up his car, hoping Aunt Jen was home. She always wanted to feed him, which was something he could use right about now.

I HATE RICE!

1956, Georgetown, Washington

Glenn and Madeleine had rented the house on Renton Avenue. It was a very small house, but at least it was better than the apartment building in Georgetown.

A dirt and gravel road gave way to a ten-by-twelve patch of weeds surrounded by an old wooden fence that housed a child's swing set, without much room for anything else. A small wooden porch with a front door to the left, led directly into a kitchen with a wooden table, and then into a living room with sparse furniture – a couple of comfortable chairs, an end table and a short book-shelf that doubled as a TV stand for the small used set. Just off the living area, were the bedroom and bath. A second room, barely bigger than a large closet, had been converted into a bedroom for their daughter. It held one small bed, a dresser, and a make-shift toy box.

Madeleine was not sure what to do. She'd fixed dinner, trying something new with rice and Cambell's mushroom soup that she'd seen on TV. She had expected Glenn home hours earlier. The rice had turned into a big mushy lump.

"Catherine, come on up here and eat your dinner. Daddy will eat when he gets home."

Four-year-old Catherine squirmed as Madeleine set her up on the chair, filling a plastic glass with milk and cooling off the rice dish on the small plate.

Madeleine was too upset to eat, upset and mad at Glenn. This was not the first time they waited dinner. More times than not, when he got home, he'd be just as happy eating a can of sardines and soda crackers, washing it down with a quart of beer.

The longer she waited, the madder she got. "I don't know why I even bother fixing dinner," she mumbled to no one in particular.

"Catherine, come with Mommy. We're gonna go see Daddy, okay?"

She should be putting Catherine down for bed, but instead, they got into the car and drove down the hill into Georgetown to Joe's bar. It wasn't the first time that she'd had to drive down here, but just that afternoon he had promised that he'd be home on time.

Pulling into the parking lot, she handed Catherine a picture book and a piece of candy and said, "I'll be right back, honey; you stay put."

Madeleine walked into the dark bar, quickly scanned the tables and then heard before she saw Glenn with two guys at the bar. She inched between the bar stools and tapped on Glenn's shoulder.

"You said you were coming straight home, tonight."

"Oh! Hi, Mad. Whatcha doing here?"

"Don't hi Mad me. I couldn't wait any longer for you. I had to feed Catherine and I got tired of holding dinner for you. I have her out in the car and it would be nice if you came home to see her for a few minutes before she goes to bed."

Without much more to say, she left the bar, letting the screen door slam behind her.

Knowing that Madeleine was angry put Glenn on the defensive. He could stop and have a beer if he damn well wanted to. He didn't need her coming down to the bar and bitching at him in front of his friends. She had no idea what kind of stress he was under. He'd had just enough to drink to make the situation volatile. He headed home.

As he came through the door, he was met with cold silence. Catherine had been put to bed. On hearing a car pull up, Madeleine took his dinner plate out of the oven where she'd been trying to keep it warm.

Glenn walked through the door, took one look at the rice dish she'd set on the table, and just stared at it. After eating rice for nearly a year in Korea and hating every minute of it, he was hoping never to have to look at rice again. He picked up the plate and threw it against the wall. "Don't you ever serve me rice again! I hate rice!"

Madeleine stared at him in disbelief, walked to the bedroom, and slammed the door, leaving him to fend for himself. She heard the refrigerator open and then shut; then she heard the top of a beer bottle coming off.

SHE'S MY DAUGHTER'S AGE

1957, Georgetown, Washington
Outside Joe's Bar

S he's just about the age that my daughter was, the last time I saw her," Ev said, as they stood outside the bar, looking at the little girl playing in the back seat.

"All this time, you and Nancy in there have been coming out here giving my daughter free peanuts and candy and spoiling her rotten, and you've never once mentioned that you had a daughter. Are you going to tell me you're married too?" Madeleine asked.

"Her mother and I divorced and I haven't seen my daughter since."

"Oh, I'm sorry, that must be hard."

"Madeleine, let me ask you something. Are you okay? I mean, I see how Glenn is sometimes when he leaves this place. When he gets home — are you okay?"

"I'm fine." She couldn't keep the ice out of her voice.

"Well, if you ever aren't fine and you need someone, you call down here and ask for Nancy. She's knows how to get hold of me most of the time."

"I appreciate that, but we're fine." Even though she said it she knew that she was anything but fine. Glenn had quit his job again and was now spending almost every afternoon and evening at the bar.

She'd taken to driving him there, to give her access to a car and to keep him from killing himself driving home drunk. With no other choice, Catherine had to wait in the car as her mom went into the bar to check on her father.

Nancy, Joe, Everett, and several other long-standing customers often went out to the parking lot to occupy Catherine while Madeleine tried to get Glenn out of the bar.

Many times Madeleine would be at home worrying about Glenn, or getting that uneasy feeling, prompting her to call the bar to check on him. At least she would know where he was and that he was safe. If he was catching a ride home and was on his way, she would know to get dinner on the table and hope that he was mellow enough not to start a fight. This seemed to be their new routine.

Whenever Ev stopped in at Joe's, he took to sitting at the nearest table to the phone, knowing that Madeleine sometimes called there. If it rang, he'd answer, hoping it was her. He liked talking to her. He liked to make her laugh. He'd keep her on the phone until he could say, "Madeleine, Glenn just left the bar with his ride. He should be home shortly. You take care of yourself. And if there is anything I can do for you, or anything that you or Catherine need, just let me know."

Madeleine always thanked him for his concern and assured him that everything was fine. But the moment she hung up the phone, fear set in. She missed having the connection with Ev. He made her feel safe — plus it was actually kind of exciting and forbidden, talking to Ev when Glenn wasn't but twenty feet away at the bar.

Ev didn't feel sorry for her, but he sure felt she deserved more than she had. He liked her. She was in a bad situation, but he liked her. He found himself thinking about her more often, and she thought about him, far more than she should.

* * *

272

March, 1958
Four months later

"Dr. Talbot, it's not exactly the most convenient time," Madeleine said, fighting to hold back the tears.

"These things never are."

"I was so sick when I was pregnant before."

"Well, Madeleine, I've got an idea about how we might handle that, knowing your history. I'm going to give you some information about something I've been experimenting with. I've had some really good results with hypnotism. Read this," he said, handing her some papers. "Discuss it with your husband and then we'll schedule another appointment soon."

Madeleine went out and sat in the car. Leaning her forehead against the steering wheel, she sat, too overwhelmed to cry, too upset to drive. She thought about what had happened during the past three months.

Things had blown up with her and Glenn. Right before Christmas he had stormed out one night, kicking a hole in the door as he left. He didn't come home for a week.

She wanted a divorce. She confided in Ev and, with his help, she secured an attorney and filed the papers.

When Glenn found out that Ev had somehow helped her, he washed his hands of the whole situation. Within three days, he had packed his things and left.

Without a job, and no money, and with no place to live, Madeleine took Ev up on his offer to stay in the Valley. She was just another bird with a broken wing. She pulled Catherine out of kindergarten and packed what little she and her daughter had into a couple boxes. Ev, with the help of his brother Howard, moved her and Catherine to the cabin.

They cleared out enough room against an inside wall of the front room to put in a bed and dresser. That's where her daughter's bedroom would be.

Ev worked hard trying to clean up and patch the cabin the best he could to accommodate Madeleine and her daughter. Never afraid of work, Madeleine tried to make it as comfortable as she could. They worked side by side, day after day, in the middle of winter.

Now, here she was, pregnant, two months later, with Ev's baby. Her divorce wouldn't be final until April, which was still a good month away. She was afraid of confronting him with this news and mentally prepared herself for rejection. She was frightened for her and her daughter, and now this unborn baby. Thoughts of going home to her dad in Montana overwhelmed her with depression.

Madeleine shouldn't have worried. Ev was happy about the baby, not necessarily about the timing. But everything was working out, and he was falling more in love with her each day. He immediately asked her to marry him, to which her response was, "Well, I guess so."

It wasn't exactly how it was supposed to work out. Ev was a really nice guy who took very good care of her and her daughter, but she never thought it was going to be long term. Lordy, she could do a lot worse. He was affectionate, always hugging, patting and touching, all endearments she was not used to. She'd grown to like it. They had fixed up the house and she had plans of putting in a garden. She liked it here in the country with him. They had fallen into a familiar and comfortable pattern. She felt secure.

Yes, she'd marry him, as soon as her divorce was final.

"Howard, how would you like to be my best man again?"

"You bet. When you gonna do it?"

"Soon as possible."

"Well just let me know; Doris and I will be there."

Madeleine had asked her friend, Lavern, if she would stand up with her, as her matron of honor and witness to the marriage. Of course, Lavern eagerly agreed.

Madeleine's divorce would be final on April 11, and she and Ev decided to get married on April 12. They made the plans, notified the people who needed to know,and waited for the divorce to come through. But then there was the issue of the wedding ring.

"Honey, I have a little money saved that I was going to use to reset the wood stove in the kitchen, but I need to get you a wedding ring, so I'm afraid the stove is going to have wait."

"That's stupid; don't you think it is a little more important that we have a stove that works than a ring that I could care less about? Besides, I already have a wedding ring and what good did that do me?"

"I need to have something to put on your finger during the ceremony, unless you want to live with a cigar band," he teased, trying to lighten the situation.

"Let's just use the gold band I have. It doesn't make any difference whether I have a new ring or not."

And so Ev agreed to place the used gold band on Madeleine's hand during the ceremony with a promise that the first time they had some extra money, he would replace it. They never had any extra money, and the ring remained a permanent fixture on Madeleine's hand.

Howard and Lavern stood up with them before the Justice of the Peace in Renton and, just as planned, they were married on April 12. They all went to dinner after the ceremony, celebrating their marriage and secretly celebrating the pregnancy. Ev and Madeleine made a pact that day that they would forever celebrate their anniversary on March 12, to avoid any embarrassing speculation by the children.

With her pregnancy, she had enlisted Dr. Talbot's help. Through use of his hypnotic suggestion, she was having a fairly pleasant pregnancy with little morning sickness. She was happy and healthy and her daughter was adjusting well.

Catherine started first grade in September and was introduced to what would become twelve years of riding yellow country school buses. She made friends with the neighbor kids and seemed to be doing just fine in school. The child had taken to country life as if it was the only life she knew. Everything that had happened before in her young life was just a fleeting image.

They hadn't heard from Glenn since he left Seattle, in January.

Madeleine was two weeks away from her due date when Catherine came down with chicken pox, along with Lavern's two children. For the safety of Madeleine and the unborn baby, they decided that Catherine would stay at Lavern's house in Seattle, at least until she was no longer contagious.

Lavern, always a true friend to Madeleine, gladly opened her arms to help in any way she could. Lavern's daughter had just recovered from chicken pox and her son Corky had just come down with it. Having another sick kid at her house was not an inconvenience and she was glad to help.

Within a day of taking her calamine soaked daughter to Lavern's, Madeleine went into labor.

Unlike her labor with Catherine, Madeleine was relaxed and in very little pain. The baby was delivered easily, largely through the hypnotic suggestion to simply relax and let nature take its course.

Ev was at the hospital when his son was born. They named him James Michael – his first name after Everett James and his middle name after Madeleine's dad. Within two days, Ev brought Madeleine and his son home. A week later, no longer contagious, they brought Catherine home.

"Catherine, I want you to meet your brother. His name is James." Madeleine removed the blanket from the baby's head and face, so she could see the baby. Catherine's eyes grew big as she looked at the red, wrinkled, squirming baby that had all of her mom's attention.

Ev walked over and picked up Catherine and put her on his lap. "Cat, I want you to know something. Your mom and I love you more than anything in the world and no one is going to take that away. Your baby brother needs you and loves you too; he is just too little to tell you that yet." Catherine's eyes warily watched the baby as her stepdad continued to talk to her. "How would you like to hold your little brother?" Catherine smiled as her mom sat the little bundle on her lap.

"Cat, this is your little brother," Ev quietly said to her. "James Michael, this is your big sister Cat." The blue bundle on Cat's lap gave her a toothless, squirmy grin, followed by two kicking feet and a little squawk.

Cat smiled at the baby and touched his little clenched fist. She was immediately enchanted with her new little brother. They nicknamed him "Jamie".

JUST KEEP 'EM COMIN'!

1957, Georgetown, Washington

When Glenn had left the Seattle area, he had a good idea where he was headed. He had always wanted to go back to California. He liked it when he was stationed there in the Army.

Driving down, he had a lot of time to think about what had happened in the last seventy-two hours. He couldn't remember what started the fight. He remembered coming home and just wanting some peace and quiet. He had been tired. Sleep had eluded him for weeks with black and white images of blown-up bodies and gunfire invading his mind. Every airplane that went overhead made him jump. He'd gone to Joe's and ordered a drink. "Just keep 'em comin'," he had said. He took a seat at the end of the bar by himself and hoped he would remain that way. He wasn't in the mood for conversation. Maybe the beer would relax him and get rid of the constant headache. If he could only put the nightmares aside for at least one night, maybe he would pass out into blissful sleep.

He didn't know he was going to be angrily confronted by Madeleine the minute he came through the door, and he didn't expect it.

No, he didn't realize it was two in the morning.

No, he hadn't eaten dinner.

No, he didn't know the grocery check had bounced.

"Well what did you think was going to happen? You quit your job and we have no money in the bank. I can't even afford groceries. How do you think we are going to pay the rent?"

"Just let it go, Mad, I'm tired."

"Well I'm tired too. I'm sick and tired of you spending what little money we have down at Joe's. Do you even care where your daughter is tonight? I took her over to Lavern's so she could at least have some dinner."

"Damn it, Mad — I don't need this shit tonight!" He swept his arm across the kitchen counter, sending a glass flying into the sink, shattering into a hundred pieces.

She angrily turned on him. "Just so that you know, I've packed my clothes and Catherine's things, and I'm going to Lavern's. I want you out of here. I can't live like this anymore."

He couldn't remember what happened after that. Did he strike her? She was crying. Madeleine never cried. She walked out, got into Lavern's borrowed car and drove off. He remembered thinking, "Maybe I'll just have one more beer. She'll be back."

The next morning a truck drove up to the house. Everett knocked on the door and Glenn, who was barely awake, answered.

"Hello Glenn, how are you doing?"

"Okay."

"Look, I've got Madeleine and your daughter out at the Valley. They're going to stay there for a while until she figures out what she wants to do."

"Good, you take 'em for a while."

That comment, along with the destruction inside the house got Everett's hackles up, but he remained calm.

"I came to pick up a few things she wants."

Glenn motioned him in with a large over-acted gesture. "Be my guest."

Everett and Howard loaded the few things into Howard's furniture truck. Nearly everything that was important to her had been given to her by her dad: her mother's sewing machine, Christmas ornaments, a chest filled with embroidered keepsakes, her mother's postcard collection. As Ev saw fit, he threw in some other things as he found them, knowing that Madeleine would regret leaving them behind someday. Then on his way out the door, Ev stopped just inches from Glenn's face. "You need to get yourself some help. Madeleine and Catherine are safe with me; I'll take care of them." With that parting warning, Ev climbed into the truck and drove off.

Glenn had to give Everett some credit for the slight confrontation. He was a stand-up guy and Glenn had always liked him. He assumed correctly that Madeleine would be filing for divorce, so there wasn't any reason to stick around. Without a job to hold him back, he took his own few possessions, got on the highway, aimed the car south, and started driving.

He finally stopped in an area outside Santa Ana, a little south of Los Angeles. He found himself a temporary job and an apartment. He moved in what little he had and never took an interest in purchasing more. The apartment was not much more than a room with a couch, a TV, and a refrigerator. That was about all he needed.

As soon as his forwarding address was registered, he got served divorce papers, as he expected. He also knew that Madeleine was still in the Valley. The Valley address was included in the information the attorney sent with the papers. It's not that he didn't think about the mistakes he'd made. As much as he could be open to love—he loved Madeleine and Catherine both—it was just that it was time to move on. Sometimes in the middle of the night when he wasn't able to sleep, he'd write letters to them, nearly always throwing them away in the morning.

In a moment of weakness, he called the Valley in the summer of 1958 hoping to talk to Madeleine for a minute. Ev answered the phone. He asked about his daughter and how Mad was doing. It was then he received the news that not only were Everett and Madeleine married, but she was expecting a baby.

They didn't hear from him again for another year when, out of the blue, he sent Catherine a birthday present. To her, it was like receiving a present from a stranger.

The minute that Madeleine had walked out of that door on Renton Avenue, she'd written him off. No good would ever come from him, and she moved forward without ever looking back. It didn't matter whether Glenn tried to contact his daughter or whether he ignored her. It irritated Madeleine either way.

The divorce stipulated that he was required to pay child support. Madeleine never attempted to collect, knowing he never had any money. And Ev was just as happy not to pursue it, alleviating any rights that Glenn might have to his daughter. Catherine had stepped neatly into the hole in his heart that his own daughter Sharon had left.

A STRANGERS VISIT

1960, Maple Valley, Washington

Two years later Glenn made a trip to Seattle. He had called the house in the Valley and Ev had easily invited him to drop by for a visit, much to Madeleine's chagrin. Jamie was almost two and Cat, Ev's nickname for his stepdaughter, had just turned eight. By then, she barely remembered Glenn.

As Glenn was driving around the circular driveway, he had a 360 degree view of the house and yard. He noticed that the house was more than the fishing cabin he had heard about several years earlier. It appeared to have been recently painted a dark brown with light green trim. Flower pots were overflowing the porch. Wild flowers and roses ran down to the river bank. Rhododendrons were in full bloom. The house still looked a little rough in places, but it had a feeling of permanency, something Glenn had never experienced except at Red's house.

Not knowing what to expect, Glenn parked his car and took in the yard one more time with the roaring sound of the river at his back. "I guess Madeleine finally got her yard," he said to himself. He tentatively got out, shut the car door, and began walking toward the back porch, when the kitchen door opened. Ev filled the doorway.

"Come on in. You want a beer?" Ev asked, after extending and receiving a handshake.

"Sure, if you have one handy."

Madeleine, who had just finished putting some dishes away, had a series of emotions run through her. As she looked at him, she found it hard to imagine that she had been married to this man for ten years. He seemed much different to her. Not only had he put on some weight, but he looked much older and sadder. It was difficult for her to find the person she'd ever married, but she refused to linger on it.

Her life had turned around in the last two years and she almost resented him intruding on her life now. She didn't care if she was cordial or not; she didn't have anything to say to him and just wanted to get through the visit.

Seeing her standing in the kitchen, he nodded her way. "Hi Mad, how you doing?"

Always an easy talker, Ev carried the conversation. "So, are you still living in California?"

"Well, I'm on my way to Portland for a job," Glenn said. "I thought as long as I was this close, I'd come on up to Seattle. I brought a present for Catherine. Is she around?"

Glenn, feeling somewhat guilty for not keeping in better touch with his daughter, had sought out and bought a boxed swing set, remembering how much his daughter had enjoyed swinging on the rusty set that had come with the house on Renton Avenue.

"Yeah, she's not too far. She's outside playing," Ev said as he reached up and pulled an army whistle from the nail beside the door. Walking out on the porch, he blew the whistle with one long breath. He listened for a response which he heard off in the distance.

Putting the whistle carefully back on the nail, he said, "As long as she's in whistle range, I figure she's not in too much trouble. Let's go outside. Bring your beer. We'll have a cigarette." As they went outside, a half-grown girl that Glenn barely recognized sized him up from across the yard.

Madeleine, Ev, and Glenn sat on the benches of Ev's newly constructed picnic table and talked while Cat and Jamie played nearby.

"She sure has grown since the last time I saw her. How's she doing in school?"

"Fine." Madeleine offered no additional information, but Ev added, "She's doing real well, Glenn — she's a smart little gal."

"That's good. You've done a lot of work on the house, Ev, it looks real nice."

"We still have a lot to do, though. An inspector was out yesterday; we just got the wiring brought up to code."

"That's good." Glenn paused and then remembered the present he had brought for his daughter. "Oh, I almost forgot, I brought a present for Catherine." Glenn got up and went to the trunk of his car. He carried the big box over and set it on the porch.

"I'll just leave it there. It's a swing set." Glenn directed his attention to his daughter. "There's a picture on the side of the box, if you want to see what it looks like." Cat came closer to the box, glanced at the picture and then back at the man who had brought it.

Clearly uncomfortable, Glenn walked over to Ev, with an outstretched hand. "I probably better get going, Ev. It was good to see you again." Ev stood and shook his hand. Then, addressing Madeleine who had refused to stand, he just nodded, turned, and walked away.

Cat had inched her way next to Ev and was hovering under his arm, as Ev subconsciously put his arm around her shoulder. He bent down and whispered something in her ear. She turned her big eyes up to him and then to Glenn. Cat had taken a tentative step toward Glenn when he met her half way. He knelt down and cautiously tried to hug his daughter goodbye. He tilted his face toward hers and whispered near her ear, "I love you, honey." Then he rose, turned and walked to his car. As he was leaving, he lifted his hand out the window of the car in a half-wave, and headed back to Portland.

When Glenn left Maple Valley that day, it was the last time Madeleine or Cat ever saw him.

Throughout the next few years, Glenn sent Catherine a birthday card when he happened to remember. He always wrote a note inside, updating them of his whereabouts and hoping that everyone was doing fine.

The last card they received from him was postmarked from just outside Portland in 1967.

* * *

Present

Not many people were inside the Starbucks coffee shop when Father Duncan came through the door with an armload of papers. "So, Father, what do you think about my story so far?" Cat asked, too excited to wait until they sat down. Father Duncan had been there for her from the beginning, always encouraging and always questioning. His opinion was important to her.

"I think it's far more than a story. I think this has been an incredible journey for you to undertake," Father said, as he handed the draft pages back to her. "I'm quite interested though in how you're going to finish this journey and what truth you might find at the end."

"Well, it isn't my truth that I'm seeking; it's just a story that loosely resembles the story of three lives."

"Oh . . . I think there is a truth that is driving you. I'm not sure you have found it yet, but there is something unresolved that's going to put this story to rest. Trust in the divine to guide you." Then raising his hand," I know what you're thinking, and I don't mean to get all holy moly on you, but something in the beyond is guiding you to finding a resolution."

"A resolution to what? I'm perfectly fine. I just find that putting all these pieces together is somehow therapeutic.''

"That's an interesting word you used. Therapeutic means 'healing'. What is it that you need to heal? I believe that you might be getting close to finding what you didn't know you were looking for."

"I don't know if that's true of not." Having ordered their coffee and moved to a vacant table, she added, "I will say though, that I do think a little differently about my father than I used to. After all, he is a part of me, all the good and all the bad."

"Yes, that's true. You were pretty young when he left, but it seems as if you were lucky to have had a good stepfather to help raise you. I think you must have had a good childhood after a rocky beginning. When you write about your stepfather, I can feel your love. When you write about growing up, I can feel your care-free spirit. So tell me your story, Cat. What was it like for you growing up that gave you such happy memories?"

"Oh, Father, I don't even know where to start. You're right about one thing though. I loved my stepfather more than anything in the world. He was everything to me. It's like he just took me and plopped me down in the country and gave me wings to fly. He's the one that nick-named me Cat. He told Mom, "Catherine is a name for a lady. This little head-strong, stubborn nymph needs a nick-name. I'm calling her Cat. And from that moment I was never anything else. Mom still called me Catherine Lee, if she was trying to get my attention. But Daddy even introduced me as Cat to my baby brother who's never known me by any other name.

"And yes, Father, my childhood was . . ." Cat searched for the right word, ". . . enviable. Every day was an adventure. I grew up with nothing, but I had everything. I know that Mom and Dad went through some very hard years, but we never knew it.

"By the time Jamie started walking, I was already on my way to becoming a real country tomboy. I know it gave Mom fits. My life was full of bruised knees and bloody elbows. I was the little girl in pigtails, climbing trees barefoot and wearing hand-me-down clothes.

"Our 1951 Ford ran, but had two old spare tires where the back seat was missing. The house was a jigsaw puzzle of completion. Someone looking in from the outside could have felt sorry for our rag-a-muffin family. Daddy never believed in carrying debt, so the house only got worked on when there was money to pay cash. Because of that, the place was always in some sort of disrepair or construction. He worked sporadically on the house, depending on if he was laid off or rehired at Boeing. We learned to live by stepping over boards and tools without even thinking twice.

"Uncle Howard came out to help Dad on the weekends. They'd scratch around old construction sites and salvage wood, old cupboards, brick, whatever materials they could get for free and use on the house. If the job was too big for Daddy to handle, he'd call Billy, an old friend of his and hire him to help. Billy was a real character. He was at our house so often it felt like he was a permanent fixture. Jamie and I liked him a lot. He was like an uncle or grampa in construction coveralls who knew how to fix anything. He used to call my dad Pete Peterson.

"'Well, if it's not Pete and Re-Pete,' Billy would say, pointing at my dad and Jamie through the window of his truck as he pulled into the driveway. Daddy would stop raking gravel long enough to wave hello to Billy and shoo Jamie out of the way of the rusty old truck.

"Billy would slide out of the cab, grab his tools and, in a gesture that had become a family joke, plop a hard hat on Jamie's head, making him giggle. He'd always give Jamie a job to make him feel as if he was helping, like hammering on a board or putting rocks in a bucket. Jamie adored him. He teased both of us unmercifully, always with a twinkle in his eye.

"Daddy could only pay Billy when he had Boeing paychecks coming in. Billy didn't seem to mind much and never complained. Every cent we had was going into the house, and that didn't leave money for much else.

"We always lived in hand-me-downs and what Mom could sew on her mother's old sewing machine. What furniture we had was old, and things had been patched over and over just to get by. The roof needed fixing and things always needed painting. It was all on the list of things to do 'one of these days'.

"I slept in the front room until Daddy and Howard built a big second story addition. I moved into the downstairs half-built room when there were still studs exposed. But, it was all a big adventure, and we were happy. We were a close family. I have vivid flashes of childhood, sitting on Daddy's lap, joking at the dinner table, camping in the back yard. We always had laughter and music. Through that haze, Jamie and I never knew that Mom and Dad were doing without. We just never knew.

"In spite of not having a pot to piss in, Dad was still a generous host and would invite anyone at the drop of pin, to dinner or to spend the weekend. Our home was always open. Someone was always staying over, camping in our back yard, or showing up for Saturday picnics. That was a trait that Mom found very disturbing at first, but I think she finally got used to it, or at least she adjusted to it. As kids, we just thought it was normal."

Father Duncan smiled as he sipped at his coffee and listened.

THE CHILI FEED

1962, Maple Valley, Washington

"**H**oney, I invited the quartet over for practice on Saturday," Ev said, alluding to his newly formed barbershop quartet. "I told them to bring their families and spend the weekend."

"Well, Lavern and Morrie and the kids are coming out on Friday night. I'm not sure where we're going to put everybody."

"We'll just pitch the tent and the kids can sleep outside. It'll be fine. Probably ought to fix some dinner for them though, don't you think? What do we have?"

Madeleine had been stretching food for so long it became second nature. A can of tuna fish could feed the family of four. Her vegetable garden supplemented every meal. Potatoes were cheap and filled up the kids. But this time the freezer was pretty bare.

"Honey, I think we've only got a pound of hamburger left and some bread. I have zucchini, tomatoes, and onions in the garden, but that's about it."

"How about if I make chili on Saturday?" Ev suggested. "All we need is a bag of red beans, tomato paste, and a couple cloves of garlic. I think I've got enough spices and everything else here."

And with a pound of hamburger, whatever could be salvaged from the garden, and the few things Madeleine needed to pick up at the store, the menu was set.

That was to be the first of many chili feeds at the house. The smell of chili spices, onion, and cumin was a common aroma wafting from the kitchen windows during warm summer days.

Ev never cooked anything small. Since his cooking skills were learned at the elbow of Brother Frederico at Briscoe, he always cooked large, filling the twelve-quart top of the roaster oven with rich, spicy chili sauce that filled the air.

Summer weekends were always full of people. It was a giant potluck with no theme. Lunches could consist of mashed potatoes, macaroni and cheese, potato chips, peanuts, and a beer keg in the old wash tub.

Kids were always in the river and camping in the back yard — music was always coming from the house in the Valley. Barbershop harmony was common, with the overtones carried by the river. Neighbors always wandered down to join in the fun. It was a place of bonfires in the evening, hot dogs and marshmallows on vine maple branches, chores in the mornings, and late nights under the stars.

Early on, Cat felt that her new little brother was a live doll to play with and seldom left him alone. As they grew older, that became both a blessing and a curse. She smothered him with love one day and teased him unmercifully the next.

As she grew older still, she became the primary baby sitter and took advantage of her new-found role as "boss". Being an easy going child, Jamie just rolled with the punches. He was very much like Ev. Unlike Cat, he could be disciplined with a short talk. He never did anything wrong and could always be counted on to tattle on his sister when she did. Cat, on the other hand, pushed the edge of the envelope every chance she got. Their personalities were entirely opposite each other, both unknowingly taking after their respective fathers. Yet, for all the differences, they adored each other.

They both competed for their dad's attention. Cat gained ground by excelling in piano lessons and school. Jamie developed a nearly perfect pitch at an early age and took an interest in barbershop singing. Cat countered with school choir and was determined to be her daddy's helper in all things, which easily got her out of household chores and helping her mother.

Both kids took to the river like they were fish, born to swim. Madeleine, still deathly afraid of water and having never learned to swim, held her breath every time they were near the river.

Summers turned into winters, school years turned over to vacations, and one holiday ran into another, the family building their own traditions.

Christmas took on certain continuity for the family. Madeleine had preserved a box of fragile Christmas ornaments that had belonged to her mother and grandmother. Through all the moves, surprisingly, very few had broken. The rest of the tree ornaments consisted of handmade paper chains and things the kids made in school, old Christmas bows, strung popcorn, and lots of tinsel and lights, which Madeleine fought to untangle every year.

"Mom, can you tell me the story again about these ornaments?" Cat was holding the box of fragile ornaments as if they were treasures.

"They were my mother's."

"And your gramma's, huh Mom?" Cat added. "I wish I had a gramma."

"Sorry, all your grammas have died."

Cat picked up one of the ornaments that had been delicately sculpted inside with a tiny manger that held baby Jesus. She poked her finger inside the ornament to try to touch the tiny sculpture.

"Get your finger out of there, Cat, you're gonna poke a hole in it." Madeleine had caught her daughter's movement out of the corner of her eye, only by accident because she was concentrating so hard on getting the knots out of the string of lights.

"Mom, how come these don't have pictures in them?" Cat was onto another box of Christmas balls.

"Because, your aunt Betty bought those for me when I was living in Billings." Madeleine paused as memories washed over the naked tree in her Billings apartment. The memory caused her to long for her family in Montana. She took a deep breath to clear her thoughts and then abandoned the Christmas lights to sit with her daughter and look at the ornaments for a minute.

"Is Daddy going to paint Christmas this year?"

"I suppose, if he has time. We'll see." Madeleine placated her daughter, trying to avoid the next hour of questions and jabber. She was sure her daughter talked just to hear herself talk.

The following morning Ev dug out his water paints and, with the flair of a commercial artist, painted holly leaves and berries in the corners of the picture window and front room mirrors. Madeleine filled the rooms with vases of fragrant cedar branches and holly with very little artistic flair — but it always looked beautiful and smelled of Christmas.

Madeleine spent the months before December sewing clothes, crocheting doilies and pot holders, knitting throws, and making candles to give as gifts. Baking Christmas cookies and fruitcake was an annual project for Madeleine and the kids.

"Cat, leave that alone. We're gonna take that fruitcake to Daddy's Aunt Jen."

"Do I know her?" Cat was scrunching up her forehead impatiently waiting for an answer.

"Yes, honey, we went to her house last year. Remember — she wanted you to dance for her, and she gave you orange candy and the little red glass of milk."

"Oh, yeah."

"She has a new house this year and Daddy wants to see her for Christmas, so we're going to visit for a little while."

Ev came into the kitchen. "ETD is in five minutes," he announced.

Ev was always punctual — always had a schedule and a plan. Both kids learned early on that "ETD" (military lingo for estimated time of departure) was no estimation. In five minutes, the family was in the car, with the fruitcake and a full tank of gas, on their way to the assisted living home in White Center and Aunt Jen.

It broke Ev's heart when he had to move her out of her home of fifty years, but she was visibly declining in health, and he and

Howard had decided that this was the best thing for her. She had reluctantly agreed. The house had become too much for her to take care of.

Ev and Howard had chosen this place for Aunt Jen because residents lived in separate stand-alone apartments that looked and felt like individual houses. Jen had been independent all her life, a trait Ev hoped to preserve for her as long as he could. While the small house felt like home, there was a community center as well as a nursing facility on the grounds that supervised all the prescription medications. It also comforted Ev to know that they had twenty-four hour medical help, if needed.

Visiting relatives and friends, the few weeks before Christmas was a tradition most likely originating with Madeline's family. Ev was never particularly close to his family, with the exception of Aunt Jen. Madeleine, on the other hand, longed to see her family. The holidays were always bittersweet, having to make do with a precious phone call and the traditional Christmas letters and pictures stuffed inside Christmas cards. She hadn't been back to Montana in years; the money just wasn't there.

Aunt Jen's house was neat and clean, with many glass figurines, pictures, and knick knacks perched on polished antique tables. Madeleine held her breath, hoping that the kids would stay put and that nothing would get handled and subsequently broken while they were visiting. With both kids full of energy, probably aided by overindulging in Christmas candy, Madeleine took them out to walk to the community center while Ev visited with his aunt.

"She takes good care of you?" Jen asked Ev after Madeleine and the kids left. Jen's voice was a little shaky from age and she had a slight tremor affecting her hands, but there was a steadiness in her stare.

"Yeah, Jen — she does," Ev said. Looking at her, his mind searched through memories. Jen! She was always there for him: sleepovers at her house when he was nine, hugs that took the place of a mother's hugs, the loans for college, and the many dinners she cooked for him when he was broke.

"Everett?" Jen looked into his eyes, "Are you happy?"

Ev felt the importance of this question and took his time in responding. "Jen, I'm happier than I have ever been in my life."

Her lips tried to play with a small smile. As she broke the stare, nodding her head, she shut her eyes, noticeably tired from the visit. Ev stood up, leaned over and gave her a kiss on her cheek. "Merry Christmas, Jen," he whispered, and let himself out.

A NEWLY FOUND GRAMPA

1963, Maple Valley, Washington

Cat lay in bed listening to her Mom in the kitchen making coffee. Without actually seeing her, she knew exactly what she was doing. She could hear the water perking, the smell reaching into her room and the sound of dishes being put away in the cupboards. She heard her mom pick up the phone.

"Yes operator, Cherry 3-8614 please."

Cat thought, over and over; Cherry 3-8614, Cherry 3-8614, Cherry 3-8614. She would never forget Lavern's phone number. Nearly every morning her mom made that same telephone call.

"Y-ellow, how're you doing?" Madeleine asked when Lavern picked up the phone.

Cat didn't pay too much more attention to the conversation until she heard her mom say, "Yeah, we haven't told the kids yet, but we're thinking about going to Montana to see 'em. Joe just got done moving Dad into a house in Fishtail. The ranch was too much for him with all the boys gone, and he's getting on in years. I guess he got himself some sheep to keep him busy." Madeleine chuckled at the thought of the cattle rancher running sheep. "Dad gave Joe the house in Absarokee." Then there was a pause as Lavern picked up the conversation, to which Madeleine responded, "No, I don't think Cat remembers. She was pretty young, but we thought we would take the train and go into Livingston. Earl said he'd pick us up and take us on down to Billings." She continued after another short pause, giving Lavern a chance to ask more questions.

"No, Frances is still there; he's still with Jane. I guess Dad's house isn't too far from Frances' ranch. Louise and Andy are still in the Philippines, but I think they might be trying to get transferred back to the States. I don't think she's felt well since she lost the baby. So, how's Maria's cold doing? Better?"

As Madeleine continued her conversation with Lavern, Cat started getting excited about the prospect of going to Montana. They never went anywhere far away, and she'd never been on a train. She strained to hear the rest of the plans.

When summer came, it was a huge adventure for all of them – the packing, the train, the excitement of going on a trip. Once in Montana, the kids were introduced to dozens of cousins, uncles, and aunts.

Upon meeting her grampa, Cat was enchanted. Mike never met a child he didn't get along with, and Cat was no different. Madeleine watched as her dad reached down to hold Cat's hand, and lead her to the corral where baby sheep were grazing. Her daughter appeared to be captivated by her newly found grampa.

Madeleine had missed her dad more than she would admit. She took in her surroundings and decided that her dad's house was perfect for him, and there was plenty to keep him busy.

Even Ev had been looking forward to the trip. He couldn't wait to go to Montana and eat a real Montana steak. Jane fed him fried chicken instead. It was always a joke after that; Ev went all the way to Montana for steak and got everyday fried chicken.

Madeleine felt better knowing her dad was doing well, and she had a great time seeing family and introducing them to Ev. The trip had been quite an experience for Ev. He was about as far away from being a cowboy as they came. But he did take an avid interest in the history of the area and, by the end of the trip, he knew more about Montana than Madeleine ever thought of knowing.

They boarded the train in Livingston and settled in for the two-day trip back home. Ev immediately became engrossed in a book he had purchased on the Beartooth Mountains of Montana, and both Cat and Jamie fell fast asleep aided by the rocking of the train.

Madeleine closed her eyes and let the sound of the train on the tracks lull her into a semi-sleep. Her old Irish dad was showing his age. A tear escaped from her eye, as she silently realized that she may have seen him for the last time.

DADDY'S LITTLE GIRL

Ev finished the new addition to the house, giving them a large master bedroom upstairs. Cat's room finally got plaster board on the walls, taped, sanded, and painted peach and white at Cat's insistence. Jamie moved into the old bedroom in the main part of the house and Madeleine finally got her front room.

As Cat and Jamie got older, their differences became more obvious. There were times that, despite Ev's influence, Madeleine could clearly see Glenn in her daughter. It caused a few anxious years for mother and daughter as Cat reached her teens. And for the one hundredth time Madeleine was thankful that she married Ev, who had the wisdom to provide the right amount of love, patience, and discipline in Cat's life.

Cat and Jamie could not have had two more opposite personalities. Cat ran wild with energy. She spent days exploring the woods. She swam like a fish and lived in the river until she could no longer feel her prune skin. It was as if it all belonged to her. Fences never stopped her. She loved freedom and was selfish with it. The whole world was hers, and she wasn't sharing. Jamie, on the other hand, had a more realistic view of his place in the world. His adventures were better planned and safe. His strong moral compass and the clearly defined line between right and wrong just pissed off Cat. More than once she would get bested by her brother. Jamie could never lie; Cat could make up stories as fast as her brain would work. She was so convincing, she believed her own lies. And then there was Jamie's love for their mom. From the moment Jamie was born, he brought calm to his mother. The bond was always stronger with mother and son than it ever had been with mother and daughter.

Cat and Jamie also loved differently. Cat was slow to trust and guarded her heart. She hurt people easily without thinking about it. Jamie loved with his whole being and believed that everyone was good at heart. Madeleine had to smile and shake her head at how she got so lucky with that one. She loved them both, but somehow Jamie was easier to love.

At age sixteen, Cat gained her self-confidence and found her stride. She also figured out, in that devious mind of hers, how to wrap her dad around her little finger.

"Hi, Daddy." Cat strode into the living room, giving Ev a kiss on the cheek, as she perched on the arm of his leather TV chair.

"How's school?" Ev asked.

"I got my report card today." She paused for effect. "I got straight A's."

"That's my girl. You see, you can do anything you want to do, if you just set your mind to it. I've seen you do that time and time again. What have I always told you?"

"To believe in myself."

"Do you know why I always tell you that? Because I believe in you. Now come down here and give me a hug. Congratulations, Cat."

"Daddy, do you think I can go down to the lake tomorrow night? A bunch of us want to celebrate that school's almost out."

"Sure, I don't see why not, honey. Do you have plenty of gas?"

"Yeah, I probably have enough." Cat knew the tank was on Empty. She had asked her mom, but had received a resounding "no" to both the party and money for gas.

Reaching for his wallet, Ev pulled out a five dollar bill and handed it to her. "You take this and make sure that you have enough gas to get home."

"Oh, thank you, Daddy. I will." Cat slid off the arm of his chair, catching a glimpse of her mother out of the corner of her eye. Madeleine caught the last of the charade, rolled her eyes, and was still shaking her head when Cat came into the kitchen with a smile on her face.

Cat had grown from an insecure five-year-old to a creative and talented young lady with a bit of mischievous fire and a knack for barely staying out of trouble.

* * *

Present

"And that, Father, was pretty much how my childhood went. I grew up as a tomboy and spent more time in the woods and the river than I did at home. I was taught to be independent and creative and expand my imagination." Cat chuckled as she remembered her childhood. "I was even difficult to punish. Once they tried to 'ground' me by telling me I couldn't leave the yard. Left to my own endeavors, I made up things to do that were great fun. I would act out complete stage plays in the back yard. I pretended to be Maria in the 'Sound of Music' or Dorothy in 'The Wizard of Oz'. I was the majorette with the baton leading a parade. I could be anything I wanted to be. I know that probably sounds stupid."

"All of the world is a stage. Most just don't take advantage of it."

"Quoting Shakespeare now, Father?" she asked. "I've probably bent your ear enough today; I'm sure God has better things for you do." And with that, they gave up their table and walked out of Starbucks. Father Duncan turned to her and asked, "So what have you decided to do with this story?"

"That's funny. Jim keeps asking me the same thing. I've decided that I'm going to write this in book format, have it bound, and give it to Jamie for Christmas. There's a lot of information in this book that represents his past. It'll be like giving him . . . his history."

"And yours as well. God's blessings to the end. I look forward to the next installment."

They parted. When Cat got home, she sat down to sketch out the chapter that she thought would be easy to write. Somehow, after all she'd learned over the past year, she was far more emotional than she'd expected.

GLENN BARKER

April, 1968, Maple Valley, Washington

As the telephone rang, Madeleine picked it up. "Hello." When Madeleine answered the phone, it usually had a sing-song quality that sounded more like "Y-ellow".

"I am looking for a relative of Glenn Barker. Is this Catherine Barker?" the strange man asked on the phone.

"No, this is her mother."

"Are you then, also her legal guardian?"

"Yes."

"Then, I'd like to speak to you for a minute. I am calling from the Colonial Mortuary and I regret to inform you that Glenn Barker has died. His records indicated a Catherine Barker as his next of kin"

"Oh my God, umm, yes that's correct, she is his daughter."

"As her legal guardian, we would like to know what your desire is as far as the burial."

Madeleine was stunned and took the caller's name and number and told him she would call him back.

Ev had been laid off once again at Boeing and had been out running errands. When he returned, Madeleine told him about the phone call.

"Honey, you know we have to go down there, don't you?" Ev asked.

"Oh, I suppose. There doesn't seem to be anybody else to do it."

"Well, regardless, that's Cat's birth father and if for no other reason, we should go to Portland because *he is* her father."

Caught between understanding what Ev was saying and her own emotions, Madeleine didn't know what to do. They could barely afford the gas to drive to Portland, let alone pay for a burial. It wasn't as if they owed Glenn anything for being a disappointing husband and an even more disappointing father.

"Honey, I know what you're thinking, so just listen to me for a minute. You know I think of Cat as my own daughter. I forget that she isn't mine. I couldn't love her any more if she was. But I don't regret that you were married to Glenn; if you hadn't been, you wouldn't have had Cat and I wouldn't have met you." Thinking about his own daughter that he hadn't seen in twenty years, he continued, "I hope someday Cat is gonna wonder about her father. Maybe she'll want to know about him, what he was like, and where he is buried. I just want to feel like we're doing the right thing for her. We can take her and Jamie to Lavern and Morrie's for a few days and do what needs to be done. Honey, it's the right thing."

"Well if we're going to do that, then I'd better pick her up from school and get her home. Jamie's bus should be coming pretty soon. I don't suppose Glenn was still working. It would be too much to ask if he had any insurance or anything," she said half under her breath.

"Come 'ere," Ev said, wrapping his arms around her. "It'll be okay. We'll take care of what we can and be back in a day or two."

They drove down to Portland and met the director at the mortuary. The only information that was available was that Glenn had been found dead in his apartment after not showing up for work at Borg Warner. Madeleine gave them all the answers that she could remember which included his military information. With the VA burial benefits, some of the money burden was relieved, and the mortuary handled the finance reimbursement.

They arranged a very small service to be held at the mortuary chapel. Fewer than a handful of people attended, two from work, his landlord, and a lady with her daughter. The officiator handed Madeleine the American Veteran Flag, the cards from the few flower arrangements, and a packet of information on Glenn's life insurance, along with a contact at Borg Warner.

Everything was settled quickly. At the time of his death Glenn had barely over $100 in assets. The attorney closed the case, saying it wasn't worth keeping it open for that small amount of money. Borg Warner released an $8,000 life insurance check, which Ev and Madeleine put in trust for Cat. They also released Glenn's final paycheck, which paid for all but about three hundred dollars of the burial fees.

The high school counselor kept an eye on Cat for any signs of stress during that time. But from the moment she heard Glenn had died, she felt nothing, as if a stranger had died. Her pat answer had become, in true Lannen tradition, "I'm fine."

MIKE LANNEN

1970, Fishtail, Montana

In 1970 Cat graduated from high school and was still home for the summer when Madeleine was called home to Montana. Age was catching up with her dad and he was not doing well. She went to Fishtail to stay with him for a couple of weeks. During that time, they moved him into a guest house at Frances and Jane's ranch. Madeleine wanted to bring her father home with her, but Mike didn't want to leave Montana. At least at the guest house, Frances would be close by and could keep an eye on him.

Madeleine was somewhat jealous that her three brothers lived close enough to her dad to visit often. They agreed that they would allow Mike to be as independent as he was able. When it came time he needed more help, they took turns taking care of Mike. Joe moved him into the Absarokee house with him and Jennie for a while, but with five kids still at home, it was difficult. Mike decided go up and stay with Earl and Betty in Livingston that fall.

Madeleine tried to do the best she could at keeping in touch with what was going on, but her heart ached to be so far away from her dad.

"Hi, Dad? This is Madeleine, how are you doing?" Madeleine asked during her weekly telephone call home.

"Okay, I guess."

"So, you're up with Earl and Betty, huh? That's good."

"Yep," her dad said, and then the phone went dead.

"God damn him!" Madeleine yelled, frantically redialing.

"Dad, don't hang up on me!" she sternly told him when he was back on the phone.

"Well, I was done talking," he drawled.

"Well I wasn't. I want to talk to you. Do you want to know how the kids are doing? (pause) Well they're both doing great. Catherine just graduated from high school and Jamie is doing real fine. Umm, we just finished putting a new roof on the house and got the attic insulated before winter. Are Betty and Earl doing okay?" She babbled on trying to evoke a response from him, just needing to hear his voice.

"Seems like it." And then the phone when dead again. He was apparently done talking. Madeleine just shook her head. At least, she thought, he could say goodbye before he hung up.

On October 20, 1970, Madeleine got the call that her dad, Mike Lannen, had died. Joe said that he had a stroke while up at Earl's and he died in the Livingston hospital. All Mike's children, now grown with families of their own, came home to Absarokee for the funeral. Louise, living with Andy in Florida, was on the first plane to Montana. Ev didn't hesitate to use his only credit card to buy Madeleine a plane ticket and she flew to Billings. Earl was close enough to drive to Absarokee, and Joe, who still lived in their childhood home, had a houseful of family that came together for the funeral. They buried Mike beside Elsie in the Rosebud Cemetery just outside Fishtail.

Mike's death caused a falling out among his children. The only thing of value that Mike owned was his land and the house in Fishtail. The sheep had long been sold; outside of a few barn cats, there wasn't much left. Madeleine and Joe sent most of their dad's personal belongings to the church charity and put the house and land up for sale. Frances and Jane offered to buy the property at half it's worth since it bordered their ranch. Joe took exception to that. He thought it should be a fair sale and, in spite of the fact that he would not see any proceeds, he set about to establish true value on the property. He had been given the Absarokee house free and clear years earlier.

Madeleine was still reeling with heartache from losing her father and was easy enough to rile up, as she'd never been too fond of Jane to begin with. Before it was all over, Frances never talked to Joe or Madeleine again. Louise had been left out of the will, presumably because she was too young when the will was written. In spite of that, Madeleine and Earl made sure she was equally represented with proceeds from the eventual sale of the property.

Madeleine remained close with Joe, Louise, and Earl, but never spoke to Frances or any of his direct family again. When asked, she didn't acknowledge Frances as her brother.

During the finalization of the probate, Mike's attorney pointed out quite graphically that their father would have been devastated to know that his death had caused this break among the siblings. He would have been sorely disappointed in all of them. Then again, the Lannens had always been a stubborn Irish bunch.

EVERETT PETERSON

1972, Maple Valley, Washington

Madeleine watched her daughter's car drive around the circular gravel driveway and come to a halt. Since Cat had started college, they didn't see her very often, and this was a surprise visit, especially coming so close after Christmas.

"Hi Mom," Cat said, coming through the door to the kitchen.

"Hi, what are you doing here?"

"I don't know; I just wanted to come and visit. Where's Daddy?"

"He's in the front room watching TV. Sit down. Do you want a glass of wine?" Not waiting for a response, Madeleine retrieved the store bought Pink Chablis from the fridge and poured two glasses. "Did your new classes start for this quarter?"

"Yeah, last week. Hey Jamie, what're you up to?" Cat asked her brother as he came through the hallway door.

"Nothing, just homework," Jamie said, grabbing a chair at the kitchen table.

"Hey Mom, how come your cupboard door is off?" Cat asked, noticing the exposed shelves and cupboard door leaning against the kitchen wall.

"Daddy fixed the hinge and just hasn't gotten around to hanging it back up."

More small talk ensued, another glass of wine was poured, and Jamie got bored with the conversation and went back to his room. He had most recently given up his small bedroom for the large basement bedroom that Cat had vacated when she left for college.

An hour or more later, just before leaving, Cat popped into the front room to greet her dad. He was sitting in his chair, his eyes closed, softly snoring. She reached over and turned the TV down, but opted not to wake him; he looked so comfortable.

"Okay, Mom, well, I'd better get going. Thanks for the wine. I'll talk to you later." Cat grabbed her coat and was about to leave.

"You know something? I'd better go back in and tell Daddy goodbye."

Cat walked back up the porch stairs, through the kitchen, and into the front room. She walked to her dad's overstuffed chair and touched his shoulder, "Hey Dad, I just wanted to give you a kiss goodbye."

"Oh, hi, honey, when did you get here?"

"I've been here for a bit talking to Mom," she said as he pulled her onto his lap. She wrapped her arms around his neck and gave him a big hug. "I'm on my way out of here, but I had to come say good night."

"I'm glad you did. You drive careful, okay?" Ev said, as he gave her a fatherly pat on the ass.

"I will. Okay, good night!" she said smiling at her dad; and she kissed him good night.

It was the last time she saw him.

Madeleine had not recovered from her own father's death when Ev died of a heart attack, at age fifty-one, in January 1972, the day after Cat had visited.

It was another devastating blow to Madeleine. He left a daughter who was twenty years old and who idolized him. He left a thirteen-year-old son, who would never know the man-to-man conversations that only a grown son can have with a father. Jamie would never quite know the man that his father was, and Ev would never see what a special human being his son would become.

He left another daughter who, even though she sent flowers to the gravesite, never once contacted him, nor told him he had become a grandfather.

Most importantly, he left a wife, the daughter of a Missouri farmer, with stubborn strength, born of Irish heritage. Madeleine handled this loss like she did all the others. She simply got through them.

LIKE IT WAS YESTERDAY

2007, Tacoma, Washington
Thirty-Five Years Later

Cat remembered it like it was yesterday. Madeleine died in 2007. Cat made the call to her mom's last living brother. "Joe, this is Cat. I just wanted to let you know that Mom died this afternoon."

"I'm real sorry to hear that, but want you to know that I applaud the decision that you and Jamie made to let nature take its course. I don't believe in prolonging life by artificial means. I saw what that did to Earl, and I don't want anyone to have to go through that again." Joe paused letting the information about Madeleine's death sink in. "When do you think you might be having the funeral?"

"I don't know yet. We need to go down to the mortuary tomorrow. She's gonna be buried out in the Valley next to Daddy, but I have a local mortuary here in Tacoma handling it. Joe, we aren't going to have much in the way of a funeral. She's outlived most of her friends, and it's just Jamie and me here. I'm not sure if you were intending to come out, but it really isn't necessary. The service is going to be very small."

"Well it ain't going to be that small," Joe countered. "Andy and I are both going to be there. So you just let me know when it is." And with that solidity of family, Cat's tears finally fell.

The funeral came and went as planned, with a handful of people showing up to pay their respects. Uncle Joe and Uncle Andy were there to represent the last of Madeleine's siblings.

Cat hadn't realized how much she had needed them to be there. It was closure.

Several months later, Cat called Jamie on the phone.

"Hey. How're you doing?" she asked.

"Okay, how are you?" Jamie countered.

"I'm doing okay. I just thought I'd share something with you. I had a dream last night. We were all at home sitting in the kitchen, and Mom and Dad were there. You have to picture this, okay? You know how they used to hug each other in the kitchen all the time? Mom would be fixin' dinner and Daddy would just walk over to her and give her a big kiss and hug right there in the middle of the kitchen? You know what I mean?"

"Yeah?" Jamie responded slowly; somewhat apprehensive.

"They were just standing there, like everything was normal and he was giving her one of those hugs. Her back was to us and his hand moved down to her butt and he just gave her a little pat on the ass, you know, just like he used to do?"

"Yeah?" He was still not sure where his sister was going with this.

"Well," Cat said seriously, "I just got the feeling that I think they're together. I think they're okay."

Jamie paused and thought about that for a while before he responded. Then in a typical Lannen short, economical response he said just two words, "Could be."

* * *

Present

The book was finished as far as Cat was concerned. This was as good a place as any to end the story. She added some of the pictures that she'd found in the old photo albums and designed a cover depicting the Irish cliffs of Moher. She sent the pages out for several copies to be printed. A local bindery had given her a good price on binding the copies, and when she picked up the finished books, she felt a huge sense of accomplishment. The book represented not only family history, but more than a year of her life in research and writing.

When she got home, she pulled out one of the copies and opened the front cover to write a dedication to her brother. It read as follows:

"This book is dedicated to my brother, Jamie.
Not a day went by throughout this past year
that I did not think of you while I was writing.
Merry Christmas, with love,
Your Sister, Cat."

She wrapped the book carefully in gold paper, tied it with a white ribbon, and put the book into a box. Then she had an afterthought and put a second book in the box for Mollie, so they could both read it at the same time. She wrapped the larger box and placed it under the Christmas tree.

The next day, she called Jamie. "Okay, so do you two want to come to dinner on Christmas Eve? Or do you want to come on Christmas day?" It was an age-old question. While growing up, Christmas presents were always opened on Christmas Eve. Her mom had always given the excuse that they went to Mass on Christmas morning and she didn't want the kids to squirm all the way through church waiting to open presents. The real reason was that Madeleine would get so excited at Christmas, she couldn't wait to open presents herself. The story was that Santa came to their house early. Weren't they lucky?

Jamie, who was just as impatient about opening presents as their mom, said "I think it would be better if we celebrated Christmas on Christmas Eve. What time do you want us to come down?"

"Why don't we plan dinner early, like at three; if you want to come around noon, that'd be fine. I'm planning prime rib, so if Mollie wants to bring a pie or something for dessert, that'd be great. I'm not much of a dessert eater, so whatever you want would be fine. Okay?"

"Perfect, we'll see you then."

On Christmas Eve, Jamie and Mollie showed up at noon with boxes and sacks of presents. They always over-bought and over-spent. While Cat had a few other gifts under the tree for them, the "big" present was the book. Mollie had brought both home-made pumpkin and apple pies for dessert. While they were trying to fit the pies into the refrigerator, the two women decided to put Jamie out of his misery and open presents before dinner. They all enjoyed sitting around after dinner talking, and it would be nice to have the excitement and clutter over by then. Plus, Jamie was already poking around under the tree, trying to see where all his presents were.

As always, the disorganization drove Cat crazy. Presents were dispersed, opened, and on to the next, before anyone even had a chance to see what was given. Cat held back on the book until everything else was opened and Jim had picked up most of the wrapping and discarded it to the garage. When there was a lull in the chaos, Cat got up to retrieve the bottle of wine from the kitchen. She refilled wine glasses and then handed Jamie the last remaining box.

He knew by her serious, yet smug expression that this was his "big" present. He was used to the drama that surrounded his sister on the holiday and looked at her with that "what have you done now?" look. He knew how this was supposed to play out, so he humored Cat. Rather than ripping the present open, he let her enjoy the suspense. He tore the paper carefully on the larger box, discovering another present inside. He very slowly untied the white ribbon and loosened the tape on the gold wrapping paper. With confusion on his face, he opened the book to the front cover where Cat had written the dedication. His eyes met hers. Jim had kept Mollie locked in conversation as all this was going on. He didn't want anything to ruin the surprise of the moment, and he knew how much Cat loved creating the drama. Jamie thumbed through the book, reading the first few paragraphs, then looking at the table of contents. As he scanned randomly through the book, he caught glimpses of photos, recognizing the work that had gone into this gift.

"I love you. Merry Christmas." Cat mouthed the words quietly.

"When did you do this? How . . .? Umm . . . I don't even know what to say." Jamie looked at his sister for answers. The moment finally got Mollie's attention and she asked Jamie, "What? What's going on?" She scrunched her face in confusion as she looked at the cliffs of Moher on the cover of the book Jamie was holding.

"Mollie . . ." Cat diverted her attention, "I just gave Jamie his last present. I wrote a book." That still sounded unreal to Cat. "It's about our family — Jamie's and mine. I guess you could call it the history of our family. It goes as far back as Ireland in the 1800s. I've spent the last year or more researching Mom's family, Daddy's family, and even my real father's. There was so much information, I just started writing it up as a book. I have to say, Mom's life really did make for a good story. Plus, I discovered a lot of things that Jamie and I never knew before."

Mollie was a reader and, as Cat knew she would, she reached for Jamie's copy of the book when Cat distracted her. "Here," she said. "Here's a second copy just for you. I knew you'd need your own. You'll probably have it half read by the time you get home." Cat smiled as Mollie opened her copy and immediately began reading.

While they were eating dinner a little later, Cat told her brother and Mollie the story behind the story. She told him about finding the attic boxes and the photo albums. They talked about Aunt Doris, and how much Cat had enjoyed Father Duncan's friendship through all this. Like all their family dinners, everyone talked and laughed at once, with Jim adding color commentary and Morgan begging for food under the table. It was the best part of that Christmas.

Mollie and Cat cleared the table and rinsed the dishes. Most of the food had been covered and put away. The evening seemed to be winding down. Jamie stood in the kitchen doorway talking to his sister as she folded up the dish towel and put the last of the glasses in the dishwasher.

"Hey, you didn't forget the biscuits or anything in the micro-wave did you?" Jamie teased with a smirk on his face.

"Nope, I think we finally got through a family dinner without something being forgotten." Cat helped Mollie retrieve the pies from the fridge, got small plates down from the cupboard, and then she turned the honor of serving dessert over to her sister-in-law. Cat and Jamie went back into the dining room and sat down. They were just pulling Jim into a conversation when they heard Mollie in the kitchen. "Oh . . . son-of-a-bitch!" she said, "I forgot the whipped cream."

Jamie and Cat couldn't help themselves. They burst out laughing. When the chuckles died down, Cat quietly thought, "Thank you, Mom. What would the holidays be without forgetting something?"

Cat knew that after Jamie left that evening and had a chance to read the book, he would have questions. She didn't expect the phone calls to begin early the next morning.

"Is it true? Is that really why Mom was afraid of water?" Was Howard really Daddy's half-brother? How did you find out that Aunt Jen had a son that died?" This would be Jamie's fifth telephone call to ask questions.

"You know what? Why don't you and Mollie come down for dinner next week? Write down all your questions and I'll try to answer them and tell you why I came to some of the conclusions. Okay?"

"Saturday?"

"Yep, Saturday would work fine. How about four o'clock?"

"That works. We'll see you then, and Cat, thank you so much. Your book is really good."

By Saturday, freezing snow flurries were falling. Cat decided to keep dinner simple and just do a pot roast and vegetables. Coming so soon after the holidays, she was still a little burned out on entertaining. A one-pot-meal sounded like good comfort food for a cold snowy day.

The minute Jamie and Mollie hit the door, she was peppered with questions. Jamie had even written down things to ask. At the top of his list, he wondered whatever happened to Maysaya? Cat explained to him that Maysaya was a fictional person representing all the Japanese friends that their dad knew in high school and college. Some of those friends had indeed been taken to the internment camp.

"I remember that Daddy was very sentimental over the Japanese incidents, and really embarrassed on behalf of the way the Americans treated them in the camps. He probably told that story to me every year when we drove to the Puyallup Valley farms to get cucumbers when Mom was doing pickles, or peaches for canning. Daddy would always get very somber and repeat the story of how the Japanese families were picked up and taken to Camp Harmony. He said we should be 'ashamed of ourselves'."

There were many questions, and Cat was prompted to share the box of photos that Aunt Doris had given her that had belonged to Aunt Jen. Among the photos were letters and notes that helped fill in pieces of their dad's life. Jamie and Mollie spent the better part of an hour reading them. The conversation continued as Cat put dinner on the table, and was sidetracked only to argue about which way to pass the food. Some things just never changed.

At length, Mollie asked, "Cat, I have a question that is bothering me. You know when you were in college and went back home that night just before your dad died? I wonder what made you decide to go home that particular night."

"I don't know," Cat replied, a little melancholy, "but, what I think is even stranger is what made me second guess myself and go back in the house to wake him up and kiss him goodbye. I never could have forgiven myself if I hadn't." The questions began to die down, with everyone deep in their own thoughts.

"It's just so hard to imagine your mom like you wrote her, in her earlier years," Mollie continued, "I only knew her when she was in the assisted living home. She sounds like she might have been fun."

"Oh, she could be fun," Jim cut in. Cat's husband was enjoying the bantering.

"Yeah, she had her moments," Cat added, as she began clearing the table.

"Too bad she never married again."

"Well she dated and had a few boyfriends from time to time. I don't think Jamie or I really liked it when Mom started dating. We never gave any of 'em a chance."

"No, it was okay that Mom dated. I just didn't like any of them," Jamie insisted and then immediately realized Cat was probably right. "Of course, I guess if the truth were known, I never did give any of 'em a chance."

Cat continued, "I had a girlfriend that I used to bring out to the Valley once in a while. We'd take Mom down to the Cedar Inn or Gloria's Club, drinking and dancing. She always had a blast when we were out. We could make her laugh till she cried, or peed her pants, whichever came first."

"Chinese food!" Jamie said out of the clear blue sky.

"Oh, yeah," Jim added. "She loved Chinese food. I remember taking her out for Chinese dinner every year on her birthday. Do you remember when we went to that Chinese restaurant, Cat, across the bridge over in Gig Harbor? She thought it was so funny when you and I got schnockered on Saki."

"And she loved barbershop music; she'd get goose bumps and a huge smile on her face when Jamie sang barbershop," Cat recalled as she was putting the last of the food away.

"I wish I had of known her then," Mollie said, rather sadly.

"Yeah, I wish you'd known her too," Jamie added.

From the kitchen, Jamie heard his sister add, "Yeah, although sometimes it feels like she's never really gone." Cat chucked as she pulled the forgotten rolls out of the microwave, walked into the dining room and unceremoniously slapped them down on the cleared table in front of Jamie. He just dropped his head in his hands.

* * *

Later that spring, Tacoma, Washington

The book had been such a large part of Cat's life for so long, it was hard to stop thinking about it. While she was writing, both Jim and

Father Duncan had wanted to know how she was going to end it. She didn't know until she wrote it — that she'd come to the end. At least she thought it was the end of the book as far as Jamie was concerned. It just seemed like a good place to leave it. But something felt unfinished to Cat.

She kept reflecting on her birth father and how it all ended so abruptly. She thought maybe she just needed to walk where he walked. The more she thought about it, the more she wanted to go to Billings and see if she could find the places he'd been. Maybe his old house was still there. Maybe she wasn't quite done yet with her own final chapter.

She decided to visit Uncle Joe in Montana. The reason for the visit was twofold: she believed Uncle Joe had more to tell, and she wanted to see him again. Plus, she wanted to look for her grandparents' cemetery and her father's old neighborhood. All of a sudden one night, she blurted out, "Honey, I want to go to Montana."

"Okay," Jim said hesitantly. "I'm assuming that's for a visit, and you'll be coming back?"

"Yes, I will. You aren't getting rid of me that easy."

"So, when do you want to go?"

"I was thinking the first part of June. I need to talk to Uncle Joe one more time and visit the cemetery where my father's parents are buried. Something still doesn't feel right. Something is still not finished."

THE ROAD BACK HOME

June, 2009, Absarokee, Montana

"Hi Uncle Joe, Aunt Jennie," Cat said as she walked into the house in Absarokee, trying to hug both at the same time. Looking around the inside of the house, it didn't escape her that this was the same house where her mother had spent much of her life.

"How's your flight?" Uncle Joe asked.

"Oh, it was good and it didn't take as long to drive over here from Billings as I thought. I'm not used to speed limits of seventy, and there's hardly any traffic on the freeway," she commented, as they led her to the guest bedroom to park her small suitcase and jacket.

"It's too bad Jamie couldn't come with you," Joe said.

"The timing didn't work out right for him, but that's okay; I'm on somewhat of a personal mission anyway. I think I told you that since Mom died, I've become more curious about my real father. I've been doing some research on his side of the family. Figures, doesn't it? You and Andy are the only two people still alive who knew him. And I never cared enough to ask about him until now."

Joe nodded, not saying anything for a good sixty seconds, then asked, "I think you mentioned you were going to stop by the cemetery in Billings. Did you find what you were looking for?" Joe pulled out a stool for Cat at the kitchen counter.

"Well, yes, I did, but it was kind of depressing. It wasn't what I expected. When I was doing research, I found information that Glenn Senior, my father's dad, and his mom were buried in Mountain View Cemetery in Billings. I had the section and plot numbers to locate them, but when I got there I was totally lost and had to ask a guy that worked there for help. We wandered around for the better part of forty-five minutes until we found the plots where they were buried; but there weren't any markers or headstones. There were headstones all around the area and just a grassy space where they supposedly are buried, or so the records say. It left me feeling empty somehow. I know there was bad blood between my father and Glenn Sr., but you would have thought one of them might have put a headstone up for Grandmother Barker."

Joe didn't respond to that, he just nodded.

"On a better note, while I was researching the family history last summer, I went through some boxes in the attic and found an address on an envelope from Grandmother Barker to my father when he was overseas. Today when I left the cemetery, I went looking for that address and I found it. I think that was the house where my father was born and raised —and it's still there, which was kind of interesting. The neighborhood is nice and the house was kept up."

Cat didn't add that she sat outside the house and could almost imagine her father at age nine, running down the steps, with the screen door slamming as he headed over to Red's house. "I drove around a little, looking for the Barker store, but there are a lot of industrial buildings and empty lots where it might have been." Cat paused for a moment.

"I never really knew very much about my father. I seldom asked Mom anything, and what she volunteered was always negative. I never cared enough to push her for the truth. But I thought it was weird that when I was going through some of her old photos, and when I took the time – stood back, and looked at them with fresh eyes as if I'd never seen them before – I realized she didn't look all that miserable. There were pictures of her up in Anchorage, smiling and laughing right after they were married, and she looked pretty happy."

Jennie handed Cat a cup of coffee. She paused for a minute and took a sip. "You know, the other thing I think is strange is that I noticed some of the pictures have my father's writing on the back. At least I believe it to be my father's writing; it sure wasn't Mom's writing. But some of the comments were very personal, like 'my beloved wife' and 'my darling'. The more I poked around in the boxes, the more I came to believe that they were normal, happy newlyweds. It didn't look to me like she hated every minute of it, as she'd led me to believe."

Uncle Joe had been listening quietly up until that point. He interjected, "Well, I'll tell you something Catherine. Madeleine never gave Glenn enough credit. Your Grampa Mike had a lot of respect for him. Dad could never thank him enough for taking Louise in and raising her without thinking twice. Nobody ever said anything bad about Glenn or Dad would stand up for him and give them the what-for."

Cat mulled that around in her head the rest of the evening as she helped Jennie with dinner. While she was setting the table, she was treated to stories about all the kids and grandkids. This was a comfortable time with the last of her mom's immediate family. Both her uncle Earl and aunt Betty had died a few years earlier and Frances had developed Alzheimer's and died even before that.

After dinner, Joe said, "I used to see Frances once in a while when he was sick, but he didn't even remember me most of the time. If he had remembered me, he didn't acknowledge it. After a while, I just quit going. I saw Jane and the kids at the funeral. She's almost totally blind now, but she's still living in the big house. She pretty much leased out most of the land. I see her once in a while in town." Joe paused for a moment and then continued, "I don't know how you feel about this, but I've seen both Frances and Dad after they died."

Cat's eyes locked on his in interest.

"Dad came to me one night in a dream and oh boy, he gave me a stern talking to. He didn't think I should have butted my nose in where it didn't belong with Frances. Yep, he was pretty upset with me. Then later on I saw Frances. He was all well, standing up straight, didn't have any disease or anything, and looked pretty much like he always did. He recognized me just fine and forgave me. And we just talked."

Joe stopped, and was quiet for an uncomfortable minute. "Well, I must not have made anybody else too mad at me, because I haven't seen anybody else since then," he teased.

Smiling, Cat felt she needed to change the subject slightly. "You know, I want to thank both you and Andy for coming to Mom's funeral. I didn't expect it, but it made a huge difference to me having you there."

He just nodded.

"Joe, I don't think I ever told you this, but one of the hardest things I ever had to do was tell Mom that Louise had died. I tried to soften it up for her by letting her know that Louise had been sick and that it didn't look good. But when I got the call that she had died, I was just sick. I thought maybe I needed to let Mom know that morning, instead of waiting until I usually visited in the evening. I didn't want her trying to go to sleep after getting that kind of news. And you know, for years after that, if I ever showed up in the nursing home unexpectedly in the morning, she'd always look at me and ask 'now who died?'"

Joe and Jennie and Cat moved to the living room and sat talking until the traveling and emotions of the day got the better of her and she retired to the bedroom. Cat couldn't help but feel the history of the house enveloping her as she lay under the hand-made comforter and dozed off.

The next morning, when they were eating breakfast at the counter, Joe asked, "So, what did you have in mind to do today?"

"Well I thought I might just take a drive around. See if I could find Fishtail and Grampa's old ranch. I thought maybe I'd try to visit the Rosebud Cemetery."

"Jennie and I'd be glad to take you. We cleared everything today, so we can drive around and do a little sightseeing if you'd like."

"That'd be great, since I have absolutely no idea where I'm going."

"Okay . . . Ready?"

Cat had to smile at his economical use of words and replied, "Yep."

They stopped first at the Rosebud Cemetery. Such familiar names ran up and down the rows of raised headstones. The Irish seemed to be in a section all of their own: Flanagan, Letcher, Flynn and yes, the Lannen family. Cat stared at the headstone for John Michael Lannen, her Grampa Mike. And next to him, the much older headstone of Elsie, the grandmother she never knew. Earl and Betty were there, close together, with Frances on the other side of her grampa. They found the headstones of Jacob and Maria Hagaman, with several cousins and extended family, whose names she barely remembered. Every time she found another headstone, it was like finding another link in her family. She thought, "This is how it should feel — a place of permanence, marked for generations to find." It was a place that made her feel connected somehow — unlike the empty feeling she had when she left her father's parents in their unmarked graves.

When they left, they drove down to the old Fishtail General Store which had been in business since 1900. They wandered around the store looking at all the antiques that reflected time long past. Joe talked about how things used to be and Cat tried to absorb every word. Then they drove up to Box Canyon to her Grampa Mike's old ranch, along with the site of the Hagaman property. Joe pointed out the little green schoolhouse where he and Madeleine had gone to "little" school. As they passed farms, he told funny stories about Uncle Ray and a long-lost, crazy Uncle Teddy.

They spent the afternoon at the mouth of the Stillwater River, hiking up the trail for a bit, taking their time coming back.

They drove past what was left of Grampa Mike's little house in Fishtail and farther on, slowed down to see Frances and Jane's ranch.

Joe's oldest daughter, Peggy, had a ranch not too far from Absarokee, so they stopped and visited there for a while. Joe had invited Uncle Earl's oldest son, Cat's cousin Mike, and his wife Carol to dinner, so they headed back home where Jennie started preparations, and Cat set the table.

Cat was just finishing the gravy when there was a knock at the door and her cousin Mike stepped through, hanging his cowboy hat on the peg by the door in one smooth move. The gesture made Cat smile. Carol was right beside him, but stepped away the moment she saw Cat. She walked directly toward her and touched Cat's face. "You look so much like your mother." For the first time in Cat's life, she had to smile at that comment, and said, "Thank you."

Cat had long since given up on counting her first and second cousins. She still had an enormous number of "relations", as Uncle Joe would say, many still living in the Absarokee area. A strange sense of belonging surrounded the family, both living and not.

She enjoyed talking with Mike and Carol, but felt a little guilty that Jennie was doing most of the running back and forth, placing food on the table, picking up used items, serving dessert, and getting coffee.

That evening, Joe regaled them with typical sibling stories about him and Madeleine growing up, throwing in a story or two about Uncle Earl and Frances. Through these stories, he introduced her to her crazy great-uncles and other characters that touched their family throughout the years. Her Grampa Mike apparently took in stray people like they were stray cats. There was always someone living up at the ranch doing odds and ends for a meal or a bunk in the barn.

The stories brought life and color to the family history Cat was now familiar with. Joe laughed and chuckled through most of the stories. He seemed to enjoy remembering all the tales — probably because he had a new audience with Cat. She had noticed Jennie roll her eyes a few times, and got the general impression that Jennie had heard these stories many times before.

At some point in the evening, Mike and Carol bid them goodbye and left, but Uncle Joe was still full of stories, continuing with Aunt Catherine and her banjo-saxophone-fiddle-playing husband Cody.

During a lull in the conversation, Joe turned very serious and said, "Catherine," using her formal name, "I have something I need to ask you. Jennie and I are very involved with our religion in the Mormon Church." He paused, searching for the right words, "And a part of our belief is in what we call 'sealing'. We believe that we on earth can seal our loved ones together for eternity. It's an acknowledgement of them being sealed to the family, so that they are able to find each other and remain together." He paused to gauge her reaction. "I would like your permission to seal your mother with your dad."

The gravity of the request did not weigh lightly on Cat, and she recognized that this was an important question. She'd never heard of "sealing" before. And because she didn't understand it all and because it made her slightly uncomfortable, she thought for a minute before she responded, "Which Dad?"

Joe broke into a big grin and said, "With your 'daddy'. I'm afraid if we tried to seal your mother with Glenn, she'd have another thing to say about that."

With the mood lightened, Cat replied, "You know Joe . . . I'd be honored. The Catholic Church never allowed her to get married in the Church with Daddy because she had married my birth father in the Church; she never forgave them for that. She might as well be sealed in death by the Mormon Church."

Cat left the next morning with family stories swimming in her head. Flying home, she knew she had one more loose end to tie up before she could bring her quest to an end. She finally realized what Father Duncan had been pushing her towards. It was clear what had been driving her — she needed to put her birth father to rest now.

GOD WORKS IN MYSTERIOUS WAYS

Epilogue

"It's so nice to see you again. What brings you to my house?" Father Duncan said, as he theatrically waved his arm in an all-encompassing motion toward the sanctuary of the church. Cat smiled as her eyes took in everything — the worn pews, the bank of red vigil lights, the Stations of the Cross. Her eyes fixed on the prayer stall and pulpit and wandered toward the two stain glass windows on either side of the cross above the altar.

"I just wanted to see where you hung out when you weren't with me," she joked.

"Actually, I wanted to tell you that you were right, and this felt like the appropriate place to do it." She slid over in the pew as Father sat down beside her with a worried but curious expression.

"You kept telling me that I was looking for something. You said I'd know it when I found it — and that it was a necessary journey for me."

"So, you've come to close the chapter, huh? Tell me. What did you find?"

"Well, I found my father. Not just found him, but found out who he was. Two years ago, I couldn't have told you anything about him, other than he left me and Mom when I was five years old. Outside of that, I knew he died when I was a junior in high school.

I might even have added, I never knew him and felt nothing for him." Cat paused to find the right words. "But, what I discovered was that he was a large piece of my life after all. He was my father and he deserved more than I gave him. I just never had asked the questions. I guess I never wanted to know."

Father Duncan's right eyebrow raised, a gesture that Cat was now familiar with. She continued, "As I was writing, I kept working through the different stages of his life, and it was almost like I could feel him changing. I started believing that there was more to him than we knew. I believe he had good intentions to make a good life for himself and Mom, but his past kept getting in the way. It consumed him. He tried to put it behind him by changing jobs and moving, but he couldn't get away from the memories of the war.

"If the truth were known, he probably had a classic case of Post-Traumatic Stress Syndrome. I did a lot of research on that condition, and it was fairly common among the soldiers during World War Two when they came home. They called it 'shell shock' or 'battle fatigue' in those days, though. He never slept because of the nightmares, and I think the drinking was just a poor attempt at trying to forget. Mom wouldn't have understood that, and he wouldn't have shared it.

"I wasn't sure if my assumption was true or not, so I went on an overdue trip to Montana to see Uncle Joe. He and Uncle Andy are the only two people still alive who really knew him. They both confirmed what I was feeling.

"You know, the military documents said my father's job consisted of 'readying planes' on the fighting fields. I didn't understand what that meant. Okay, I thought, he got planes ready to fly out. But Uncle Joe explained that his job included emptying and cleaning blood and body parts from the fuselage — from those planes that had been in active battles. Joe told me he'd seen my father break down once and talk about 'the boys no older than sixteen and seventeen' whose blood was hosed out of the belly of the airplanes." Cat paused for a minute to catch her breath and wipe an escaped tear from her cheek.

Father Duncan could see she was struggling. "No wonder he was depressed and angry. Those visions in his mind probably haunted him throughout the balance of his life. You mentioned several times how he couldn't sleep. He was suffering."

"Yes, and he medicated himself with alcohol. My mom saw how he'd changed, but she never wondered why. Even my Uncle Joe told me that Mom never gave him the credit that he was due. So, in that vein, neither did I.

"When I came back from Montana, I felt different about my father. I felt like I knew who he was. And knowing him left a huge hole in my heart. I had never mourned him and I never said good-bye."

"And have you now . . . said goodbye?"

"Oh, Father . . . if I told you that, I'd ruin the end of the story for you." She wore a smile on her face as she handed him a small set of typed pages, adding, "I think you have to read the rest yourself. I don't think I can go through it again. I've subtitled it, 'Cat's Closure'."

Father took the pages, rested his back against the pew and began silently reading. Cat turned her eyes toward the crucifix and slowly breathed in and out, letting the church absorb her.

FOUND

Cat's Closure

Cat always knew where her father was buried. When her mom and dad had come back from Glenn's burial in 1968, Madeleine had given her the small cardboard box containing her father's United States Veterans Flag.

More than 40 years after he died, Glenn's daughter needed to see the grave. Maybe she needed to say goodbye or mourn. Maybe she just needed to make sure it was there. She wasn't sure what it was, but there was something inside her that was left unfinished.

Cat sat down at her computer and brought up the Willamette National Cemetery website to see exactly where it was located and was somewhat surprised at how close it was. The cemetery was outside Portland, not that far away. She noticed a button on the web site, titled "locator". Following the path, she was asked to type in the name of who she was looking for. She typed in 'Glenn L. Barker'.

When the name immediately came up, she just stared at it. There was some sort of finality to actually see his name among the death records: *Glenn L. Barker, born Oct 31, 1921, died Apr 16, 1968 S section Sgt US Army Air Corp, site 63.* She carefully wrote down the information and put the note in a side pocket of her purse.

That night, over a dinner of leftover pizza, Jim asked, "There's a car show in Bend, Oregon next week. How would you like to go with me?"

Coincidences had come often during the past year. Cat sometimes chalked it up to divine intervention; whatever it was, she needed to follow it. Driving to Bend would take them through Portland and very near the Willamette Cemetery.

"Yeah, I'd like to go, but I have a favor to ask. On our way down, can we take a quick side trip and swing through the Willamette Cemetery to see if I can find my father's gravesite? I think the cemetery is only a couple miles off I-5."

"I don't see why not. I think that would be the right thing to do. It's probably about time you visit him, and I'd consider it an honor to take you."

There was a lot to do before the weekend to get ready for the show. Jim spent his time making reservations and planning the trip. He did some last minute detail on his car and they got it loaded in the trailer. As the weekend drew near, they discovered some friends were also going down to Bend with their cars. At the last minute they made plans to caravan together.

After taking Morgan to the kennel, packing an ice chest and loading up the truck, they left Tacoma on Friday morning.

When Cat had originally decided to stop at the cemetery, she hadn't anticipated they would be caravanning with other people. Jim and Cat talked while they drove, and changed their plans slightly, agreeing to stop at the cemetery on their way back after the car show. They would be coming back by themselves.

They checked into the Bend hotel, unloaded the trailer and tried to get their bearings. The hotel was across the street from McMenamins, a converted Catholic schoolhouse called Old St. Francis School. It was complete with classrooms that had been turned into lodging, a pub, brewery, bakery, movie theater, and restaurant. They stopped for lunch before heading to the park where the cars would be staged and viewed.

The temperature was a sweltering one hundred degrees and thankfully, McMenamins had good air conditioning and cold beer.

The high temperatures weren't something either of them was used to. Even walking to the park, which sat along the Deschutes River, was a tiring walk.

In spite of the heat, the show was packed. There were five hundred incredible street rods and classic cars, music, venders, entertainment, and a carnival atmosphere. It was an adrenaline packed weekend. By Sunday night, they were exhausted. The heat had done in both of them, and they were more than ready to go home. They packed up the trailer that evening, stopped for a quick dinner, and went back to the hotel to get some sleep. On Monday morning, they loaded the rest of the truck, including Jim's trophy for "Best '56 Chevy", punched the air conditioning on high and left Bend behind. It was a quiet drive through the central mountains of Oregon, both still exhausted from the weekend.

As they got closer to Portland, Cat pulled out the instructions and map to the cemetery. Once they pulled off the freeway, the two-lane road was much harder to navigate with the twenty-one-foot trailer, and the cemetery was farther off the interstate than she expected. They both became very frustrated trying to find the right road. Cat had always been directionally challenged, so was of little help in navigating.

After several wrong turns, they finally arrived at the main gate. Trying to be efficient, Cat thought she should go to the office and have them direct her to the site, to avoid wandering around lost. They followed signs for the office and grave locator, but when they got there, the front door was locked. Cat went around the side of the building to another door, but it was locked too. She looked through the windows, looking for a sign, or a light, but there was none. She was tired and feeling more frustrated every second. Staring at the locked door, she couldn't stop the tears; she'd come so close. Now it looked as if she wouldn't be able to find him. She just stood there staring at the lock — finding it symbolic somehow.

She had this vision of wandering around and not ever finding his grave. She felt lost. There was no other way to explain it. The bottom just dropped out from underneath her. She was nearly ready to say "let's go home" when Jim put his arm around her. He knew if they left now, she'd never be able to put this to rest.

The piece of paper that Cat had in her purse indicated that her father was buried in section 'S-63', and Jim remembered driving past a sign that pointed to Section 'S'.

"Let's go back up the hill where that sign was and see if we can find the 'S' section." Even Jim's optimism didn't cheer her up. But he was persistent.

"Come on, Honey, let's just give it a try."

After twenty years of being married to your best friend, Cat just knew that Jim could feel her pain and disappointment as clearly as if it were his own. She knew that his heart hurt for her; he wanted to be a part of giving her this resolution, as much as she needed it. Without having to say a word, Cat leaned into him for strength. They stood in the middle of the parking lot and he held her until the hurt went away . . . and her tears dried.

With a new deep breath, they decided they'd give it a shot. They got back in the car and started toward section 'S'. They found it and parked. Getting out of the truck, Cat just stood there and stared. There were hundreds of graves around a huge flag pavilion. They all looked alike. There was no way they could go through hundreds, possibly thousands of headstones in the hopes they would stumble across her father's. The information she had said he was buried in site 63, but she had no idea how to find it.

Cat walked slowly to the middle of the field as if she was in some sort of trance. She made a complete turn, taking in all the directions. There were grave markers as far as her eyes could see. She closed her eyes for a moment and bowed her head, looking at one of the graves; in the upper right-hand corner of the marker, she saw a number — "865". She looked to the left. The next marker had a number "864". The numbers were too high. She must have misunderstood the site number, or there was some other type of section coding. The frustration tore through her; the tears came again, but she kept walking.

This one says "978", Jim said to her from several rows away. She walked on the other side of him down a few more rows, to one that read "1403."

"The numbers are too high, honey, let's just go" she said resigning to the frustration. She started walking the other direction. Tears were clouding her vision and she had a hard time reading the numbers, but as she found them she started calling out the numbers to him. He was walking in another area calling out numbers to her.

"402" He called, "401" the numbers were going down.

Cat found a row that had numbers in the 200s and kept walking.

She called out, "98. They're getting lower." Then that row stopped and she walked over a couple more rows. "86 . . . 82 . . . 76" . . . the tears came again, "69 . . . 65 . . . 64" and then, in a whisper ". . . 63". The marker read "Glenn L. Barker". Cat's knees buckled and she hit the ground. She couldn't read any more of the marker for the tears. She started picking the grass away from the edges to clear the etching.

"I found it, I found it." It was simply a tear laden whimper, but Jim heard it. He caught up to her, tears in his eyes, and watched her for a minute before he bent down to help her clear off the stone. Cat whispered, "Oh God, thank you, Mom. Thank you for doing this for me."

They both stood up and silently stared at the marking:

Glenn Lee Barker
Montana
S Sgt 88 Recon SQ AAF
World War II
October 31, 1921- April 13, 1968.

Jim put his arm around Cat, willing strength into her. She felt as if she'd just run a marathon. She couldn't breathe. They sat down in the grass, under a nearby tree and just looked around. They saw the mountains off in the distance, the manicured gardens and the very quiet rolling hills. The rhododendrons were in bloom, the grass had been recently cut and edged, and that's when she caught the scent — tea roses. She looked around for a rose bush and saw none. Still, the scent was as clear as if the flower were beneath her nose. It was the scent of Evangeline, Glenn's grandmother. He hadn't been alone all these years. Now, Glenn's daughter and her husband sat there quietly and breathed in the scent.

Jim finally got up and went to get the truck since they had walked a considerable way through the section. He pulled it around and parked close to where they had been sitting. They walked around a little bit and absorbed the sobriety of it all. Then they walked back, circling around to her father's marker once more to pay their last respects before getting back in the truck.

Cat sat for a moment and took a deep breath, staring in the direction of the grave site —a grave site that had never been visited by family before.

"Are you ready?" Jim asked.

"Yes . . . and thank you. You don't know what this means to me."

"Yes, I do." He reached over to squeeze her hand.

It felt like the chapter was finally closed. Cat felt okay. No, she felt centered. Everything felt right. They drove slowly out of the cemetery, through the main gate, and quietly, each of them in their own thoughts, drove home.

At some point during the time that Father Duncan was reading, Cat had left the Sanctuary of the church and was sitting on the steps outside. She felt, rather than heard Father Duncan approach. Knowing he was standing behind her, she said, "Father, you were so right; there was something driving me and it was a journey I needed to take. I didn't realize that the journey wasn't a destination, but closure. And now I guess I can put it all to rest."

"How lucky you are," Father said, after a few quiet minutes. "You have met generations of your family through your research, discovered a father you never knew and filled your heart with love. St. Teresa, the Saint of the little flower, said, *"What a comfort it is this way of love! You may stumble on it, you may fail to correspond with grace given, but always love knows how to make the best of everything."*

Father sat down on the step and continued, "I believe I can also tell you that Evangeline more than likely had St. Teresa's help in sending down that shower of roses from heaven. After all, Catherine," reverting to her formal name, "St. Teresa is said to shower the blessed with roses. It *is* what she does." He paused. Then he smiled and asked, "did you know that different flowers have different meanings?"

"No, I don't Father. So, what is the meaning of the tea rose?"

"It means . . . *I'll always remember you.*"

Father and Cat sat for what seemed to be a long time. The sun had clouded over and a chill was building in the air. They stood and walked down to her car. She opened the driver door, but stood for a moment, looking up at the steeple.

"Yes," Father Duncan added, reading her mind. "God does indeed work in mysterious ways. So my friend, Cat, where do you go from here? What is your next project?"

"Well, it's funny you should ask that Father, I have a new idea for a book. It's going to take a lot of research though." She paused for a moment to form her thoughts. Then with mischief in her eyes, "It's about an offbeat, unorthodox, slightly funny, but everso-likeable Ukrainian Priest."

Father Duncan burst out laughing. "So, I guess we need to do coffee next week?"

ACKNOWLEDGEMENTS

I would like to thank my family, present and past. Without them, there would have been no story.

A special thank you to Father Michael Durka who inspired me to use his character as a friend and confidant in this book.

And, as always, to my husband who has supported me in all of my crazy and creative endeavors.

Visit the author's website at

www.glendacooper.com

Glenda Cooper lives in the Pacific Northwest with her husband Jim and their Old English Sheepdog Reilly. She is a journalist and author of short stories, poems, humorous lyrics, and a family recipe book. The inspiration for "The Road to Lost and Found" began with an unexpected discovery of old family photos in an attic. Published in 2012, it's a poignant tale of love and loss across four generations.

Glenda is currently working on her second book; a story that came to light at a recent high School Class Reunion. More information is available at www.glendacooper.com.

14258520R00206

Made in the USA
Charleston, SC
30 August 2012